UNHEDGED □ □ □

UNHEDGED

A Killing in the Market

STEPHEN L. WEISS

Stephen L. Weiss:

UNHEDGED

A Killing in the Market

ebook ISBN 9780786754755

Print ISBN 9780786754748

Distributed by Argo Navis Author Services

Also by the Author □ □ □

Other Works by the Author include:

THE BILLION DOLLAR MISTAKE

Learning the Art of Investing Through the Missteps of Legendary Investors

THE BIG WIN

Learning from the Legends to Become a More Successful Investor

Author's Note

□ □ □

This book was a long time in the making and there are many people I have to thank for their assistance and encouragement. To put this in perspective, I actually started writing UNHEDGED when oil was trading at thirty-five dollars a barrel, envisioning a major move to seventy, at the time a seemingly unattainable level. But reality can often humble a fertile imagination, as was the case here. None of the characters I mention in the book are real, although each is an amalgam of people I have met during my career. At the risk of losing sales, I gave various versions to friends for their comments and found it amazing how many of them asked me if they were the model for Jeremy. I either need new friends or friends with smaller egos. To officially put their speculation to rest, this was not the case. However, the settings are very authentic, from the trading room to the Gulfstream.

The genesis of this book was in a conversation with my wife, Lauren, and my daughters, Lindsay and Shelby. Immediately after I finished reading a work by one of my favorite authors or especially, by one of my not so favorite authors, I would opine, "I can do that." They got tired of my Walter Mitty moments and challenged me to write a book. I accepted and UNHEDGED is the outcome. The challenge, however, actually yielded even greater productivity, resulting in two investment books, The Billion Dollar Mistake: Learning the Art of Investing Through the Missteps of Legendary Investors (Wiley, January 2010) and The Big Win: Learning from the Legends to Become a More Successful Investor (Wiley, May 2012). Mistake has been translated into Chinese, Korean, and Japanese, languages I unfortunately don't speak.

My family continues to be my inspiration and motivation and Lauren is the best I could ever hope for in a partner and wife. Howard Jurofsky, my closest and oldest friend, read so many versions of UNHEDGED that he probably could have written the final version if only ESPN ever went dark. The Reinliebs, Lulu and Roger, were also very supportive despite Roger's affinity for more erudite literature–or so he says. Jen Escott did a great job editing the final version and Susanna Margolis is always a reliable and insightful resource. Susan Ginsburg of Writers House is one of the top agents in the business and her counsel was extremely helpful.

Epigraph □ □ □

"All the money you make will never buy back your soul."
  Bob Dylan

  "A billion here, a billion there, pretty soon it starts to add up to real money."
  United States Senator Everett Dirksen

  "Greed and corruption, that's what this trial is all about."
  U.S. Federal Prosecutor Jonathan Streeter
  at the insider trading trial of a billionaire hedge fund manager

Chapter 1

□   □   □

The trading room fell quiet as Vernon Albright stormed across the floor, the thick carpet doing little to mute the anger evident in each step. The traders had seen him this way before and feared the worst. They tried hard to fade into the background, averting their eyes and punching phantom stock symbols into their keyboards. As Albright passed each desk, the dread of being his next victim gave way to barely contained sighs of relief.

Albright stopped at the desk of Parthenon's newest employee, towering over his target. His booming voice echoed off the walls. "Sell the fucking stock."

"But the shares are only down a quarter. I know they'll go higher."

The portfolio manager's first mistake was putting on the two-hundred-million-dollar position but that was, after all, what he was hired to do. His second misstep, perhaps the more egregious error in judgment, was talking back to Vernon Albright. Freedom of speech was an unknown concept at Parthenon Capital, where only one opinion mattered. That and bottom line results. He had been at Parthenon for all of three weeks, but it was not the first time he regretted leaving his highly paid position at Morgan Stanley.

"What don't you understand? This isn't open to a vote. I said to sell the fucking position. And by the way, you moron, on twenty million shares, that quarter is costing me five million."

The man was dazed; he felt like he had just been smacked across the back of his head with a two by four. He knew Albright's reputation for churning employees and had aired it as a concern during the recruiting process. Albright's response now echoed in his mind. "I never should have hired those people; they didn't have your experience. You're different, much more accomplished, someone I can trust and give complete autonomy." He took the job. *What's my downside? Even if I get fired after a year, I'll have made more money than I earned the last five.* Against the advice of many, he rejected a substantial counter bid from Morgan and accepted Albright's more generous offer.

"This isn't what we agreed upon. You said I could trade without your supervision."

"Tell you what, genius," Albright responded in his most condescending tone, "going forward you can trade all you like without my supervision because we're done. Actually, you're done. Down five million in less than one month is a record. I have no intention of letting you pad your legacy."

He knew it wasn't unusual for tempers to flare when the market got hit although he had never witnessed, nor been the victim of, such a public flogging. He also realized that offering further rebuttal was senseless. Composure barely intact, the best defense at this point was to grab a cup of coffee and hope the incident would die down until it could be discussed in more private surroundings. He pushed his chair away from the desk, gaining distance from Albright's menacing glare. As beaten down as a chastised puppy, he rose from his seat and started toward the pantry. From Master of the Universe to poor bastard in less than a minute.

"You're going in the wrong direction, just like the stocks you buy," Albright bellowed as a wry smile spread across his lips. "The elevators are that way." He extended his arm and pointed toward the reception area.

Joseph, Albright's personal bodyguard and head of Parthenon's small security detail stepped in. "It's probably best to do as Mr. Albright suggests," he advised in a voice that was slightly above a whisper. "He doesn't usually change his mind. Your personal items will be sent to your home."

His humiliation was pushed aside by anger, rage evident in his eyes and the clenching of his fists. He took a step toward Albright but Joseph's vise-like grip caught his arm, holding him in place.

"Time to go," Joseph said while placing his other hand on the man's back, directing him toward the exit.

"Parthenon isn't for the weak or the stupid," Albright remarked for all to hear as the latest casualty exited through the glass doors.

And so ended another "career" at Parthenon. It wasn't the shortest tenure on record. That distinction belonged to a portfolio manager who lasted all of three days. His mistake? He went out to lunch and returned an hour later. The markets didn't take time off during the trading day and neither did Parthenon. He didn't even make it past the lobby when he returned. His electronic building pass had already been voided.

Albright was still incensed as he returned to his office. He was tired of these high priced hires squandering the opportunity he had given them and damn tired of having to go through the inconvenience of bringing in someone new. He sat at his desk and mentally ran through a list of ten potential replacements, portfolio managers at other firms he had met with in the event the inevitable occurred. Almost out of reflex, the process of compiling a list of candidates began immediately upon the first misstep of the latest hire. After a few minutes of deliberation, he settled upon a name.

"Get me Jeremy Cranford." Albright barked to his secretary.

Incredibly, and in defiance of all precedent, that was three years ago; Cranford had survived the odds but he would soon have to outlive more severe threats than those to his career.

Chapter 2

□ □ □

The black-clad figure blended invisibly into the shadows of the tall trees that formed a protective barrier around the staid Tudor style home. In this affluent, almost rural area of New Jersey, the landscaping was lush and mature, providing all the gunman could have hoped for in the way of cover. Right arm braced against torso, left elbow resting on bended knee, his near-perfect form provided steady support as he sighted through the night scope affixed to the long metal barrel. Like the pictures he had seen of other true marksman, both eyes remained open but he concentrated his vision through the right one, peering intently at his subjects, who sat in the house across the street. Sneering at the image of familial bliss, he tightened his finger on the trigger.

***

Sunday evening was intended to be a time to relax. With sorting through the week's mail as the only scheduled chore, it even started out that way. Their two young daughters finally tucked into bed, the Cranfords settled into the first floor study. It was a nicely appointed room, its décor enveloping the family in a warmth that bred comfort and togetherness; the only nod to its dual function as an occasional home office was the mahogany desk positioned in the corner. As a partner at a very successful hedge fund, Jeremy's position required an intense amount of focus when he was at the office, but when he was at home he applied that same devotion to his family.

Jennifer curled up on the couch next to her husband. It was always hard for him to concentrate when she did this, but never more than now as she reached across his chest for one of the two glasses of wine that sat atop the end table. She gently planted a kiss, more sensual than casual, on Jeremy's lips.

"You're making it tough for me to get my work done, Jenn." He was the only one to ever call her Jenn and she liked it that way.

"Sorry," she replied, the mischievous smile on her lips belying any real contrition. "I'll just sit here and read my book."

"Just a few more minutes, honey," Jeremy assured her, adding a sly grin of his own, "and then I will be all yours until five a.m."

Jennifer was a natural blonde with striking, topaz eyes and skin tanned the color of honey; her workout regimen and genetics created an athletically toned body that would serve to preserve her youthful appearance for years to come. Now in her early thirties, she and Jeremy had been married for ten years. He often thought of her as the girl next door with the prurient appeal of a centerfold. Their time together had done nothing to dampen that notion, and Jennifer's feelings about Jeremy were very much the same. With his boyish blonde good looks, baby blue eyes and similarly fit physique, they were as appropriately matched physically as they were emotionally devoted to one another.

***

Uncertain who to take down first, the gunman moved his sight back and forth between the two figures who appeared so comfortable in their cozy home. He warmed to the thought of Jeremy helplessly watching his lovely wife writhe in pain as the blood drained from her body. Wasn't that the point of this excursion to this godforsaken cesspool of a state? To make Cranford suffer as he had when his family abandoned him? Or should he go for the most direct path to revenge and take out the person so clearly responsible for his misery?

***

Oblivious to the danger lurking outside, Jeremy reached for a letter that seemed to protrude from the pile that lay on the squat glass table in front of the sofa. He noticed that the envelope bore no sign of a postage mark or stamp and hoped the similarity to the letter he received in the office last week was just a coincidence. Instinct spoke otherwise. He had dismissed the prior missive as harmless venting from some crank but immediately began to reconsider his nonchalance. Jeremy was still upset with himself for trusting the Wall Street Journal reporter who attributed a quote to him bashing Datatech stock. Publicity brought out the crazies and a lot of unwanted attention. The author of the article, Bill Sundrick, promised that he wouldn't be mentioned, agreeing to label him "an informed source who spoke off the record." Of course Jeremy was pleased that on the day the article came out it caused the price of Datatech stock to decline by twenty percent. The stock collapsed by another forty percent over the following week as every analyst on Wall Street pulled their buy recommendation. Parthenon booked a nice profit on their short position.

Like most other tech-savvy people, the Cranfords received more emails than actual letters so Jeremy decided to move to the desk before his wife noticed what he held in his hands. He sat down and quietly ripped open the sealed flap. Just like the prior letter, this one was typed on a single white sheet of paper. He vividly recalled the wording of the first one calling him a "graveyard dancer who profited from the misery of others." The language in that letter was clear; the man had lost everything in the market and Datatech had been his last, best chance to recoup his losses. He wrote that he had been on his way to winning his family back, proving to his wife that he was a great trader and that the initial gains he had made investing their savings were not a fluke, that despite a period of bad luck he was a moneymaker.

Datatech had tripled after he first bought it and she was finally coming around, coming to her senses, until... *"until you started bad mouthing the story and screwing me over. And then all those sycophants, those amateur traders that follow your every word just because you work at Parthenon, started bashing the stock, too."* It had ended with a threat, but no one could have possibly taken it seriously. Jeremy certainly hadn't.

He stared at the paper in front of him, his expression reflecting the concern he felt, his concentration so intense that he didn't notice Jennifer had followed him to the desk and was now reading over his shoulder.

The letter began with a typical salutation: *"Dear Mr. Cranford."* The words that followed were the cause for alarm.

"Remember me? I'm the one who you screwed!!! I'm the one who lost his family because you made me lose all my money!!! I'm the one who will get even. I'm the one who wants you to suffer!!! You're the one who won't know when or how it will happen!!! Give my best to Jenn and the girls!!!

Yours truly, Mr. Datatech"

The glass of red wine hit the floor as Jennifer's hands went to her face, barely muffling the gasp that was still so very audible. It was immediately apparent that whoever this psycho was, he had gone to the trouble of finding out where they lived and already knew way too much about their lives. Jeremy rose and embraced his wife as she sobbed on his shoulder.

***

The man in the shadows looked on, a sick grin of pleasure forming on his face. He knew he was responsible for the scene he was watching and decided to savor his targets' misery for a moment more. Slowly, he brought the rifle down to his side, acting upon what he had known all along; now was not the time to act irrationally. All in due course, he reasoned, controlling his emotions as would every good trader. And he wasn't just good, he was the best. *Don't let the game control me, I control the game,* he reminded himself. First he had to recoup his money. Then it would be time to act upon his future plans for Mr. and Mrs. Cranford. For now he would have to be content with this visual benchmark of their anguish.

***

They didn't speak much before they went to bed, unsure of what to say. Jennifer had confidence that her husband, their protector, wouldn't let anything threaten their family. Still, she was afraid.

Sleep would not come easily as their thoughts returned to the letter. Silently, they each recalled the words in vivid detail. *"I'm the one who will get even."* Jennifer pulled her husband's arm tightly around her waist while they lay in bed, bodies touching, fitting into one another as if sculpted together. *"I'm the one who wants you to suffer."* Jeremy heard the sniffles as his wife fought back the tears of fear. *"Give my regards to Jenn and the girls."*

Jeremy had always kept up a brave front, no matter what the circumstance. He sometimes felt the burden of doing so while always recognizing the necessity. Eyes vacantly focused on the darkness, his thoughts went to the time when their first child, Alexandra, was born. It was the first time the brave front had really mattered.

It had been a tough delivery, an emergency C-Section, and the doctors weren't sure the baby would pull through. Jennifer was anesthetized but still mostly conscious, there being no time to put her out. Jeremy stood at the end of the birthing table holding Jenn's head, her line of vision, but not his, obscured by a foot high white sheet that was purposely positioned on top of her lower chest. She sensed all was not right but remained largely oblivious to the actual danger as the newborn was lifted from her womb with the umbilical cord wrapped around her neck, her little body a pale shade of blue.

The medical staff, nurses and doctors, proceeded without any sense of drama lest they give an indication to the new parents that this was anything but normal. It was important for Jennifer to stay calm, to keep her blood pressure within an acceptable range. The attending obstetrician dispensed with ritual and cut the umbilical cord himself so that he could quickly remove the impediment to the newborn's air supply. Nothing was lost on Jeremy. Fighting back emotion, he knew he had to stay calm. Everything was going to be all right; he was sure of it.

"It will be okay, won't it?" Jennifer whispered tentatively, bringing Jeremy back to the present.

"Of course it will. This is just some harmless kook. I'm sure it's not the first time he's lost money on a stock yet I don't recall reading about any hedge fund managers being mysteriously killed by a Mr. Datatech."

"So you're not worried?"

"Worried? Not really. I'm pretty sure this will turn out to be nothing," he responded, at once surprised and disappointed that he could speak the words so sincerely despite not believing them.

Jeremy's mind returned to the trip home from the hospital after mother and daughter were given a clean bill of health. There she was swaddled in her blanket, peering out from under the little knit cap she wore to help maintain her body temperature. He held her tight, afraid to drop her, as Jennifer sat down in the wheelchair that would bring her to the lobby doors. He gave his daughter one more kiss as he placed her in Jenn's lap, the smile born from pride and happiness never leaving his face.

Jeremy couldn't wait to be a dad. His father had died when he was only nine years old and he never saw much of him when he was alive. It wasn't that his father wasn't a good parent—quite the contrary. He was a very loving, family man who, if he had the option, would have spent all his time with his wife and son. But he was an uneducated, albeit hard-working, immigrant who never made much money. Out of adversity comes strength and from that early age, Jeremy vowed to succeed, to be in a position to give his family everything they could possibly want and to dote ceaselessly on his children. He would renew and embellish this vow as he got older. He would be there to tuck them into bed each and every night. When they got older, he promised himself that he would sit with them at their desks and help with their homework. When they went off to college, he would visit as often as they would let him. And when they had children of their own, he would not be held back from spoiling his grandkids rotten.

But now, the smile that had always accompanied Jeremy's perfect picture of family life had evaporated, replaced by the blank stare of someone worried about an unseen, unknown menace. The visions of joy were pushed aside by a dark foreboding, the fear that the lives of those he loved the most were in danger and that he would be unable to keep them safe.

Chapter 3 ▫ ▫ ▫

The Gulfstream 550 flew smoothly over the low white clouds that marred an otherwise clear blue sky. Buck Hendricks pressed a button, lifting the shades that covered each of the cabin's eight windows and peered out at the landscape 35,000 feet below. He mindlessly jiggled his left leg, repeatedly banging it against the underside of the highly polished wood table that extended from the cabin wall.

The rhythmic thumps carried to the front of the elegantly appointed interior where Dina, the stewardess, sat on a small couch.

We still have two hours to go, Mr. Hendricks, she thought. *It's too early for even you to be jumping out of your skin.*

***

Despite the comforts provided by his forty-five-million-dollar jet and a flying time of only four hours, Buck couldn't wait to deplane. While not clinically hyperactive, he nonetheless thrived on constant motion. This was not the only characteristic he shared with another predator, the shark. They both also had an instinct for the kill. Buck peered ahead to the front of the cabin and turned on the flat panel screen. A map appeared, tracking the jet's flight pattern and time to destination. It was not a feature he often used, reasoning that there was a direct correlation between his perception of the flight's duration and the number of times he checked the progress. He preferred to watch a movie to pass the time or use the airphone to check on his business dealings and social life, both of which were very active. But having idle time wasn't always all bad since it provided Buck with an occasion to plan his next deal. It was late Saturday morning in New York and a good time to call Vernon Albright.

***

Albright reached into his pocket to retrieve the ringing cell phone that brought him to the attention of everyone in the exhibition room on Sotheby's first floor. His wife joined in the chorus of annoyed looks that shot his way.

"Yes," Albright said in a hushed tone, clearly irritated at the interruption.

"Is that any way to greet your favorite cowboy and top investor?"

Buck's voice was instantly recognizable. He spoke with a strong Texas accent, a product of his upbringing. He was pleased with this facet of his persona since Texas was synonymous with oil and oil was the foundation of his massive fortune. But an accent was one thing and language was another. He had worked hard to eradicate any down-home colloquialisms from his speech. Every so often a *y'all* would slip out but that was okay; kind of endearing, actually. And although he would occasionally toss out a sarcastically tinged *dang it* or *hogtied* to someone he knew well, his general thought was that those phrases connoted a lack of sophistication and would inhibit his access to the upper echelons of finance where all the big deals were made. That would be unacceptable.

Albright walked through the glass doors and onto York Avenue, gaining distance from his wife's angry glare. Not that he particularly cared what she thought, but it was worth suffering through the minor dust up sure to follow as a result of taking Hendricks's call. Conversations with him usually turned into profits for Parthenon.

"Buck! How the hell are you?" Albright inquired over the roar of city traffic. "I would love to catch up but I'm with my wife."

"Let me guess. It's Saturday morning, so that means your wife is dragging you to some gallery on Madison Avenue. Please don't tell me you're letting her waste all that money I helped y'all make on a grade-school finger painting."

"Ah, that charming Texas twang does it again." Albright had grown to like Buck, always amused by his phony Philistinism. "Actually, I was looking to see if they had an old Remington lying around that I could purchase on your behalf. A couple of million would be a small price to pay for owning some of your down-home culture."

"Appreciate the thought, but I didn't call to discuss art with you. Besides, I prefer Charles Russell's broad brush strokes to Remington's cast iron sculptures."

"Touché, Buck," came the response, accompanied by an almost inaudible laugh. "So tell me...how are we going to make money this week?" Albright was accustomed to discussing only one topic when Buck called.

"I'm afraid this isn't that kind of call either."

"That's disappointing. I so look forward to your pearls of investment wisdom."

"I really hate disappointing you, Vern," Buck parried in kind. "Why don't you let me make it up to you with dinner tomorrow night?"

"I don't typically schedule anything for Sundays. Why not make it for one night during the week?"

***

Vernon looked forward to Sunday nights. He caught up on his business reading and used the quiet time away from the office to think about how he wanted to position the fund in the week ahead. It was a routine he had reluctantly embraced after he was felled by a heart attack two years earlier. He had been eating and drinking to excess—a function of stress, not gluttony. Then one day, during a particularly difficult time in the market, he had experienced significant pain in his chest that turned out to be two blocked arteries requiring an emergency angioplasty.

After the surgery, Albright's doctors had warned him in no uncertain terms that if he didn't start taking better care of himself, he had no better than a fifty-fifty chance of seeing his sixtieth birthday. Not usually prone to accepting another's advice, he had nonetheless embraced the notion (after prodding from his current spouse, trophy wife number three, her concern about a pre-nuptial agreement that hadn't yet matured outweighing any worry about his health). He then embarked upon a fitness program with the same intensity he gave to his business, pushing himself so hard that his doctors had occasionally reminded him that his heart had suffered permanent damage and it would be wise to ratchet down his regimen. Mindful of his family history of heart disease and desirous of avoiding another close call, Vernon had finally cut back his seven day work week. He had learned to use Sundays very effectively, even slotting in a few conference calls with key employees. For him, that was relaxation.

Such an all-consuming work ethos had not always been the way Albright lived his life. He was raised by his father and never really knew his mother. She had abandoned the family when Vernon was just ten years old, bitter at her philandering and abusive husband and resentful that her beauty pageant looks had lost out to childbearing and alcoholism. Life went on for Mortimer Albright, largely uninterrupted by any parental responsibilities. He had parlayed a charismatic personality into a successful investment banking career as a rainmaker. The example he had set for Vernon was simple: pour a stiff drink, tell a few jokes and maintain a low handicap. And always have a different, and younger, woman, on your arm. Further underscoring the message that hard work was not the only path to success, it was solely through his dad's connections that Albright, a bright but underachieving student, got his first job. While personality is not scientifically tied to DNA, Vernon relied more on his own brand of charisma to climb the corporate and social ladders, his surname helping more than a little.

Eventually, he fell in love, something his friends regarded as a virtual impossibility for the avowed playboy, but she had everything he desired. She was beautiful, brilliant and the progeny of a very wealthy family. She was also very accomplished in her own right, a fast-rising star at a large New York hedge fund. He proposed, she accepted, and three months before the big day, they began living together in the apartment she had bought with her own earnings.

Perhaps they should have continued living apart because, unfortunately for Vernon, his fiancé was much more ambitious than he. She came to realize how ill-suited they were together; she would leave for work while he was still sleeping. He would be out partying with friends while she worked late. Vernon didn't even see it coming when she kicked him out and took up with her boss. It wasn't long before they married. Vernon was emotionally crushed and, soon thereafter, financially devastated. A mere two weeks later, the senior Albright died of a heart attack. With his father's passing, Albright's already tenuous hold on his job slipped away. He held out hope that his father's estate would provide a financial bridge to the next phase of his life, one that would allow him to move on professionally and emotionally from his dire straits but Mortimer's legacy contained more debt than savings. So instead of moving on, spurned love and a rapid descent to near poverty bred an extended period of introspection. He decided that he would go through life alone, that falling in love would only lead to eventual betrayal; he saw it with his parents and with his one true love. A behavioral disdain for women would eventually turn him into a serial divorcee, marriage was just a longer rental period than dating. Nor would he ever rely on anyone ever again, for the one person he had depended upon, his father, had, in the end, left him with nothing.

Bitterness became fortitude, revenge became inspiration and desire to regain past comforts became motivation. He decided to show *her* that he was ambitious; he could and would outwork and out earn both she and her new husband

and do it at their own game. Albright vowed to become the new star of the hedge fund world. And he didn't need a woman by his side to do it.

Thus the legend of Vernon Albright was born. Multiple wives, multiple billions and incredible adulation—well, it was addicting. And the harder he worked, the more his wealth increased, the more women he dated—increasingly younger as he got older—and the more self-absorbed he became. But that one taste of failure never quite washed away. That was the real motivating factor, definitely the most powerful—an intense fear of failure that would last a lifetime, controlling his every move in every facet of his life. Like an addict who required more frequent and higher doses to achieve a satisfactory high, Albright's elixir was ever-increasing wealth.

**

Buck sighed, having danced with Albright many times about the sanctity of his Sunday nights. "Sorry, Vern, I forgot about you and Sundays. How about Monday night? I know its short notice but its the only other time that works for me. I'd consider it a favor. Bring the wife along. We'll go to one of your favorite restaurants. You know, one of those places that charges way too much for way too little that you New Yorkers all seem to love."

"Monday works but you're going to have to be satisfied with only me."

"Good enough. Come to my place at six."

Buck placed calls to two other fund managers where he had sizeable investments. With business out of the way, he dialed another number.

"Hey there Cowgirl! Y'all missin' me?"

"Buck! Seems like you're doing the calling so I guess it's you missing me."

Buck enjoyed Marty's strong personality—up to a point—and it was one of the reasons they got on so well. He was a billionaire accustomed to getting anything he desired, but she made him work for everything, from benign praise to a sexual encounter. Tough minded, independent and as ambitious as a Kennedy entering politics, she enjoyed the challenge of being in a relationship with someone whose personality exhibited similar traits. Buck felt the same way. Not merely beautiful, Marty was the vision of what every East coast male would conjure up if given the go ahead to design a cowgirl of their very own. Her body was full but not full figured, firm enough to be considered tight but soft enough that it begged to be touched. Light brown hair and a taut butt that looked good no matter what she had on. On this transplanted Texan, fifty-dollar Levi's worked as well as two-hundred-dollar jeans minus the fancy stitching and too cute name on the back pocket.

"Guess I do miss you, which is why I'm on my way to New York."

"I'm so happy and you're so full of shit. You must have other business in the city."

"Never could pull one over on you, but let's just say I have two damn good reasons for coming to New York. I'll pick you up for dinner at eight."

Marty paused before responding. "I don't know, Buck. It's been a long week."

"A long week of what? You're a lady of leisure. Tell you what—let's make it easy. We can dine in at my place."

"Well, it would be sort of nice to see you."

"That's my girl. I'll see you tonight."

***

Marty turned to the bathroom door. "Time for you to hit the road, Tom. Been a hoot but my man's coming home."

***

Buck's thoughts returned to Albright and padding his own considerable wealth. Convincing Albright to accept additional funds would be difficult, but Buck was accustomed to getting his way, and Parthenon was the best vehicle to accomplish his purposes. There weren't too many funds that had the size and reach to invest in any geography and into any instrument without attracting the attention of government regulators, particularly after the financial debacle in 2008 when Washington was caught napping, or perhaps more accurately, in a deep, deep sleep. Buck needed the cover that Parthenon could provide; Albright's reputation and connections would keep his firm above reproach.

Restless and mentally spent from contriving a realistic plan, Buck switched on the satellite television hoping to clear his mind, but his thoughts never wandered to the intended distraction. Then, in an "ah ha" moment, something clicked. He suddenly felt energized. The velocity of his knee moving against the underside of the table increased, this time from excitement, not restiveness. In his mind, it fit together perfectly. Albright would go along, he was sure, willingly or otherwise. Buck preferred a velvet glove but was not above lacing up the figurative eight ouncers when needed, although that had never been the case with Albright. Nor did he believe it would be effective. Billionaires were not easily bullied.

While Buck regaled himself with his self-ordained brilliance, the plane knifed through the clouds and began its approach. After the Gulfstream's wheels touched the runway, Buck pulled on the custom-made cowboy boots that were his trademark. He wore them with everything, including a dinner jacket. Made out of ostrich skin and dyed black, the two-inch heels added unnecessary height to his six-foot-two-inch frame.

Buck headed aft to the bathroom, hunching over slightly to avoid hitting his head on the cabin's low ceiling. He felt more alert after splashing his face with cold water. In lieu of a comb, he ran his fingers through his sandy brown hair and stared into the mirror at his weathered reflection. The facial lines he'd acquired while working in the oil fields under the bright Texas sun added character to his rugged good looks, also serving to make him look slightly older than his fifty-one years. Despite the bloodshot eyes, Buck was pleased with what he saw.

***

The foundation for the relationship between Albright and Hendricks had grown more and more entangled since their initial meeting less than nine years earlier. It was a marriage of sorts but Albright's attraction was the dowry, not the desire to spend the sunset years of his professional life in a partnership with Hendricks.

It was nearly a decade ago that Parthenon had sat upon the precipice of failure, the victim of ingesting a poisonous cocktail of arrogance and ego. Albright wouldn't accept that he could be so wrong so he had kept doubling down, pressing his bet, trying to will a different outcome. He had thought this was in his power. After all, he was Vernon Albright. *The* Vernon Albright. But of course no one is right all the time; the markets are too fickle for one person, no matter how smart, to win on every trade. This is why the best money managers don't bet the farm on any single outcome. But Albright had succeeded many times with this strategy. It had worked until it didn't.

How can I be wrong? I've never been this wrong! The rest of the world is full of idiots. Fuck them!

Albright picked up the phone and pressed a button that connected to his then head trader, Vincent Garmeillion.

"Buy two million more Palmo Energy bonds. Do it now!"

Albright's order was met with silence.

"Are you deaf? I said buy two million more Palmo Energy bonds."

"No, Vernon, I'm not deaf. I'm out of firepower. None of our brokers will trade with us until we satisfy the margin calls."

"I'll pretend that you just misspoke since I know I pay you more than enough to keep those assholes in line."

The trader took a deep breath. "We're frozen until we pay down our balances and there's nothing I—or the brokers—can do about that. Instead of buying more bonds, why don't we sell a portion to raise cash and give us some breathing room?"

"Since when are you making investment decisions? When I want infantile advice I'll call the local elementary school. I'm not selling anything at these prices and booking a loss."

"Maybe getting some outside advice is not a bad idea the way you're going. Those kids couldn't do worse. You've lost a fortune in Palmo and most of the other bonds you bought." Garmeillion paused to let his words sink in. "What do we know about bonds? We should have stayed with stocks."

Albright shouted into the phone. "Who the fuck are you to tell me what we should do?"

"You know what, Vernon, I've had enough of your insults. You may pay me enough to keep the brokers in line but nowhere near enough to take your abuse. And I'm tired of fielding calls from those brokers asking when we're going to pay them back. The bonds you bought keep going lower and our debts keep going higher. I quit. Hell, given the fund's performance this year, you won't be paying me a bonus anyway."

"Get the hell out. I don't need you. Go on, get out!" Albright slammed the phone down and fell back into his chair. His hands began to shake as the stress started to take an increasing toll. The circumstances were even worse than Garmeillion's most dire thoughts.

Albright had placed almost fifty percent of his fund into a series of corporate bonds that appeared to him to be incredibly cheap. But the bonds kept getting cheaper and the companies he had invested in wound up spiraling into bankruptcy. And if that alone wasn't bad enough, he was not legally allowed to invest in bonds as stated in Parthenon's contract with its investors. Were the limited partners, that is, the investors, ever to find out that Vernon had lost money doing what he was expressly prohibited from doing, he would have been personally liable not only for the actual losses but also for any punitive damages the courts sought to impose. Parthenon would have been put out of business and Vernon would be standing in line at a homeless shelter waiting for his next cup of soup and bragging to whoever would listen that he used to be one of the country's wealthiest men. And if the offense rose to the level of fraud, a distinct possibility post Bernie Madoff, Albright might very well have traded his 36 room apartment for a 36 square foot cell.

It didn't take long from the time that Garmeillion quit for Albright to finally accept what he had known for some time; he wouldn't be able to trade his way out of the mess he had created, begrudgingly admitting to himself that his investment acumen wasn't transferrable from stocks into bonds. He began to search for someone who possessed enough financial wherewithal to bail him out; someone who would be discrete, someone who—well, someone who was as consumed by wealth as he was. Somewhat reluctantly, but without any other option, he knew it was time to re-connect with Buck Hendricks. Less than six months earlier, Hendricks had secured an introduction to Albright through another hedge fund manager. Although not looking for new investors, especially because their due diligence process would likely uncover Parthenon's unauthorized investment issues, Albright took the meeting upon hearing that Buck had earned his billions by transforming a successful family business that owned a few oil wells into an energy behe-moth. Desperate to recoup the money he had lost betting on the bonds of Palmo and other energy companies, Albright had hoped to glean an edge on the direction of the price of crude. Hendricks, however, had a different agenda; he wanted to discuss an investment in Parthenon on surpris-ingly favorable terms. When Hendricks intimated that he knew something was amiss at Parthenon, Albright was at first clearly taken aback but he rallied quickly, launching a blistering offensive at this stranger who dared insult him.

"Com'on now, Vernon. You think I just dropped in on you out of the blue? The CEO of Palmo is a buddy of mine.

Our daddies used to wildcat together. Nothing happens in
the oil business that I don't know about. You've been buying
those bonds from up here," Hendricks raised his hand high
over his head, "to down here." He brought his hand toward
the floor, slapping the surface of the antique end table for
effect. "I happen to be pretty damn good with numbers and
I figure you lost a fortune in Palmo and the bonds of those
other oil companies you own."

"That's crap and you know it. Crude prices have been
going straight up and so have my investments."

"Com'on now, Vernon," he repeated. "There's more to
making money in bonds than the price of crude going
higher. Palmo had already sold all their production at lower
prices and then dug too many dry holes with borrowed
money. I wish we knew each other before you bit on their
bullshit. I could have kept you out of trouble." Buck paused
and looked directly into Albright's eyes. "But maybe I still
can."

"How's that?" Albright inquired, calmer and clearly
curious.

Hendricks put forth a proposition that Albright found
completely untenable—at least as long as there was still
a sliver of hope that he could independently dig his way
out of his troubles. They both held their ground and parted
amicably, neither one interested in leaving the other with
hard feelings.

Hendricks continued to keep abreast of Parthenon's
declining fortunes while Albright kept pushing on a string.
Finally, after exhausting all options and unwilling to revisit
the failure he had known early in his life, Albright reached
out to the Texan and they struck a deal. Hendricks agreed to
make good Parthenon's losses without the limited partners
ever finding out in exchange for a significant discount on
the fees Albright charged and participation in Parthenon's
future profits. Hendricks also negotiated a hefty say in the
firm's investment decisions. For the first time in Parthenon's
storied existence, Albright would not be the only one call-

ing the shots. Needless to say, he was none too pleased at this arrangement, often paying lip service to Hendricks's "suggestions" rather than acting upon them. Without anyone on the inside, Hendricks had no way of knowing this and Albright took comfort that he was smarter than the rich hayseed from Texas.

Were trading profits the only measure, their union would have been regarded as the perfect marriage. Hendricks fed Albright important information about the oil markets and certain oil company stocks that always led to winning investments. In fact, Parthenon generated its best performance after Buck came on board. To investors and the outside world, the legend of Vernon Albright continued to grow. However, all was not as it seemed and Albright's occasional dissatisfaction with the partnership grew more frequent. But he knew Hendricks would never agree to a dissolution of their interests—at least not willingly.

Chapter 4 □ □ □

For most people, Sunday night sleep patterns were different from the rest of the week. Ironically, studies revealed that it took longer to drift off on the biblical day of rest than any other night. Experts attribute this to apprehension about the workweek that lay ahead. Whether a function of his even-keeled personality or being accustomed to never taking a break from thinking about his portfolio, Jeremy seemed immune to the Sunday night effect. Recently that had begun to change, and on this night he became another statistic. He lay in bed for hours, restlessly turning, trying to find the perfect position that would bring a welcome state of slumber. Despite mental and physical fatigue, his limbs seemed strangely possessed, as if they wanted to separate and run off. So as not to wake Jennifer, he went into the guest bedroom where he tried reading, then watching television but was much too tired to focus on either. They were an annoyance, failing to possess his thoughts for even a moment. Jeremy finally surrendered and ingested an Ambien, ten milligrams, a remedy he was drawn to with increasing frequency. He hid this from Jennifer; he hated causing her to worry.

Twenty minutes later he was out, but not completely, slipping into consciousness off and on every thirty minutes before awakening for good after only three hours. Jeremy had become accustomed to functioning quite well on only five to six hours of sleep, but it was usually peacefully uninterrupted unless his portfolio happened to be going through a particularly rough period. His mind racing, he faced the ceiling and sought a solution. He was in a continuum of time where the minutes ticked by endlessly, never seeming to move forward. Morning would never come.

But come it did. Streams of light filtered through the linen curtains as the early summer sun shone over the horizon. Jeremy wanted to reassure himself that his family was safe so he peeked in on his daughters. He arrived at Alexandra's room first and caught her wide awake.

"Daddy," she screamed in delight, bringing an instant smile to Jeremy's face. "Is today Sunday again?"

"No, baby," he chuckled. "Daddy just wanted to check on his girls but I didn't expect you to be up so early."

"Some birdies were outside my window making lots of noise," Alexandra replied, pointing to the window. "Let's make waffles. Mickey Mouse waffles."

"I'm sorry honey but I have to go to work."

"Pretty please, we never have breakfast together on days you go to work. We can wake up Melissa and she can help. And then we can surprise Mom."

Exhausted from lack of sleep, he was looking for any excuse to avoid working out and this was the best that he could hope for under any circumstance. "That's probably the greatest idea I have ever heard."

"Yippee!" She wrapped her arms around her father and everything seemed right with the world again as they headed to the kitchen.

Jeremy placed Alexandra in her chair at the table. "Wait here, honey, while Daddy grabs the newspaper."

He opened the front door and headed to the bottom of the driveway where the newspapers sat, each one in a different colored plastic wrap. As he turned back toward the house, his eye caught on something that protruded from the mailbox. *Too early for mail*, he thought. A sense of dread hung in the morning air as he reached for the object, a plain white envelope, unsealed, no writing on either side. Slowly, he extracted a single piece of lined, yellow paper and unfolded it.

"Good morning, Mr. Cranford. Just wanted to let you know I stopped by." It was signed, simply enough, *"Mr. D."*

Jeremy ripped the paper in half, then half again. He snapped his head to the right, then back to the left, hoping to see his tormentor. His fists clenched tight, he scanned the neighbors' yards, but nothing disrupted the stillness of the morning. As he panned the area, he noticed the front door was ajar. *Oh my God! What if....* Panic set in and he dropped the newspapers and the torn note, the pieces of paper scattering in the breeze. He ran to the house, expecting the worst.

Chapter 5 □ □ □

Hours before the market would open in New York, trading had begun at the International Petroleum Exchange where the majority of the world's oil is priced. By operating out of London, however, it bridges the time difference between the United States and the rest of the world.

Trading in oil futures, particularly Brent crude, was brisk, hovering around one hundred dollars a barrel for the last five months but now it was over one twenty. The talking heads had a veritable smorgasbord of reasons for the surge in oil prices. Among the favorites were the global economic recovery, gas guzzling SUV's and the emergence of China and India as industrial powers. Although some of their reasoning was credible, a twenty percent price increase in such a compressed period was extremely unusual, particularly considering the already elevated levels.

***

Brendan McNamara and Chuck Nettles, the youthful managing partners of two other hedge funds in which Buck was invested, had both set their alarm clocks for 4:45 AM Eastern Standard Time, anxious to call their brokers in London. They had a particular view about the inventory levels for crude oil that were released every Wednesday. Lower inventory levels indicated greater demand portending higher energy prices. Lately, Brendan and Chuck always seemed to be on the right side of the trade, betting that demand would continue to be strong. They loved having Buck as an investor. His information was golden.

The phone rang at the trading post of Fahnstock &

Moore. A clerk stood at the ready, pencil and order book in hand. To the uninitiated, the screaming and shouting that went on in the trading pit might seem like pure chaos, similar to a birthday party for a group of four year old boys, but the system was actually highly orchestrated and carefully controlled.

As a safeguard against disputes, generally occasioned by disreputable traders attempting to renege on a bad bet, each incoming and outgoing call was recorded. Brokers were repeatedly admonishing their girlfriends and wives (sometimes one of each) to keep their conversations clean. Replaying the tape while investigating a trading dispute could provide shocking entertainment such as the time one intern, unaware of the custom, was taped discussing in glorious detail a night of kinky sex with a guy she had met only hours before.

"Fahnstock," the clerk necessarily yelled into the phone above the background noise. Conversations on the order desk were kept brief. A delay in placing an order into a moving market had a cost.

"Brendan McNamara from Energy Venture Partners. Brent crude. Where's it trading?" He had a live feed wired to his PC at home, but preferred to get a real picture from the pit where qualitative information also flowed.

"Last trade was at one hundred twenty even. Hardly any contracts for sale."

Damn, Brendan thought. Trading had just opened and crude was already up a dollar. He was pleased that his current holdings had been appreciating over the last couple of months, but he didn't yet have a full position, not with the new money that Buck was investing into his fund. And now, with nothing being offered at the price of the last trade, he would have to pay up to buy more. He didn't really mind, though, since he just kept on making more money. Not married and young, making money was all he cared about. That and having a good time.

"See what you can do at a hundred twenty-seven but I'm

willing to pay a little more to get in a thousand contracts." The total cost of the trade would be at least twelve million U.S. dollars.

The clerk confirmed the trade in a staccato stream of words. "Right. Buying a thousand contracts. Brent. Using a top of one twenty-seven with a little room."

"Correct." Brendan would receive a call when the trade was complete or if his price limit was too low. In the meantime, he took a shower and prepared to go to the office.

***

Chuck Nettles could never get the markets out of his mind, dreaming about them more often than not. He even went to the expense of hiring a researcher from MIT to develop a device that would allow him to take a quick look at the overseas markets during the night without having to leaving his bed. A wireless transmission of his heartbeat was sent to a receiver built into a Bloomberg terminal. Once his pulse quickened to a certain level, indicating that he was coming out of REM sleep, a signal would be dispatched triggering a mechanism that would have a screen, showing his entire portfolio, swing out from the wall directly into his line of vision, the amber lights clearly visible in an otherwise darkened room. Through constant repetition, he had become quite good at fixing his eyes on the exact right spot. This gizmo, let alone an obsession with work, had cost him more than one relationship over the years.

Before the start of the trading day, Nettles made sure he was completely alert. Rising out of bed when the alarm sounded, he immediately took a cold shower. Fifteen minutes later, he placed a call to his broker at Smythe Brothers, located on the opposite end of the pit from Fahnstock.

"It's Chuck Nettles. Give me a price on Brent."

"Let me get a fresh look." The Smythe employee stole a glance at his monitor and observed the action taking place no more than fifteen feet from where he stood. "Looks like it's starting to heat up again. There's a large buyer lurking. Five hundred already traded up two dollars today."

"Go along for five hundred."

"Right. Buying five hundred Brent contracts alongside the market."

The order was input into the system and wirelessly sent to the broker who would execute the trade. Nelly, a large man with a barrel chest, stood at the edge of the crowd and read the message appearing on his handheld screen. He buttoned his khaki colored cotton broker's jacket and stepped into the pit, elbowing his way to the center.

"Listen up mates. I'll buy two hundred right here." Nelly held back part of the order hoping to get a better price.

The response to the offer came back just as loud. "I got three hundred for sale at one twenty-seven-fifty. All or nothing."

"I'll pay twenty-two-fifty for the whole lot. Take it or leave it."

"Done."

Nelly played possum hoping the price would come in without him as an active buyer but even if he had to pay up to complete the order, Chuck Nettles would be pleased with his average cost. A significant commission generator, it was important to keep him happy.

Meanwhile, two more orders were phoned in from other funds in the U.S. seeking to acquire positions of similar size. The brokers met in the center of the pits, their voices getting louder and more determined with each new bid.

By the end of the London trading session, the price for Brent would settle comfortably close to one hundred twenty-eight per barrel. This would provide a nice lift to Vernon Albright's portfolio since he had some very big stock positions in companies whose fate was directly correlated to the price of crude.

Buck Hendricks had a downright uncanny ability to forecast the price of oil. Every time he told Albright that the price was about to move higher, he would add to Parthenon's already significant energy positions. Albright came to believe—or rationalize—that the Texan was somewhat of an idiot savant when it came to the energy markets. It also didn't hurt, Albright reasoned, that Buck was pretty well connected both domestically and abroad. This didn't necessarily indicate that he had inside information, but rather possessed industry knowledge that was (hopefully) perfectly legal to share. Buck was also helpful in another way; he knew which companies Albright should buy shares in, which were, coincidentally (wink, wink) the same ones that Buck owned. Albright never questioned Buck's relationship with these companies, perhaps afraid of the answer. Providing information on the commodity was one thing, doing so on a specific company was a gray area. Greed was a great motivational technique that helped Albright overcome his cynicism; no one was right all the time.

Resulting from the spike in crude, the value underlying Albright's small energy companies had increased by five percent, most of the work being done while he slept. Five percent would be an excellent return after six months and here it was 'earned' in mere hours. But what was good for Albright wasn't so good for the rest of the market or the economy, for that matter.

Chapter 6

□   □   □

Albright left the office earlier than usual so he could stop at home and say a quick hello to his wife before meeting with Buck. She never liked it when he had business dinners during the week. It was one of his issues with a much younger trophy wife; they always wanted to be out on the scene and be seen, not left home alone. Deciding to enjoy the temperate summer evening, he gave his driver the night off and walked from his thirty-six-room duplex apartment on Seventy-Third Street and Fifth Avenue to The Carlyle Hotel on Madison and Seventy-Sixth. Located in one of the most affluent neighborhoods in the world, The Carlyle was the resting place of choice for the rich and famous that cared more about their privacy than having their whereabouts deliberately reported in the gossip columns. In addition to rooms and suites for transient but well-heeled visitors, there were also permanent apartments for those fortunate few who could afford to maintain them. The hotel didn't offer discounts for their long term residents pushing the average rent in excess of a hundred thousand dollars a month.

Albright entered the lobby and was immediately noticed by one of the several discreet security officers. Conservatively dressed in navy blue suits, the better to blend in with their surroundings, they walked a delicate line between maintaining vigilance and allowing visitors to come and go without feeling they were being scrutinized.

"May I help you, sir?"

Albright answered without breaking stride as he moved

toward the elevator. "No, it's quite all right. I know where I'm going,"

Tension appeared to pervade the atmosphere surrounding Vernon Albright—he had that air of elitism about him—effectively warning people to approach with great caution. It was almost as if a sign hung on his back that said "I'm too important to be bothered by the likes of you." However, when charm was the order of the day, Vernon could turn it on like a faucet.

The guard quickly determined that the silver-haired gentleman in the finely tailored suit and Hermes tie didn't represent any type of threat and wasn't about to tolerate being hassled. He faded away as unobtrusively as he'd approached.

Albright knocked on the door to Hendricks's Penthouse apartment and was greeted by Rick Galloway, a hulking figure perennially dressed entirely in black. He was Buck's driver, bodyguard, and general factotum. Galloway ushered Albright into the foyer where Carla awaited his arrival.

"Good to see you again, Mr. Albright. May I offer you something to drink? Perhaps an iced tea or coffee? Maybe something stronger?" Carla hadn't spent four years at the University of Texas training to be a waitress but her distaste for some of the aspects of being Buck's administrative assistant were more than offset by outsized compensation and excitement.

"So good to see you, too, Carla. Iced tea will do just fine."

"Very well then. Mr. Hendricks would prefer for you to wait on the balcony while he finishes an important call."

Certainly no stranger to the trappings of wealth, Vernon still marveled at the luxury of The Carlyle's apartment suites. Resting upon an ancient Persian rug was a piano, framed by two antique love seats upholstered in rich dark velvet allowing for a small audience to enjoy an impromptu concerto, although the idea that such an event would ever take place in Buck's home struck Albright as nothing short of hilarious. The windows were swathed in taupe silk draperies held open by matching sashes, giving the room's occupants an unimpeded view of Central Park one block to the west. A Bidermaier desk and a few tasteful antique accessories completed some anonymous interior decorator's vision of what a room furnished with old money should look like.

Albright stepped through the sliding doors onto the balcony, coming to a stop at the low wall rimming the terrace. He bent over slightly, peering down on the passersby below. Even though he stood thirty-four floors above the street, this was still New York and the traffic noise along Madison Avenue muffled Hendricks' arrival, announced with a squeeze of Vernon's shoulder. Startled, he jumped back.

Buck laughed, but Albright wasn't amused.

"Easy there, Vern. Why so jumpy?"

"Not jumpy at all, just a bit startled. I didn't hear you coming up behind me." Albright was in fact skittish, always on tenterhooks around Hendricks though he would never admit it, not even to himself.

"I've never been accused of being light on my feet, especially in these shit kickers," Hendricks responded as he lifted his foot off the ground revealing his Texas footwear. "Let's go inside."

Buck lowered himself onto the sofa while Albright sat opposite, his back to the door. Carla brought their drinks, a scotch for her boss and an iced tea, as requested, for Vernon, then left them to confer in private.

Buck got right to the point. "Did you come to your senses about letting me put more money in the fund?"

"Listen, Buck, you know I love doing business with you but I don't want to have this same conversation every time we get together." Vernon paused, trying to stem his impatience with discussing Hendricks' seemingly favorite topic. "The fund is still closed. Nothing has changed. Besides, it wasn't that long ago that I made an exception and took in another hundred from you. If I do it again, what will my partners think? Jeremy will start asking questions if an additional five hundred million suddenly appears on the books. I've told you what he's like—Mr. Upstanding Good Citizen, and not much gets by him. Right now he's entirely focused on his portfolio and I want to keep it that way for obvious reasons. Be patient, I'll figure out how to take the money eventually without raising any suspicions. It would mean more for me too."

"Sorry, Vern, but that doesn't sound right. You're the big kahuna, the top dog. Tell your partners it's a done deal. This could add another thirty million to the bonus pool. I'm sure you pay them really well but nobody's rich enough to turn their noses up at that kind of dough."

Vernon shifted forward in his seat, set his jaw and spoke. "You don't give up, do you? It's not the right time." His comments had an edge that he didn't intend. He slid back against the cushions and softened his tone. "Soon, Buck. Soon but not now."

"Hey, you can't blame me for trying. In my business, that's the only way to succeed. If I had stopped drilling every time some dirt came up on the bit, I'd never have hit a gusher. And then you and I wouldn't be sitting here talking about hundreds of millions, would we? Do me a favor and think about it because I guarantee that a lot of good information comes with that money. I know you have more millions than I have cattle on my tiny spread in Texas but this is pretty easy money." Buck let out a laugh and Albright politely joined in.

"You make some good points, but my hands are tied for now." Albright shifted in his seat. "So, did you ask me to stop by because you missed me or is there something else we have to discuss?"

"Don't flatter yourself, Vern. You're not exactly great company," he shot back. "Of course we have more to discuss and this is something you will thank me for."

"I can't wait to hear it."

Buck smiled at the sarcasm. "You're always complaining

about some of the folks that work for you. Well, I have an answer to your prayers."

"I so appreciate you looking out for my best interests. It warms my heart."

"I'm damn pleased to help out." Buck paused to take a sip of his cocktail. "My cousin just moved here from Texas and she is looking for a job."

"I'd be happy to meet with her and offer some guidance. What does she want to do?"

"That's easy. Marty is a huge fan of yours and wants to work at Parthenon. She seems to know everything about your firm: how you got started, your investment strategy, your biggest trades. Called you a genius. Guess you are a legend," Buck offered, deliberately pandering to Albright's weak point, his ego. "She knows I'm a large investor in the fund but that's all she knows and it's best to keep it that way."

"I'm flattered and while I'm sure any relative of yours would likely be a welcome addition to Parthenon, we do have a rather stringent screening process all candidates must go through."

"Com'on, Vernon, don't I look familiar to you?" Buck didn't wait for a response. "Probably not, because you must be mistaking me for someone who didn't bail your lily white, city slicker ass out of trouble." A sardonic smile efficiently communicated the implied threat.

Although sometimes necessary, Buck disliked having to remind any of his fund managers that if it hadn't been for him they were likely one bad trade away from the welfare line or a prison cell. He believed that gratitude should have a long memory, and although it wasn't his preference to cast himself in an adversarial position with his "partners," he had no problem being the bully.

Two weeks prior to this meeting, their relationship hit its first rough spot when Buck initially told Vernon he wanted to put another five hundred million into the fund. Vernon refused; he was already becoming uncomfortable with the relationship and didn't want Buck becoming a larger presence in Parthenon. At first Buck wasn't too concerned since Albright had always initially balked at taking in any additional money only to eventually succumb to an insatiable desire to make more money that he would never need. But after a second refusal and a very different tone to Albright's voice, he decided it was time to ratchet back Vernon's increasing obduracy. He had decided that going forward, he would give little ground, no matter what the issue.

Buck continued on without giving Albright an opening. "Marty is a very bright woman. Attended the London School of Economics and then spent some time at Goldman Sachs. After Goldman she went to work for a hedge fund in Dallas—much smaller than yours—in an operations role." Buck paused. "Her parents passed on when she was real young, and with no other close relatives, I took her in and raised her like my own daughter. Taking her under your wing would be a tremendous favor to me." He sat forward in his seat and stared hard into Albright's eyes. "I'm sure you can get this done for me."

"Of course we can find something for her," Albright capitulated, realizing that, under the circumstances, he couldn't refuse such a simple request. It was actually serendipitous; Paul Robbins, who ran the firm's operations and administrative functions, had been looking to add to his staff. It was the perfect position for a courtesy hire, far away from the investment process. "We're always looking for bright young people but I would like to meet her first—purely as a formality. You understand that I'm sure."

"Yessir, that's what I expected and why I went ahead and told Marty to come by for dinner tonight."

"Always thinking ahead, Buck. If this oil thing doesn't work out for you, maybe Marty will hire you at Parthenon to be her assistant."

Buck chuckled but it wasn't at Albright's poor attempt at humor. He wondered if Albright was a fan of Greek mythology but it wouldn't matter; Marty was one helluva Trojan horse.

Chapter 7 □ □ □

Seated with his back to the door Vernon was unaware that someone else had entered the room until Buck stood.

"As usual, your timing is perfect."

Gentleman that he was, Albright rose and turned just in time to see Hendricks pulling a lithe, exotically beautiful young woman into a warm embrace, placing a gentle kiss on her cheek. Smoothing his jacket as unobtrusively as possible, Vernon stepped around the sofa and waited to be introduced.

"Vernon Albright, meet Marty Jagdale."

Vernon accepted Marty's outstretched hand, gently encasing it in his grasp. "It's a pleasure to make your acquaintance," he said with absolute sincerity.

She was not what he had expected. In a short black dress that hugged the contours of her perfect body, Marty was both more striking and sophisticated than he would ever imagine any relative of Buck's to be. With hazel green eyes, a flawless, tawny complexion, and straight black hair falling slightly below her shoulders, she exuded an intriguing combination of aloofness and sexuality. This dinner was starting to look far more interesting than he had anticipated.

"It certainly is an honor, Mr. Albright. My cousin has told me many wonderful things about you, but I confess that I have been a fan of yours for some time."

Charming as well as beautiful with the faintest hint of a difficult to place accent.

"Please call me Vernon," he said without any indication of humility.

"Vern and I were just discussing your interest in Parthenon," Buck interjected. "Now it's up to you to convince him to give you a shot. That's why I suggested y'all have dinner."

"Dinner is an excellent idea," Albright intoned, having clearly warmed to the suggestion. "It will be much easier to have a conversation without all the interruptions I would have to deal with in the office."

"Get on your way," Buck said, gently placing a hand on the small of Marty's back as he ushered them to the door. "I had Carla make a reservation at Le Bernardin. Hope you don't mind, Vern."

Much as he might resent the presumption, Albright certainly couldn't fault Hendricks for choosing one of New York's finest restaurants.

As they stepped outside onto the sidewalk, Rick was already waiting in Buck's car as the doorman held the rear door open.

"You seem to have a slight accent that I'm having trouble placing, although I'm pretty sure it's not from growing up in Texas."

Marty laughed softly, bringing her hand to her mouth as if to stifle her amusement. "I'm sorry, I didn't mean to find that funny, but it seems that everyone assumes that since I'm Buck's relative I should be wearing boots and jeans with straw sticking out of my hair."

Vernon chuckled. She wasn't far from the truth given what his expectations had been.

Marty continued. "Actually, I've spent most of my life overseas, first attending boarding school and then graduate classes after university. My mother, you see, wasn't from Texas. She was originally from the Middle East. Like Buck, my father was in the oil business, except he worked for Exxon in their Saudi operations. That's where my parents met. My accent has a little bit of everything from Texas to Europe to the Middle East."

They arrived at the restaurant shortly after six and

were greeted warmly by Lawrence, the maître d'. "Bon soir, Monsieur Albright. What a pleasure to see you again. I have your table ready."

Albright scanned the room, conscious of being seen with a beautiful woman who was even younger than his wife. She knew he had a business dinner but wondered if she would believe him were one of her friends to see him and report back. As he considered the possibility, he realized he only cared to the extent that he wanted to avoid the hassle of dealing with another argument.

"How about a table in the rear so that we can speak privately." He slipped a fifty dollar bill into Lawrence's hand.

"Of course, Monsieur Albright."

Lawrence grabbed two menus from the side of the podium that stood near the entrance and led the way to a quiet table. Richly textured curtains hung from the twenty-foot-high ceiling protecting the well-heeled diners from gawking passerby. At the table they were greeted by two waiters dressed in dinner jackets standing behind two slightly oversized chairs covered in dark brocade. As Vernon and Marty took their seats, the waiters pushed their chairs closer to the table, then lifted the napkins that lay next to the decorative chargers, and gently dropped them into their laps.

"So good to see you this evening, Monsieur Albright," said Phil, Vernon's regular attendant. It amused Albright to know that Phil, a Brooklyn native, had a command of French that began and ended with the menu and a few generic expressions.

After Marty tendered her drink order and Phil assured "Monsieur Albright" that he would bring his regular martini, Vernon turned to his young companion. "Tell me more about yourself."

Marty leaned forward, chin cupped provocatively in the palms of her hands, fingers flat against her cheeks, elbows resting comfortably on the table. "What would you like to know?"

"Whatever you think would help me decide where you might fit in at Parthenon."

"Hmmm...." She uttered coyly.

Unsure if she was being flirtatious or if it was just a case of nerves, Albright took the initiative. "Tell me if I have it right. You attended the London School of Economics. Goldman was your first job and then you decided to make an honest living and went to work at a hedge fund." He paused. "Have I hit the highlights?"

"Honest living? Some would say that my honest living ended when I left Goldman and came over to the dark side."

"Fair point," Vernon conceded with a chuckle.

"My cousin seems to have laid it out well. What else did he tell you?"

"That's pretty much it." Vernon took a sip of his martini. "How familiar are you with Parthenon?"

"Everyone who knows anything about investing knows Parthenon and Vernon Albright," Marty stated as if a fact. "You are a legend, a true pioneer. I've read everything about you that I could get my hands on. Your firm manages approximately twenty billion dollars and it is all in stocks. My cousin told me he is one of your largest investors." The words came out of Marty's mouth innocently, not in any way bragging. "Parthenon has a great track record," she continued, "probably the longest and best in the business. Yes, Mr. Albright...I mean, Vernon...your reputation as a market wizard is well entrenched. Small and mid-capitalization stocks are your forte while your partner, Jeremy Cranford, invests in larger companies."

"I'm impressed." And duly flattered, he might just as well have added. "Since you appear to know us so well, where do you think you could be helpful?"

"I'm only twenty-eight," Marty demurred. I'm still young, and while I have some practical experience, it was at a much smaller shop than yours. Anything you can find for me would be great."

Vernon found himself taking a liking to Marty. She reminded him a bit of Jeremy when they first met in that she was clearly smart and driven but in no way arrogant, a refreshing alternative to all the self-important Harvard MBA's he interviewed over the years. He knew he had no choice but to offer Marty a position, but she was making him feel better about the circumstances.

"How can I go wrong? Great education, relevant experience, and I get to keep my largest investor happy." He handed her his card. "Can you stop by tomorrow?"

"Tomorrow? As in Tuesday?"

"Yes. That tomorrow."

"Absolutely. I've been waiting for an opportunity like this for a long time."

"Perfect. Stop by in the afternoon. I want you to meet Jeremy and Paul Robbins, another senior member of the firm."

Seemingly out of impulse, Marty grabbed Vernon's hand as it rested on the table, letting it linger. "Thank you so much, Vernon. I promise that you won't be sorry you gave me this opportunity."

Albright began to feel pretty good about his new hire. The two, five thousand dollar bottles of Petrus they consumed were making it easier for him to believe that the idea had actually been his.

Marty couldn't help but smile. Buck would be pleased but not nearly as pleased as she was. She had imagined Albright being a difficult adversary but now she spied a weakness, the same vulnerability she had been able to so adeptly exploit in those other wealthy old codgers she had come up against. As with them, he would have more difficulty overcoming his ego and libido—she knew what he wanted—than anything the markets threw at him. But Buck—well, that was a different story.

Chapter 8

□ □ □

It was 5:30 a.m. and the sky was just beginning to lighten outside the windows of 105 Park Avenue as Vernon Albright emerged from the elevator onto the sixtieth floor, where Parthenon Capital Limited had their offices. The warm feeling from last night's red wine had morphed into enough of a hangover to put him in a rotten frame of mind. Not even another two dollar spike in oil prices lightened his mood despite the sizeable lift it would provide to his vast holdings of energy stocks. The smile on his face was misleading. It was a habit that had turned into a reflex every morning when he saw his firm's name through the glass doors leading into the reception area.

Who wouldn't smile in Albright's position? The money he managed for a group of extremely wealthy individuals, corporations and endowments, who anted up the minimum twenty-five-million-dollar investment, generated substantial fees. As soon as Albright turned the lights on every January 1st, the three percent management fee he took off the top of the twenty billion earned him six hundred million dollars. This payment was just for the privilege of investing in his fund. Then, if Parthenon made any money for its investors, and it always did, Albright would get an additional twenty percent of those profits. In his best year he had earned a shade less than a billion, a sum that exceeded the gross domestic production of a number of small African nations. Jeremy Cranford was the only other employee who made eye-popping money but he was nowhere near Albright's level.

In just a few hours the now-empty reception desk would

be occupied by two very beautiful, stylishly dressed young women. Their bright smiles, Frederic Fekkai haircuts and cultured voices, along with the eight million dollar Picasso hanging on the wall behind them, provided every visitor's first impression of Parthenon. All were an essential part of a carefully cultivated image. Vernon wanted everything about the reception area to say that Parthenon was where money—a lot of it—was made.

Making his way through the reception area, Albright flipped on the light and stopped to glance at the most recent issue of Forbes magazine, casually opened to the listing of the Forbes Four Hundred. Despite his huge ego, Vernon generally did his best to avoid publicity, but the annual appearance of his name among the world's four hundred wealthiest people was beyond his control. Next to each name on the list there was a thumbnail description including age, source of wealth, and family status. Albright's read: *Vernon Albright, 62, divorced twice, remarried. General Partner, hedge fund.*

The picture that accompanied the caption on page 173 in the magazine captured the essence of the man. From his perfectly cut silver hair to his bespoke suits, understated but instantly recognizable Hermes ties, and Lobb shoes, Albright wore his wealth well. At an even six feet and fit from his daily workouts, he appeared to have avoided the wear and tear that constant stress can have on even the most driven of men. It was his eyes that were the true windows into his soul. A piercingly bright blue, they could express either unwaveringly gracious attention or fiercely unbridled anger, often within minutes of one another.

This morning, however, Albright could have passed for any reasonably well kept middle-aged executive as he headed to the company gym. Albright endeavored to be the first to arrive every day. It was his way of defying the odds, as well as reminding his employees that he wasn't slowing down and they best stay on their toes. Albright noticed that it had become something of an unspoken challenge among certain members of his staff to try to arrive at the gym before he did. Since he relished a competitive atmosphere, nothing could have made him happier, although he had no intention of letting them know he was onto their little game.

The state-of-the-art work out facility was a great recruiting tool for the firm. It was cool to have a fully equipped gym, including personal trainers, located inside your office space. But as healthy as it was to exercise, it could be extremely damaging to the well-being of one's career to make use of it during Parthenon's workday. Company lore included one oft-repeated story of the day Albright, walking in the hallway at lunchtime, heard the whir of a stationary bicycle from behind the closed gym doors. He called his head of Human Resources from the first phone he saw. "I want you to go into the gym and fire whoever is in there working out. I don't care who it is. Just throw them out. In fact, don't even let them shower. No one takes time off when the market is open!"

Everyone knew not to approach the boss while he was exercising unless he initiated the conversation. Otherwise his early morning workouts would be accomplished not to the tune of piped in music but to the much less mellifluous sounds of employees kissing his ass. One conversation that always took place, however, was the briefing Albright received from the only people who were not wearing workout clothing. They were the night traders who were responsible for overseas markets. Their workday ended shortly after the sun came up, but not before they had filled Vernon in on events occurring on their watch that might affect the firm's holdings. Getting sprayed with the boss's flying sweat as he took a turn on the treadmill was an occupational hazard the night traders were well paid to withstand.

Jeremy Cranford and his best friend Paul Robbins, Parthenon's Chief Operating Officer, were already peddling on side-by-side stationary bikes at the far end of the gym when Albright arrived.

Jeremy leaned toward Paul and spoke quietly. "There's something I have to discuss with you. I received some letters..."

"Hold on a second," Paul interrupted while nodding toward Albright. "Our boss is looking a little ragged this morning."

"And none too happy," Jeremy agreed. "It's definitely one of those mornings when it's best to keep your distance. I hope these kiss-ass associates have the sense to stay away from him. I'd hate to have to interrupt my workout to peel one of them off the floor."

A few minutes later, the gym doors swung open. "Oh shit, it's Janowicz and he's looking kind of sheepish. The night desk must have screwed the pooch somewhere," Jeremy hissed through gritted teeth. "He's going right for Vernon. This is not going to be pretty."

Larry Janowicz was responsible for trading stocks in Asia and Europe.

"Bet you're right. Clear out the women and children," Paul said sarcastically as he followed his friend's gaze. "Call me crazy, but judging from his pained expression, I don't think Larry is going to be telling Vernon he made him any richer overnight."

"Vernon is really loaded for bear. If Larry were smart, he would do an about face and get the hell out of here before it's too late."

They turned, eyes front, pretending to be absorbed in the television monitors affixed to the handlebars of their bikes. Regardless of where they focused their attention, they knew they would not have any problem overhearing the conversation taking place on the opposite side of the room.

"Honda got away from me," Janowicz confessed meekly.

Vernon didn't break stride. "What do you mean it got away from you? Is that a joke? You must be referring to one of those cheap little cars they make. That's what must have gotten away from you. Couldn't be the stock. You get paid too much money to let the stock get away from you."

Head down, unable to look directly at his boss, Janowicz responded. "I wish I was joking but I'm not. I missed the trade."

Vernon's glare reduced Janowicz to an even smaller man in stature than his five-foot-five height exhibited. "Isn't that just great! Honda got away from you. Exactly how many shares transacted out of your grasp?" His voice had not yet risen to higher decibels but the anger was apparent in his condescension.

"Two million shares." Janowicz whispered.

Albright was having a tough time controlling his mounting anger as he draped his towel over the handrail and stepped onto the exercise machine. His dismissive attitude made Janowicz even more uncomfortable. "You only bought fifty thousand out of the two million that traded. It's a virtual impossibility to fuck up that badly. You certainly have a special talent. Where the hell is the stock now?"

"In dollars or yen?"

"Am I speaking Japanese?"

"Sorry. Fifty-seven."

"Fifty-seven? We had a six top. How the hell did that happen?" Albright yelled, popping the veins in his neck. "We've been buying that stock for two damn weeks and now you fall asleep on me! What the hell is wrong with you?"

Even though he was not the one working out, Janowicz started to sweat. "Can we go to your office and discuss this?" he begged. "It will be more private."

"I want the others here to listen to this. This is a teachable moment that they can learn from so that they don't fall asleep on their responsibilities. Besides, this will not be a long conversation," he said in a lower but still edgy tone. "This is the second time you've screwed up this week and its only Tuesday. I guess you are tired—maybe too tired to do this job any longer. I sort of feel bad for you, having to stay up all hours of the night for the measly half million dollars I pay you to do the job a wide-awake sixth grader could do." He let his words sink in for what seemed an eternity to Larry. "So I'm going to do you a favor; I'm going to make sure you get lots of sleep. You're fired. Go home. Go to bed. Don't even bother packing up. We'll send it all to you." His voice revealing indifference, Vernon had lost interest in the conversation. "Now get out of here and let me finish my workout."

Jeremy was stunned. Still looking straight ahead, he spoke to Paul in a hushed tone. "That was pretty harsh, even for Albright. Larry's been here a long time."

"Man, I agree. I've seen Vernon fire guys before but never like this. He put new meaning into the word asshole with this episode," Paul responded, feeling uncomfortable, the thought of being Albright's next victim never far from the surface.

Head down, shoulders slumped, Janowicz lumbered back to the trading desk to get his jacket. He'd known it would come to this eventually, but this job paid far more than any other he could have found on the Street. Relief at the realization that he would never again be the subject of Albright's abuse quickly dissolved into disappointment as he faced life as an unemployed fifty-year-old searching for a job in a younger man's business. Like a junkie who wants to quit using but is addicted to the high, Janowicz was tethered to the dollars and could never bring himself to resign despite wanting to many times. His only regret, the one that would linger with him for quite some time, was that he was intimidated into silence even though he had vowed that when this inevitable day came, he would tell Albright what he really thought of him, often imaging the very words he would use. Instead, he once again had allowed Albright to humiliate him; the difference this time being that he didn't have a job at the end of the tirade.

Before he left the gym, Janowicz took a quick look around the room, his eyes briefly coming to rest on Jeremy. Why hadn't he interceded instead of allowing Albright to so publicly berate him? He couldn't even be bothered to stop his workout to get involved. Was that a smirk on Cranford's face? He was sure it was. What a two-faced scumbag! At least he always knew where he stood with Albright, but Cranford.... Well, Cranford was now at the top of his list.

Jeremy stopped pedaling as the door closed behind Janowicz. "I'm going to say something. That's no way to treat anyone, particularly someone as loyal as Larry who's been taking his shit for so many years."

Paul grabbed Jeremy by the shirt. "Easy there, buddy. Go back into the phone booth and take off the cape and tights. What's done is done. Besides, Larry's been well paid for taking Vernon's shit. Nobody needs to hold a benefit for him. And he did screw up."

Jeremy smiled at Paul's Superman reference, but knew his friend was right. He also knew that, of the two of them, he would always be the crusader while Paul would remain more pragmatic—it was one of the differences that had made them such good friends and such perfect foils. Still, as he and Paul finished their workout, showered, and had their morning coffee in Jeremy's office, he was finding it difficult to forget the ugly scene he had just witnessed. The bloom could come off his own rose one day, putting him in Albright's crosshairs, a well-known occupational hazard at Parthenon. Still, Jeremy wanted to keep his job; it paid well and there was no guarantee that the office politics would be any better anywhere else.

***

Paul had been looking out for Jeremy ever since they met almost seven years ago in the training program at Salomon Brothers. Jeremy was already married to his high-school sweetheart. Paul was single and the more streetwise New Yorker, born and raised in Brooklyn, having only recently moved to Manhattan. He reveled in his new status as an eligible and relatively affluent young man on the Street. Even his slicked-back hair, dark good looks and whippet-thin build were in direct contrast to Jeremy's more wholesome, blond, all-American features and athletic physique. Jeremy projected an intensity that bred success; a personality that was warm yet measured. He was someone that you instantly wanted to trust. Each providing the yin to the other's yang, their different but complimentary personalities provided the foundation for the type of relationship that is usually the bastion of brothers. Both exceedingly intelligent, Paul had an affinity for technology and systems while Jeremy remained more interested in the investment side of the business. Upon graduation from Salomon's training program, they were both placed in the firm's asset management division. Wall Street, the ultimate meritocracy, had no requirement for a specific period of tenure so Jeremy's talent was quickly recognized and rewarded. Paul's career path and remuneration lagged; operations people were perceived to be less valuable than portfolio managers who were directly responsible for generating profits

Jeremy had met Vernon Albright when pinch hitting for a colleague at a business dinner. The bi-weekly event was sponsored by one of the brokerage houses and brought together a number of senior hedge fund managers for the purpose of sharing thoughts on the stock market and the economy. Jeremy had eventually secured his own place at the roundtable and so impressed Albright that he had offered Jeremy a job at Parthenon. Jeremy hadn't wanted to leave Paul behind, but it was at his friend's urging that he ultimately accepted the position.

"I don't know about this, Paul. Albright seems to run through employees almost as often as I change socks," Jeremy had worried aloud.

"You're as good as anyone, and you're being offered an incredible opportunity to work with one of the best in the business. The guy's a frickin' legend; a regular at the Barron's Roundtable." Barron's, the weekly bible of the Wall Street community, published an annual roundtable issue to which only the best and brightest money managers were invited to contribute their views. "You have to take the shot.

There's just one thing.... "

"What's that," Jeremy had asked, expecting a word of caution.

"Remember to hire me after you make it big," Paul had said, smiling but nonetheless serious.

In short order, Jeremy's performance had exceeded Albright's high expectations and he was rewarded with a partnership on his first anniversary at the firm. Jeremy had remembered his promise to Paul when the senior position in the back office, overseeing the technology for the accounting and trading systems, became available.

"Vernon, I know just the person for Macmillan's spot."

"Who's that?"

"My friend, Paul Robbins. You've met him a number of times. He does the same job at Sollie. He's smart as hell and lives and breathes the business."

"Done. Hire him."

"Just like that?" Jeremy asked. "Don't you even want to sit down with him?"

"You're a partner here. If you tell me he's the best person available for the job, I trust you. I'd much rather hire someone we know than bring in a stranger."

It made sense to Jeremy, and he was pleased that Vernon trusted him enough to make the decision. However, Vernon's thought process was a bit different than what he had expressed to Jeremy. He really didn't care who worked in the back office. As far as he was concerned, even the senior role in operations was purely a clerical position. With everything computerized, there was little chance of a significant administrative screw up. The important jobs belonged to those on the front line who made the investment decisions and brought in the revenues upon which the firm's reputation was based, and upon which Albright's income was dependent. Back-office pencil pushers were considered second-class citizens.

"I appreciate the vote of confidence but there is one more thing."

"And what's that?" Vernon briskly pulled his shirtsleeve back to glance at his watch; he had already spent more time on this issue than it merited.

Jeremy took note of Albright's narrowed eyes, his clenched jaw, and knew he was treading heavily on Albright's patience. "Since Paul has a senior role at Salomon we should bring him in as a partner."

"A partner!" Albright said. "No one has ever come into my firm as a partner. Why should I do it now?"

"First of all, Paul's the best at what he does. He's an animal when it comes to controlling costs. Let me give you an example: He renegotiated every single one of Sollie's vendor contracts saving them millions a year. Near as I can tell no one has ever done that here and that's cash coming directly out of our pockets. I guarantee Paul will pay for himself within weeks, but he's not coming here unless the offer includes a partnership."

Vernon thought it over carefully, warming up to the suggestion. *What the hell is the difference if I make him a partner*, he reasoned. *And if he can do what Jeremy says he can, it won't cost me a penny. Hell, I might even come out ahead.*

***

Jeremy, Paul, and Vernon were the only named partners at Parthenon, but neither of the younger men was under any illusion that the title bestowed equality with Albright. Although outsiders might logically have assumed otherwise, Vernon had made it perfectly clear from the beginning that Parthenon was not, and never would be, a democracy. Only one person made important decisions and was privy to the firm's entire database of information. That said, however, having the title conferred status and, from a practical point of view, should bring a larger bonus at the end of the year. Although Jeremy's compensation was still considerably more than Paul's, both their pay packages were determined by Vernon, and the formula for determining bonuses was the same all over Wall Street: generously remunerate your stars and pay everyone else a dollar more than required to keep them from looking elsewhere. It was an art, not a science.

***

Janowicz exited Parthenon's building and stopped. Increasingly anger and bitter, he debated returning to the office and telling Albright and Cranford what he thought of them. "Fuck them. This isn't going to end like this." He went through the doors and approached the turnstile, pulling out his I.D. card, glad that he had forgotten to leave it in the office. He swiped the card through the reader and a buzzer sounded. Two security guards approached.

Janowicz spoke first. "There must be something wrong with my card. It worked this morning."

"Do you mind if I take a look?" The guard took the card from Janowicz's outstretched hand. He pulled a piece of paper from his pocket to make sure that he had the right name. "I'm sorry, sir, but I am going to have to keep your building I.D. since you are no longer an employee of one of our tenants. It might also be a good idea for you to leave the lobby. Sorry."

Humiliated, his anger reached a higher level. He almost didn't recognize himself as his thoughts uncharacteristically turned dark and vengeful. *Two can play at this game. This is not over.*

Chapter 9 □ □ □

Vernon's hangover had largely dissipated by the time he got off the treadmill, but firing Janowicz had only further aggravated his foul mood. Not that he felt bad about doing it. Janowicz had it coming; it was just a hell of a way to start the day. Now he had another problem to straighten out.

Vernon barged through the door of his young partner's office, oblivious that Jeremy and Paul were in the middle of a conversation. When money was on the line, Vernon was single minded, and right now he was more than a bit unhappy about one of Jeremy's positions. "What's the thought process behind your position in Intel? Is your plan to hold onto it until it gets to zero?" he blurted without so much as a nod in Paul's direction.

Jeremy had purchased two million shares at thirty-five dollars per share. The stock was now down more than three dollars a share on the seventy million dollar position.

Startled, Jeremy looked up as he gathered his thoughts. "I'm not wrong on this trade," he responded calmly, in determined self-defense. "It's unfortunate the stock's traded down but we'll make good money on the position. I want to hold it."

Paul did his best to blend imperceptibly into the background.

"And I want you to sell it," Albright shot back. "I've lost enough money for one day as a result of Janowicz's screw up and I'm not in the mood to lose any more. You're already down six million. I'd say that takes it to a higher level of concern than unfortunate."

"Give me a minute to explain why I bought it," Jeremy tried once more but when Albright was so worked up, explanations were impossible.

The telltale veins in Vernon's neck had already started to pop, indicating that he was about to lash out, when an excited voice came over the open line that connected directly to the trading desk. To accommodate the quick movements of the market, this line was always on speaker mode; there was no ringing to announce an incoming call, only the bellowing of the trader alerting the portfolio manager to any movement or news that could affect one of Parthenon's positions.

Jack Knowles spoke in his familiar staccato cadence. "News on Intel. Just announced a major contract extension with Dell. Hasn't hit all the wires yet, only Reuters. Stock's up a dime in pre-market trading."

Even before Knowles had finished delivering his message, Jeremy was punching the ticker symbol for Intel into his Bloomberg keyboard. Wasting no time, Albright took over. "Jack! Buy another three million shares and try not to pay more than thirty-two and a quarter. Let me know when it's done," he shouted into the open phone line.

No one had to tell Vernon what was going on. Raising the position size to well over $150 million took balls the size of the globe that descended in Times Square on New Year's Eve, but Vernon knew that as soon as the rest of the wire services picked up the news the stock would trade significantly higher. With its strong brand name and dominant market share, it was a company that virtually every institutional and retail investor felt comfortable owning. Parthenon would eventually earn more than forty million dollars for its limited partners on this trade. With a carry of twenty percent of the profits, the firm would pocket eight million dollars, most of it, of course, going to Albright.

Jeremy was pissed. First Albright tells him to close out the trade and in the next second, he takes it over as his own. He was ready to let loose when Vernon once again beat him to the punch.

"I'm sorry Jeremy. I know you were getting ready to do the same thing, but even after all these years, I still can't contain my excitement at such a great trade. You stuck with it when I would have probably closed it out. Nice job."

"Thanks," was all Jeremy could say after that unsolicited apology and compliment. He knew he shouldn't have wasted any time pulling up a quote on his Bloomberg. The price of the stock was moving quickly and every second of delay led to paying a higher price. Albright had done the right thing, and it was those kinds of decisions that had earned him his well-deserved reputation as both a genius and a shark. He could walk into a situation he didn't know all that much about, but when the action started, he reacted instinctively and correctly—in this instance quicker than Jeremy despite it originally being his trade. Jeremy had confidence in his own instincts but Vernon took gut trading to a whole different level.

Albright wasn't finished. "So now that you've had your little ego massage, let's call a spade a spade. When a position goes against you like that, you either sell it because you were wrong or you take advantage of the decline to buy more. You did neither. The bottom line is that you got a little lucky."

Compliments from Albright never came without a twist of the knife, but this time Jeremy knew better than to get into an argument he stood no chance of winning. He bit his tongue and stayed silent.

Albright turned on his heels and moved down the hallway, a bit of a spring in his step as he allowed himself a mental pat on the back for having one-upped his younger partner. It was difficult to ascertain whether Albright reveled more in the victory over the market or Cranford. But he would never admit to the ego gratification, rather he regarded it as a teachable moment in the mentoring process. After all, Jeremy was one of his all-time favorites.

***

"Well, it certainly looks like this is going to be a banner day for Parthenon," Paul remarked as soon as Vernon was out of earshot. He was relieved to have dodged two vituperative bullets so far that morning, but the day was still young. "I don't know how you do it sometimes. At least I can hide in my office and, as long as the trades get settled and the bills are paid, I know the old man will leave me alone. I don't think he even saw me sitting here."

"He did the right thing. No questions, no discussion, just bang! He pulled the trigger before I could even get the words out and it was my trade. He can be a real asshole but he's still the best in the business."

"You're not being fair to yourself. I've seen you do exactly the same thing hundreds of times. You're every bit as good as he is."

Jeremy shrugged. "The bottom line is it worked out and I'll get paid two ways on the trade; my investment in the firm increases and my bonus should be bigger since I'll get credit for the trade. As far as I'm concerned he can have the moment of glory. I'll take the cash. But you shouldn't concern yourself with the mundane issues of making money. What's on your schedule today? Books to balance? Hard drives to swap out?"

"You're a funny guy but not funny enough to get me off the subject of Vernon shitting all over you."

"Easy there, buddy. He's—"

Mid-sentence, Jeremy's computer screen suddenly flickered and Albright's face appeared. "It's eight o'clock. Assuming you're finished basking in the glory of the Intel trade, how about gracing me with your presence for our morning meeting?" Without waiting for an answer to a question that didn't require one, Vernon's face faded from the screen.

"Case in point, right there. You're a rock star stock picker. You could start your own fund and not have to listen to his garbage."

"He gave me my big break, and I feel a certain amount of

loyalty to him. But aside from that, if I had my own firm I'd be working even more horrible hours than I do now, which would mean less family time. Maybe when the kids are a little older...." his voice trailed off.

"Screw the loyalty. You've paid him back a billion times over—literally."

Jeremy grabbed the notebook that he always took to his meetings with Albright. With one foot in the hallway he turned back to Paul. "I appreciate your concern, I really do, but did it ever occur to you that I may have other things on my mind?"

It was the first crack in Jeremy's unflappable demeanor that Paul had ever witnessed. He knew something was not right.

Chapter 10

□ □ □

Albright was still feeling pretty good about his Intel trade when he reached his office. There was one more matter to attend to before Jeremy arrived for their morning meeting. Still feeling good, he discarded his suit jacket and sat down behind his massive desk. Suzie Clintock, his administrative assistant, had already delivered his morning espresso, which, of course, was a double shot. He rubbed a fresh lemon rind around the edges of the demitasse then dipped an almond-flavored biscotti into the dark liquid. The office was cavernous, the adjoining private bathroom likely as big as most of his young staff's studio apartments. Atop the burled wood desk sat four flashing monitors that constantly updated the price of Parthenon's holdings as well as real-time price changes for every financial market in the world.

One of the companies in Parthenon's stock portfolio, Alpha Systems, was significantly underperforming. In fact, its price had been cut in half since Vernon first purchased the shares. He continued adding to the position as the stock price declined so he now owned almost twenty percent of the company. He had originally purchased the stake after a couple of conversations with the CEO, Michael Generau, wherein Generau had laid out his blueprint for revitalizing the operations. It was a realistic plan. However, Vernon reasoned, if Generau were not able to execute it effectively, the company could be liquidated allowing Parthenon to recoup its investment.

Albright had participated in a number of conference calls with Generau and his management team, but they did little to assuage his concerns. Improvement in the operating results remained elusive and he was out of patience. Moreover, Generau was sick of being harangued by Albright and chose to not take any more of his calls. Generau had underestimated Albright's persistence, a miscalculation that he would soon regret. As the first salvo in what would be a nasty proxy fight, Albright penned one of his trademark letters.

Michael Generau, CEO
Alpha Systems, Inc.
500 Merrick Road
Merrick, NY 10280

By Messenger

Mr. Generau:

Parthenon Capital Limited, LLC currently owns a 20% interest in Alpha Systems, Inc. Regrettably, this stake provides us with the dubious distinction of being Alpha's largest shareholder. Giving credit where credit is due, perhaps we should be grateful that your repeated acts of malfeasance have created the opportunity to buy shares at lower and lower price points. However, we generally prefer that the management of a company we own not run a perpetual fire sale on their own stock.

We have tried to contact you by phone but our entreaties have been continually stonewalled by your less-than-professional secretary who, I have learned from reliable sources, owes her job more to her skills as your consort, unbeknownst to Mrs. Generau I might add, than to her ability to type at a breakneck pace of 20 words per minute. Continuing to employ her at a salary of $100,000 per year not only makes her the corporate world's highest priced call girl but is demonstrative of only one of the many ways you have chosen to squander corporate assets. We also question what value your eighty-five-year-old mother can bring to the company at a compensation level of $250,000 a year. Although we would like to delve into your Oedipal complex a bit further, it is not a good use of our time. You have been running Alpha as if it *were your personal cookie jar rather than a public company that should be run for the benefit of shareholders.*

Alpha's Board of Directors, perhaps more appropriately called Board of Marionettes since you appear to pull all their strings, has repeatedly breached their fiduciary obligations to shareholders by not dismissing you years ago. You are to be commended for recruiting such a blatantly sycophantic board of corporate stewards. We intend to file lawsuits against all of them.

Your incompetence is not only reflected in your lack of simple communicative skills with your shareholders but also in the myriad missteps you have taken in the execution of your duties. The only consistency you have exhibited since you have been at the helm of Alpha has been your uninterrupted track record of blunder after blunder. The legacy you have created is defined by the spectacular 85% decline in the company's stock price since you assumed the title of CEO. We feel fortunate to have participated in only part of that downward spiral.

Michael, it is time for you to retire and leave the company in the hands of professional managers who have been absent for far too long. At this point in your career, you must be exhausted; doing such a poor job cannot come easy to anyone. From a shareholder's perspective, your time would more effectively be spent on the golf course reducing your handicap than continuing to ensure your inclusion into the CEO Hall of Shame. Given that you long ago sold any stock you held in the company you lead, we are sure you share our lack of confidence in the management team.

Please feel free to contact me directly to discuss my concerns.
Warmest regards,
Vernon Albright
Managing Partner
Parthenon Capital Limited, LLC

Albright read the letter over once more before asking Suzie to call for a messenger. He enjoyed the attention his correspondence received after it was leaked to the Wall Street Journal and wanted to be certain that this effort was up to his usual standards. Of course, it would also undoubtedly have a positive effect on the stock price, because anyone reading the letter would surely believe that Alpha was now in play; the company was up for sale.

***

Without breaking stride, Jeremy said a quick hello to Suzie as he moved past her desk in the reception area directly outside Albright's office and into the inner sanctum.

Albright motioned to a chair abutting his desk. "Come around here so we can both look at the screens." His tone was a complex mixture of command and invitation.

"What's going on with Don's portfolio?" Albright inquired as Don Jackson's portfolio and investment returns appeared on the screen to Jeremy's left. "It was down again last week which makes it three in a row."

Jackson was a junior portfolio manager being trained by Jeremy. He had joined the firm as a research analyst two years earlier but had recently been promoted.

"He had a few positions go against him but he's not managing much money so the losses are minimal and won't impact my bottom line."

"If he can't manage the limited capital he's overseeing now, how is he ever going to be of any use to us?"

"You know the process. It's way too early to draw any conclusions."

"Fire him."

The order, though softly spoken, was still shocking. Jeremy was momentarily stunned. "Fire him? You have to be kidding!"

Albright braced his right foot against the edge of his desk and leaned back, casually reclining in his chair. "Does it appear that I'm joking?" Albright paused before repeating his order. "Fire him!"

Jeremy was trying to figure out what buzz saw he had just walked into. First, Larry Janowicz and now, Don Jackson. What the hell was going on? This was much more than a bad mood. They had been through rough markets before, but Vernon had never let them get to him in this manner. He took his distance from Albright by moving to the other side of the desk.

"I can't do that. Don's going to do well but he needs more time. He and Emily just had their second child, and you know the story with their little boy." Jackson's first child was autistic.

Albright took his foot off the desk and brought it down to the floor. In response, the seat back sprang forward. He rose from the chair and leaned forward, hands flat on the desk, and stared directly at Jeremy, his eyes flashing their infamous fire. "This isn't a charitable institution or the fucking government. We don't keep people around just because you like them or they have issues at home. Either perform or get the hell out. It's too bad about his kid, but it's not my fucking problem. Or yours!"

"Be reasonable. You can't throw Don out. He is too well liked and everyone is aware of his situation at home. It will kill morale. And you've already fired one person this week." Jeremy took a breath.

"I wasn't aware I had a quota."

Jeremy tensed at Albright's snide remark but all he cared about was saving Don's job. "Don works for me and his portfolio's performance gets rolled into mine. You can take his losses out of my share of the profits."

"Your profits? What exactly are your profits? I'll answer that for you. Your profits are what I tell you they are."

Jeremy shook his head from side to side in disbelief. "My value to this firm is pretty damn clear. Don stays. I'll run the fund with him until he gets on track."

"And am I supposed to be reassured by that?" Albright asked, his voice dripping with sarcasm.

Jeremy stepped forward and leaned on the desk, closing the space between him and Albright. Bending forward to get even closer, he spoke with quiet fury, "What's that supposed to mean? You want to fire me, too?"

The anger faded from Albright's expression. He began

waving his hands back and forth, as if trying to erase his last comment. "No, no, no. Of course not," he sputtered. "All I'm saying is that your portfolio isn't performing as well as it usually does."

"Have you noticed the markets? The Dow's down fifteen percent, the S&P is down the same, and NASDAQ is under water by twenty-five percent. Considering that my stocks are up five percent, I'd say that's pretty damn good. It certainly puts us in the top tier of all hedge funds."

"I don't give a shit what other funds are doing. They don't put any money in my pocket—or yours," Albright shot back. "If we don't make money for our investors we don't get paid and this job is way too hard to do for free."

"Let's talk about your side of the business for a change," Jeremy proposed, tired of being beat upon. "How is it that you're doing so well, up twenty percent on the year?" The question was posed as a challenge, as if to say that he was skeptical of the numbers.

"Are you questioning my marks?" Albright fumed. "I hope that's not what you're doing."

The majority of Vernon's holdings were in smaller companies with little or no trading volume in its shares. Without a sufficient public market, it was up to Vernon to determine the price, or put another way, mark them to the market. There was a check and balance on this valuation mechanism and it lay in the hands of the outside auditors. But few of them had either enough knowledge to disagree or the incentive to question the decisions of the man who paid their very large retainer. Marking up stocks to a price that exceeded its true value was a tempting exercise since the higher the stock price, the greater the profit and the fatter the hedge fund management fees.

Albright continued. "All of a sudden you're interested in what my stocks are doing? Do us both a favor and worry about your own holdings. I'm not Don Jackson; I don't need your help."

What Jeremy didn't realize was that no matter how

much interest he had shown, there was not a snowball's chance in hell that Albright would ever let him get under the hood. In fact, there was some information that even Paul, who ran the firm's operations, wasn't privy to, although Paul had no way of knowing that.

"I'm a partner at this firm and I have a right to look at our portfolios. Maybe I can learn something," Jeremy added, clearly tongue in cheek.

"You're a partner—and I use the term loosely—only for as long as I say and only for what I want you to do. Right now you're partnership responsibilities don't include looking over my shoulder."

An awkward silence

"Jeremy, I didn't mean to..."

Jeremy held up his hand, clearly sending Albright the message that he didn't care what else he had to say. "Look, Vernon, I don't think either one of us really wants to take this conversation any further. It's almost 9:30 and I have to get back to my office before the market opens." He turned to go, leaving Albright slack jawed.

"Jeremy, I apologize. It's been a rough market lately. I have a lot on my mind and the situation with Larry this morning put me in a rotten mood."

Jeremy waited for the follow up comment, the one where Albright twists the knife, essentially retracting his apology, but it never came. His ire was somewhat mollified at the first true sign of contrition Albright had ever shown. "Let's move on for now. I really have to get back to my screens."

"Hold on a second, there's one more thing we have to discuss. I hired the cousin of a close friend. Her name is Marty Jagdale. I haven't met her yet but I've been told she's exceptionally bright and has relevant experience. Paul has been looking to add a body to his staff and the back office is a good place for her to start. She's coming in today to meet with Paul, and I would like you to say a quick hello to her."

"Fine. I'm sure he'll be happy for the help."

"She gets treated like any other employee. I promised to give her an opportunity, not lifetime employment. If she isn't up to Parthenon standards, we'll cut her loose."

"If she did her due diligence on the firm, she knows that's a real risk," Jeremy offered before leaving Albright's office.

Out of Albright's line of sight, Jeremy paused by Suzie's desk, speaking in a whisper. "What's wrong with him today? He's borderline rabid."

Before she could respond, Albright bellowed from his office. "Get Buck Hendricks on the phone."

"Right away," she replied in a more conversational tone.

Jeremy stayed silent as Suzie connected the two parties. He listened to their conversation from the vantage point of Suzie's desk.

"Morning Buck. It's settled on my end; I don't anticipate any issues."

"That's damn good news, Vern. Marty was real excited after your dinner. I'm glad she won't be disappointed."

"Who is Buck Hendricks?" Jeremy inquired, still speaking softly.

"Buck Hendricks? You don't know? Why am I not surprised? One day you have to get your head out of your portfolio and pay attention around here."

"Okay, okay. Point taken—believe me. Now who is Hendricks?"

"The firm's largest investor, that's all. Texas boy. Big oil money."

Jeremy was taken aback, a bit embarrassed actually, but maintained a stoic demeanor. He thought he knew most of the firm's important investors, particularly those with the biggest balances, but the name "Hendricks" didn't even sound faintly familiar. Before he could follow up with another question, Albright came out of his office.

"I forgot my coffee," Jeremy said as he placed his hand over the top of the cup, covering Suzie's lipstick imprint.

"I guess we're on the same page after all, Jeremy" Vernon responded, handing his cup to Suzie. "I could use a refill."

**

Alone in his office a few minutes later, Vernon was fuming. First his night trader had screwed up, and then the argument with Jeremy, who was not only the best portfolio manager he had ever hired but also the first employee who he had ever felt close with. It wasn't completely lost on Albright that his affection for Jeremy had a high correlation with the performance of his portfolio. He hoped Jeremy wouldn't revisit their conversation in the future; he didn't need him nosing around. And then there was Buck, who was becoming more of a nuisance. It was a hell of morning—not very productive. *I'm too rich and too old for this shit.*

Underpinning his anger was concern. Parthenon had been returning to its investors an average profit of thirty percent a year, a track record that had no peer. Until recently he had never received even one question from any of his investors about how he was able to generate such consistently strong returns. But then Bernie Madoff happened and Allen Stanford happened and there was seemingly a story a day in the newspapers about the investment fraud du jour. So his phone started ringing. And ringing. And ringing. Albright understood the concern and was uncharacteristically patient at first despite the vast majority of these queries coming from his smallest investors. But as the volume of calls increased and the line of questioning became more inane, he told the callers that he would rather lose an investor than reveal his proprietary trading strategies. He welcomed them to redeem their investments if they were uncomfortable with the lack of transparency, and they would receive their money the next day. Not even one investor elected to cash out.

Secrecy was a high priority in the competitive world of hedge fund investing. Vernon's motivation, however, was not only the obvious desire to achieve better returns than other firms but also to stay out of the SEC's crosshairs. That was one of the reasons recruiting Jeremy had been such a coup. He was a great stock-picker but could care less about other aspects of the business. Paul was a different story. His role required him to be involved in some of the areas of the business that Vernon would rather keep private but Parthenon was so large that Paul's view was from 30,000 feet, leaving the details—and the devil is always in the details—to his minions. Albright was convinced that the lowly paid back-office paper shufflers couldn't recognize an irregularity if it jumped off the computer screen and started dancing on the keyboard. Albright did take one other precaution, which was outsourcing various portions of the work to a number of different firms. Outsourcing was fairly standard in the industry and Paul was a fan since it made his job more manageable.

Despite the precautions, Albright understood that his empire was built on shifting sands and that the foundation could crumble at any point. Head in hands, Albright felt the pressure collapsing upon him. He knew Hendricks wasn't about to give up on his quest to have him accept more money, and if he acceded to the request, the risk would ratchet higher to an even more imprudent level. As much as he liked Buck and enjoyed the benefits of their relationship, he was beginning to think that it might be time to put an end to it. Albright knew that someone would ultimately sneak behind the great Oz's curtain; that best-in-class stock picking hadn't been the sole reason for the outsized investment returns that Parthenon generated. He got the first hint of that in the discussion he'd just had with Jeremy.

Returning Buck's investment wasn't going to be easy. Buck would refuse to be bought out or demand such an incredible price that it wouldn't make sense. But even if he eventually acquiesced, Albright had no idea how he could raise enough cash from the portfolio to pay him out. The small energy companies that now made up the bulk of his portfolio didn't trade very often—there wasn't enough liquidity in the market to absorb the selling pressure—and the private enterprises in which he had invested didn't trade at all, absent a sale of the entire company. To make matters worse, he had bought into many of those companies at Buck's direction. Maybe it would be easier to part ways with Jeremy.

Vernon ran a finger nervously across his dry lips. At this point he wasn't really sure how long he could keep on juggling without dropping a ball, and doing that could not only cost him his financial future but also put him in prison for fraud and insider trading. Well, Vernon Albright was smarter than all of them, he reassured himself, and he had no intention of going to jail like those morons in the headlines every day. Vernon liked himself in stripes but preferred them to be vertical and crafted by his own tailor rather than the Federal prison system.

***

The familiar beep drew Paul's attention from his paperwork. It was an instant message from Jeremy, using the initials of his wife and kids as his screen name.

JAM: "congrats on ur new hire"

"?" was the shorthand response from F360, in honor of Paul's new sports car. The Ferrari 360 Modena was a $200,000 gift to himself.

JAM: "vernon hired a friends cousin 4 u"

F360: "wud have been nice to have met him first"

JAM: "yup but wudnt have mattered. anyway he's a she. be happy 4 the help. besides doesn't sound like vernon met her either which means shes prob harmless"

F360: "hope she's cute. not surprised anyway. not the first time. and i cud use the extra body"

JAM: "little downside for you. vern said if she doesn't work out, she's gone"

F360: "so she's a favor to someone and the old man cud care less about her"

JAM: "you got it. urs to do with as u want"

F360: "great. anything else up"

JAM: "old mans really got a bug up his butt today. wanted me to fire don. we got into it"

F360: "no shit. not a great day to be working here. i better hide or i'll be next"

JAM: "gtg. mkts about to open"

Chapter 11

□ □ □

Buck Hendricks was sound asleep when the hotel operator delivered his wake-up call at seven in the morning.

"I'm up, I'm up," he said into the handset in a raspy morning voice.

"Shall I ring you again, Mr. Hendricks?" the operator inquired as she did every morning.

"No, Ma'am. I'm up, thanks."

"Glad to be of service, Mr. Hendricks. It will be seventy degrees and sunny today." The weather report was a small benefit of hotel living.

Hendricks hung up the phone without another word. Throwing off the covers, he stood. *Buck naked*, he thought with a wide grin as he walked to the mirror that hung on the outside of the bathroom door. Turning slightly sideways, he admired his trim, muscular body. It was a somewhat startling contrast to his weathered face, but his vanity prevented him from noticing.

After a workout with his personal trainer, followed by a steam and a shower back upstairs in his penthouse apartment, Buck appeared in the living room where Carla had already been at work for the past half hour. A breakfast of egg whites and dry wheat toast was waiting on the table, just delivered from room service and kept warm by silver domed covers. A small carafe of fresh squeezed orange juice sat next to a larger pot of coffee. When Carla heard the door to the bedroom open, she poured the hot brown liquid and added just a dollop of warm skim milk. Always famished after a grueling workout, Buck consumed the juice in two large gulps, then scoffed down the eggs and toast in just a few bites. Carla trailed him with the coffee as he moved into his study and sat down at an antique desk positioned between two walls of bookshelves. Buck was far from being a voracious reader, but the decorator had convinced Carla that it was an appropriate old money look and "would emit the right message of sophistication."

Buck punched the letters C-L-A C-O-M-M-O-D-I-T-Y on the Bloomberg keyboard, and the price of crude popped up on the top of the screen. In active trading, the price was hovering just near one hundred twenty-nine dollars a barrel. Buck smiled as he raised the cup to his lips and reached for the stack of newspapers Carla had placed on the corner of his desk. Passing over the Dallas Morning News, Houston Chronicle and New York Times, he pulled the Wall Street Journal from the bottom of the pile. The perfect start to his day became history as he read the feature article on the right side of the first page.

Economic Terrorism: The Oil Boom

by Bill Sundrick, Special Correspondent

What are the real reasons for the recent unrelenting rise in oil prices? The experts we interviewed were divided into two distinct schools of thought: some pointed to the increasing consumption of crude in India, China and the United States, while others felt that the increase was the direct result of traders aggressively bidding up the commodity to create a sense of scarcity of supply. Some may term it manipulation. We don't disagree.

According to Senator Barney Mylar from Idaho, the 40% price increase in crude is financially devastating to the consumer and every non-energy producing business. "....[T]his is a potential disaster for the American farmer. The cost of filling the gas tank on a John Deere tractor has risen 40%. The cost of heating a home has increased a similar amount. A trip to the grocery store, which may be 30 miles away from some of these farms, has become prohibitively expensive. People are prisoners in their own homes. And come winter, their homes will be very cold."

Benjamin Baker, an economist at Loma House, a conservative think tank, takes it one step further. "The increase in energy prices has significantly crimped most household budgets, pushing the country to the brink of a double-dip recession. The economic recovery that we have experienced over the last eighteen months has come to an abrupt end."

Senator Mylar has a distinct view on the root cause of the crisis. "The assault on the well-being of our economy is a deliberate act of financial terrorism in which OPEC and oil speculators are complicit. The SEC must seek out and discipline those who make their outsized livings on the trading floors by inflating the price of oil, effectively gouging the consumer. The President must request that Bill Lindsay, the Energy Secretary, release some of the nation's oil reserves to help bring down the price...."

When interviewed by....

The article continued on but Buck had read enough. He hoped that Mylar was only playing politics, but it was an election year and this rhetoric could increase. Could they really launch such an investigation? He pondered the question. Castigating the Saudi's, our biggest Arab ally, wouldn't happen and going after the commodities traders would be too much of a stretch. This country is built on capitalism and many capitalists live in the President's home state of Texas. *Damn it! It's our oil money that got him elected.* Hell—the President's family is in the oil business. *Nah, nothing is going to happen,* he concluded. Having worked out the issues to his satisfaction, Buck sat back, breathed a sigh of relief, and reveled in the glow of his Bloomberg as the price of Brent continued to climb.

Chapter 12

□ □ □

The Gisele Bündchen look-alike prepared to greet the visitor as the elevator doors opened into Parthenon's lobby. Sitting at the sleek receptionist's desk, she offered the visitor a toothy smile, showcasing near-perfect cosmetic dentistry she had splurged on in hopes of jump starting a modeling career.

"Welcome to Parthenon Capital. How may I help you?'

Stylishly decked out in a Chanel business suit, Marty approached the desk. She was all business. "I'm here to see Vernon Albright."

"You must be Miss Jagdale. Mr. Albright is expecting you. I'll tell his assistant that you're here. Please have a seat."

Only a minute or so had passed before Suzie Clintock entered the reception area. She introduced herself to Marty before leading her back to Albright's office, making small talk along the way. As they passed the first glass enclosed conference room, a picture hanging on the wall caught Marty's interest.

"Impressive," Marty remarked as she nodded toward the artwork. "A Picasso in the reception area and another in a conference room."

Suzie had come to believe that if someone didn't offer a comment, they were either oblivious to their surroundings or they incorrectly assumed that the self-portraits were copies. Either state of mind had a high inverse relationship to a successful meeting with Albright. Marty passed the first test.

"Mr. Albright is an avid collector. He occasionally rotates pieces between here and his homes."

Albright, always chivalrous, came around his desk to shake Marty's hand. The last thing he wanted to do was set a precedent of greeting an employee with a kiss even though the prior evening had ended with a friendly peck on his cheek. Vernon moved to a chair upholstered with butter soft brown suede while Marty sat down on the neighboring couch, assembled from the same hide. She settled into the cushions and elegantly, deliberately, crossed her legs.

"Before you meet with Jeremy and Paul, I wanted to go over a few points. We have a policy of not hiring the relatives or friends of investors but because of my relationship with Buck, I made an exception for you. No one needs to know that, so the party line will be that you are the cousin of an old friend of mine from business school, James Backus. Secondly, as far as anyone knows this is our first meeting."

"Why is that important?"

"Don't worry about that," Albright responded curtly, unaccustomed to anyone asking for the thought process behind his directives. "I also want to keep our relationship in the office at arm's length, meaning that while I enjoyed dinner last night, in the office we are employer and employee. I'm not a casual guy around here with anyone and that's how it will be with you. Don't take it personally."

Marty's vision of life at Parthenon just morphed into something less comfortable. And she knew her job, getting close to the three partners, just got significantly tougher. What Albright said made sense—Buck had already cautioned her not to reveal their true relationship to anyone at Parthenon—but his condescending manner suggested to her that it would be a different game.

"Of course not. This is business. I understand that."

"Good. Since you are already familiar with Jeremy's background and what he does here, let's spend a second on Paul Robbins. Paul manages all the non-investment related activities including technology, accounting, trade settlement—everything administrative that has nothing to do with making money. I'm sure you won't be surprised to learn that our operation is surely quite a bit more complicated than your prior fund, although the core procedures are likely similar. We would have a hell of a tough time functioning day to day without Paul." Albright was more agnostic about the value of both Paul and his department but he couldn't confess that to Marty, not when that was the area where she would be working.

"I know you have my best interests at heart, Vernon. I'm very comfortable in your hands."

Vernon liked the innuendo in her answer, particularly coming from such a beautiful woman, but restrained himself from responding in kind. He was not a fan of mixing business and pleasure, never needing the office as a source for his liaisons.

"If there's anything on your mind, speak up now because once you get in front of my team, I want you to exude confidence and make the best possible impression upon them."

"Thank you but I did my homework. I don't see any problem getting their support."

"That's exactly what I want to hear. Confidence is important in this business." Vernon rose from his seat. "I'll walk you over to Jeremy's."

***

Jeremy stood to introduce himself. "It's a pleasure, Marty."

Marty peered over his left shoulder at the pictures that sat upon the credenza. "What a beautiful family."

It wasn't the usual discussion Jeremy had come to expect from a new employee, even at a hedge fund that attracted the highest caliber recruits. Marty was well versed in multiple areas of investing, allowing him to conclude that she was clearly qualified for the position. He was relieved that she had turned out to be more than a courtesy hire. His only trepidation was discomfort with Marty's lack of reverence.

It wasn't that he needed to be shown deference, not at all, but overconfident young employees could portend a management headache.

Twenty minutes into the conversation Jeremy stood, anxious to return his focus to the market. Interviewing a candidate that had already been hired wasn't a good use of his time during trading hours, particularly someone with whom he would have minimal interaction.

"Paul's next. I'll take you to his office."

Paul's office was more reflective of function than his position as a partner. He sat in a large, open room, his desk no more than six feet from his staff, most of whom were separated by four-foot-high charcoal gray cubicle walls. Wealthy but watchful of his money, Albright chose not to spend Parthenon's considerable profits on an area that investors didn't see. Maintaining immediate lines of communication was another factor in the set up. Paul's desk was positioned so that he faced the wall, ensuring that casual chatter between boss and employee was kept to a minimum. He wasn't the type who liked being sucked up to.

Jeremy tapped on the door. Without looking up, Paul held up one finger as if to say, "give me a minute." Jeremy tapped again. This time Paul turned around and immediately smiled at his visitors, pleasantly surprised at the appearance of the newest addition to his staff.

"Let me call you back," he said into the phone as he stood to face Marty. "Hi. Paul Robbins. It's a pleasure. If we can get rid of the third wheel here," he nodded toward Jeremy, "you and I can spend some quality time discussing your role."

In an almost hypnotic trance, Paul and Marty spent the next hour getting to know each other. He threw out a number of questions, testing her knowledge. She handled them adeptly. The business part of the interview out of the way, he turned to her social life. Paul knew this wasn't a job interview—she was already hired; it was more of a get-acquainted session. Did she have a share in the Hamptons;

where did she hang out in the City, culminating with the politically incorrect question as to whether or not she had a boyfriend. She said she didn't.

"Excellent! No relationship translates into more hours at the office," he said with a mischievous smile. "And what about Vernon? Will he be upset with me if I work you too hard?" Paul inquired, probing their relationship.

"Having met him for the first time this morning, I don't know him well enough to answer that and it seems unlikely I will ever get to know him."

"Why is that?"

"He's *the* Vernon Albright and I'm a nobody. He also didn't seem particularly interested in anything I had to say."

"He's like that with everyone except Jeremy."

"I'm just going to keep my head down and stay out of his way," Marty offered, pleased at her acting ability.

As much as he enjoyed the banter, Paul had work to do. He drew the conversation to a close and stood up. "Can't say this hasn't been fun but unless I get my work finished, Vernon may give you my job. I'll take you back to his office."

"I hope I have as much fun once I start working here." Marty flashed a smile.

Paul regarded the flirtation and then reconsidered his interpretation, realizing that he thought every attractive woman who smiled at him was flirting. Walking down the hallway, they heard loud voices coming from Jeremy's office. Marty turned to Paul with an inquisitive look.

"Is that Jeremy?" she asked, "He struck me as so even keeled."

"None other."

"That's the person I just met with? What gives?"

"Let's go see."

With Marty in tow, he paused in Jeremy's doorway. Paul extended his arm, offering commentary to accompany the image of Jeremy in action. "He's our very own superhero. Clark Kent until the market opens, and then he turns into the man of steel, able to conquer declining markets, unable to be deterred from finding the truth about stocks. He becomes a man possessed. Nothing gets in the way of him making money." Paul caught Jeremy's eye and he waved them toward chairs that occupied the far side of the office. "Let's watch him in action. There's no one better at this than him."

The flashing stock quotes on the Bloomberg monitor, red and green, reflected in the window behind Jeremy's desk. He paced back and forth as he tossed a small blue ball in the air, slapping it into his grasp as its flight turned downward. Jack Knowles's booming baritone belied the fact that the volume on the speakerphone was only in the middle of its range.

"You're not helping me here, Jack. The damn stock is down five percent and you can't find out why? Why the hell do we pay out all those commissions? One of those lazy-ass sell-siders you talk to has to have heard something even if they're not smart enough to realize it." Five percent translated into almost three dollars a share.

"We're talking about Pepsi, Jeremy. What the hell could be wrong? They make frickin' soda. You've been waiting for the stock to trade down to your price for three months. It's fifty-five a share. Just buy it. It never stays down for long."

Despite the quickening pace of his words Jeremy remained in complete control, his voice never rising above a loud, but firm, conversational tone. "I'm not buying it until I know why it's getting beaten up. What if the SEC is on their ass? It could collapse another twenty percent in a heartbeat. You stick to trading and I'll take care of the portfolio management. Now get me some information."

Jeremy punched a button on his phone console. One buzz and his new secretary, Karen Phipps, answered. Her predecessor couldn't take the stress of the job and lasted all of two months. "Get Rich Barker on the line—ASAP!"

Barker was the Chief Financial Officer at Pepsi. Jeremy had known him for years, having been a large shareholder of Pepsi during his time at Salomon Brothers. Barker was always willing to speak with Jeremy because he was under the impression that Parthenon also had a large position in Pepsi and Jeremy did nothing to persuade him otherwise, even though he had never owned it at Parthenon.

Fifty-four and a half. The stock continued to trade down. Either it was a great buying opportunity or something was really wrong.

Jeremy punched another button on the phone, this time connecting to Jamie Jurofsky, one of his research assistants. "Check the wires and see if there is any news on Pepsi. The stock's getting clocked. Check Coke, too. Maybe something's happened on the competitive front."

Jamie punched in the ticker for Pepsi, P-E-P. "Damn! It's getting crushed. I'll get right on it."

Fifty-four and a quarter. Down another twenty-five cents. On the four million shares that Parthenon would ultimately buy, the firm would have already lost three million dollars if Jeremy had taken Knowles's advice and was long the stock at fifty-five.

Karen's voice shot through the speaker. "Barker on one."

"Hi, Rich. Thanks for taking my call."

"Always happy to take a shareholder's call."

"What's going on with your stock? The market is up two percent today and you've given up over five."

"Wish I knew. We haven't made any announcements. What have you heard? You're better connected to the Street than I am. Anything from our friends in Atlanta?" Coke's headquarters were in Atlanta.

"Nothing on the wire services. Someone had to start a rumor somewhere."

"Could be one of your more distinguished hedge fund brethren is short our stock and looking to make a quick buck by spreading some shit about us somewhere."

Jeremy stared at his screen. Fifty-four and a half. Ticking back up. Was this the turn? "Could be. I'll let you know if I hear anything."

As soon as Jeremy hung up with Barker, Knowles's excited voice reverberated throughout the office. "Got it! Trading desk at Morgan said that they heard that Burger King is about to boot Pepsi and sign Coke for all its restaurants."

Fifty-four and a quarter. The downtrend resumed. The uptick could have been a head fake.

"That explains why Coke is up and Pepsi is trading lower. I have one more call to make."

Marty whispered to Paul. "This is so exciting."

Jeremy buzzed Karen again. "Get Barker back on the line."

"Is there any truth to the scuttlebutt that Burger King is cutting you loose?"

"Well, yeah. But it's not a big deal. Their business wasn't that profitable for us. At most, after costs it works out to about forty cents a share."

Jeremy thought, *Forty cents a share! That's pretty damn significant in my book. Did this idiot think I wouldn't find out?* There was no point in getting angry with Barker—he was still a valuable resource. "I agree. Contracts come and go. All it means is that you'll get one of Coke's customers to switch. I may add down here."

Barker let out a sigh. "I wish all my shareholders were as smart as you."

Fifty-four and a half. The stock was trying to level off.

Jeremy resisted the urge to laugh. "Gotta hop so I can put an order in with my traders."

"I can't believe he's going to buy that liar's stock," Marty remarked quietly.

"Don't be so sure."

Paul and Marty could almost see Jeremy doing the math in his head.

The stock is valued at twenty-five times earnings. If I subtract forty cents a share out of their forecasted earnings for this year and multiply that by twenty-five, the stock should be down at least ten bucks. And that's before it gets penalized for

not issuing a press release as soon as the company received the
bad news from Burger King.

Jeremy muttered a derogatory term for Barker under his breath as he called Knowles. "Jack, short two million Pepsi and hurry up."

"Short it? I thought we were buying it."

"I'll explain later. Just get it done. And buy three million Coke. You have discretion." Jack could decide at what price to execute each trade.

Marty feigned confusion. "I don't get it. Jeremy acted like he was Barker's best friend. Now he's shorting his stock. He doesn't seem like the type to...."

"To what?" Paul stated rhetorically, picking up where Marty paused. "To be so disingenuous? You heard Barker. He would have had Jeremy buy shares when he knew there was bad news coming and the stock would trade down. That's being disingenuous."

"I guess they were both being a little dishonest."

"I guess hedge funds in Dallas work with a different definition of dishonest than Wall Street." Paul chuckled. "He was only doing unto Barker as Barker did unto him. Jeremy needed information to protect our investors. He's known Barker for years and the guy has never been up front with him, and wasn't going to start today. He never actually lied to Barker, and I'm sure he will buy the stock at some point, but first we're going to make a boatload on the short."

"All I can say is that I'm impressed."

"Lesson over. Off to Vernon's so I can get back to work."

Marty walked out of Jeremy's office with more than just an appreciation for his trading ability; she also found herself attracted to the man.

***

Carla brought Buck the phone while he lunched on the patio.

"Marty's on the line."

Buck pushed the button on the portable and spoke into the handset. "Your first day at work and already making personal calls on company time. Forget your lunch box?"

"Not very funny, Buck, especially since you're the one who wanted the mid-day update." Marty spoke impatiently as she strode through the lobby of the building on her way to pick up lunch.

Buck leaned back in his chair and twirled a butter knife around his fingers. "Okay. What have you learned so far?"

"Cranford is an interesting character; sort of a study in contrasts. Not an easy one to figure out."

"If anyone can figure out some guy, it's you. What's that mean for me?"

"Just listen. According to Paul Robbins, who runs operations, Jeremy can be pretty ruthless when it comes to making a buck. But he also claims the guy is as honest as the day is long."

Buck leaned forward and put down the utensil. "Forget what the ops guy told you. What's that pretty little gut of yours say?"

"Don't know enough to say just yet but he certainly seems that way. I saw him being a real hard-ass one minute and a perfect gentleman the next. He's pretty damn complex but Robbins is easier to figure out, and I had no problem connecting with him. I couldn't even get a smile out of Cranford."

"Well, then it's not all bad because Robbins is someone you're going to have to get close to—real close."

"I know what I have to do, Buck."

"Relax, darling. Just trying to help with your social life." He paused to let out a low laugh. "Now what about Cranford?"

Marty felt like saying "didn't I just tell you what I thought, you moron," but thought better of it. "Too early to tell if he's driven by the almighty dollar or by the chase. Definitely a family man; that's for sure. A lot of cross currents but I will get it figured out. I like the challenge and I'm well aware that he can either help us or get in the way."

"I have no intention of letting him get in the way. Don't care what it takes."

"I'm with you—whatever it takes. I have a lot at stake here, too."

"That's right. Listen, it can't be that complicated. After all, he works with Albright and we know what he's about. If Cranford is as sharp as you think he is, then he has to know that old Vernon ain't the most lily white guy in the room even if he doesn't know—and I'm sure he doesn't—what Vern and I have working on the side."

"You're probably right."

"You have to work the bit deeper and faster. The markets aren't waiting on us so the longer it takes to get to the bottom of what really makes that place tick, the smaller the opportunity. Keep your eyes wide open."

"Open for what," she wanted to know.

"For a weakness. For anything that we can use to get to Cranford in case he is a boy scout and gets in my way. Robbins too. I want to know if Albright is trying to pull one over on me or if those other two are really resistant to taking in more money. Hell, Marty, I want to know if those two even matter."

"I got it, Buck. Have to go." Marty folded her cell phone shut, ending the call.

Buck pushed away from the table, leaving his lunch unfinished.

"Carla," he shouted across the hotel suite, "get Albright on the phone."

Buck started the conversation in a friendly enough manner. "Another day, another nice move in Texas tea. I sure love that black gold, don't you, Vern?"

"It is a pleasant circumstance," Albright responded coolly. He tended not to get excited about intraday moves. Anything could happen during the course of the day to change the market's direction.

"Damn right it is. Our oil stocks are following just like they should."

"*Our?*" Albright chafed when Buck portrayed himself as someone involved in the portfolio process. It grated against his ego and, more importantly, reminded him of the risk that he ran in their relationship.

"They're green, if that's what you mean."

"Easy there Vern, I'm just making conversation."

"You never call just to make conversation. We are both too busy for idle chit chat."

"My sources tell me crude's got a long way to go on the upside. I don't know why you keep resisting more money. Neither one of us needs to make more dough but we both sure as hell want to."

"I'm sure you didn't call to give me a commodity market update. How about moving on to a topic we are both willing to discuss, like your cousin?"

"How's she doing? She pass muster with your partners?"

Albright hadn't caught up with either Paul or Jeremy yet but it didn't matter. "She had good meetings with both and is no doubt going to do very well here."

"I'd like to meet Cranford."

"That's not a good idea."

"Why's that? I have a fortune tied up in your shop and he's your top lieutenant. I'd like to know who is looking after my money."

"It's not a good idea. It presents too much risk."

"So you're afraid I can't handle the conversation?"

"Of course not, but why put ourselves in a situation that brings attention to our relationship? Jeremy's incredibly perceptive. Even one innocuous comment and he'd analyze it up and down until he connected the dots. That's what he does for a living. Even I have to be careful what I say around him, and we've known each other for a few years. A virtual stranger—well, it's not worth the risk."

Buck thought that Cranford was sounding more and more like a good candidate to bring into the fold. Albright had already made his fortune; Cranford was on the way up and, according to Marty, hungry and driven. Cranford was more like the others on his team: younger and still trying to acquire immense wealth. He viewed winning him over as a challenge, as long as it didn't take too much time. If it did, there was a second option, a contingency currently in the planning process. But gaining his cooperation through financial inducements would be much tidier than using other means.

Albright continued. "This is really about the five hundred million, isn't it? You figure if you meet Jeremy, you can make him an ally. But guess what, it's not Jeremy's decision, it's mine."

Buck tested the waters and now it was time to change the subject. If he wanted to meet with Jeremy, Albright wasn't going to stop him. "Let's back burner this debate and make some money. Cherokee Drilling. Ticker's CDC. Trades on the Big Board. Some associates of mine own a chunk of the company. Buy some for the fund"

Albright input the ticker into his Bloomberg. A description of the company, as well as all relevant statistical data, instantly appeared on his screen. He liked what he saw. "What's so interesting about this company?"

"I got a look at the geologist's report and the company is about to announce a huge find that will increase their production from 50,000 barrels a day to near 200,000. That'll take the value up to two billion—easy."

According to the Bloomberg market data, the company was presently valued at $400 million, bite size. Albright did the math in his head and figured out that Parthenon could buy thirty percent over the next couple of weeks and become the controlling shareholder. He would be getting in deeper with Buck but he couldn't resist these easy opportunities to increase his fortune. He was torn. Was he in so deep that one more trade wouldn't matter? Or was every move taking him one step closer to ruin? Conversations like this caused him to doubt his control of the firm. His firm!

He could easily cash out any other investor, but there were too many strings attached with Buck.

Nope, getting rid of Buck would not be easy. Vernon's portfolio was tied up in small capitalization stocks that didn't trade very often. He could never cash out Buck without liquidating a significant portion of the fund— something that would be virtually impossible in a short period of time. And if other hedge fund managers found out Parthenon was selling, they would short those same stocks. Since Vernon would still own a large percentage of these companies, he had no interest in harming his own investments. The relationship with Buck had served Parthenon well. But as good as it was to build upon his enormous net worth, Albright understood that one day it could all end badly. He resigned himself to one last trade and then he would deliberate anew on how to rid himself of the Texan.

While Albright chafed at his lack of will power, Hendricks reveled in his ability to bend the man to his will. Hendricks had no reason to deliberate over the relationship for he knew it was about to enter a new phase and Albright would be going along for the ride—whether in the passenger seat or, if need be, in the trunk.

Chapter 13 □ □ □

The phone in Jeremy's office broke the early morning silence. The person on the other end remained a mystery only as long as it took him to take note of the caller's name on the LED display. "Feeling okay?"

"Pretty much. Why?"

"You skipped the gym on Monday and you weren't there today, either. You never miss a day, but now you missed two in three days."

"Thanks for the concern but I'm fine. I had a rough night getting to sleep so I decided to take it easy and have breakfast with the family."

"Are the kids sick? I know you weren't tossing and turning, worrying about the portfolio." As intense as Jeremy was during market hours, he was usually able to bifurcate his life and leave any issues with work at the office. He didn't want to compromise the time with his family.

"No, that's not it. Everyone's fine. Just one of those nights."

"You never have one of those nights; at least not since I've known you. Why don't you tell Uncle Paul what's on your mind."

Jeremy considered his response. He had intended to raise the issue of the letters with Paul on Monday, but as he got through the first part of the week his angst had settled down. But last night, he had a terrible dream that had startled him awake. As he lay in bed, fully alert, all sorts of visions danced through his mind, none of them good and all of them involving Jenn and the girls.

"Actually, I do want to talk something over with you. How about a beer after the close?"

"As long as you're buying, count me in. I'll come by around four thirty."

"Deal."

***

Suzie Clintock answered on the first ring. "Vernon Albright's office."

"Michael Generau calling for Mr. Albright."

"Please understand that Mr. Albright will not accept this call until Mr. Generau is on the line."

This was one of Albright's pet peeves; if you were calling him then you should be on the line—end of story. To him, the tactic smacked of self-importance and arrogance, common ground between him and Generau as well as ignorance of the fact that they each possessed them.

A different voice came through the receiver. "This is Michael Generau."

"One second, Mr. Generau," Suzie said as she rose from her desk. She put the call on hold and walked into the doorway of Albright's office. "Mr. Generau is on line one."

Albright looked up from the flat panel screens that sat prominently upon his desk. "Well, well, well. I guess he does read the Wall Street Journal." Not surprisingly, the letter that Albright wrote had found its way into the day's paper. "Put him on permahold. And when he calls back tell him I went into a meeting. You know the drill."

Suzie did her part, deploying Albright's tried and true negotiating strategy. Step one: permahold. Generau would hang up after two minutes (the unofficial record was actually six minutes). Then he would call back.

"I am so sorry, Mr. Generau. I thought Mr. Albright had picked up."

"Well, you thought wrong. Tell him I won't be hanging on this time."

Generau's sour mood was understandable. His wife had just informed him that he would be terminating his current assistant and that she would be the one hiring the replacement. He would also be spending the rest of the week at one of the corporate apartments that Albright believed was an unmitigated waste of shareholders' money.

Suzie came back on after nearly a minute. "I'm sorry, Mr. Generau, but he just went into a meeting. Is there a number where he can reach you?" Step two.

"What do you mean he went into a meeting?" Generau responded, his voice getting louder. "He just had me hold on for five minutes, then you put me on hold again and he doesn't even have the courtesy to pick up the phone? Get him out of that meeting right now!"

"I'm afraid he can't be disturbed but I would be happy to have him return your call later this morning. However, he is quite busy today so it may have to wait until tomorrow." Steady and even came the rhythm of her response, like repeatedly hitting a tennis ball against a wall.

"That won't do." Generau slammed down the receiver.

The script had played out perfectly. By the time Generau called again, which, in an attempt to save face, would be late the following day, he would be so angry that Albright would be able to take advantage of his adversary's irrational mindset. Generau would "retire" with a decent, but not lavish, severance package and Albright would install his own person as CEO of Alpha Systems. The employees would eventually be fired and the company's assets, including some very valuable real estate upon which the headquarters sat, would be liquidated, fetching a sum far in excess of the depressed stock price. Parthenon would ultimately reap a fifty percent return on its investment. To ensure that any potential critics, and his wife's friends, did not focus on the wrong issues, such as firing thousands of people, Albright would make a large, and very public, donation to the Foundation to Benefit Inner City Children.

It was another victory in Albright's guerilla war against CEO's. Ironic that such a skilled fighter didn't see his own bloody battle looming.

Chapter 14

□ □ □

It seemed that the next time Jeremy took his eyes off the screens was when Paul tapped on his office door at 4:30. His suit jacket was casually thrown over his shoulder, finger hooked inside the collar.

"Ready to go?"

Jeremy fell back into his seat and let out a breath of air that seemed to deflate his body into relaxation. "What a day! I don't think I've seen that much action in a long time. This market is clearly setting up for some big moves."

"You can tell me all about it over a beer. Where should we go?"

"Hannigan's."

Although in the heart of midtown and surrounded by lots of trendy places, they still preferred to have their beers in a good old fashioned bar surrounded by low key individuals taking the edge off before boarding the 5:45 for the burbs. Since the birth of his children and moving out of the City, it was now a rare occasion for Jeremy to spend time in a bar rather than at home, but this was important and the conversation was best held away from the office.

The sidewalks were crowded with commuters heading home. They queued up at the corner and waited for permission from the flashing red light to cross the busy intersection. Suddenly, Jeremy felt a jab in his back, the force of which pushed him off the curb and into the street. He tumbled to the pavement and a small delivery truck bore down on him, oblivious to what was in its path. He tried to scramble to his feet but slid on the oil-slicked street, falling to his knees and hands. The truck continued on a collision course with little room to maneuver on the busy thoroughfare. In Jeremy's mind, he was frozen, helpless to prevent his death. An image of his family flashed into his thoughts.

Paul saw the truck and reacted, stepping off the curb and grabbing his friend's extended hand, yanking him to safety just as the van swerved away, the driver shouting obscenities as it sped by.

Jeremy finally rose to his feet. A woman noticed blood on his hand and asked if he was okay.

"I'm fine. A little shaken but otherwise okay." He took the handkerchief from the breast pocket of his suit jacket and wrapped it around the open cut. Then he dusted off his pants.

"Holy shit! That was close. You almost bought the farm with that little stumble," Paul remarked excitedly.

"I didn't stumble, I was pushed. There was definitely a hand in my back and it didn't feel like an accidental brush. It was pretty damn firm."

It could have been an accident but nobody offered an apology and the push, although not terribly violent, was much too forceful to have been unintentional. Jeremy quickly scanned the sidewalks to see if anyone was hurriedly moving away from the scene, but at this hour of the day, everyone was in a rush. The near death experience brought sweat to his brow and soaked through his shirt. Jeremy had just been warned.

"That's crazy. Why would anyone push you? I'm sure it was an accident." Paul said, convinced Jeremy was overreacting. "Hey, maybe we should just forget about the drink and get you home. You seem pretty shaken up."

"Are you kidding? Now, I really need that drink," Jeremy responded, the trace of a smile trailing his words.

"If you're sure you're okay...."

"I'm fine. And maybe you're right. It was probably someone running to catch a train."

Pulling open one of two outer doors, Jeremy was relieved to see that the bar area was fairly empty, not un-usual for a weekday evening. Typical of most neighborhood taverns, Hannigan's had not updated its furnishings since serving its first beer nearly half a century before. The shelves behind the bar were lined with all type of spirits, although the owner would not be surrendering space to kiwi infused vodka anytime soon. Good old whiskey and beer, fifty varieties from every corner of the globe, were the mainstays of this tavern. Cobwebs clung to old lighting fixtures that hung from the stucco ceiling. A dartboard was nailed to the wall above the last booth, a dangerous place to sit, particularly right before last call.

There were two seats at the near end of the long wooden bar, a worn but shiny mahogany surface scarred by the calligraphic doodling of patrons memorializing their visit. Paul and Jeremy straddled a couple of stools and ordered two mugs of Samuel Adams.

"I guess you don't want to talk about my date last night."

Jeremy had just missed getting intimate with an unattractive delivery truck and was not in a laughing mood. "This is a tad bit more serious than that."

The bartender threw down a couple of three-inch square coasters. Two frosted mugs of beer found a place on the small pieces of cardboard as foam seeped down the sides of the glass.

"Cheers, Gents."

Paul lifted the mug and placed his lips on the rim. He slurped the top layer of foam from the glass. "Ah, that's good." As he swiveled on his stool to face Jeremy, he ran his tongue across his upper lip removing the foamy white residue. "You seem distracted lately."

"It's that obvious?"

"To me it is, but then I know you better than most."

"There's a lot on my mind and you're the only one I can confide in."

"You mean aside from Jennifer, of course."

"Of course, but not on this."

"If I didn't know you better, I would say that you're about to tell me you either have a girlfriend or want a divorce. And if it's either one, I'm going to deck you."

Jeremy shot Paul a look of disbelief. "Do you really think...."

"You do work for a guy that's on his third wife and has almost as many women as he has dollars. You never know what rubs off on someone."

"I'm about to deck you, asshole."

Paul laughed. "Do you really believe that I think you would cheat on Jennifer? Not that I would mind because it would give me an opening to sweep her off her feet and make her forget she ever knew you."

"Okay, that's enough. Mind if we have a serious conversation?"

"Shoot."

"What do you know about Buck Hendricks?" Jeremy lifted his beer and took a short sip.

"Is Buck Hendricks the reason you were visiting Mars this morning?"

"My trip to Mars, as you put it, and Buck Hendricks are different issues. First, talk to me about Hendricks, and then I'll tell you what else is on my mind. Who is this guy? How much do you know about him?"

"Not much. Next to Vernon, he's our largest investor and has been with Parthenon for a very long time. That's really all I know."

"Have you ever met him?"

"Nope. You know I don't meet our investors. I'm just the back-office geek." He paused and shot Jeremy a puzzled look. "You've met him, haven't you?"

"Never had the pleasure. Strange, isn't it?"

"You got that right!" Paul took a couple of big gulps, almost emptying the mug. "But why bring it up now? Hendricks was with the firm long before we arrived."

"There are some strange things going on. I can't really point to anything specific other than a couple of conversations—one I had with Vernon and one that I overheard."

"A fucked-up conversation between you and Vernon isn't anything new."

"That's true but this is different. Vernon seems very unsettled. I've never really seen him that way before."

"We've also never seen markets like this and never struggled like this to make a buck. It changes the way people act." Counseling understanding was out of character for Paul. He wasn't particularly philosophical.

"No, this is completely different."

"Different how?"

"I don't know yet which is why I need your help in figuring it out. I want you to pull some data together."

Jeremy turned the mug around and around in his hands, intermittently taking a small sip. Paul was more focused, finishing the beer in two long gulps. He held up his hand to signal the bartender that he was ready for a refill.

"You know I'll do anything that I can. Tell me what you need."

"A copy of his portfolio, for starters."

"Hold on. I thought that's what you and he talked about in your morning meetings."

Jeremy was almost too embarrassed to respond. He knew the answer Paul was expecting; what the correct answer should be—but the truth was that he never really paid much attention to anything outside his own world. Why bother? It's not as if Vernon would be open to advice. Besides, Jeremy had often rationalized, he barely had enough time to manage his own portfolio, no less check up on the person who hired him and built the firm into the behemoth that it is. He had to trust him.

The bartender placed another Adams in front of Paul who quickly made it disappear.

"I haven't really taken the time to focus on Vernon's holdings. Sure he'll occasionally mention a stock or two that he owns, but we usually spend our meetings discussing my positions. After all, it is Vernon's firm and I've got plenty to do without sticking my nose into his business. Until the last couple of days, I never really had any reason for concern. Frankly, I'm not sure I do even now."

Paul stuck his index finger into Jeremy's chest. "Listen, Bud. I'm going to tell you what you would tell me. It's your job to know what's going on. We can't only do the part of the job that we want to. We have to do it all. Sound familiar?"

"Point taken, and that is exactly why we're discussing it now. I want to get as good a look at his portfolio as possible. And there are some documents I also want to see."

"Why not ask Vernon directly?"

"I thought of asking him but you know how he is. It would only lead to an argument because he would accuse me of checking up on him. He hates that."

"I also know how you are."

"Meaning?"

"Meaning that you're not telling me everything. I'll attribute it to your analytic neurosis and need to withhold judgment until you have performed all the work."

"Look at you, Mr. Accountant. You're more anal than anyone."

Paul playfully jabbed Jeremy in the shoulder. "I know but it felt good to give you the line you always throw at me."

"Okay. Now that you got your jollies, here's what I need." In addition to Vernon's portfolio, Jeremy asked for Buck's investor applications that each limited partner completed before being accepted into the fund. "And since Hendricks is such a large investor and apparently close to Vernon, he probably negotiated better terms than our average investor. There has to be a side letter in his laying out those terms. I want that too."

"I should be able to round up all those docs."

"Let's make sure you have it all. Portfolios, investor contracts including side letters, personal info—anything and everything in the files on Hendricks."

"Whoa! How about writing these things down? Drinking beer this quickly affects my powers of retention. First thing tomorrow, I'll start with the portfolios. Now, what else is on your mind?"

Jeremy retrieved an envelope from the inside pocket of his jacket and handed it to Paul, who removed the letter and laid it down on the bar, rubbing his palms over the paper to smooth out the creases. It only took a few seconds to read it through.

Paul let out a low whistle. "This guy is a sicko. When did you get this?"

"Over the weekend. It's the second one. The first one came to the office almost two weeks ago. I threw it out, completely ignored it, but then this one arrived at the house. Plus he left me a little reminder yesterday. The fucker knows where I live."

"It's not too difficult to find out where anyone lives these days, especially a highly paid Wall Streeter. The search can be narrowed down to a handful of areas—the city, and the high-end suburbs; Greenwich, Scarsdale, Short Hills, Summit—that's about it. And don't forget that you are listed."

"Fair enough but it's still kind of creepy that someone would go to the trouble of tracking me down." He paused a beat. "Now do you understand why I thought I was pushed?"

"I get the paranoia, although I'm still not convinced it was anything more than an accident. But putting it all together, the letters and if it was someone pushing you— well, we shouldn't ignore it completely. Have you brought this up to Vernon?"

Jeremy nodded his head from side to side. "Not yet."

"Why not?"

"I intended to show it to him this morning but never got

the chance. He was still in a shit mood and it was the wrong time to throw fuel on his fire. You know how he feels about anyone speaking to the media."

"You're kidding me! You didn't show him this letter threatening your family because you didn't want him to know you spoke to some reporter? Tell him tomorrow. He should know about this." Paul looked down at the letter and read it again.

"No, that wasn't it. We were arguing and at that point I wasn't sure I wanted to get him involved."

"What about Jennifer? Has she seen it?"

"Unfortunately, yes, but I really downplayed it. In fact, we haven't discussed it since Friday."

There was concern in Paul's expression. "It seems pretty clear that if this guy really is serious then you're the only target, but I would still tell Jennifer to keep her guard up." Paul paused, realizing he was verging on being too much of an alarmist. "Hopefully this will turn out to be nothing, but you never know. Go to the cops. Get their perspective."

Jeremy had barely touched his beer. "There are thousands of people who own stock in Datatech. The police aren't going to question every one of them."

"You don't know what their response will be. What's the downside? Suppose this nut isn't only trying to scare you. Suppose he means business? What if he was the one who pushed you? You just said he took the trouble to find out where you live, where you work and your wife's name. This could be some serious shit."

"I know, I know. Maybe Tom Wichefski can help me."

"Suzie's fiancée?"

"Yeah. The FBI must deal with this type of situation more often than the police. And with Tom I can trust that this won't wind up in the newspaper."

"Jeremy, listen to me. Take care of this right away and speak to Jennifer. You'll be filed with regret if something happens that could have been avoided."

"Okay, okay. You're right. I'll take care of it."

Paul drained the last ounce of beer from his glass as Jeremy threw a twenty on the bar, signaling that the conversation was over.

"Let's go. I want to beat at least some of the traffic through the tunnel."

They walked out onto the street, squinting as the darkened room gave way to the bright sunshine still in abundance despite the early evening hour.

Chapter 15 □ □ □

Jeremy drove his car up the ramp and out of the garage beneath the building housing Parthenon's offices. His commute never changed except on summertime Fridays, when the usual roads home turned into parking lots filled with Jersey Shore regulars embarking upon their pilgrimage south. He directed his silver BMW west. The first traffic light he came to turned red, stopping him right in front of the crosswalk on Park Avenue and 40th Street. The loud roar of a broken muffler drew his attention to a beat up old Chevy that pulled alongside, its fenders rusted through. The vinyl top that once provided a rich offset to the painted metal body was in tatters. Jeremy caught himself inadvertently staring at the unkempt man sitting in the driver's seat; his return gaze unsettling. Turning his attention straight ahead as the light turned green, Jeremy continued to the Lincoln Tunnel.

After traveling a few blocks, Jeremy developed the uncomfortable feeling of being followed. He looked in his rearview mirror and saw the Chevy a car length behind. He convinced himself that he was mistaken; the Chevy was just another Jersey-bound commuter, although the New York license plates somewhat contradicted that rationale. *I'm losing my fucking mind*, he thought. *Get a grip.* Jeremy chose not to consult his mirror again until he was in the queue approaching the mouth of the tunnel, not that he needed to, anyway; the rumble of the Chevy's broken exhaust caused a mild vibration in his car. Jeremy eased up on the accelerator, slowing to a pace that was even more sluggish than the trickling flow of traffic. He stayed in the lane that fed into the tunnel. At the last possible second, he gunned the accelerator, turned away from the tunnel and sped away. He wondered if the Chevy would follow.

Ernest Varko had had a long day but accomplished what he had set out to do. He had no doubt that Cranford now believed that he held the power. It would make the next step in his plan so much easier. He continued to New Jersey—it was a nice night for a drive.

***

Jeremy was not pleased. He had become a paranoid mess and it was all due to a couple of letters from some crank. Thousands of cars go through the Lincoln Tunnel every day. He laughed out loud about how ridiculous it was for him to believe that he was being followed, or that someone wanted to kill him. The unnecessary detour to evade a phantom pursuer would add twenty, maybe thirty minutes to his ride home. He was not pleased.

His brief respite from concern didn't last long. Once in New Jersey, he drove along the viaduct that fed the Turnpike, and tried to make sense of everything that had happened during the day. Not normally a worrier, he nonetheless thought through the events: the scene in the gym, Vernon taking his arrogance to an intolerable level, the push from behind into oncoming traffic—he was back to believing he was pushed—the conversation with Paul and, of course, the letters. Jeremy was so preoccupied that he didn't even remember passing the usual landmarks on his way home. He hadn't bothered to turn on the radio nor have his daily call with the night traders to discuss early action in the Asian markets. As the commute dragged on, he became less worried about himself and more concerned about his family. *What if this Datatech guy really intends to harm my family?* The children, especially, had to be protected, and that would be tricky. Even if they could understand the danger, explaining it to them would only chip away at their innocence.

How, he wondered, would he explain this to Jennifer?

It's not as if he was in a dangerous line of work. Stress was the only occupational hazard he had signed up for.

Jeremy's thoughts swung back and forth like a pendulum with increasing momentum. Maybe being nudged on the street was just an accident and he was making too much of it. If someone really wanted him dead, it would have been easy to accomplish. A harder shove to his back into oncoming traffic and the speed of the truck could have....

He again wondered if the crazy guy had been following him. The guy in the Chevy had been staring right at him. His gaze possessed emotion, even anger, not the usual casual glance reserved for passing the time while stopped at a light. Jeremy's eyes darted from the rear view mirror to the road in front. *This is crazy! Get hold of yourself.* He took in a deep breath then exhaled, trying to calm his nerves. He couldn't walk into his house so visibly frazzled.

Jeremy reached for his cell phone, seeking the reassurance of Jennifer's voice. After four rings, the answering machine picked up. His family was always home at dinnertime. His mind began to wander, imagining the worst, and he cursed himself for taking the detour, extending his commute. He dialed her cell. No answer. Jeremy punched the accelerator to the floor and held it there until he realized he was going much too fast. His foot lifted from the pedal, slowing the car but his grip on the steering wheel never relaxed. Jennifer was probably in the front yard with the kids and couldn't hear the phone. They often waited outside for him. He pictured pulling up to his house and hearing the welcoming chorus of "Daddy! Daddy!" and his thoughts brightened. Seeing Alexandra and Melissa drawing chalk pictures on the driveway while they awaited his arrival was the favorite part of his day.

"This is all crazy," he said aloud. "Calm down, damn it!"

Exiting Route 24 at Hobart Road, he approached the traffic light at the top of the ramp, a light that never seemed to be green at the right time. He lowered his window and let the fresh air fill the car. He was only eighteen miles from New York City and the air wasn't all that different but Jeremy inhaled as if he were in the Rockies. It was how he always started his weekends—a relaxing first breath. He called upon that routine now. With that first breath he could feel the tension that had built up over the past five days evaporate from his body. It was a simple exercise that confuted its significant impact. In a neighborhood of stately homes dating to the early 1900's, with their rolling lawns, the Cranford house seemed to stand out. The pale yellow paint was nicely framed by a white front porch that ran the length of the house, highlighted by a swinging bench suspended from the cantilevered ceiling. Older, uniquely shaped trees and bushes provided the landscaping that new money could only hope to imitate. It was here that Jeremy would always stop and, for just a fleeting moment, appreciate his good fortune. A loving family, a beautiful home and more money than he ever thought he would have. In the back of his mind he hoped it wasn't all about to end.

Jennifer's car was in its customary spot at the top of the driveway but she and the kids were nowhere to be seen. He guessed they were now back in the house eating dinner. But the kitchen, clearly visible from the street, looked empty. His mind ran through some troubling scenarios and his pulse quickened. He jammed the transmission into park while simultaneously releasing his seat belt with his left hand. The car door flew open; he jumped out and sprinted across the lawn. He tried the knob on the front door but it was locked. He fumbled around in his pocket for the keys.

The heavy wooden door slammed into the wall behind it. "Anyone home? Jennifer? Girls? Anyone here?" No reply.

Jeremy raced around the main floor and saw the pots on the stove, the table set and plates filled with food. Jennifer's cell phone lay on the counter. "She never leaves home without her phone," he remarked aloud, troubled by the image. His heart rate quickened from stress and exertion as he ran up the steps, taking them two at a time. He heard noise coming from the upstairs family room and went there first. It was just the television tuned to Nickelodeon. A quick reconnaissance of the bedrooms; they were empty too.

He consciously reverted to his professional training, tried to be analytical, reviewing the facts, hoping something made sense but it still didn't add up. Despite realizing that it was most likely an overreaction Jeremy felt he had no choice. He dialed 911.

An official sounding voice came on the line after the first ring. "Nine-one-one operator, what is the emergency?"

He hurried the words, running them together. "I know this may be a slight overreaction but it's my family, they're not home and they should be. I have reason to believe they may be in trouble."

"Okay, sir. You're going have to repeat what you just said except slower so I can understand exactly what you're telling me."

"Okay. I'm sorry. I said my family's in trouble."

"I'm going to need some details such as who you are, where you're calling from and the reason why you believe something happened to your family."

Jeremy slowed his speech to make his reply more intelligible. He responded to the requests for information in the same order they were put to him, culminating in the circumstances for his concern.

The emergency services operator listened carefully but was skeptical. Nonetheless, she didn't want to read her name in the New York Post calling for her head if there was something truly amiss. "There's a patrol car only a couple of blocks away. Please wait outside for them to arrive. Would you like me to stay on the line?"

"No, no, it's okay. I'll be out front."

A few minutes later, a police car arrived, siren off but roof lights flashing. The cops, there were two of them, opened the doors of their patrol car and got out. Seemingly in unison they placed their hats upon their heads, then hitched up their pants before adjusting their holsters. One of the officers was extremely well muscled, his large biceps accentuated by the blue uniform material that appeared to be painted onto his arms, a tattoo of an eagle peering out from beneath. His partner had quite the opposite appearance, with a distended stomach stretching the seams of an unyielding uniform.

The taller, less fit of the two, spoke first. "I'm Officer Danby and this is my partner, Officer Kramer. I assume you're the one who—"

Every second mattered. "Yes, yes, I'm the one who called."

Danby pulled a pencil and pad, covered in black leather, from the pocket that ran down the leg of his dark blue uniform pants. "Tell us what's going on."

"I came home and my family's not here." Jeremy quickened the pace of his speech. "They're supposed to be here. They're always home at this time."

Serious crime just didn't occur in Summit. Probably a worried husband and nothing more. "Couldn't your wife be running an errand? Why do you suspect something criminal?"

"Her car is still in the driveway and she wouldn't walk a couple of miles to the market, dragging along two toddlers. Look, I'm sure you think that I'm overreacting but there's more to this."

Officer Kramer interrupted. "Sir, can I ask if you and your wife live together?"

Anger nudged worry aside. "What the hell does that have to do with anything?" Jeremy snapped. "Yes, we live together and to answer your next question, no, we have not been arguing. Now, are you going to help me or not?"

Danby took back the lead. "Of course we will but first tell me why you suspect that something is wrong."

"I'll do better than that. I'll show you."

Jeremy started toward his car to grab the letters as a black GMC Yukon pulled into the driveway. Jennifer thrust her door open and flew out of the passenger seat. Deep concern was evident on her face as she ran to her husband.

"What's wrong? Are you okay?"

"Yes, yes. Of course I am," Jeremy answered, immediately feeling foolish.

The officers exchanged knowing looks.

"Then why are the police here?"

"I called them because I was worried. I saw your car in the driveway and dinner was on the table but no one was home. I don't know...I guess I just wanted to be sure everything was okay."

"Didn't you get the message I left on your cell phone telling you that Lauren came over, and we were taking the kids for ice cream?"

Danby had heard enough. It was simply a case of another overzealous spouse hitting the panic button because things weren't exactly as he thought they should be. "Sir, if it's okay with you, we'd like to move on."

"Sure, sure. I'm sorry to have dragged you out here for nothing." If Jennifer weren't standing there, Jeremy would have shown the police the letters. It would help assuage his feeling of embarrassment and provide a better ending to the story the cops were sure to tell their buddies.

"No problem; we understand. I would have done the same," Kramer graciously responded although he knew that he would not have panicked like the rich banker that was standing in front of him.

As the officers walked to their car, Lauren, seeing everything was okay, let Melissa and Alexandra out of her SUV. They made a beeline for their dad and tangled themselves onto his legs.

"Daddy, Daddy. Why were the policemen here?"

"They wanted to see where the two cutest kids in the neighborhood live."

He was relieved that they felt none of his concern and regretted his reaction. After all, what really were the chances that someone would go to so much trouble over one stock bet gone bad? He would soon find out that the odds were pretty damn good.

Chapter 16

□ □ □

Ernest Varko had been up since five o'clock in the morning. That was when the big boys on the Street awoke and he was every bit as good as they were. Unfortunately, he reasoned, he was suffering from a run of bad luck. The basement where Varko now lived had one small window in the upper portion of the wall against which his cot was placed. This dump was all he could afford on a night watchman's salary. Until he was back on his feet he would have to tolerate these ramshackle conditions. Living in this hellhole would not break his spirit; he had lived under far worse conditions when his wife first kicked him out. But he was determined never to return to that shelter on the Bowery. Cranford was responsible for putting him there before, but he wasn't going to do it again.

The only items his wife had allowed him to take were his clothes and a beat up old television. It was actually the cops who finally convinced the witch to let him have the stuff. He was still upset with himself for telling her he was coming back to the apartment to retrieve his belongings. She then made up some lies about how he had tried to kill her; he was only trying to shake some reason into her. The cops were waiting when he arrived. Varko had no idea how she was able to bamboozle some judge into issuing a restraining order. He hadn't been home or been allowed to see his children since.

The television was precariously balanced on a small chest of drawers he had salvaged from the curb up the block from his building. He turned it on; it was already tuned to channel 15, CNBC. At least basement living provided one thing to be thankful for and that was the ability to hack into all the wires that fed the apartments on the upper floors. Without good credit, it was the only way for him to get cable access, even if the reception was spotty at best.

Asian and European market news were all that these dopey anchors talked about at this time of the morning. The good stuff didn't start until six. Nonetheless, he knew that smart investors had to keep up on all financial markets whether they were involved with them or not. While Ann Wong reported from Singapore, Ernest went to the bathroom and washed up.

He was dressed and in his chair, which, aside from the bed and set of drawers, was the only other piece of furniture in the room, exactly when *Market Talk* came on at the top of the hour. The futures indicated a softer opening but it was still early; stocks would not start trading for another three and a half hours. He sat there the entire time, transfixed as the futures continued to sell off. Datatech was his biggest position. He had owned it for almost a year and was sure he knew the stock better than anybody. It wasn't just another internet company. They had a real product, or so he thought. At one point, his fifteen thousand shares were worth half a million dollars. Actually, not quite since the number of shares and the profit were imagined. His actual profits approximated only a few thousand—and that may have been a stretch. As Datatech's price declined, he used margin to buy more. The company told him business was absolutely great. He spoke to management directly; they wouldn't lie to him. The company blamed the bear market and short sellers for the stock price decline. Short sellers like Parthenon were no different than the crooks at Lehman Brothers or Enron. They got rich at the expense of others. Ernest vowed to make it right. Jeremy Cranford would either tell the world the truth about Datatech or regret that he had ever heard of the company.

The market opened lower and continued to decline during the first hour. Ernest wasn't happy but being the pro that he was, he would ride it out. Rookies and retail investors got nervous and tended to capitulate at the bottoms of markets but not him. Not Ernest Varko. He was a professional, as good as any of them.

***

The proof of Varko's investment acumen sat right there in the corner, the written records he kept of all his phantom trades. Over the last four years he had filled eighty-two legal pads with every trade he would have entered into if he had had the money. Each line, in a scrawl legible only to him, contained the stock ticker, the date and price of each purchase and sale. At the bottom of every page he totaled his paper profits, transferring those figures to yet another pad. He had compiled a remarkable track record with only one out of every 15 or 20 pages indicating a loss. Hindsight and revisionist history always trumped actual performance. *I meant to sell it last week but I forgot to write it down* was one of his oft-employed tactics that allowed him to record a profit instead of the loss that should have been noted.

The pads, yellowing and worn, lay in three neat piles but for the occasional page that partially protruded from the perforated spine of each. Prior to committing more funds to his brokerage account, he reviewed his "performance" with his then wife, she being no more of a realist than he and absolutely naïve about any type of investment. It wasn't until their electricity was turned off and the city marshal served them with an eviction notice, both occurring on the same day, that she realized she had been living in her husband's delusions for years, although it was his dishonesty that widened the chasm between them, ultimately causing her to leave.

Varko hadn't always been so delusional. He had once been a moderately successful stockbroker, having followed his father into the profession. Vocation and surname weren't the only similarities they shared in their adult life. The bloodlines were a conduit for the father's bipolar disorder. For most of his life, Ernest had managed the disease with medication, religiously following the regiment prescribed by his doctor, increasing the dosage in periods of significant stress.

During the market meltdown in 2000, the internet stocks that Ernest and his clients had made so much money investing in substantially declined in price—some of their holdings, their largest positions, losing all their value. He was almost completely wiped out, financially and professionally, as every single client abandoned him. Without a book of business, he was dismissed from his job. The popping of the internet bubble reverberated through most firms on the Street and massive layoffs ensued; Varko was unable to find another job. There were a few firms, hedge funds, that profited handsomely from the demise of the market. They were smart enough to have been short a large number of overvalued internet stocks, the same ones that Varko had fallen in love with. He read article after article about the wealth these individuals had accumulated at his expense and it angered him. It was only because of his deficiency in capital relative to their massive funds that they were able to drive those companies into oblivion. He vowed to one day make enough money to get even with the "shorts" who ruined his career and destroyed his family.

Varko took what little savings he had left and plowed it back into the market. His investment acumen had not improved and his account was nearly depleted but, strangely, not his confidence. By this time, he had been stretching his medication, skipping a dose here and there, in an effort to save money on the prescription. His tenuous grip on reality eroded with longer episodic instances of irrational behavior. Under a cloud of psychosis, Varko regarded his options. He decided to take one more shot at the market, defying a Family Court order to allocate a portion of his unemployment check to health care insurance for him and his family. Without any insurance to offset the cost of his pills, he succumbed to his illness and it infiltrated his every waking hour.

Varko studiously reviewed his voluminous records, jotting down his most successful trades on still another pad. One particular stock had repeatedly generated more profits than any other. It said it right there on page after page. In fact, the total profits generated from his trading in this one company were obscene. Datatech, ticker DTCH, was his horse; he clearly knew it better than anyone else. He would put everything he had into that stock and eventually, probably sooner rather than later, make enough money to convince his wife that his run of bad luck was over.

Chapter 17 □ □ □

A chime sounded on Jeremy's PC.

F360: "man, is she hot!!!!!!!!!!!"

JAM: "whos hot"

F360: "my new employee. thats who"

JAM: "keep the employee part in mind. its not good to shit where you eat"

F360: "i think she's attracted to me"

JAM: "her 2? thats 5 this week that can't keep their hands off u. its been all of one day. stop fooling around"

F360: "whos fooling around? this is serious"

JAM: "i don't have time for this and you don't have enough job security for it. plus i can tell when ur pulling my chain"

F360: "had you going for a little. admit it"

Marty had quietly come up behind Paul and quickly read the transcript of the IMs before making her presence known. "Sorry to interrupt but do you have a minute?"

"Hey Marty. Give me a second so I can finish this email." Paul typed in "gtg" before closing the dialogue box. As he turned around, his embarrassment was evident in his slightly hued, red cheeks. "Okay. I'm all yours."

"All mine?" she asked coyly, smiling.

Paul momentarily deliberated on his reply, deciding which way to take the conversation. Jeremy, as if sitting on his shoulder whispering in his ear, won out.

"How can I help?"

"The firm I worked for in Dallas was so much smaller than Parthenon, so I'm sure we did things a lot differently than you do them here." Marty responded, more measured.

A trusting relationship took longer than a day to build. "I don't want to mess up so would you mind giving me a brief rundown on your ops?"

Marty had performed her due diligence. It was pretty clear. Within the limited circle of large hedge funds, Paul was widely regarded as one of the industry's best business managers. He was bright, thorough and forward thinking. The feedback that was most impressive was that unlike his peers, Paul understood the investment aspects of the business. While that did not qualify him to be a portfolio manager, it was invaluable in managing his unit for maximum effectiveness with as little slippage as possible.

"I would be glad to."

"Perfect!" She said enthusiastically.

"Since I really don't know what you do or do not know, I'm going to be very basic about this. If I notice your eyes glazing over, I'll take it as a sign you're bored."

"Basic is good for now."

"Great. First of all, you're absolutely right. Because of our size we had to customize most of our systems. That alone makes us different than most of our peers who use off-the-shelf technology."

"No wonder people say you're the best. I can only imagine how difficult it must be to stay on top of the technology, the people—everything."

Paul enjoyed the flattery, particularly since it came from Marty, but didn't quite know how to respond so he continued on with an overview of his department's mandate.

"This is where we process the wires. Are you familiar with wiring?"

"Of course but are people still trusting you as much with all their banking information since Madoff?"

"That asshole should have been shot instead of imprisoned."

"He'll have a long time to figure out where he screwed up."

"Interesting perspective," Paul responded, lifting one eyebrow. "I would think he would spend his time regretting that he screwed so many people and caused his son's suicide rather than how he could have perfected his scheme."

"Of course. That's what I meant," Marty said, embarrassed at her misstep.

"I know what you meant," Paul offered, noting Marty's discomfort. "None of our investors have pulled back. We offer them significant transparency and have too many safeguards. Vernon, Jeremy and I are the only ones with access to all the investor data."

"Jeremy? What does he need access for?"

"He's one of the partners. If something should happen to Vernon he's next in line to run this firm." Paul cupped his hand over his mouth, facetious in his indication that he was letting Marty in on a big secret. "But between us, neither Jeremy nor Vernon has ever accessed the system. Hell, I would doubt they even know their passwords."

"Passwords? Like a login to a computer?"

"Similar, but the system is a lot more advanced in terms of levels of access. The three of us have our own codes, four digit numbers that I assigned to them. I made them easy to remember. At some point you will have your own password but it will only entitle you to certain parts of the database."

"Ooh, how exciting. Can I pick the numbers all by myself?"

Paul chuckled. "Aren't you the comedienne? Let's move on."

And so they did. Marty was the perfect pupil, hanging on to every word, periodically asking questions to show that she was paying attention.

"You seem to have a pretty good grip on these procedures but there's one more to discuss and that is the transference of cash to pay for our trades. A fortune travels through this office every day. We could never keep up with the workload manually, so the small trade settlements are automated—I'll spot check them depending on how busy I am—but the larger payments require my signature."

"Hope you have a good firewall to prevent someone hacking into your accounts."

"The best."

"I know something about firewalls. Which company do you use?"

"HPS. Stands for Hack Proof Systems. We actually liked the product so much that we bought stock in the company."

Marty noted the company name.

Paul turned to look at the clock sitting on his desk. "I know this is going to crush you, but I have to rush off to a meeting. I can circle back later in case you have any questions."

Paul didn't tell Marty that even after two years at Parthenon he still had questions. He wasn't completely comfortable with the custom reporting requirements for a few of the limited partners. And sometimes it seemed to him that certain information was written in a code he couldn't understand. Vernon was kind to spare him the necessity of unraveling it by farming out most of the reporting work on his small company portfolio to an independent consultant. It was a legacy he accepted when he arrived at Parthenon and, given his heavy workload, he saw no reason to initiate any changes. That would be Vernon's decision.

"You make it all sound so uncomplicated. I already feel more comfortable."

"With your background, this should be a snap."

Marty hadn't learned anything new. The only thing she didn't know was which bank and financial custodian Parthenon used. She would find out. Unfortunately for Parthenon, Marty was a very good student and a brilliant technologist.

Chapter 18

□ □ □

From the time he sat down at his desk with his morning cup of coffee until the market opened, Jeremy did nothing but read. Although he had an online subscription to each of the four newspapers he read—Wall Street Journal, New York Times, Washington Post and Los Angeles Times—he still preferred turning pages to poking the keyboard on his computer or stabbing the shiny glass of his iPad. Perhaps it was a sentimental feeling from when he used to read the Sunday comics with his dad as a kid, but he still liked the feel of newsprint in his hands.. Next he would quickly skim through the hundred plus emails he received every morning, most sent by brokerage firms regurgitating the prior day's business headlines, adding nothing of value. As much as he wanted to delete his entire inbox, he was an information junkie always searching for that one piece of information that he could parlay into profits.

Jeremy's system was comprised of four twenty-inch monitors connected to two very powerful PC's. One screen accommodated his emails; another displayed the market indices, bond, commodity and currency prices as well as the tickers of over seven hundred stocks, their direction on the day indicated by red or green; a third presented the real time profit and loss of Jeremy's portfolio; and the last screen, furthest to his left, scrolled live headlines of all news stories from various wire services, including Bloomberg, Reuters, the Associated Press and Dow Jones. For most people accustomed to working with only one monitor, Jeremy's set up would be sensory overload but for him they were easily managed and necessary data sources.

On this particular day, the overseas markets were all down. The U.S. exchanges followed suit. The declines weren't significant relative to the run up over the last couple of days and a little profit-taking surprised no one. However, companies that depended upon oil as a feedstock or operational necessity saw their stocks suffer more significantly. The price of Brent Sea Crude was still moving higher after already experiencing one of its historically biggest moves. Initially, the markets took the rising price in stride, opting to believe it was temporary, but the day's action indicated greater concern. The only beneficiaries of higher oil prices were the energy companies themselves, the stocks of which Albright owned in size.

Intently watching his monitors, Jeremy was pleased that his portfolio was making money as the general market declined. Despite having little insight into Vernon's portfolio, Jeremy was sure that his partner was also having a profitable day since there was no evidence of an eruption coming from down the hall. Jeremy sat back in his chair, eyes darting across the four monitors as if he were viewing a tennis match from mid-court. It was a huge amount of information to digest but he was good at it. It was then that one of the headlines caught his attention.

Wal-Mart announces that their weekly sales estimate has been revised from plus 1% to negative 2%, citing the impact of higher fuel prices on their customer base.

Sitting up straight in his chair, Jeremy placed his right hand on top of the mouse and dragged the cursor directly over the headline. He clicked on it twice to reveal the full text of the Wal-Mart statement.

Our core customer has been hurt by skyrocketing fuel prices. We anticipate year over year same store sales continuing to decline at an average rate of 2–3% unless oil prices begin to recede. Particularly hard hit areas are housewares, clothing and toys. We have also noticed a decline in the average receipt for food. Customers have already begun to trade down from brand name merchandise to less expensive goods.

The wire services followed the brief company release with commentary from a noted economic pundit:

Wal-Mart has been a reliable window into the financial health of the American consumer and what they are telling us is that families are being forced to make the choice between putting food on the table and buying clothing for their children, usually cutting back on both. We fear for them and the general economy, once winter arrives, should prices remain at current levels.

Jeremy let out an audible sigh. One thing that always bothered him about the hedge fund business model was how often he was in a position to profit from other peoples' misfortunes, sometimes even rooting for the negative event to occur. He once doubled his money when a company fired five thousand employees since it reduced their cost structure, thus making it much more profitable. Now, since he was short stocks like Wal-Mart, he stood to make another killing off the backs of those unable to navigate both rising energy prices and the inflated cost of life's necessities.

Jeremy continually reminded himself that he wasn't the one responsible for anyone's misfortune; he didn't create the event, he was just astute enough to anticipate a profitable trade. It was his job. Ignoring the opportunity wouldn't make anyone feel any better. Still conflicted, he assuaged his residual guilt by making significant donations to various charities, mostly youth organizations. In contrast, Albright never provided a hearing. His charitable impulses were fueled by ego; the thrill of seeing his name above the doorway at some hospital or attached to some cause that drew the spotlight of fame. Albright negotiated his donations as if they were business transactions with more strings attached than a soccer net.

***

Further uptown, Buck was surveying the markets. He sat in the living room of his apartment at The Carlyle, a large plasma television tuned to CNBC. In a box in the lower right hand corner of the screen the numbers and captions changed every two seconds. The S&P 500 was down five points; NASDAQ was down fifteen; the Dow Jones average had declined by fifty-six. Bonds were going in the opposite direction, as was oil. Buck couldn't help but smile. *Damn if it ain't working like a charm.*

"Get Hallwood on the phone," Hendricks called out to Carla, who was perusing the morning newspapers in the nearby kitchen area, always within earshot of Buck's beckoning. Even though they spent a lot of time together, Hendricks wasn't a big fan of small talk and would rather be in a room by himself than share his space. Less than a minute later, Carla appeared in the living room. It was okay for Buck to shout from room to room but everyone else was required to observe proper decorum.

"Hallwood is on line one."

Buck lifted the remote control from his lap and pointed it at the television, then pressed the mute button. Reaching to his left, he placed the remote on top of an eighteenth century end table, exchanging it for the telephone handset.

"Scottie. How's it going?"

Hallwood, based in Dallas, was the general partner of SH Asset Management, LLC. It wasn't until the paperwork was complete and all the legal and accounting fees paid that he realized the acronym was none too flattering, SHAM being the worst possible adjective to pin on any financial company. But that's what SH Asset Management had turned out to be.

SHAM had been sending out falsified statements to its investors that showed an increase in their investment account whereas their actual balances had declined by nearly eighty percent, a result of poor trading results. However, Hallwood was unwilling to forego the good life even if it meant authoring a bit of financial fiction. It was a foolish attempt to buy time until he could figure out a solution to his cash drain, since each instance of fraud was subject to a twenty-year prison term. He didn't need to employ his MBA in Finance to understand that with nearly one hundred investors in his fund, immortality would be the only way he would outlive his sentence.

Buck had a relatively minor investment in SHAM and would periodically call Hallwood for an update. During one such conversation, Hallwood took Buck through a trade he had just put on with the expectation he would double his money. SH bet big on soybean commodity contracts breaking out to new highs. The Midwest had been experiencing severe drought conditions for over a month. All the weather forecasts predicted more of the same for weeks to come. As a result, soybean supplies in the U.S. were very tight, causing a major increase in price. The scenario played out exactly as Hallwood had predicted, making him look like a genius. That is, until the government made a deal with Brazil to ship their excess harvest, which was plentiful, to the U.S. Soybean prices collapsed on news of the agreement. Buck asked Scott if he had been able to get out of the contracts in time. Scott said he had and Buck, with no reason to disbelieve him, continued to receive his monthly statements showing a positive balance. It wasn't until Buck heard from his banker that Scott was defaulting on some loans that he became suspicious and paid a visit to SHAM's office with Rock in tow. Rock, a former college football player, was nearly as wide as he was tall, his tight black tee short accentuating an intimidating physique. He had a simple place in Buck's organization; driver and bodyguard, a role that on occasion extended to enforcer.

For both Hendricks and Hallwood, the meeting ended better than it began. The threat of legal repercussions wasn't enough to convince Hallwood to fess up so Buck tried a different tactic, sitting back as Rock temporarily assumed the role of lead negotiator. Hallwood decided he didn't like the sensation of having his fingers broken one by one and enthusiastically accepted Buck's onerous terms, ceding complete control of his firm in return for a bailout. Hallwood would now be working for Hendricks. For Buck, SHAM was just another vehicle he had commandeered to execute his plan. Two years later, Hallwood was grateful that he had avoided jail and appreciative of his increased wealth.

"We're long and going strong. The black stuff is hitting another new high and we are definitely participating. How long are we gonna ride this horse?" The glee in Hallwood's voice was evident.

"A while yet. Just stay in the position until I say otherwise."

***

As the lunchtime lull in trading approached, Jeremy decided to stretch his legs and pay Vernon a visit. He had spent the morning commute thinking about the prior day's conversation, concluding it was time to pay more attention to the business end of Parthenon. Additionally, Paul's comments over drinks had resonated; with his family's financial security at stake, it was irresponsible not to be more involved. He also had a fiduciary responsibility to investors. Should something go wrong, and that was always a possibility at complex investment vehicles such as hedge funds, the law would not allow him to hide behind apathy or the excuse that it was Vernon's firm.

"Morning, Suzie. Is Vernon busy?"

Suzie turned from her paperwork to face her favorite Parthenon colleague. "Good morning to you too. Did my boss invite you over?"

"Nope. This is a self-initiated friendly fly by."

"Well, your timing is perfect. He just finished a call." She pointed her pencil toward the open door. "Go right in."

Albright looked up as Jeremy entered his office. "Just the person I want to see. I've got great news. The bonus pool should grow nicely with the additional funds we took in."

"From whom? How much?"

"Buck Hendricks," Vernon responded casually. "Five hundred million. It sounds like a bigger number than it is since it works out to less than a 3% increase in our assets."

"Didn't it occur to you that this was something we should have discussed? We've been turning down other investors for months. The market is acting like garbage and you want to throw more at it? That's crazy! Besides, I don't even know this guy."

"You don't need to know him; I know him! He's been a great friend of the firm and as our largest outside investor—and most loyal—he's entitled to some special treatment. And it's not that we couldn't handle any more money, it's that we—mostly you—don't want to. To make it more manageable, we'll each take half into our portfolios. That's another quarter billion from which you can generate fees and add to your bonus."

"So this is a done deal?"

"Look, Buck's a great strategic investor. He's very plugged in to the oil and gas markets. Everything he's told me has worked out. With more money invested with us, he'll have more incentive to keep that dialogue going."

"Please don't tell me that he's giving you inside information and that you're using it to trade. Tell me I have it wrong."

"No, no of course I'm not saying that. It's not like that at all," Albright protested, using his hands to wave away any suggestion of the sort. "For Chrissakes, he's an oil man. He grew up in the business. It's no different than some of your sources. Do you think I'd jeopardize this firm and the people in it for a couple of bucks?"

"When you're talking about sums of money equivalent to the Gross Domestic Product of a medium sized third world country, it's bullshit to call it a couple of bucks. If you're telling me everything is on the up and up and a decision has already been made, then there's not much I can do. At the very least I should meet him, particularly given how important he is to the firm and my livelihood."

"I'll try to arrange something next time he's in town, but his schedule is always very tight." Albright was not particularly concerned that Jeremy would follow up; he never showed interest in anything that drew his attention away from the market.

"Vernon, this is the second time within a week that you've treated me as if I'm just another hired hand and I'm getting tired of it. First you hire Marty and now this. Put yourself in my position. You would feel the same way."

"It's incredible that you're getting this worked up about my hiring another flunky for the back office or taking in a few hundred million when we already manage twenty billion. That's a damn rounding error. What *is* important though is how much this firm earns and the size of our bonuses. That's where the focus should be. Besides, I wouldn't have agreed to take the money if I didn't have complete faith in your ability to put it to work."

Jeremy took a couple of seconds before responding, a tactic that became a reflex when he traded, ensuring that his emotions didn't override his judgment. "I'm flattered by your faith in me," he said sarcastically, adding "you're too kind." Jeremy turned and left, confused about the recent events but determined to sort them out.

As Jeremy walked to his office, he thought through the exchange with Vernon. He had misgivings about the sarcastic response he offered; a more straightforward reply would have better expressed his viewpoint. He was also disappointed with himself for allowing Vernon to obfuscate the real issue by belittling Jeremy's desire to be more involved in the firm.

Vernon bristled at Jeremy's impudence. Anyone else would have been immediately terminated but Vernon was more hurt than offended. He viewed himself as Jeremy's mentor and friend, and, of course, his benefactor in a way, having made him a very wealthy man. Perhaps it was confirmation of his suspicion that Jeremy was on the cusp of resigning from Parthenon, something he would never let happen. If Jeremy left, it would be Albright's decision. No one had ever walked out on him except Vince Garmeillion but that was years ago and he was a lousy trader anyway, a half-step ahead of the broom.

As Vernon continued to ponder his relationship with Jeremy, he reminded himself that to keep his edge he had to maintain his discipline. Buy a stock, make a boatload on it, and get so comfortable owning it that you don't ever think about exiting the position—that was a default strategy that always came back to bite him in the ass. Why was Jeremy different from any other successful trade? Perhaps he had kept Jeremy on the shelf long after his Sell-By date had expired. He was becoming a real nuisance and might ultimately inhibit Albright's ability to capitalize on his more profitable relationship with Buck. Albright turned to his screens; it was not yet time to make a decision but that day was fast arriving.

Chapter 19

□ □ □

Ernest Varko had the wild-eyed look of an addict who was working hard on his latest crack-infused binge. Always disheveled, his rumpled clothes hung loosely on his near skeletal frame. His full head of wiry red hair went in every direction, dander falling to his shoulders as he repeatedly clawed at his scalp. Varko feverishly paced back and forth across the tattered rug that provided partial cover to the basement apartment's cement floor. He nervously wrung his hands each time he looked at the television, trying to erase the image on the lower right hand corner of the flickering screen that showed the market averages continuing to plummet. He was pissed off at his broker, Al Manero, for not returning his calls. Varko wanted to take advantage of the market's decline by buying more Datatech stock, but first he had to speak with Manero. Another broker finally accepted his call.

"Your account's frozen, Bud. You need Manero to go to bat with management so you can trade again."

Varko was not one to take no for an answer. He dialed his broker's number again.

"Alan Manero speaking."

"I've been trying to get through to you for an hour. How am I supposed to make any money if my broker doesn't return my calls?"

Manero recognized the voice and immediately regretted not having had his sales assistant screen the call. Varko was one of the firm's smallest customers yet the biggest pain in the ass. Manero had tried to push him off on another broker but they all knew he was a whacko and would not go anywhere near his account. The branch manager would have closed the account but for the recent newspaper articles that were critical of the way large investment banks treated the small investor. He feared being a poster boy for greedy brokerage firms, so he repeatedly told Manero, "You're stuck with him. Deal with it."

"It's been a crazy morning and the phone has not stopped ringing but I have a minute now. What can I do for you?"

"Where's Datatech trading right now, right this minute?"

"It's down a buck. The whole market is getting clocked."

It couldn't be. He couldn't afford for this to happen. "There's nothing wrong with this company. You must be reading the quote wrong."

"I know how to read a quote. The stock is down a dollar. Why don't you sell this piece of garbage before it goes to zero?" Manero had long ago run out of patience.

Varko channeled the restraint that he knew was the hallmark of a successful trader. "I need a favor.... "

Manero's other phone lines were ringing and he had to move on. He was on straight commission and stood no chance of earning another penny from this poor shmuck.

"We've been through this before. There is no way in hell that this firm is going to extend additional margin to you. There's hardly any equity left in your account now and with what's happening today, you might even have to pony up more cash."

"Listen, asshole, don't you understand the game? By the end of today Datatech will be a lot higher and you'll wish you owned it. I'm warning you not to screw me on this. I need some buying power and I need it now."

"I don't have to take any more shit from you. This conversation is over. And don't bother calling my manager anymore. He won't talk to you either."

White foam bubbled at the corner of Varko's mouth and the spittle that shot off his abnormally large tongue covered the mouthpiece on the handset. "It used to be that you couldn't do enough for me. Told me I was one of your biggest accounts. Now you treat me like shit. Not a good move, Mr. Manero, not a good move at all."

"Don't threaten me, you psycho. Listen carefully. There's no more money here for you. In fact, I can't wait for the margin call so I can sell what's left of your precious Datatech. Just a few more ticks down and poof. Say bye-bye to Datatech." Manero slammed the receiver back into its cradle.

Varko tightened his grip on the handset, the cord dangling by his side. He looked at the television and saw the market begin to recover. DTCH, the ticker symbol for Datatech stock, was periodically displayed on the scrolling ticker tape at the bottom of the screen. The last price noted was four dollars even. Not that many shares ever changed hands in this company so it was ten minutes before he saw it flash by again. Now it was ten cents higher, moving up with the market.

"Damn that fucking broker," he shouted at the top of his lungs. "He just cost me a fortune!"

The loud tap-tap-tap from the floor above let him know that his upstairs neighbors had tired of listening to his rants. Varko grabbed the broom that was leaning against the wall and started jamming the handle hard into the ceiling, causing loose pieces of plaster to rain down upon his head. "And fuck you, too," he screamed at his faceless tormenters.

Over the next hour, Varko watched the market complete its recovery and move into positive territory. Datatech stock went along for the ride, ultimately ending with a nice gain on the day. Markets being what they are, the reversal could be short lived. No matter, this was not foremost on his mind. DTCH would always do well. Varko knew it. He put on his baseball cap, grabbed his keys and walked out the door. It was only a ten-minute subway ride to midtown. He would arrive right before lunch.

Chapter 20

□ □ □

Jeremy had two calls to make when he returned to his office. He looked up Suzie's direct line in the company directory, keying in through the Microsoft Outlook icon on his desktop. He usually reached her through Vernon's extension, a number he long ago committed to memory, but didn't want his number to appear on caller ID. Jeremy was uncomfortable initiating a clandestine conversation with Suzie but didn't feel he had any other choice. They always had a great rapport and, intuitively, he believed that if she were not so egregiously overpaid, she would have left Vernon a long time ago. Terming Vernon a difficult personality was akin to saying a piranha had sharp teeth; both were major understatements.

"Hello, Jeremy. This must be special. I think the only other time you called on my line was six months ago when we were planning a surprise party for Vernon."

"I'm not sure I would call this special. I'm only calling because I wanted Tom's number."

"When did you two become telephone buddies?"

"I'm afraid it isn't that kind of conversation."

The cheer in Suzie's voice settled into a more somber tone. If Jeremy was seeking out her fiancé, it most likely was not a good thing. Despite her curiosity, she sensed Jeremy's discomfort and chose not to pry. "Call him on his cell. It's the best way to get in touch since he spends most of his time in the field. The number is 917–555–1286."

Jeremy was tempted to tell Suzie about the letters but didn't want to compromise her position with Albright. He believed Tom would feel the same way. Additionally, his position as a special agent with the FBI trumped his status as Suzie's future husband when it came to keeping a confidence related to his work.

Jeremy's next call was to Paul, forgoing their usual method of communicating over the internet. All the firm's data, including emails and IMs, were captured and held on the firm's servers for at least three years, whereas only calls to and from the trading desk were recorded.

"Any progress on your project?"

Paul spoke quietly into the receiver. "Coming along but slower than I would like. Marty has been on me non-stop, asking question after question. I don't want her to know what I'm doing. Don't want to risk it getting back to Vernon."

"I wouldn't worry about that. She knows you're the risk manager. It's only natural that you periodically review all the portfolios and trades. Christ, it's part of your job. Sneaking around will only make her suspicious."

"Good point. *I* am the master of my domain," Paul said with a half-hearted laugh.

"Exactly! Pull together what you can and bring it by later."

"I should at least be able to provide you with a list of the securities he has in the portfolio as of yesterday. Today's trades won't be in the system yet. And the investor information you asked for will have to wait awhile."

"Concentrate on the portfolio and don't worry about the investors for now. Let me know when you have something."

"No problem. I remain your best friend, high level clerk, and faithful servant."

"Well, two out of three isn't bad," Jeremy responded, unable to resist the friendly jab.

"Pretty funny. You'll miss me when I'm gone."

"You're right. I couldn't do any of this without you," Jeremy spoke sincerely before adding a jab that had a place in most of their dialogue "I am a mere pawn in your plan to take Parthenon to the next level of greatness."

"Finally—you get it! I'm getting back to work. Later."

***

"Wichefski."

Tom Wichefski always practiced formal decorum when he answered his cell phone whether it was during the day or in the evening. An FBI agent in the white-collar fraud unit was never off duty. And lately he was very, very busy.

Jeremy pressed the privacy button on his phone in case anyone inadvertently picked up his extension. "Tom, this is Jeremy Cranford. Suzie gave me your cell number. I hope you don't mind my calling."

"Not at all. She just called me with a heads up although she seemed to be in the dark about the subject matter."

"And if it's okay with you, I prefer to keep it that way."

Any thoughts by Tom that this was a social call immediately dissipated. With all the corporate scandals and hedge fund shenanigans making headlines recently, he had to offer a disclaimer.

"Before we go any further, I would just caution you to take my position as a special agent into account. Please don't continue if you believe what you are about to say will compromise either one of us."

"Wait? You think....? No, no, it's nothing like that. Nothing like that at all."

"That's good," he responded, relieved that Jeremy wasn't calling about Parthenon. "So how can I help?"

"I received a couple of threatening letters. At first I didn't think anything of them but then something strange happened yesterday and I thought it would be a good idea to get your perspective."

Normally, Tom would end the conversation quickly by suggesting that Jeremy first go to the police, but given Suzie's job at the firm that wasn't an option. He also liked Jeremy and wanted to help. "What do you mean by strange?"

"Actually, scary would be more like it. Paul and I were walking on the street and we stopped at the crosswalk outside our building, waiting for the light to change. The next thing I know is I'm almost flat out in the street with a truck bearing down on me. I could swear I felt a hand push me from behind."

"And you believe that incident is related to some letters that you received. Tell me about those. What do they say, how did you get them? I need some details."

"The first came to the office and the second one was sent to my house and it specifically mentioned Jennifer and the kids. He also snuck a note in mailbox. I think I'm being targeted because I gave an interview to the Wall Street Journal, about how I thought this one particular stock, a company called Datatech, was a core short. I pretty much said it was a piece of junk and anyone that owned it should sell it. The stock went down the next day and has continued declining. Whoever wrote those letters no doubt owns the stock and is blaming me for their losses. What has me worked up is that this kook went to the trouble of tracking down my home address. It would have been a helluva a lot easier to mail them to Parthenon."

"I understand your concern even though these matters usually turn out to be nothing. I have seen it dozens of times; someone gets pissed and fires off an emotional letter. The second was most likely sent to your home because the person who wrote it didn't want to take a chance on your secretary tossing both letters before you saw them. Same with the one he delivered. Wanted to make sure you received it although, candidly, that does make me a bit uncomfortable."

"So what do you suggest?"

"First tell me about the pushing incident. What time of day did it happen?"

"After work."

"I know you guys work late. Was it during the evening rush hour?"

"Yup."

"So rush hour, crowded corner, people in a hurry to

get home. The corner was probably pretty crowded at that time of day. You're a pretty levelheaded guy; think about it. Don't you think that maybe it was accidental? I've been in those types of crowds. Someone's always impatient and trying to bust out of the pack."

"You're right about me being levelheaded; the last thing I want to do is overreact to anything. But this was no accident; I was pushed. I felt a hand in my back. But even if you put that aside, someone went to the trouble of finding out the names of my wife and children, and where I live. Isn't that combination of factors, or even if you take these incidents separately, enough to cause me some concern?"

"Absolutely. I'm just trying to get some perspective. I want to make sure that the letters aren't driving you crazy, seeing shadows behind the shower curtain—that type of thing. And I'm not trying to play down those letters. I want to take a look at them."

"I only have the most recent one. I tossed the first one and tore up the note he put in my mailbox. I know it was a dumb thing to do but I wasn't thinking about preserving evidence at the time."

"Okay. We'll work with what we have. It's probably too late now, but be careful how you handle them. Actually don't handle them anymore. Use tongs or a tweezers to put the letter and envelope into a larger envelope. I want to see if we can lift some prints off the paper. If you have it with you, I'll stop by and pick it up."

"It's here. When can you come by?"

"Either in the next hour or it will have to be tomorrow."

"Are you sure you don't mind getting involved?"

"Don't worry about it. I'm happy to help."

"That's great. Can't tell you how much I appreciate it." The tension in Jeremy's voice eased for the first time. "I hate to ask you this, but would you mind if I gave them to Paul to pass on to you? I have a meeting with Vernon and if I cancel—I will if I have to—he'll want to know why, and I'm not ready to tell him about this."

"Don't worry. You've told me pretty much all I need to know for now. I can meet with Paul if you're busy."

***

His door open, Vernon raised his voice slightly to get Suzie's attention. "Suzie, could you call Marty and ask her to come to my office?"

"Right away."

Marty arrived at Suzie's desk a few minutes later.

"Go right on in. He is expecting you."

Without so much as a thank you to Suzie or a friendly smile, Marty walked right into Albright's office. "You wanted to see me, Vernon?"

"Yes, I did. Please close the door."

Suzie noticed that Marty didn't exhibit any of the nervousness typical for a new employee meeting with the top boss. It took almost a year of working for Vernon before she felt comfortable addressing him by his first name and only after he suggested it. Albright cut a commanding figure, his reputation providing the foundation for a person's discomfort even before being in his presence. Either Marty was more familiar with Vernon than Suzie had been told, or she was unusually confident. Whatever the reason, it didn't much matter. Marty just rubbed her the wrong way. Maybe it was her less than modest wardrobe, her seeming lack of deference to the partners, her unfriendly personality or, most likely, a combination of all those factors.

After a relatively brief meeting, Marty left Albright's office just as Tom Wichefski arrived to say hello. Albright was always gracious when he saw Tom but less than warm. He had no intention of inviting the fox into the chicken coop. Albright didn't like Tom hanging around for too long so he always came up with a time sensitive task for Suzie aimed at shortening her fiancé's visit.

As Albright escorted Marty out, he greeted Tom with a firm handshake. "So how are things at the FBI these days? Still keeping America safe?"

"We are doing our best, Vernon."

Marty's eyes momentarily stuck on Tom. Although she was immediately concerned about an FBI agent's presence at Parthenon, she liked what she saw—a dark-haired man with strong good looks. Slightly over six feet tall, he had an impressive build that spoke to his passion for competing in triathlons. Conservatively attired in his Bureau uniform, he wore a dark gray suit, white shirt and nondescript tie. The shine on his black wing tips was almost blinding. Marty decided she would do her own due diligence on the FBI's apparent interest in Parthenon and asserted herself into the conversation.

"Hello. My name is Marty Jagdale. I'm brand new at the firm."

"Excuse my rudeness," Vernon interjected, taking over the introductions. "This is Tom Wichefski, Suzie's fiancé." Vernon turned to Tom. "What brings you here? Working on a case in the neighborhood?"

"As a matter of fact it's a fairly big case. I got a lead on a girl scout gouging customers on Thin Mints," he responded, eliciting laughter. "Actually, I was in the neighborhood and thought I would pop in for a quick hello."

"I'm pretty busy, honey," Suzie said. "I'll see you at home later." She hoped she had avoided a lecture from Vernon about socializing during business hours.

Tom took a different route back to the reception area, passing by Jeremy's office. He approached the open door-way and loudly cleared his throat, pulling Jeremy's atten-tion away from his screens. As he moved to the door, Tom motioned to the cell phone he had removed from the clip on his belt, mouthing the words "call me" and held up five fingers. As Jeremy waited out the proscribed time period, Suzie called on behalf of Vernon requesting his presence.

"Tell Vernon I need a few minutes to finish up a trade." He hung up with Susie and picked up his cell. "Hi, Tom. It's Jeremy. Did you see Paul?"

"No. Vernon gave me a cool reception so I thought it was best to say a quick hello to Suzie and leave. I'm at the

Starbucks in the lobby. Can you come down?"

"Unfortunately, I can't. I have a meeting with Vernon but Paul will come down."

"No problem. You and I can catch up later."

Jeremy called Paul and quickly got him up to speed.

"I thought you were just humoring me when you said you would call Tom. Glad to see you listened and got someone involved who knows what they're doing."

"Why don't you run your victory lap past my office and grab the envelope. I'll leave it in the center drawer."

***

Tom was sitting at a table in the corner, nursing a cup of coffee, when Paul entered. He nodded at Tom as he strode to the counter in search of his own caffeine fix. Starbucks was effectively an outsourced employee lounge for Parthenon. Although snacks, coffee, and soft drinks were available to everyone at the firm free of charge—it kept people in the office and productivity higher—if someone wanted to take a quick break, they went to Starbucks. At the rich price of four dollars a cup, it was almost like paying membership dues.

With the manila envelope securely tucked under his arm, sugar in one hand, iced coffee in the other, Paul walked over to where Tom sat.

"Sorry we're not meeting again under better circumstances but good to see you anyway." Paul set down his coffee and stirred in a packet of sugar. "I really appreciate your getting involved."

"I'm glad to help in any way I can." Tom pointed to the envelope. "Is that for me?"

"Yes. Here you go."

Tom opened the flap and peered into the large envelope. He was pleased to see that Jeremy had put the letter into a plastic zip lock bag. He pulled it out and held it in his hands.

"Hopefully we'll be able to classify this incident in the better safe than sorry category," Paul said with a slight smile.

Marty walked into Starbucks as Tom was reading the letter. She quickly moved to the far end of the counter where she still had a good sight line but would be able to fade into the crowd if she needed to obscure her position. She wondered what they were doing together, her curiosity piqued as she observed the FBI agent reading a document through a plastic bag. To Marty, or anyone else who had ever watched a police show on television, this only could mean one thing; the discussion was all business. Slightly shaken and significantly curious, she ducked out of the store through the door that led directly to the street.

Chapter 21

□ □ □

Upon returning to his office, Paul logged onto his instant messenger. He kept his comments cryptic.

F360: "all set. hes on it"

The chimes drew Jeremy's attention to the blinking light at the bottom of the screen. He clicked on the icon to display the dialogue box.

JAM: "and..."

F360: "and he's going to see what he can do and how quick he can get it done. he doesnt seem too sure what to make of it"

JAM: "meaning what exactly"

F360: "that came out wrong. he doesnt know if its real or not but told me to tell you that these things usually turn out to be nothing to worry about"

JAM: "what about the push? that wasnt nothing to worry about"

F360: "his initial take is that its likely unrelated and accidental but his advice is to be careful until he figures it out"

JAM: "great. that makes me feel better. NOT!"

F360: "he will take care of it and get it done quickly. he knows youre concerned but my gut tells me he doesnt think u should be"

JAM: "k. thanks. now please get me the other things i asked for"

F360: "k. i already did a bit of checking to make sure i had all the info i need and its all up to date. wont take much time"

Paul's phone buzzed. It was Jeremy. With his door wide open he spoke in a quiet voice.

"I wasn't comfortable having the rest of the conversation over IM."

"Good thinking," Paul offered, looking around to see if anyone was in earshot.

"Listen. Once you get it all together, note how many stocks are in the same industry. I want to see how Vernon is making his money and if he is taking too much risk by owning too many of the same type of stocks. See if anything else sticks out, like common ownership. You know the drill."

"Got it. None of this should be a problem but I will need a few more days. He owns a ridiculous number of stocks."

"I can only imagine. Call me when you're finished. I would prefer not to receive it piecemeal. And don't rush so much that you make mistakes. It's much more important that it be correct and complete."

"I feel like James Bond. I'll take care of this little clandestine operation and you get back to work making money for me."

For the first time since Jeremy called, Paul looked at his monitor and saw Marty's reflection behind him. She always seemed to just show up and he wondered how long she had been standing there. If she weren't so attractive, her clinginess could be a real pain in the ass.

"Hi Marty, what's up?"

"You look like you're pretty busy. Anything I can do to help?"

"As a matter of fact, there is. I have a project for you," he said almost reflexively. "The background is that an important part of my job is risk management which is another way of saying that I'm supposed to make sure that we keep the portfolio within certain guidelines, so we don't put ourselves at risk by placing too many eggs in one basket."

Marty reached out and playfully punched Paul's shoulder. "Duh. I think I understand the role of risk management."

Paul's embarrassment was palpable. He knew that Marty was not only smart but also possessed relevant experience. It was actually a pleasure to work with someone who didn't have to be force-fed every little detail of the job. Eventually he thought he might even be able to take a day off without calling in every hour. Marty was going to work out fine.

"Do I detect a little redness in your cheeks," she kidded.

"I doubt it," he said dismissively with an *are you kidding* expression accompanying his response. "So here, in the most sophisticated terms, is what I want you to do."

Marty picked up a pen and a lined yellow pad that sat on Paul's desk. "Can I borrow this? I want to take a few notes."

"Sure... I'm going to give you a copy of one of the portfolios and I want you to note the sector affiliation and market capitalization of each company. Then crosscheck the management and shareholder list of each, looking for commonalities."

"But, what if, after doing significant due diligence, Vernon decides to buy a number of stocks in the same industry? Isn't that okay? Isn't that what Parthenon is supposed to do?"

"Yes, absolutely, but not to the point of having such a significant concentration in one industry that if his thesis turns out to be wrong, we'll lose a boatload of money. That could put us out of business so I have to stay on top of our exposures and make sure we stay within our risk guidelines."

"So it comes down to Parthenon's particular appetite for risk and your ability to keep Vernon and Jeremy in line?"

"Sort of, but it's not my job to tell Vernon or Jeremy that they can't own too much of any one sector. My role is to hedge out the risk through options or other positions."

"Now I understand. So is this a routine analysis or are you looking for something specific?"

"This is a pretty routine risk analysis. In fact, it's so basic that there is a software package on each workstation that can be used to compile the report. I should have some more data for you tomorrow that will make this even easier. The turnaround time should be fairly quick."

Marty was pleased that she seemed to be making headway with Paul. He was giving her more responsibility, which would allow for easier execution of the plan.

As Marty walked away, Paul instantly regretted his decision to enlist her help. It was a reflex to feeling flustered at her sudden appearance; a response to her being in the wrong place at the right time. But, he rationalized, Jeremy specifically admonished him not to sneak around. And what better way to allay any suspicion Marty may harbor than to bring her into the fold. Vernon had made it clear she was just another employee, a favor hire and she in as much confirmed this when she admitted that she and Vernon had never met before she joined the firm. Jeremy's desire for a quick turnaround trumped any unsubstantiated concern about Marty. It would all be fine. Convinced of the absolute correctness of his logic, he placed his trepidations aside and went to work.

***

Jeremy was finishing a cursory read of the latest annual report from Jarmat Industries, his focus heavily skewed on the financial section. He was interested in building a portfolio position in Jarmat and this was the first step in his analysis. Row after row of fine print was taking a toll on his eyes so he wasn't about to complain when the incoming call offered a momentary respite. Vernon's extension revealed itself on the console.

"Yes, Vernon. What's up?"

"I wanted to check in with you before I left for Europe in the morning. Is there anything we need to discuss?"

Once a year, Albright traveled to Monte Carlo where he and five friends, all renowned hedge fund managers, met to discuss their views on the markets and the most attractive investment opportunities for the year ahead. Situated on the French Riviera, Monaco, the capital city, was the perfect place for the rich to gather during the summer. The small principality catered to the extremely wealthy and the world's "A" list celebrities. Its ultra-expensive accommodations and restaurants provided an almost impenetrable barrier to anyone who actually had to work for a living versus those who chose to. Although a very social gathering, having six of the world's top investors swap ideas always made the trip extremely profitable. It was an excursion that none of them had ever missed.

One thing I don't need is another discussion with you this week, is what Jeremy thought, wishing he had the nerve to say it. "No, I think we're fine. I'll send you an email or call your cell if I need you," he responded instead, taking a less confrontational route to the same conclusion.

"I trust you to handle matters, but given how volatile the markets have been I feel a bit funny leaving. I'll make sure to call in regularly."

Jeremy laughed. "Of course you will. I wouldn't expect this time to be any different."

"Good point. I guess you do hear from me more when I'm on the road than when I'm in the office."

Vernon was unabashedly a control freak when it came to his business, but who wouldn't be with billions of dollars on the line every day? And it wasn't as if Jeremy could manage Vernon's portfolio in his absence. That was out of the question.

***

Marty made it back to her desk and did all she could to keep herself from laughing out loud at how ridiculously easy it would be to take a fortune out of Parthenon without them ever finding out. If Paul was the best in the business, then the hedge fund business was staffed with idiots. But she couldn't completely discount the possibility that even he could screw up the plan, as remote as the chance seemed. She thought about sharing this new bit of information with Buck, as well as telling him about the little get together in Starbucks, but had no interest in being castigated for not having more facts. She decided to wait and maybe, just maybe, she would use the information for her own benefit. The smile vanished from Marty's face as she realized that it was inevitable that someone would get hurt; there was too much at stake. It wasn't a completely distasteful thought— it worked the last time—as long as it wasn't her.

Chapter 22

□ □ □

Varko slipped his token into the turnstile and waited for the Number 4 train to pull into the station. The Lexington Avenue subway line was the city's busiest so the wait was brief. As he stepped into the middle car his disgust was evident to anyone that looked his way. Varko resented having to take mass transportation while other, less talented traders rode in limousines or big fancy Mercedes. He toughed it out only because he knew his time was coming.

He walked through a couple of cars before coming upon an empty seat between two people who apparently believed that their lives depended on never missing a meal. The tight spacing on the Japanese made railcars made it impossible for everyone to be comfortable. In alternating order, one person leaned forward while their neighbor sat back against the hard plastic. That's how it is on NYC subways but Varko had no intention of respecting convention. He threw his body back, jamming his shoulders against his co-riders, who responded with expressions of bewilderment. But mere action was not enough for Varko as he cursed under his breath. The other riders were well aware of the dangers of confrontation on a subway so they moved to the far end of the car.

Watching the pillars in the darkened tunnel fade into the distance, Varko wondered where Datatech's stock price would be when the market closed and how much his portfolio would profit. He picked various price points and did the calculations in his head. Then he doubled that amount, figuring that would be how much he would have made if Al Manero had only been more reasonable. That would be the penalty he would extract from the brokerage firm. That was what they owed him.

The subway slowed as it pulled into Grand Central Station. Before Varko stepped out onto the platform, he grabbed a copy of the Wall Street Journal that another rider had left behind. Proceeding slowly up the stairs, he opened the paper to Bill Sundrick's column. He occasionally picked up some interesting information from reading *About the Street*, such as the real scoop on who was working against him on Datatech. Seeing nothing of interest, he casually let the paper drop to the pavement as he continued walking west to Fifth Avenue.

The receptionist recognized Varko as he tapped on the street level glass doors that opened into the offices of Tinker Blistrom & Company. He gave her his best smile and she buzzed him in.

"Who are you here to see today?"

"Al Manero but don't tell him. It's supposed to be a surprise. I have a present for him."

The receptionist responded innocently. "Oh, is it his birthday?"

"Nope. I just wanted to show my appreciation to him for being such a great broker."

"Isn't that nice. I wish we had more clients like you." Despite being disappointed that there would not be any birthday cake she hit the button that released the locked door.

Having been in Tinker Blistrom's offices on multiple occasions, Varko knew exactly where Manero sat. He made his way down the short hallway that led to the bullpen area where all the brokers were gathered in an open space. Manero had a distinctive look, drawing Varko's gaze. A poorly executed comb over only partially covered Manero's large pate. A loud purple tie extended midway down his shirt, lacking enough material to transverse his distended stomach. His diamond pinky ring reflected the neon overheads as he twirled the phone cord in his hand. The vision was almost too much for Varko to bear as Manero casually leaned back in his chair, propped his feet up on his desk and jabbered away on the phone acting like a real big shot. Anxious to get their meeting off on the right foot, Varko pressed the palm of his right hand on the upper left corner of Manero's chair, causing it to tilt further backwards. Startled into believing he was about to fall over, Manero sprung to his feet to the accompaniment of the cackling laughter behind him. He turned to see the identity of the practical joker and was shocked to come face to face with Varko.

"W-w-what are you doing here? How did you get in?" Manero stammered.

"I'm a valued client stopping by to check on my portfolio," Varko responded sarcastically.

Manero began to regain his composure. "But guests are not allowed back here unaccompanied. Why don't we go to the conference room in reception and discuss this matter intelligently."

"Are you saying that if I stand here and talk to you that means I'm stupid? We don't have to go anywhere. You and your firm owe me some money and I want to collect. Simple as that."

"Oh, so you finally want to close out your account." Manero reached for some forms. "Fill these out and we'll take care of it right away."

A dark look took over Varko's face. "No, you idiot. You owe me the difference between what I made today on my Datatech stock and what I would have made if you provided the margin I was entitled to."

The other brokers in the bullpen stopped making their cold calls. As inconspicuously as possible they directed their attention toward Varko and Manero. The entertainment factor on these episodes was high since the odds favored escalation from harsh words into something more disruptive. This was a bucket shop, not Morgan Stanley. Tinker Blistrom had lower standards for accepting accounts.

If the prospective customer had a pulse and any level of income or savings, they could open an account.

"I'm happy to talk about it but I'm late for a meeting. If you wait in the reception area until I'm finished, we should be able to settle this to your satisfaction. I shouldn't be too long."

"You must really think I'm stupid. I'm not someone you want to mess with. I can sue you or even worse...."

Varko didn't notice the two security guards coming up behind him. They each grabbed an elbow, firmly but not aggressively, as one of them spoke. "Sir, we're here to escort you off the premises. Non-employees are not allowed in this area."

"I will leave when I'm ready. I'm in a meeting with my broker," Varko said through gritted teeth, struggling to break free.

Emboldened by the guards' firm grasp on his tormentor, Manero took a step forward and pointed his finger squarely in Varko's face. "No more you're not. This is the final act of insanity. If there is anything left in your account after today you'll get it back just as soon as we can close it out."

"Sir, you will have to leave now or we will call the police." Security was trained to defuse these confrontations as quickly as possible.

"Fine, I'm out of here. This place has cost me a fortune."

The guards relaxed their grip and Varko turned to leave the way he came. With security trailing a half step behind, he quickened his pace until he was out of the building. He couldn't afford to let them call the police; he was already on probation for violating his wife's restraining order. If the court found out about this, he would never gain custody of his children. Manero may have won this skirmish, but Varko decided that this was not the end of their discussions. It was still only lunchtime so he decided to hang around for a bit and gather his thoughts. He didn't feel guilty about not going back home or to one of the local Charles Schwab offices to watch the ticker tape since even traders were allowed to take an occasional break. Varko bought a hot dog from a street vendor and waited on the corner, losing himself in the lunchtime crowd.

Only ten minutes elapsed before he spied Manero coming toward him. Varko guessed he was heading to the same deli where Manero had taken him for their first meeting. "Klein's is the best deli in the world," he recalled him saying. Varko faded into the throng of people and let his now ex-broker stroll past, slowing down as the red *Don't Walk* sign on the corner began to flash red.

The broker came to a stop right at the edge of the curb. Looking around, Varko saw that he was in luck. This was going to be perfect.

There was no way for the bus to stop in time. The man seemed to come out of nowhere, the driver would later tell the police. The rear fender of the cross-town bus caught Manero sideways, violently twirling him into the front of the oncoming FedEx truck, his momentum halted only when he collided with the windshield before dropping down to the pavement. The front right tire rolled over his upper torso, crushing his chest, killing him instantly.

It turned out to be a good day for Ernest Varko after all. By the time the markets closed, the price of Datatech stock would nearly double. And Tinker Blistrom would have to assign him a new broker; Manero had been officially terminated.

Chapter 23

□ □ □

Date night for the Cranfords. Saturday nights were a time to be with other couples but their weeknight out was an opportunity for them to be alone. No children, no friends, just the two of them. It was a particularly good release for Jennifer, who was home with the kids all day long. Around mid-week, she began to crave adult conversation.

Jeremy was diligent in ending his workday at four-thirty on Wednesdays, leaving a sufficient buffer to ensure he would still be home before six so that he could sit with the children while they ate their dinner. Since Alexandra's and Melissa's bedtime ritual was his favorite part of the evening, it was moved up in the schedule to accommodate date night.

After the children had their bath, the entire family would crowd on top of Alexandra's big-girl bed—that was what she called it. It was her first full-size bed after she outgrew her small training cot. Melissa would sit there, legs folded, back propped up against Jeremy's chest as he lay on his side, while Alexandra turned the pages of her favorite Dr. Seuss book, making up words to go along with the pictures. Ever so bright, Alexandra would slow her pace as she moved through the book, realizing that when it was done it was off to sleep. This was Jeremy's cue to take over. He stayed with the script provided by Dr. Seuss but used a different voice for each character. This always got a giggle out of the girls. Melissa, being younger, typically lasted only a few pages before Jennifer whisked her off to bed in an adjacent room.

Alexandra wasn't yet ready to go to sleep. "Just three

more pages Daddy," she held up three fingers to illustrate her point, "then, I promise, I'll go right to sleep."

With Alexandra, everything seemed to come in a package of three. "Just three more minutes Daddy." Or, the calculated request of "can I have three more kisses?" Jeremy always laughed when Alexandra negotiated with him. He knew that at some point she would realize that her father had built a fudge factor of three into everything.

Once the children were safely on their way to dreamland, the sitter would take over and the Cranford evening out would begin with dinner at one of the local eateries. They weren't fancy people, preferring a casual setting. Despite the proximity, they hardly ever traveled the half hour into New York for dinner. Jennifer would have preferred an occasional change of scenery but understood that Jeremy had no desire to travel into the city twice in one day.

In a sweater and jeans that were tight enough to conform to her athletic shape but not offer the image of someone trying to relive her teenage years, Jennifer still held Jeremy's attention. Every so often he wondered why his attraction to her hadn't waned. Wasn't that supposed to happen after so much time together? Hadn't he heard that it happened to most married people at some point? Still, he couldn't envision it ever happening to them.

Their usual waiter, Roger, stopped by the table and exchanged pleasantries with his favorite patrons. "How are the girls?" he would always inquire. They had stopped looking at the menu a long time ago and Roger could have written down their order without even asking for it. Two organic mesclun salads to start; one with the dressing on the side; grilled shrimp, no oil for her; black spaghettini with shrimp in a spicy red sauce for him; side of spinach and a bottle of sparkling water. Skip the bread.

"How was work today?" Coming from Jennifer, the question was sincere, not an icebreaker.

"Tough markets but fortunately the portfolio is doing okay," Jeremy answered while watching Roger uncork their bottle of wine. "We won't be making a lot of money this year but we're holding our own."

"Anything else going on?"

"Why do you ask?"

"Because you're acting strange. You don't seem like yourself."

They raised half-full glasses, gently touching them together in a silent toast. Each took a sip.

"I guess I can't get anything over on you, can I?"

"Nope, and no point in trying. So fess up."

"It's been a tough couple of days dealing with Vernon but nothing necessarily new about that."

"What's he done now?"

"He hired a friend's cousin without telling me beforehand."

"Are you okay with that? Those type of hires don't always work out."

"Yeah, I'm fine with it. She seems pretty bright and it's only a back-office position. It's the way he went about it that got under my skin." Jeremy averted his gaze, a sign that maybe he wasn't being completely forthcoming.

"You don't seem fine with it. Did you say something to him?"

"Of course I said something but I'll admit that it wasn't the most satisfying discussion that we've ever had."

"What does that mean?"

"He's been acting a little strange."

Jenn put down her salad fork and reached for the wine. "What do you mean by strange?"

"I don't know. Maybe it's the markets, maybe it's this damn business but there's something not right. Maybe it's me."

"Maybe it is you." She was holding the glass, gently rolling the stem between her fingers.

"What's that mean?" Jeremy refilled their glasses while waiting for his wife's answer.

"You've always talked about being your own boss. It could be time to do something about it. The little things that are starting to gnaw at you now will only take on a bigger profile later on. And it won't stop there. Everything will be magnified and the parting will be uglier than if you do it now before it hits a crisis point."

"Vernon gave me my shot and he's paid me very well. I know I've talked about leaving, but I don't know if I could do it right now. Maybe when things calm down or when the market stops declining."

"It's your call, honey. I only want you to be happy and you don't seem like you are." Jennifer raised the glass to her mouth, barely wetting her lips, and then placed it down on the table as she resumed picking at her salad.

"There is one piece of good news at least. Vernon is leaving for his annual Masters of the Universe gathering in Monaco. It'll be nice to have some time without him in the office."

"Good luck with that. He always seems to be more of a pain in the ass when he's on the road," she said, half joking.

With the second glass of wine taking effect, using the anonymity posed by the tablecloth, Jennifer slipped off her shoe and rubbed the inside of her husband's leg. It was just the right display of affection to snap Jeremy out of his funk. He reached across the table and took her hands in his. He spoke just above a whisper. "Let's get the check and hope the kids are asleep when we get home."

Chapter 24

□ □ □

The moonlight shone through the wall of windows, softly illuminating the couple nestling inside. Buck and Marty were a glass away from their second bottle of Cristal.

"How are things at the office?" Buck inquired with a smirk.

"Going well. Jeremy is a fascinating person."

"You're not sweet on him, are you? It's not good to shit where you eat."

"Don't be jealous, my dear." She caressed his cheek with her hand. "Jeremy is too much in love with his wife to look at me."

"Knowing you, that's the challenge not the end."

Marty threw her head back and laughed. "You may not know me as well as you think. Maybe Paul Robbins is the one you should be watching out for. Each day we get a little closer. More importantly," she added with a seductive smile, "he's unattached, good looking and as jazzed up on testosterone as anyone I have ever met."

"Can he be valuable to us?"

"I believe so, but didn't you just tell me not to poop where I eat?"

"Poop? That's rich. Since when are you such a lady?"

"You tell me if I'm being a lady now." Marty continued to play with Buck, lightly dragging her fingernails across the back of his neck. His arm tingled in response. In return, he stroked the inside of her bare thigh, starting at the knee and running up under her short skirt, his fingers ever so lightly touching the thin, silky fabric of her undergarment.

"What else can you tell me about your *co-workers*?" Buck added with an obnoxious emphasis. He was in rare form tonight.

"Aside from Vernon, those are the only two who matter. Robbins runs all the operations including risk management, wire transfers and so on. I haven't performed all my due diligence but there doesn't seem to be too many safeguards built into the process of accepting funds or transferring them out."

"Now is not the time for that. It's secondary to what I have going on. Whatever you can get your greedy little hands on will pale in comparison to what that firm means to me. Maybe at some point but not now. Now tell me about Robbins."

"Sometimes he seems smart and sometimes not so much, but in any case he knows his job well. And you two have something in common." Marty ran her tongue along Buck's lips before sensuously sliding it into his mouth.

"I doubt that," Buck stated dismissively. "He's a glorified pencil pusher and I'm a billionaire Texan who does whatever the hell I want."

Marty giggled. "Ha! You're jealous. Very flattering but I would never give myself to another. Unless you give me a reason to, that is."

"Hardly jealous but you know I hate to share unless it's my idea," he responded with a wink and a smile.

It was another tick of Buck's that she was put off by, and she felt like gagging in response, but understood that such a show of disdain would only jeopardize her own plans.

"Now tell me what else you know," Buck continued.

"Paul and Jeremy are very, very close. They talk or send each other instant messages all day long."

"Instant messages? I thought that was for teenagers."

"That's what I thought too, but everyone on the Street seems to use it and it is pretty effective."

"I'll take your word for it. Tell me about Cranford."

As she ran her fingers through Buck's hair, Marty placed her lips on his ear and whispered. "He's good looking and real bright; cool under pressure and very focused on making a lot of money." She pulled back, a momentary respite from the tease. "But he's also quite the family man. You don't see that combination too often."

"I like dealing with family men; their Achilles heel sits right on their desk in a nicely framed photo. Continue."

"Vernon trusts him implicitly. It's almost like a father-son relationship. They even bicker occasionally. I was surprised to find out that he oversees more money than Vernon but I'm sure you knew that."

"Of course I know that." Buck said, catching himself before his anger bubbled up further. "What I want from you are the details that Albright doesn't share with me and that I can't ask him about."

Buck continued to fill Marty's glass after every few sips. As the first bottle of champagne relinquished its last drops, he uncorked another. The froth rolled over the top as Marty reached for it. She seductively ran her tongue up the neck of the dark green bottle, catching the dripping bubbles as they ran over Buck's fingers. Buck lifted Marty's chin with his index finger and brought her lips to his. They exchanged a passionate kiss.

"Back to your boy, Cranford. I should get to know him."

"I agree. I'll keep my eyes open," she said with a sarcastic emphasis, "for the right opportunity."

Marty filled Buck's glass. It had become a contest, each plying the other with alcohol, seeking secrets from a looser tongue.

"When will my job be done, Buck?"

Marty ran her hand firmly over Buck's crotch while bringing her mouth to his. She was doing her best to catch him off guard.

More focused on Marty than on her question, Buck's answer was as brief as possible. "When I say so."

"I wish I knew more about what it is you want me to

do. I wish I knew what *you* were doing." Marty continued. "The three of them are so smart that I wonder if your plan—whatever it is—will work out."

The champagne, the seduction and Marty's concern about Buck's ability to go tête-à-tête with the senior team at Parthenon conspired against Buck's will to keep his thoughts private. "Don't worry about that. I already have ol' Vern beat."

"How so?" Marty asked coyly.

"I'm going to let you see for yourself."

"I'd love that."

Buck leaned over to the table and grabbed the phone, dialing a number from memory. "Evening, Vernon. I'm not calling too late, am I?"

"No, Buck, but it is getting late. Can we speak in the morning?"

"I'm in meetings all morning but if you want to pass on this one, that's your call." He paused a beat. "If you're too tired to make some money, then sweet dreams."

Marty reached over and pushed the button on the speakerphone allowing her to hear both sides of the conversation.

"Okay Buck, what's this evening's can't-miss oil investment idea?"

"Put aside your attitude for a few seconds and hear me out. Universal Oil and Gas. I heard from one of my sources in Texas that they're sitting on one of the largest finds ever discovered in the North Sea, but because it's a real small company, they don't want word to get out until they raise enough cash to fund their drilling plan. Once they are sure they can fund the drilling then they'll step up and buy a chunk of their own stock. After that, they tell the public and boom—off to the races. Thought you might be interested, that's all."

"It sounds promising. Thanks for the heads up. I'll take a look first thing in the morning. Now if it's okay with you, I'm going to bed."

Marty pushed the off button on the phone, ending the call. She turned to Buck. "That's it, darling?"

"No, of course that's not it. He'll ask me about it again in the morning, real early, before my meetings start, and I'll give him a little more but swear him to secrecy. These hedge fund guys all talk to one another so I know once Vern has his position he'll whisper it to others to get them to bid up the stock price."

"Just like you are doing."

"Don't jump the gun."

"Sorry, baby."

"Next, I tell him I'm negotiating to buy the company's leasehold and was considering bringing in a partner to offload a portion of the risk. He then just about begs me to let him in. After hemming and hawing I agree. Now, he's taken the bait, swallowed the hook and I'm reeling him in like a big old catfish. He speaks with the company, puts in twenty mill and buys more shares in the open market. It takes years to drill a well. The money will be long gone before he realizes he's been had. In the meantime, word will spread from the brokers that Parthenon uses to execute its trades that the great Vernon Albright is buying Universal. Oil prices keep going up, and everyone is looking to find energy stocks that have the most exposure to rising crude prices, so more and more money pushes Universal higher and higher. And by the way I don't see the price of oil coming down anytime soon."

"But you're an investor in his fund so he's using some of the money that you have invested with him to pay for this. If he loses, you lose too." She moved even closer, putting her bare leg over his.

"Nice to see you're paying attention. The twenty mill he's gonna pony up is spread out among all his investors in a twenty-billion-dollar fund, so my actual hit is equal to the weekend tips I give to the doormen downstairs. But, and this is a key part of my tale, I own a big slug of Universal directly in my holding company. That's where I'll make my killing. And who do you think will be selling stock to Vernon's buds after he touts it to them?"

"And because he believes you have money at risk in the deal from your investment in Parthenon, he doesn't really look at it too closely. So it's a simple pump and dump scheme? That's it?"

"Was that meant to be an insult, little girl? I'm a helluva lot more sophisticated than that. There's more."

"I'm all ears, baby."

"Vernon is now convinced that this investment is worth more than he paid for it so instead of carrying it on his books for twenty million, he marks it to market at forty million. It's thinly traded so he can make the case that the true value is not reflected in the price of the stock. He could put down almost any value he wants to, within reason. Do you think his accountants know what a North Sea oil and gas company is worth? Besides, in a twenty-billion-dollar portfolio that is leveraged, these names are little gnats on an elephant's ass. They won't hurt the overall fund too much but will cause the price of stocks like Universal to skyrocket. The key is for me not to get too piggy about these deals; not with everything else that I'm working on."

"Brilliant. So you get the twenty million from big bucks Vernon and whatever else his buddies spend to buy the stock from you except they don't know you're the one selling it to them. But what if his investors ever want to cash out of Vernon's portfolio at Parthenon? What happens then?"

"Parthenon never had any real redemptions, aside from that one time when he needed me to bail him out. His investors stick with him like dog shit on the bottom of my boot. Every month they see their statements and see how much money they've made. Most have been with him for years. They can't get those returns anywhere else so they don't ask questions. Vernon is so wealthy that he would just as soon kick an investor out of the fund than be harassed by them with mindless questions. They all know this and choose to trust him. Parthenon has plenty of folks waiting on the sidelines to invest. It's no different than the latest hot spot New York restaurant. Everyone wants in but no one knows how the food tastes."

"But if they do want to get their money out?" Marty persisted.

"A well-kept secret and the chink in Albright's armor. It would be ugly. There are not many buyers for these illiquid stocks. He'd suffer devastating losses if he had to sell in a hurry which is why he's stuck with me. He can't give me my money back or everyone gets hurt, most of all him."

"I thought there was something else going on between you and Parthenon." Nothing turned Marty on more than big money. As she moved her leg up and down Buck's thigh, she noticed that her excitement was contagious.

"Don't know what you're referring to," he offered in coy response.

"Come now, Buck, my darling. You can tell me." She dipped a finger in her glass of champagne and ran it across her lips before seductively putting it in her mouth.

"There's nothing to tell," he offered in a less than convincing tone.

"I may have a bit of *gossip*," she spoke the word in an affected tone, "that you might find interesting."

"Lay it on me, gorgeous."

"Not quite yet. First show me you don't just love me for my brains."

Marty straddled Buck's lap and they brought their mouths together sharing a violent kiss. She remained on Buck's lap and pushed her hair back behind her ears. "I guess that will do," she sighed, content for the moment. "Jeremy asked Paul to pull together a bunch of data on Vernon's portfolio. He wants Paul to check for common shareholders, overlapping business interests and so on. Paul said it was their normal risk management review but I know that's not true."

"How do you know that? Hedge funds go through that exercise all the time."

"I know because I saw the IMs they were sending to each other and then they switched to the phone so there wouldn't be any record of their calls. Is that good enough?" Marty responded, indignant at being doubted. "Plus he asked me to work on the project with him so I should know a lot more tomorrow."

"Good work, girl. I knew I put you there for a reason."

Marty grinded her body against Buck pushing her butt down on his crotch. She stood and took a few deliberate steps toward the large picture window. In the darkened room, the brightness of the full moon cast a silhouette around her shapely figure. She reached behind her back and pulled down the zipper of her tight, almost sheer, black dress, lowering her shoulders just enough to allow the garment to slide to the floor. She stood there naked but for a black thong that rested high on her hips, accenting her perfectly firm and shapely rear.

***

Vernon climbed into bed next to his wife.

"Who was on the phone, honey?"

"That damn cowboy. Drunk as hell and blabbing about some little stock that I have no interest in at all."

"Seemed like a quick call."

Vernon rolled over on his side and turned off the light. "It was quick but only because I let him believe I was interested in what he had to say. He's turning into a real nuisance."

"Show him the door like you've done with others."

"It's a bit more complicated than that but rest assured I'm considering all my options."

Chapter 25 □ □ □

After another restless night, Jeremy rolled out of bed an hour earlier than usual and threw on his gym clothes. He was damn tired but hoped that a workout would be energizing. On his way into New York, he stopped at the 24-hour neighborhood diner for a large coffee to go. After five minutes or so of banter with the owner, he jogged down the steps from the restaurant and toward his car but stopped a few steps short.

What the fuck? I could swear I left it running! He stood there bewildered while in the near distance a loud rumble pierced the quiet of the pre-dawn morning. He knew it was a broken muffler struggling to stay alive but couldn't understand why he was so drawn to the noise. Jeremy pulled open the door to the BMW, but the sound still nagged at him like a déjà vu as the memory of it came into focus. Jeremy shook his head, trying to clear away the anamnesis, as he reached to the ignition but the key was not there. He felt his pockets, simultaneously looking in the center console and passenger seat. Nothing. He continued scanning the interior and a lump formed in his throat, a bead of sweat on his brow; there, in the back seat, were his keys.

"How the hell did they get there," he wondered aloud, trying to decide if he was losing his sanity, if for the first time, the pressure was getting to him. Then fear set in. *The muffler. The Lincoln Tunnel—that's where I heard it before. My God!*

Jeremy's eyes darted around the parking lot, looking for his stalker but of course no one was there so he listened for the noise, hoping to hear it again and track it down so he could finally confront the asshole who was making him crazy. Then a thought hit him and he jammed the key in the ignition, started the car and sped home. Everything looked normal as he pulled into the driveway. Jeremy pulled the keys from the ignition, sprang from the car and locked the car doors. He opened the front door and began to recon the house, room by room, starting upstairs with the children's rooms, careful not to wake them or Jennifer. Everyone was asleep. He exhaled, set the alarm, which was something he never did when he left for work, and returned to his car. Jeremy sat in his car and wondered if he was coming apart. Then another thought. He ran to the mailbox hoping not to see another message. He didn't.

As Jeremy walked back to his car, he laughed aloud. *This is so fucking ridiculous. Pull it together, man, and stop imagining things.* He decided that this was not an episode he would be sharing with anyone, not even Paul.

The man in the shadows across the street was not pleased to see his prey having such a good time at his expense.

***

Paul walked into Jeremy's office at 9:45 a.m. "Shit, Jeremy. The Dow's down three hundred right out of the gate. What the hell is going on?"

"First of all, genius, I've told you that we don't focus on what the Dow does. That's just thirty stocks and the only ones who pay attention to it are retirees and bad business writers. If we cared about any index it would be the S&P, which contains 500 stocks."

"All right, professor. I stand corrected. The S&P is down forty ticks. Why?"

Forty points was significant. It was over a three percent drop in price.

Suzie's voice, embellished with a sense of urgency, reverberated over the intercom. "Vernon is on line two for you, Jeremy."

Jeremy picked up the handset and pushed the blinking light. "That didn't take long. The market's only been open for twenty minutes."

Paul had already turned toward the door. "I'll get out of your way."

"What the hell is going on?" Albright was loud and on edge. "I was about to get on the plane until I heard the market is getting trashed. I'm coming back."

"You can't come back. They're expecting you in Monaco."

"I'll fly out after the close."

"If you leave the office at four, you won't get to Teterboro until at least five o'clock—and that's with no rush hour traffic, which is unlikely. That means you probably won't take off until six. And between the time difference and time in the air, you won't land in France until eight in the morning.

"Do you really want to miss tonight's dinner? You can make more money for us by brainstorming with your buddies than I can possibly lose today." Jeremy laughed at his self-deprecating wit.

"You're right." Vernon ignored the humor and considered the logic. "I'll stick to the schedule but what the hell is going on?"

"I can sum it up in one word: crude. Damn commodity is on a tear. Funds are selling stocks like crazy. Anything that's sensitive to the consumer spending less dough on discretionary items and more on filling their cars is getting whacked."

"So it's more of the same but at least we're participating on my end. I think oil keeps going higher." Calm returned to Albright's tone. "I'll touch base before I take off."

Albright told Joseph, his bodyguard and driver, to continue on. A former high-ranking officer in Israel's intelligence agency, the Mossad, and prior to that, the elite Israeli commando forces, Joseph did not come off as a particularly imposing figure in his nicely tailored suit. He could be mistaken for any other executive who preferred the gym to happy hour. But if he felt that his client was in danger there would be no misinterpretation of his intention or actions.

The world had changed since Albright helped pioneer the hedge fund industry. Ever since the stock market boomed in the late nineties and CNBC became Wall Street's Oprah in popularity, the best and wealthiest hedge fund managers became celebrities in their own right. They mostly shunned the fame but when someone earns billions of dollars, fame seems to find them. And that kind of wealth attracts individuals who harbor more harmful ambitions than collecting an autograph. As hairdressers are to models, bodyguards are to billionaires; a required accessory.

The guard stationed just outside the airport gates recognized Joseph and waved him onto the short road that led directly to the runway where Parthenon's converted Boeing 737 was waiting. The limousine came to a stop at the stairway that protruded from the jet's fuselage, where two porters stood ready to greet Mr. Albright and take his luggage from the car.

Vernon climbed the steel steps and made his way into the cabin. He gave his sport coat to the stewardess, a Parthenon employee, took off his shoes and fell back into one of the heavily cushioned leather chairs. The satellite television was on CNN and he quickly switched it to the CNBC channel. On the table top next to his usual seat was a keyboard and mouse configured for remote access to the system that resided in his office on Park Avenue. The data from those four monitors would be replicated on one of the Boeing's large plasma screens.

Carole Shaw had worked for the firm for four years after spending two years with United Airlines. The pay was just as good but the hours were much better. She was young and extremely attractive, but also very good at being unobtrusive, a necessary quality in small quarters. Her skirt was shorter and her blouse tighter than her United uniform had ever been.

"Should I serve lunch after takeoff?"

"Yes. Then I'll try to grab some sleep for a few hours so I can acclimate to the time change." Despite his intention, he would not be able to sleep while the market was tumbling.

"Is there a particular wine that you would like with your meal?"

Before responding, he looked over the menu that was left on his chair. "I'll leave it up to you."

The stewardess pulled the table top out of the arm rest and put down a piece of fine white linen fabric for use as a place mat along with a full setting of silverware. Next, she gingerly placed a napkin, cut from the same linen cloth, on Vernon's lap.

Albright dialed Jeremy's number. "How is the portfolio holding up?"

"I have the right stocks and exposure so the portfolio is performing surprisingly well. I was just thinking about covering some of the shorts and booking the profit. Maybe even buy some stocks that have been really beaten up."

Albright felt like he was in an information vacuum. "Still believe that oil prices are wreaking havoc?"

"Crude just broke through one thirty-five a barrel. As if that's not enough, some low life hedgie who is probably short the S&P index is adding to the decline by starting a rumor that Warren Buffet was selling all his equity holdings. IBM has been down big the last couple of days, and that's his largest position, so it made sense to some people. Crude is only partly to blame. The Market is getting oversold so we're probably overdue for a bounce."

"Being out of the office is agony when the market is acting crazy like this."

"I can handle it Vernon."

"I know you can. I would just rather be there. If you're sure that the selloff is overdone, start nibbling."

"I got it Vernon," Jeremy said, getting short on patience. "What time do you take off?"

"We're weather delayed for another half hour. I'll call you back right before takeoff. Transfer me to Paul." There were other, albeit, smaller portfolios, to check on. "How are we holding up?"

"We're in pretty good shape," Paul responded without delay. "Our NAV is up nicely." NAV was the net asset value of the fund, a real time indicator of how much money was being made or lost.

Albright felt more comfortable that everyone was paying attention. "Damn good. If things change, call my cell or the air phone. I may be out of touch for a while until we hit cruising altitude, but I'll check in later."

"Have a great flight."

***

Jeremy looked at his screen. The market was stabilizing. He hit the button that connected to Parthenon's trading desk. "Jack. Get me a look at Dell and Mickey D's."

Virtually every technology and consumer stock was under pressure but Dell and McDonald's were suffering the largest declines. Cranford already had a small position in Dell and he was short McDonald's, a negative bet made in the aftermath of his daughters' no longer wanting to eat at the fast food chain. This prompted him to do more extensive research. A Parthenon research analyst called a number of franchise owners to inquire about business conditions and concluded that McDonald's was losing share to competitors who had recently freshened up their menus with healthier fare. Jeremy put on the short position but with the stock down thirty percent from his entry point, it was time to cover and book the profit.

Jack Knowles called back in under two minutes. "Dell is looking twenty-nine to a nickel. One million up. Sell side has been fading." Buyers were willing to pay twenty-nine dollars for one million shares but the sellers were offering to sell the same amount of stock five cents higher.

"Lift the offering for the million. Take a dime discretion

in case it moves against us. And I would buy another two million at a dime or better."

Knowles had been overseeing the daytime trading desk for three years. With an undergraduate degree from Yale, he didn't conform to the old stereotype of what a trader was thought to be: whiskey-drinking tough guys earning their diplomas from the school of hard knocks. They usually got into the business through someone who knew someone in the back office of some brokerage firm and made an introduction. Times change. With information king and technology driving trading, it was now important to have a trader who understood the markets almost as well as a portfolio manager.

"Got it. I'm lifting the twenty-nine-five offer for a mill and in the market for another two million. Keeping a dime in my pocket." Too much money was at stake not to repeat every order. "Mickey D's is looking better to buy. Thirty-two-and-three-quarters to the figure. Two million by a million-five. I'd pull the trigger right here in a hurry."

Jeremy didn't hesitate. A quick response in a moving market was critical to success. "Take the offer at the figure if you have to but a quarter of a point is a big spread for this stock."

"It sure is but you can bet it will tighten up in a second or two, which is why we should step up now," Jack shot back. "You're done on Dell. We cleaned up a large seller. You own two and three quarts. Here comes the report on the burgers. Done there at a quarter. Wish it could have been lower but it was the right thing to do. Anything else?"

"Sit tight for now. Great job as usual. My other line's ringing. Gotta hop." He picked up the handset.

"Mike Casey." Casey was a research salesman with a large investment bank.

"Anything important, Mike? I'm in the middle of a trade."

"Yeah. My tech analyst just called in from a meeting he's having with the management of IBM. He gets the sense that

IBM is about to announce that they're going to miss the next quarter's earnings estimates."

"Did he say why?" Jeremy calmly inquired.

"Dell cut prices on their servers again. IBM will have to cut prices too, but because their manufacturing is all in the U.S., they can't go as low as Dell. My analyst is positive that IBM will definitely lose share."

That explained why IBM stock was dropping. Buffet had nothing to do with it. It was just another Buffet rumor, the third one this week.

"Great call, Mike. I don't know if I'll do anything but I appreciate your hustle. Tell your trading desk to expect some business from us." He hung up without waiting to hear Mike kiss his ass.

Jeremy immediately called Jack. "Where's another million Dell trade? I'm not interested in getting cute and missing it. There's news coming."

"I can get a fill on most of it right here but the bid seems to be building. I may have to pay up for the balance."

"Buy it."

"Got it. Buying another million Dell. Doing what I have to." Jack frantically punched the button on his phone that connected him to the exchange floor while also buying what he could electronically.

Jeremy waited and hoped Mike Casey's information was good. If not, he'd be calling his boss and asking for a new salesperson.

Knowles' voice shot over the speaker. "You bought them all at a quarter. We got lucky. Total of three and three quarter million on the day. Nice trade. Stock's already lifting. Story must be making the rounds."

"You're the best, Jack."

"No, Jeremy, you are. I'm just here to do your bidding," laughing with the knowledge that Parthenon was already profiting on the trade. "Before you go, you may want to do something on Datatech. It's down another buck. Do you want to cover this piece of shit?"

"Why would I? It's going to zero."

Chapter 26

□ □ □

Paul returned to his office and finished pulling together the information on Albright's holdings; the first step in the analysis. He counted over two hundred stocks, an unusually large number of companies for one portfolio manager to keep track of, even with the assistance of three analysts. Satisfied that he had fully reconstructed Vernon's entire portfolio, Paul scanned the ten double-spaced pages. Although the list was complete, there was still a lot of information that was missing, information critical to assessing the actual level of risk. The seven columns on each sheet required that the pages be turned sideways in order to accommodate all the information.

Paul couldn't help but notice that a very large number of the company names contained either the word "Energy," "Petroleum," "Gas," "Oil," or "Exploration and Production." He tensed at the sight and the muscles in his neck began to tighten, although he couldn't tell if it was from bending over his desk for so long or from stress. No matter. He made a mental note to schedule an appointment with Maria, his three-hundred-an-hour masseuse and stood to stretch. Paul extended his arms to the ceiling and took in a deep breath, then let the air slowly escape from his lungs. Somewhat looser, he turned his gaze to the Bloomberg to get a fix on the market. The five hundred plus stock symbols that occupied his monitor page were flashing and changing price at a slower pace than earlier in the day, indicating that market activity had returned to a more reasonable level. It seemed like a good time to call Jeremy and inform him of his findings.

"Looks like the excitement is over for now." Paul took a quick glance at the firm's P&L. "Wow! You're having a good day."

"Did okay, I guess. Rather be lucky than smart."

"Whatever you say," Paul responded dismissively, unwilling to attribute Jeremy's skill to happenstance. "I finished pulling together Vernon's portfolio."

"And...?"

"I know you don't want the information piecemeal but I took a quick look and I'm not happy with the lack of diversity in his holdings. If crude has even a moderate correction, say goodbye to your Beemer and hello to the subway. I've seen the old man make some very concentrated bets but this really pushes the envelope."

As much as he respected his judgment, Jeremy kept Paul's training in perspective. Risk managers were a lot like lawyers and accountants who thought they were paid to always say no; any risk was too much risk

"Define concentrated. Is it Paul-like concentration or is it something that I would be concerned about?"

Paul chuckled at the dig. "Can't tell for sure until I get into what some of these other companies do for a living but for now I'm only waving the yellow flag of caution. But it's a very bright yellow."

"Okay. Say your first read is dead on. We still have to be absolutely sure that it portends issues other than a short-term bet on energy. With Vernon's set of cojones, he likes making those bets and the strategy has served him well over the years."

"Understood but let's not forget that you're also making some of the same bets in your portfolio, which is essentially doubling down on the risk."

"Sure I own some energy stocks and put on a few derivative plays, like being short Ford and Toyota, but I'm hardly irresponsible. It would be crazy to have any type of oversized concentration in any one theme. There's no way

I would do that without a guarantee and we both know there's no such thing as a guarantee in this business."

"Not that you would ever consider it but there is another way: inside information. That's about as close to a guarantee as you can get."

"Sure is but we don't do illegal."

"You won't get any argument from me. Don't forget that I'm the risk manager—that is when Vernon lets me be, which as far as his portfolio is concerned seems to be never. If he ever let me look at his holdings, I wouldn't have to be going through this back-door process." Paul said with resignation.

"Poor baby, self-pity on seven figures a year," Jeremy teased. "Put aside the woe is me for a second and let's get back to Vernon's stocks. He's been real bullish on energy, but I had absolutely no idea that his portfolio was dangerously concentrated. That's something he would never do without possessing a real edge."

"It does seem a little strange that he hasn't tipped his hand to you at all."

"Yes and no, I guess. Occasionally he mentions his view on crude but since he owns so much of it, it wouldn't make sense for him to get me all bulled up, too. But I am surprised that he hasn't at least used me as a sounding board. That's something he used to do all the time."

As Jeremy spoke, Paul considered mentioning Marty's involvement but decided it wasn't the appropriate time. He was certain it was not an issue since he hadn't provided her with nearly enough information to connect the dots and, of course, the risk analysis was in the ordinary course of business.

"We can talk more later," Paul offered instead. "Right now I want to get back to work. With a little bit of luck and a lot of elbow grease you may have it all tomorrow."

He turned and walked toward Marty.

"Ready to go?"

Marty was sitting back from her desk revealing long,

lean legs, crossed at the ankle, extending out from a very short skirt. Paul was transfixed, surreptitiously—hopefully, surreptitiously—following her smooth limbs from the upper end of her thigh down to the black pumps that finished off her seductive pose.

"I'm always ready," she responded, clearly noticing Paul's interest.

Paul snapped out of his trance and handed over a document. "This is the portfolio I mentioned yesterday. Just to be safe, let's review what I need you to do." He moved behind Marty so that they could read along together. "I want you to go through every company on the list." He paused. "I guess I shouldn't ask if you know how to use a Bloomberg."

"I've had access to a Bloomberg since college."

"Right, of course. Why am I not surprised?" He inquired, rhetorically. "Here's what else I want you to look for...." He finished the list with "...compare the holder's list for each stock."

"Mind if I ask why that's so important?"

"I hate giving you information that you already know so I'm going to let you answer that."

"You got me. I'll bring it over to you when I'm done."

Marty turned her back to Paul and began poring over the pages and hitting the keys on her Bloomberg terminal. An hour elapsed before he checked back with her. She was proceeding with no issues but did have an unrelated question.

"Why does it seem so quiet here today when the market is so volatile? I haven't heard a peep out of Vernon."

Paul smiled. "That's because he's on his way to Monte Carlo. He'll be back early next week."

Chapter 27 □ □ □

Marty had worked hard to show Paul she was enthusiastic and more than competent; her efforts had not failed. She did marvel, however, at why he would have anyone with more than a high school diploma working on this analysis. The task couldn't be more basic, but she knew that she wasn't there to be trained or pursue a career. She already had a job and it was to keep her eyes and ears open for anything that her "cousin" would find interesting. She quickly scanned the list of stocks and noted all the energy related companies. Some of the names sounded familiar.

The exercise was much more time consuming than she had anticipated, although the tedium was not a shock. She took her first trip to Starbucks an hour in and ordered a double espresso in the hope that a stiff jolt of caffeine would keep her awake. It barely worked but she pushed on.

Marty took advantage of Paul's absence to call Buck with an update. "It's pretty much as I thought. It's Vernon's portfolio for sure."

"And exactly why are you so confident about that?"

"Simple. It's a small cap portfolio with mostly energy stocks. That's what the old man specializes in, isn't it?" It was spoken as a question but was more of a statement.

"There is just no fooling you, is there?"

Marty hated how often Buck used that phrase. "One more interesting tidbit and then I have to hang up before someone walks in. Albright is on his way to Europe."

"I give a damn about his travel schedule?"

"You should if it means meeting Jeremy Cranford. I watched him in action again today and he is really, really good. The market was getting destroyed and he just sat there picking his spots, making money left and right. Calm as always."

"He's a professional. I'm tickled he's doing his job."

"Buck, stop being such a jerk. I don't have a lot of time."

"I guess office work really doesn't agree with you. Seems to have killed your sense of humor."

"He was more than doing his job," Marty responded, trudging on. "He's a money maker. You could really use him. He can handle much more money than the old man. You said you wanted to meet with him and now would be the perfect time. Albright's not around to get in the way."

Buck digested the information. He was always looking to add another manager to his stable, and bringing Jeremy on board would also alleviate some of the risk associated with Albright. Albright was not like the other managers who he had either seeded or kept in business. They were younger and hungrier and knew they would not exist if not for him. Nettles and McNamara only cared about being rich and had no qualms about doing whatever was required to achieve that goal, gladly taking both direction and money from Buck. Albright, on the other hand, was established and independent. Buck felt his grip over him starting to loosen; his initial resistance to taking more money only one indication of the future.

"What do you suggest?" he demurred, uncharacteristically.

"Call Albright's office. When his secretary tells you he's traveling and can't be reached...."

Hendricks interrupted, regaining his form. "I get it – she'll transfer me to wherever he is. That's a great fucking idea."

Marty raised her voice; something she didn't often do. "Damn it Buck! Do you want to hear this or not?" She paused but hearing no response, continued. "He barely wants to speak with you when he's in the office. Do you think she's going to transfer your call to his jet?" She paused again, taking a breath, trying to stay calm and keep her anger at bay. "Did you notice the markets today? The volatility is insane! You're supposed to be a serious investor with a lot of money at stake. It would hardly be unusual for you to call for an update. When Suzie tells you Albright's not around ask to speak to Jeremy but don't be obvious."

"I told you I got it."

Marty held the phone away from her ear and took a deeper breath.

"Hello? You still there?" Buck asked.

"Regrettably yes. Invite Jeremy to go with you to Robin Hood tomorrow night. It's such a big Wall Street event, I'm sure he's already planning to go. Ask him to sit at your table with his wife."

"That's a damn good idea! Guess the old adage about the blind squirrel is true."

"Thanks Buck." She added under her breath, *"you moron."*

Chapter 28

□ □ □

"Mr. Hendricks is calling for Mr. Albright."

"I am terribly sorry but Mr. Albright is traveling and unreachable," Suzie braced for the fireworks sure to follow.

"Please hold on," Carla replied indignantly.

Predictably, the next voice on the line was that of Hendricks. "Look here, I need to speak with Vernon. The markets are gyrating wildly and I want to know how the fund is doing. Call him wherever he is and get him on the phone."

"I'm sorry, Mr. Hendricks, but that's not possible. He's on an airplane and won't be reachable for quite some time. Is there anything that I can do to help you?"

"Ha. I really doubt it."

Suzie felt like teeing off on the condescending bastard but it wasn't worth risking her job. "Well, sir, I may not be able to help you but perhaps I can find someone who can."

"Who's in charge when Vernon's not around? That's who I want."

"That would be Jeremy Cranford. I'll see if he is available. Please hold on."

Suzie was unable to see the smile on Hendricks's face.

Jeremy picked up the handset. "Hi Suzie, what's up?"

"It's Hendricks. He's concerned about how the firm is coping with the market and wants to speak with Vernon. I told him Vernon is in the air and offered to take a message but that wasn't acceptable. He said he wants to speak to whoever is in charge when Vernon's out and that is you, fella."

"No problem. Put him through to my line. Thanks."

"Hello, Buck. This is Jeremy Cranford. I'm one of Vernon's partners. Susie mentioned that you were looking to speak to Vernon about how the fund is handling today's volatility. I can handle that if you'd like."

"I'd appreciate it. I'm not the nervous type but when the market goes down three percent and then right back up, all within an hour, I get a little uncomfortable."

Jeremy spent the next few minutes going through his thought process. He mentioned that market swings of today's magnitude give him cause for concern as well "... but given that the market collapsed on very light volume then recovered on much higher volume, this is actually a very bullish sign."

"The way you put it seems right," Buck responded, impressed. "I appreciate your insight but there's one more thing I need to put me fully at ease."

"Hopefully I can help with that."

"I'm sure you can. Vernon and I have known each for a long time but you and I have never met. With the size of my investment in Parthenon and your involvement in overseeing it, well—that also makes me a little uncomfortable."

"So what do you suggest?"

"Vernon said he would schedule a meeting for us to get together, but why wait? You must be going to Robin Hood tomorrow—it seems every hedge fund manager is going. Why don't you and your wife join me at my table?"

The brainchild of Paul Tudor Jones, one of the world's richest hedge fund operators, a Robin Hood event raised more money for charity than any other by a wide margin. Parthenon, and the other large hedge funds, usually bought two tables, equating to a $500,000 donation. Jeremy and Jennifer hosted one table of Parthenon employees and Paul the other, although he graciously ceded this year's tickets to junior people at the firm. Despite the top-drawer entertainment, Robin Williams was the Master of Ceremonies and Bruce Springsteen the entertainment, it was the live auction that generated the most oohs and aahs. Last year's offerings were particularly special. Ron Perelman, the billionaire owner of Revlon, paid a hundred fifty thousand for his son to take a one-hour hockey lesson with Sidney Crosby. The deal included an autographed hockey stick so maybe it was a bargain. An anonymous donor lent their private jet to the cause, along with a visit to five couture houses in Paris. That went for a million to some lucky bidder. If you were still hungry after the event, you could pay six hundred thousand for a chef from a top New York restaurant to come to your house and cook for you and six of your closest friends as one investment banker did. Despite the fact that a McDonald's franchise cost about the same, the bidding was ferocious on this and all other items. And up for grabs during the last auction of the evening was the right to wear the appellation "Robin Hood" for the entire year. A million and change won this feverish bidding contest. Green tights were not included.

Albright was beyond the point where he needed to be seen; it fed his ego more to be the mysterious non-attendee. He wrote the big check, had his name in the program and that was good enough. Jeremy didn't usually attend either but Jennifer had wanted to see Springsteen perform. He was inclined to accept Hendricks's invitation and didn't believe Jennifer would mind the new seating arrangement. It was important for him to know more about this Buck Hendricks character.

"Jennifer and I will be delighted to join you."

"I live at The Carlyle Hotel. Come by at six for cocktails and we can head over together. Should be a fun evening."

It was a relatively brief conversation and Buck came away from it feeling good about this Cranford character. They seemed to view the markets in a similar light; hopefully they viewed the path to wealth in the same way. The last thing he needed, or wanted, was another self-important nuisance on his hands. That, he would not tolerate.

Chapter 29

□ □ □

Jeremy called Jennifer to inform her of their change in plans. "It will be a good opportunity to spend some time with the firm's largest outside investor. He has a place at The Carlyle and invited us over for drinks before heading off to the event."

"Won't your people be disappointed that you won't be sitting with them?"

"Nah. All they care about is the event. They probably prefer it this way. It will give them a chance to let their hair down and have a good time without worrying about how they're acting in front of the boss. Paul can sit in for me and he'll make sure everyone has a great time. He's a lot looser than I am."

"No kidding."

"Listen I gotta hop. Market's starting to heat up again and I have to make sure Paul is available. Give the kids a kiss."

"Will do. Love ya."

Next, Jeremy clicked on F360 in his Instant Messenger address book. A message box opened on his computer screen and he typed in the words that would surely make his buddy's day. Paul had been lamenting that he wasn't going to Robin Hood this year, not because of any charitable yearnings, but because virtually every model in New York would be in attendance. Most of them were on the lookout for some rich hedge fund manager as a retirement package when they were inevitably pushed aside by the next pretty face.

JAM: "its ur lucky day"

F360: "yes o great 1?"
JAM: "ur on 4 2morrow"
F360: "the hood? u got 2 b kidding me"
JAM: "nope. ur in. come by when u can"

It didn't take long for Paul to arrive at Jeremy's door. "How come you're bailing on tomorrow night?"

"I'm not. Jenn and I will still be there but we'll be sitting at the table of the mystery man, Buck Hendricks. It will give me a good chance to get to know him. You've got two tickets. Who will be the lucky girl?"

"Is that a serious question? There are so many great looking women there that bringing a date to Robin Hood would be like taking a snowball to the North Pole."

"All well and good but don't forget that you're management and can't be seen acting like a hormone infused college kid. You have an image to uphold and project. Actually," Jeremy added with a grin, "you have an image to change."

Paul's expression turned from elation to a frown. "Man, leave it to you to kill a good time—and the party doesn't even start for another twenty four hours!"

"I don't want you to get in trouble with the old man, that's all. You know he's a stickler about image."

Paul thought for a second. "Maybe I'll take Marty. She's probably never been and should get a kick out of it."

"Keep it professional."

"No worries, Bud. Thanks again."

Just as Jeremy was wondering why he had not heard from Vernon for a few hours, he was on the phone. He didn't know why, it shouldn't be a big deal, but for some reason he felt unsettled about his upcoming evening with Hendricks.

"Hello Vernon. Thought I would hear from you a little sooner."

"You would have if we didn't get stuck on the damn runway for so long. Looks like the market is doing better. Did our gains hold?"

"Certainly did and then some. Worked out exactly as I thought it would. Surprisingly enough, I received a helpful call from one of our brokers and added to a couple of positions. Made a few mill and counting. Now we can afford to pay for your flight," he added lightheartedly.

"That's good news. Nice job. I'm going to try and get some shuteye. I'll call you later."

"Before you go, there is one more thing. Buck Hendricks called in looking for you, pretty concerned about the sell-off. When Suzie told him you were unreachable he demanded to speak with me. I offered an explanation for today's volatility and it seemed to have calmed him down. After we finished discussing the market he invited Jenn and I to join him at Robin Hood."

"Are you going?" Albright's intonation reflected more than just normal curiosity.

"Yes, I'm going. I thought it would—"

Albright cut in with a word of caution, words he instantly regretted. "Be careful—that's all I'll say. Now, if it's okay with you, I'm tired and want to nap before we land."

"Careful about what? I've dealt with plenty of investors."

"I don't mean to imply anything sinister, but Buck can be a pretty crass individual. You can take care of yourself, and I'm sure you and Jennifer will have a good time. Let me go and I'll try to check in later."

Albright realized there was nothing he could do or say from forty-five thousand feet above the ocean without sounding like an alarmist, alerting Jeremy to issues that he didn't know existed. But now that he had likely piqued Jeremy's curiosity, it was unlikely that he would leave things alone. While it was convenient and prosperous for Albright to take a don't ask, don't tell approach to his dealings with Buck, Jeremy wasn't about to be as easy going about the relationship. He had no desire to wind up a headline like Jeff Skilling from Enron or Bernie Ebbers from Worldcom. If those guys had been a little smarter and a lot less greedy, they would still be living life on top of the world instead of spending their last years in a jail cell. They were also part of large public companies always under the scrutiny of government regulators and shareholders. That was the real difference, Vernon reasoned. Hedge funds weren't tightly regulated and he was the only shareholder who mattered.

However, there were elements of his relationship with Buck that caused him concern. The velvet-gloved demand that he hire Marty was a shot squarely aimed at his ego. It was Buck's way of reminding him who had the upper hand in the relationship. *I'm Vernon Albright, for Chrissakes! I don't need this country bumpkin anymore!* Vernon closed his eyes and tried to massage the tension from his temples knowing that there would be no divorce. Buck's information was too profitable, and putting up with his cowboy ways was a small price to pay. Maybe it was a rationalization. Albright had enough money; building more wealth wasn't what drove him. He could live fifty lifetimes and never have to sacrifice any part of his luxurious lifestyle. It was the chase, the conquering of markets, the desire to go down in history as the best investor ever to play in the markets. He wanted to be mentioned in the same breath as Warren Buffet or George Soros. Soros brought the Bank of England to its knees by betting against the British pound and winning. But Soros exited the trade easily; the British currency was incredibly liquid. Vernon could never cash out all his chips. He was on a treadmill that couldn't stop and he was getting very tired.

Maybe Jeremy was the issue? How important was he to Parthenon? He damn sure didn't make more money for Parthenon than Buck did.

Chapter 30

□ □ □

Despite strong headwinds conspiring against the powerful thrusts of the private jet's twin Rolls Royce engines, the pilots maintained their estimated flying time at less than seven hours. Although Albright's fascination with the markets had made his avocation a passion rather than a job, he loved the solitude of flying and the insulation from email, phone calls and fluctuating markets. It was during these flights that he was usually able to get his most peaceful rest. Configured with all the amenities of a small luxury apartment, Albright retired to the bedroom in the rear of the plane where another plasma screen was located. Behind the bedroom was a full bathroom, complete with gold plated sink and tiled shower. Marble was the decorator's first choice but the stone was much too heavy when considering all the other equipment on the plane. Occasionally Vernon would tune in to a news show offered on satellite television, but more often than not he would select a DVD from the vast collection kept on board. One of Parthenon's investors was a well-known Hollywood producer who had arranged for all new releases to be sent to Vernon's office before they even hit the theatres. Some were then forwarded to the plane and others to Vernon's apartment. He hated going to movie theaters; too pedestrian. His home theater was so much more comfortable and technologically advanced. On rare occasions, the screen in the main cabin was employed for videoconferencing, making it a seventy million dollar mobile office.

Lunch was over and it was time to get some sleep. "What time would you like to be awakened, Mr. Albright?" Carole inquired.

"An hour or so before landing."

"Yes sir. And should I have dinner waiting when you wake up? Suzie called ahead and requested this menu."

Carole handed Albright a menu scripted in perfect old world calligraphy. The meal commenced with a Caesar salad followed by a taste of lemon sorbet to cleanse the palate. The main course was lemon sole meunière accompanied by steamed spinach. Each course was complimented with a different bottle of wine. Albright never had bread with his meal, having no interest in ingesting so many carbohydrates.

"I have a dinner engagement planned."

"Then a light snack prior to arrival will be waiting for you when you wake up."

"Perfect."

Albright shut the bedroom door. He wasn't particularly tired but wanted to be rested for the evening's activities. He lifted a book, eschewing modern technology for old school substance, from the nightstand hoping to read himself to sleep. It was the same novel he was reading at home. Suzie arranged for a duplicate copy to be on board. Ever so detail oriented, she had spoken with the Albright's housekeeper so that a bookmark could be placed where Vernon had left off.

Still five hours away from touching down in Nice, France, Albright finally gave up on getting any real rest. He continued to be bothered by the thought of Buck and Jeremy spending an evening together, not knowing what would come up in conversation or where it would lead. He considered taking an Ambien but shelved the idea—he feared the effect wouldn't wear off in time. It would be better for him to be exhausted when he crawled into bed at the hotel so that he could offset the time difference and avoid jet lag. The discussions he and his friends would be having the next day required absolute mental acuity or it could lead to embarrassing gaffes. Each one was smarter than the next and if someone didn't meaningfully contribute, he may not be invited back. The same standards were not in effect for the dinner and gambling Vernon would be enjoying upon arrival.

Monaco is such a tiny country, measuring just three quarters of a square mile, that it didn't have an airport capable of accommodating a jet. He would land in Nice, France and then take an eight-minute helicopter ride to the hotel. Albright rose from his bed and settled into a seat in the middle of the main cabin. Trolling through the on-demand movie library he opted for his favorite, "Wall Street." Albright regarded the drama as a comedy and motivational tool. "Greed is good," he said aloud, echoing the film's most memorable line of dialogue and a mantra he practiced. After he finished watching the film, he reviewed his notes for the upcoming summit.

The wheels of the 737 gently touched on runway three at Aeroport Nice Cote D'Azur, the second largest airport in France. A customs official came on the plane and stamped Albright's passport while posing scripted questions about the nature and length of his visit. The pilot trailed Albright, suitcase in one hand, leather garment bag in the other, across the runway to where a shiny blue helicopter was waiting. As he boarded the Bell 430, Albright's thoughts turned to the victory lap he would take for correctly calling the huge run up in oil prices. He settled into one of the four seats in the spacious wood paneled cabin and accepted the proffered glass of Champagne. The Mediterranean Sea glistened in the moonlight as they glided over the water and landed on the shoreline of the French Riviera. From above, the city seemed crowded, the buildings appearing to touch one another, their combined lights illuminating the shoreline.

Chapter 31

□ □ □

With Albright out of town and Joseph at his disposal, Jeremy arranged for him to pick up Jennifer in Summit and bring her to the office. Worried about potentially getting caught in the first wave of rush hour traffic, Joseph gave himself a cushion and left the office at three thirty. He breezed out to Summit in a hair under forty-five minutes. The return trip took no longer since they were traveling against the flow. Joseph didn't mind getting out of the office, and enjoyed the novelty of being regarded as more of a commuting partner than a chauffeur. There wasn't a pretentious bone in Jennifer's body.

The chime sounded above the elevator in Parthenon's lobby, warning the receptionists to put away their high gloss fashion magazines and be ready to welcome visitors.

"Good afternoon, Mrs. Cranford. It's nice to see you again. I'll call Jeremy and tell him you have arrived."

"Thank you," Jennifer responded with a smile.

Jeremy was at the front desk so quickly it seemed as if he were waiting just around the corner. "Hi, honey." He kissed his wife on the cheek as he whispered into her ear. "Wow! Don't you look hot."

Jennifer hoped the receptionists didn't see her blush. She was pleased that the two days she had spent shopping for the right outfit had paid off. Strapless and clingy enough to be provocative while still maintaining the standards of refined, good taste, it was sure to turn a few heads. Walking down the hallway toward Jeremy's office, they heard Paul's voice and decided to drop in. He was in the middle of a conversation with Marty but rose to greet them.

"I hope your husband will let you have one dance with me this evening."

"He won't be able to stop us."

Paul turned to face Marty and brokered the introduction. "This is our most recent addition to Parthenon, Marty Jagdale."

"It's nice to finally meet you Jennifer," she said while extending her hand. "I love working with your husband. He's fantastic," she gushed.

As they continued to Jeremy's office, Jennifer shared her thoughts. "For someone so new to the firm, Marty seems pretty comfortable."

"She definitely doesn't appear to suffer from a lack of confidence, does she?"

"I know the type. Paul should be careful with that one, she's a schemer."

"What is it about beautiful women that they can never trust one another?"

"So now you think she's beautiful?" Jennifer playfully thrust an elbow into her husband's ribs. "You better watch out, too."

Chapter 32 □ □ □

"Good evening Mr. and Mrs. Cranford," Carla said as she opened the door. "Can I take your wrap?"

"No, thank you. I'll hold onto it."

"May I interest you in a glass of champagne while you join Mr. Hendricks on the patio?"

"Absolutely, thank you." Jeremy accepted the offer for both of them.

Jennifer whispered to her husband as they walked across the living room. "Is this a hotel suite or a palace? My God!"

"Nice, isn't it?"

Hendricks greeted his guests as they stepped outside. "Thank you for coming. It's a pleasure to meet the man I have heard so much about. I'm also pleased to meet you, Mrs. Cranford." He reached for Jennifer's hand first and gently kissed the top of it.

"Please call me Jennifer." Her eyes ran along the contour of the balcony, taking in the view. "You have a lovely place."

"Thank you. Wish I could take credit for putting it together but that wouldn't fool anyone."

Over the next half hour, Buck regaled them with tales of his youth, doing chores on the ranch and working in the oil fields. He was charming and amusing. Jeremy began to wonder about the basis for Albright's concern.

"So what's your story, Jeremy? I assume that you didn't grow up with a wad of tobacco stuffed in your cheek like me."

"That's a very good guess. My background is definitely a bit different from yours. I'm from—we're both from," he motioned toward Jennifer, "a little town outside Buffalo, New York."

Buck interrupted. "Ah, high-school sweethearts?"

"In fact, we are."

"That's nice."

"My family didn't have much but I can't say I ever went without. They weren't sophisticated people but did a great job preparing me for life. Taught me all about values and hard work. I'm fairly uncomplicated."

"No hobbies? No interests?"

Jeremy shrugged his shoulders. "Who has time? Two young kids and a twenty-four-hour-a-day job. My hobby is my family. There's nothing I enjoy more, so why spend Saturday and Sunday on the golf course when I would rather be with them?"

"You sound more like a saint than a hedge fund manager."

"What my husband didn't say," Jennifer interjected, "was that he is one of the most competitive people you will ever meet, which is one of the reasons he works so hard."

"I plead guilty to that," Jeremy laughed. "I love beating the market and every other manager in the game. What else can I say? It's the ultimate high. Trillions of dollars and all those people going one way and I'm going the other. It's a lot of fun; not that it's without stress."

Jennifer's comment resonated with Hendricks, overshadowing Jeremy's avowed commitment to his family, believing that to be a small obstacle to his plans. Buck decided to help him find a way to overcome that flaw in his character whether Jeremy wanted to or not. He couldn't imagine someone with his personality, market acumen and drive being content staying a junior partner to Vernon Albright.

"There's no shortage of money managers that love to win but still wind up losing fortunes. What's your edge?"

Jennifer rolled her eyes and smiled. "Big mistake. Now

you got him started. We might as well dig in for the night and call room service."

"I won't let him go on too long." Buck showed a knowing wink.

"Actually, Buck, I was being a bit facetious," Jennifer said somewhat apologetically. "Once you get to know my husband better you'll find out that he's not a big talker, particularly when the topic is him."

Under most circumstances, Jennifer's words rung true. But with Jeremy being first up at bat in the conversation, and the purpose of the evening was to get to know Parthenon's largest investor, he decided to open up a bit with the hopes that Buck would reciprocate.

"Obviously Jennifer knows me quite well." Jeremy reached over and patted his wife's knee. "There's no mystery to what I do. I keep emotion out of my decisions and I try to have timelier and higher quality information than the competition. Being as successful as you are, Buck, you must go about your business the same way?"

The irony of the remark wasn't at all lost on Buck and for a second he wondered if Jeremy was letting him know that he was well informed about his relationship with Vernon. "But tell me how you get that real solid information," Buck responded, brushing aside the compliment cum question.

"By outworking the competition. The good old American way."

"Isn't that the truth! God Bless America."

"Let me ask you a question. Why pay us such exorbitant fees to manage your money when you could hire a few smart people to work directly for you. You're clearly better connected in the oil patch than we could ever hope to be."

"You're too kind. I'm just an ol' country boy who was lucky enough to be born into the right family." Buck's response was accompanied with a sardonic grin, an unintentional manifestation of his strong ego.

"Sure and I'm just a kid off the streets who lucked into

working at the most successful hedge fund in the world. We both worked a plan. What's yours?"

"My father always told me that there is no such thing as a free lunch. If I want to deal with smart people then I have to pay them. And the last time I looked there was only one Vernon Albright out there, and he wasn't ready to close up shop and come work for me." *Well, actually he is working for me.* "I also needed diversification; can't have all my money in oil. I thought owning some stocks would be a good thing but I'm a babe in the woods when it comes to the stock market."

"Your dad was a smart man. We love having strategic investors in the fund. They have significant incentive to ensure we're current on their industries. Their knowledge and experience give us an edge on their sectors."

"Exactly right," Buck agreed enthusiastically. "If I can provide some helpful insight into my little corner of the world, then everyone wins."

As if on cue before the conversation took a deeper turn, Buck's date arrived. Jennifer instantly recognized her from the cover of *Cosmopolitan*. For a model, Alana was relatively short, measuring a hair under five foot ten inches in heels. She was, however, strikingly beautiful, if somewhat offbeat. Hair dyed jet black with a page boy cut in the front, the back of her head almost shaved. Lithe, Alana had long, lean limbs and smooth, almost translucent skin. Jennifer remembered reading an article touting her as the next big supermodel. Using a single name moniker, she was on her way. Compared to what Alana was wearing, an almost sheer top and a skirt that had less material than a washcloth, Jennifer suddenly felt dowdy. Sitting next to her all night was not going to be much fun.

Chapter 33 □ □ □

The Cranfords never traveled by limousine, favoring a low-key lifestyle, but, as Buck's guests, they had no choice. Their discomfort ratcheted up a notch as the stretch Maybach, a half-million-dollar automobile, came to a stop in front of the Javits Center, where they were expected to step out onto the red carpet. A velvet rope held back a large throng of celebrity seekers and paparazzi.

"Is this a movie premier or a charity event?" Jennifer inquired.

The crowd that waited for the occupants of the shiny black limousine had no idea who was inside, but that all changed when Alana's publicist shouted her name. "Oh my God, it's Alana."

The flak did her job, fueling a clamor among the onlookers and ensuring that her client's picture would be in tomorrow's New York Post on Page Six. The wolf pack of photographers moved in unison toward the source of the excitement. Having no interest in being jostled and photographed as they made their way into the building, Jeremy briefly considered asking the driver, Rock, to drop them off down the block but abandoned the idea, concerned about insulting his host. Instead, they waited for the crowd to move with Alana toward the entrance before disembarking. Having given Buck a brief head start, they moved quickly, following him to a table at the front of the large room.

"Look who's arrived." Paul pointed Marty in the direction of the Cranfords, who were now sitting three tables away. "Let's go say hello."

Out of the corner of his eye, Jeremy saw Paul and Marty

approaching from the other side of the table. He raised his hand and waved, Jennifer doing the same. Their reactions to Marty, who returned their acknowledgement with a smile, were very different.

"She certainly is an attractive woman," remarked Jennifer.

Coming up from behind, Marty noticed Alana playfully twirling the back of Buck's hair, and her smile faded. Continuing around the table, she caught his eye for the first time. Unaware that Marty would be attending, Buck had the sheepish look of a child being caught with his hand in the cookie jar. Two can play at this game, Marty decided as she put her arm through Paul's, pulling herself into his side. Paul wondered what was behind his good fortune.

"They seem to be getting along very well," Jennifer remarked with obvious displeasure.

"Perhaps a little bit too well. This goes on the list of items to discuss with my overheated partner tomorrow."

"I'm not so sure he's the aggressor. It looks like she's the one on the offensive."

"It's still worth a conversation but it will wait until tomorrow," Jeremy remarked as he stood to greet his friend. "Enjoying yourselves?" he said, the sarcasm not lost on Paul.

Marty pulled back her arm, realizing the mistake. "Yes, it's a lovely evening. Thank you for the tickets." Her attention veered from the Cranfords as she attempted to keep an eye on Buck and Alana.

"My pleasure." Jeremy turned to Paul. "Say hello to Buck Hendricks."

"Hi, Buck, I'm Paul Robbins, one of Jeremy's partners." He was almost shouting in an effort to be heard over the noise. "And this is Marty Jagdale, the newest member of the firm."

"Nice meeting you both."

Before the conversation could continue, Robin Williams took the stage and began the auction. Buck thought a silent prayer, grateful that the increasing noise level made further conversation impossible. As they walked back to their table, Marty shot an unhappy look over her shoulder toward Alana and Buck, a reaction caught by Jennifer.

"Marty seemed distracted by Buck and his date. It almost seems as if she knows them."

"You're imagining it. It's just a case of one young woman checking out another. After all, Alana is a famous face."

The auction was the main event, and it took place while dinner was being served. The highlight was a walk-on role in Steven Spielberg's upcoming film, the winning bid of two million dollars offered by the wife of a hedge fund operator from London. The forty-five minute bidding war for the next ten items raised over nine million dollars for the charity. Another three million came from ticket sales. Right before Springsteen took the stage, the auctioneer announced that a particularly generous attendee, who wished to remain anonymous, would match the evening's take, bringing the tally to twenty four million. After listening to Bruce perform two classics, the Cranfords stood to say their goodbyes but Buck wasn't about to let them leave without first talking a little business.

"We'll walk out with you. Rock will drop us and then drive you home."

"I appreciate the offer but we can call for a car."

"I insist. You're my guests this evening."

Reluctantly, Jeremy accepted.

As they walked toward the door, Buck grabbed Jeremy's elbow to slow his pace, falling behind Jennifer and Alana. "You have a very lovely wife. Alana and I enjoyed the evening."

That's odd, Jeremy thought, *Alana couldn't have said more than five words to either of us since we met at The Carlyle.* "Thank you," he replied. "It was a very nice evening."

"And thanks again for spending time on the phone with me yesterday. It was helpful. Your insights tonight were right on target, too. You're an impressive guy."

Uncomfortable being the recipient of such praise,

Jeremy quickened his pace, trying to catch up to Jennifer. Buck took hold of his arm again; their conversation wasn't over.

"Ever consider hanging out your own shingle?"

"You mean start my own firm?"

"You should strongly consider it. I would definitely consider backing you."

Jeremy stopped in his tracks and faced Buck. "I'm happy where I am," he said sternly. "Parthenon is a great place to work and Vernon's a great guy to work with." He looked at Buck quizzically. "I thought you two were friends."

"I guess I misjudged you. Seemed to me that a man like you would want your own deal but not everyone's cut out to be a chief. The world still needs some Indians."

Jeremy was tempted to tell Buck to take his offer of a ride home and put it where the sun don't shine, but held his tongue. He was already worried about possible repercussions with Vernon. Regardless of his building dislike for Buck, it would be inappropriate for Jeremy to completely alienate him. Buck was too important to Vernon and the last thing he wanted to do was to make matters worse than he may have already done with his tactless response.

Hendricks was angry that he had wasted an entire evening but even more upset with Marty for her idiotic idea and lack of judgment. He would deal with her later. A bigger concern was that he was now more exposed than ever before, and with Cranford being every bit as sharp as advertised, he had to go on the offensive. Quickly, decisively. It would likely get ugly, but not for him.

Chapter 34 □ □ □

After dropping Buck and Alana at The Carlyle, Rock continued to Summit. "I'm going to give you some privacy and raise the soundproof partition."

"Thank you, Rock."

"At least his driver is a decent person," Jennifer offered. "This has been a special evening. I think I've had more interesting conversations with Alexandra's friends than Alana."

"Now, now, honey. That's not nice. True, maybe, but not nice."

"What did he want to talk about with you?"

"If you can believe it, he offered to back me in my own fund if I would leave Parthenon. When I said no, he got pissed."

"So he thinks that you would trade a partnership with Vernon for a partnership with him? Doesn't sound like a great deal to me."

"I don't disagree but why don't you think so?"

"After all you said about how you look at life, he thinks you would screw your partner—the one who gave you your start? The only type of person who would think like that has to *be* like that."

"I have to say it was a flattering offer and since work sucks right now, particularly dealing with Vernon, it was worth considering for half a second. But, I had the same thought as you." He very gently prodded his wife. "No surprise there, huh?" They smiled at one another and Jennifer gave Jeremy a peck on the cheek. "Vernon didn't seem to want Buck and me to get together. Now I know why.

He doesn't believe Buck is someone he can trust, which then begs the question as to why he has him in the fund."

"I wouldn't want him as an investor."

"I don't know if I would either but it's not my choice."

Jennifer relaxed, resting her head on her husband's shoulder. "I don't know. Maybe we're too straight laced for this business or maybe our values are too old world. It seemed that half the crowd tonight wasn't even old enough to drink."

Jeremy put his arm around his wife, affectionately squeezing her into his body. She turned to face him. "You were the sexiest woman there tonight." He kissed her passionately. "Even if you were the oldest," he added and recoiled, waiting for another shot to the ribs. He wasn't disappointed.

"Hotter than that teenage nymph the cowboy was with? Or your new employee?"

Jeremy just threw his head back and laughed. "Jealousy doesn't wear well on you my dear but yes, hotter than every woman there—even if they were all at least a decade younger."

Rock took it all in. Buck would enjoy listening to the tape.

Chapter 35 □ □ □

Marty was particularly tired when she opened her eyes; the mild hangover and the four hours of sleep no doubt to blame. She considered staying in bed but there was too much at stake for her to indulge herself. Marty sat up and leaned against the cloth headboard, the sheet slipping down off her bare breasts. As she attempted to shake off the haze of a partial night's sleep and too many flutes of Dom Perignon, she pondered the prior evening, replaying both the good and not-so-good highlights. Marty's principal lament was not so much the drinking; the hangover would be gone by the second cup of coffee. Nope, that wasn't it. And she didn't regret spending the night with Paul. That was actually very pleasing. It was her public display of affection for Paul that gnawed at her. Nothing against Paul; his wild side pleasantly surprised her. But hanging onto him throughout the evening was just a knee jerk reaction to Buck preening with that damn model. Marty knew she should have been in better control of her emotions. She detested her own weakness.

Marty turned to look at Paul, who lay beside her, still passed out. Apparently he was not as adept at holding his liquor. He was an excellent lover, good looking and well built. She was tempted to wake him for one more go but thought better of it. Instead, she slowly got out of bed and followed the trail of her clothing into the living room. She decided to head home for a quick shower and then a fly by at Buck's apartment, ostensibly to recap his evening with Cranford but also to find out more about Alana.

Slightly more than thirty minutes later, she arrived at

The Carlyle. "Good morning, Carla. Is Buck awake yet?"

"I was just about to wake him," Carla said as she started toward the bedroom.

"Don't bother, I'll do it." Marty hurried past Carla, too quick for her to object.

Already awakened by the doorbell and the hotel operator, Buck was in the process of getting out of bed when Marty walked in. He immediately went on the offensive, not waiting nor caring to hear why she stopped by.

"Your judgment was way off last night. Cranford has no balls. There's no way that boy can cowboy up. He's no more a man than that pretty boy you were hanging on all night."

"You're one to talk."

First Cranford shit all over him and now Marty. Buck flew into a rage, his tone getting louder with each word. "That show of affection was bullshit. Did you sleep with him? Did you risk everything for one night, you stupid, jealous bitch!" He drew back his hand and brought it across her face. It was only because of Marty's quick reflexes that she was able to avoid most of the impact.

Marty had walked into The Carlyle resolute in her game plan; she would go on the attack first, believing the best defense is a good offense. Buck beat her to it and his anger was real. She was worried about what he might do next. "I'm sorry Buck. I know I was out of line last night but seeing you with that witch drove me crazy." She paused and rubbed her cheek, her tears begging for sympathy but none was forthcoming. "And I didn't sleep with him. You know how I feel about you."

"I'll give you a pass this time but only this time." He embraced her and wiped away her tears. "Your insecurity can be a real pain in the ass and there's no reason for it. And this deal is way too important to me to let petty emotions get in the way."

Looking over Buck's shoulder, Marty couldn't help but notice a red thong lying on the floor, partially obscured by the bed. *Bastard*, she thought. *You should be asking me for forgiveness.*

***

Buck and Marty weren't the only ones recapping the prior evening. Jeremy decided to broach the subject with Paul while they were working out. Pulling rank on his best friend was always uncomfortable; he decided that having a discrete discussion in the gym would lessen the formality.

"What got into you last night? I thought we had an agreement."

Paul threw up his hands, exasperated. "Hey, it wasn't me. I'm the wronged party here. Something got into her when we came over to your table. All of a sudden, she grabbed me. There was no warning, nothing. Not that I minded but it was a little weird."

"Is that the best you can do?" Jeremy said, sitting straight up on his bike, clearly incredulous. "Are you saying she latched onto you out of the blue? Maybe stuffing her with drinks had something to do with it."

"Look I admit we had a few pops, but that was it. After we left your table, she came to her senses and apologized. It was back to employer/employee. I'm being good but it's not so easy. She's a looker and has a great personality to boot."

"So that's it? That's all you did? You held hands like school kids and then went your separate ways?"

"Yup. That's pretty much it." Paul immediately felt guilty about the deception, but what was done was done. He knew the relationship was wrong and intended to nip it in the bud before it went any further—and before Jeremy found out any more details.

"Pretty much can mean a whole lot of things. Tell me the rest."

Embedded in the ceiling was a speaker that delivered Paul's reprieve. "Jeremy, pick up line one. It's Vernon."

Jeremy dismounted from his exercise bike and went to the phone. "I'll go to my office so I can be in front of the screens. Hold on a sec."

Before leaving, Jeremy turned to Paul, "You're an adult so I'm not going to tell you how to run your life, as long as it doesn't affect our business. We'll drop it for now." He grabbed a fresh towel to wipe the sweat from his forehead. "I have to take this call from Vernon."

He ran down the hall to his office. It was already midday in Monaco. "How's the trip so far?"

"It's been great. Winning at the tables and, more importantly, we've been brainstorming investment ideas non-stop. We'll discuss them when I return. How's the portfolio doing?"

"We made a few shekels yesterday and should be fine today."

"That's always good to hear." Vernon added. "How was your evening?"

"It was fine," Jeremy responded, having anticipated the question. He preferred a face-to-face discussion with Vernon so that he could gauge his reaction when he told him about Buck's offer. "You know I'm not a big fan of those Wall Street events. The important thing is that they raised a lot of money for a good cause."

"Sounds fairly uneventful."

"It was. Why? What were you expecting?"

"I had no expectations but Hendricks is a key investor so I wanted to follow up. I'm pleased it went well."

Jeremy saw right through Vernon's smokescreen of nonchalance. Ironically, he was more disturbed by this tactic than if Vernon had come right out and asked for his impressions of Buck. He didn't know what Vernon was trying to hide but had no problem coming up with a number of possibilities—none of them good.

Chapter 36

□　□　□

Toward the end of the day, Jeremy stopped by Paul's office where he found him in a discussion with Marty.

"Hey, Paul. How do you stand on that project? Far enough through for us to have a discussion?"

"How about knocking?" Paul responded, clearly feigning annoyance. "Can't you see we are deep into an extremely important conversation?"

The comment elicited a smile from Jeremy

Paul continued. "It's coming along pretty well. A couple of more i's to dot and t's to cross and it's done. What time are you out of here today?"

"Don't kill yourself finishing it up for today. I didn't get to see the kids last night so I'm leaving right after the close. We can sit down first thing tomorrow."

"That works. I'll take the rest of the day to put the finishing touches on the documents and be ready to go in the morning."

Once Jeremy left, Paul resumed the conversation with Marty. "Let's wrap this up. There's a minor amount of data to drop into the spreadsheets and then we're done. You should be out of here in no time."

"Perfect. Then you can buy me dinner to celebrate."

"Listen, Marty, I've been meaning to talk to you about last night."

"I had a great time too."

"No, that's not what I was going to say." He paused, avoiding eye contact. "I mean, I did have a really good time but it's better if we move on. Office liaisons are not good for anyone."

There was a lot at stake and Marty had worked too hard cultivating her relationship with Paul to let it end. Compared to dealing with Buck, cozying up to Paul was actually enjoyable. He was a much more generous lover—and a lot closer to her age.

"Hey, I'm a woman. They put scarlet letters on us, not the guys. I intend to be in this business for a long, long time and don't want to risk my career on an office affair with my boss. I still can't believe we did what we did. I'm sort of embarrassed, and as good a time as we had, we can't ever do it again."

Paul breathed a sigh of relief.

Marty continued. "But isn't it customary to have a celebratory dinner after completing a big project? I'm not suggesting some romantic night out; I'm talking about a harmless business dinner to reward someone—namely me—for a job well done."

"You do have a point and we shouldn't let the pendulum swing too far the other way. Dinner's a good idea but only as long as we're both on the same page about it staying strictly business."

Marty smiled coyly. "Of course. No monkey business; only hedge fund business. I wouldn't have it any other way."

"Excellent!" Paul exclaimed, "Now look at this," he said, pointing to his computer screen. "One more task and it's a wrap." Marty quickly scanned the columns of data as Paul proffered his final instructions. "It shouldn't take long. I'll send you a copy of this file from my database and all you have to do is combine the columns. Once that's done, sort it according to the instructions on the first sheet."

Marty held her reaction in check; the compilation of the data was more damaging than she had thought. Deleting the file wouldn't work, not unless she could also erase it from Paul's hard drive, and there was no plausible way to do so, at least not before it was presented to Jeremy. Unable to decide upon a course of action, she excused herself and went to the rest room. She checked under the doors of each stall to make sure she was alone. Confident of her privacy, she pulled out her cell and hesitated. She knew that once she shared what she had just learned, there would be no turning back. Worse than that, the result would be irreversible. Marty pushed aside a modicum of pending guilt and made the call.

Chapter 37 □ □ □

After a final review of the analysis, Paul went home to clean up and change into more casual clothing. He had sent Marty home almost half an hour earlier with the plan to meet up later.

By the time Paul showered and shaved, it was seven-thirty and he was right on schedule. He pulled on a pair of khaki slacks and a bright blue polo shirt that hung tightly to his sculpted physique, the bright cotton weave accentuating his finely toned musculature. He never lifted heavy weights, assiduously avoiding the look of someone too muscle bound, fearing he would be stereotyped as someone with more brawn than brain. Besides, successful Wall Street types weren't supposed to have enough spare time to craft intimidating physiques; their time was better spent using their wallets and intellect to influence others.

He stared at his reflection in the mirror, highly confident that Marty would approve. As he conjured a vision of her lithe body, he realized for the first time that the color of his shirt was almost identical to that of the dress she had worn in the office. On his feet were brown Tod's loafers. At a cost of five hundred bucks for what was essentially a pair of moccasins, they were instant status symbols easily recognized by those who knew fashion. While he hoped he didn't look too preppy, he wasn't going to waste any more time worrying about it. As instructed, he called before he left his apartment, checking on Marty's progress getting ready.

"I'm leaving my place in about two minutes."

"I need a few more minutes. How long will it take you to get here?"

"Depends on how deep the garage buried my car but probably no more than fifteen minutes."

"It's probably not a good idea to take the car."

"Why not? It's a beautiful night to drive with the top down."

"That's true but there aren't any garages where we're going, assuming that you're okay with a slight change in plans."

"Depends on the change."

"I was able to get us into Rao's. Is that okay?"

"Okay? I've always wanted to eat there but could never get in. How'd you pull it off?"

Rao's was located on 114th Street and Pleasant Avenue in East Harlem. Founded in 1896, it was one of New York's oldest restaurants and, with a reputation as a "mob joint," also one of its most storied. It was only a couple of years ago that Louie "Lump Lump" Barone shot another alleged mob solder who had mouthed off to him at the bar. Mixing in with the blue collar crowd were the Hollywood elite and pro athletes. The true stars at Rao's were those that had reservations in perpetuity, slots doled out by the owners for a specific time and evening each week of the year. It was up to those who "owned" those reservations to ensure that their table was always filled at the appointed time or risk losing their slot. It never seemed to be an issue since a reservation was near impossible to come by.

"Let's just say I know people who know people. But it can be expensive and they only accept cash so I'll understand if you want to go somewhere else," Marty added sheepishly, knowing full well that money was not an issue.

"I think I can handle the expense but I need more cash. There's an ATM in the building next door. I'll make sure to withdraw enough so that you won't have to wash the dishes."

"We can always go Dutch," Marty parried. "After all, it is a business dinner."

"I'm glad you haven't forgotten that. I'll pick you up in a cab in twenty."

Paul pushed his bankcard into the slot outside the small vestibule that housed two ATM's. The red light on the doorframe turned to green signaling access was granted. Before the door closed, another customer rushed in, startling Paul and causing his heart to momentarily flutter. He casually looked at the stranger and felt relief that the well-dressed man posed no threat. While silently chastising himself for being so jumpy, Paul tapped his PIN into the designated box on the touch screen then went about providing the other requested information. The significant account balance he maintained allowed for daily withdrawals up to ten thousand dollars but that would be overkill so he withdrew only two thousand, pleased that the machine dispersed hundreds instead of twenties. Adding that to the cash he already held, he was in good shape for the evening.

"I'll take that," the stranger said in a menacing yet steely calm voice.

Alarmed, Paul turned to see that a gun was pointing directly at his chest.

The well-dressed man spoke again, this time more threatening, the hand in which he held the gun still and unwavering. "I told you to give me the cash."

Paul was frozen by fear. He started to speak, to say, "Take it. Take everything" but never got the words out. The gunshots echoed loudly in the room that was no larger than a closet. Paul slumped to the floor, his heart working hard to save him but paradoxically hastening his demise as it pumped the blood from his body.

Chapter 38

□ □ □

The ringing pierced the silence of the night, startling them awake. Incoming calls after midnight didn't usually bring good news, and with the Cranfords each having an elderly mother living on her own they suspected the worst. Jeremy hoped it was a misdialed number as he reached for the phone. He put the receiver to his ear but what came through was largely unintelligible although it didn't take long for him to realize it was uncontrollable sobbing.

"Hello, hello. Who is this?" Jeremy's concern ratcheted higher as he strained to decipher the caller's identity.

"It's... it's me. Paul's mother. I didn't know who else to call." Paul was an only child; his father had passed away many years before. "Oh, Jeremy, Jeremy. What did they do to my boy?"

"Mrs. Robbins! What's wrong? Is Paul okay? Did something happen to him?"

"They...they...they shot my boy. They shot him, Jeremy, they shot him."

Jennifer had been stirring since the telephone rang. Now the emotion in Jeremy's voice brought her to a full state of consciousness. "Jeremy! What is it? What's wrong? Did something happen to Paul?" Tears streaked down Jeremy's cheeks and the effect was contagious. "Oh my God! Something terrible has happened! Jeremy, tell me, please, tell me what's going on!"

Reflexively, Jeremy put his arm around his wife, seeking and providing comfort. "Is he going to be okay? Tell me where he is."

"It's too late. He's gone. Paul is gone."

"Gone? What do you mean gone?" He asked, panic in his voice. "Oh, no! Oh, no! I'm so sorry."

Jennifer buried her head in her husband's chest, her body heaving uncontrollably as she gasped for air.

"The police asked me to come to...to identify the body. They called him a body, Jeremy. Paul's not a body, he's my son," she sobbed between words, "but I don't want to see him that way. I want to remember him as my beautiful boy. Can you come with me?"

Jennifer was hysterical, inconsolable, but Jeremy knew he had to pull himself together; he had to be strong enough for all of them. "Of course. I'll be there right away."

Chapter 39 □ □ □

The veil of sadness that engulfed the Cranfords hung heavy, stifling the air and closing out the light. In the days that followed, they barely slept, and consuming any nourishment was a tasteless chore as their appetites waned. Jennifer's mother took Melissa and Alexandra to stay with her until some semblance of normalcy returned. Jeremy was haunted by the image of Paul's pale and lifeless body stretched out on a stainless steel gurney at the morgue. It's not how he wanted to remember his friend.

Writing the eulogy was a mixed experience. On one hand, it was cathartic as he relived the best times of their relationship, often bringing a smile to his face, but it was also depressing as he periodically focused on the end of their time together and the manner in which Paul died. It took nearly the entire night; writing and editing, deleting words from the text only to add them back again—over and over. He wanted it to be perfect; to ensure that everyone who came to pay their respects really understood Paul's essence and remembered him as Jeremy did: a happy, bright and giving person.

"Paul was a brother to me. Now I know that close friends often say that at a time like this, but anyone who knew us knew it was true. He was an uncle to my children, a brother to my wife, and a son to my mother. His personality was contagious, always infecting others with laughter and the zeal to enjoy life. It is the ultimate injustice to deprive the world of someone as good as Paul Robbins. Where is the justice and comfort for his mother, whom he cared for and spoke with each and every day? Where is the justice and the comfort for the children at the Foundling Home, where he donated his time and money so that they could live better lives? We all are far worse off today than we were when Paul was with us. But we should be grateful for the time we had with him...."

Pausing often to regain his composure, it took Jeremy almost twenty-five minutes to get through the fifteen minute tribute. Mrs. Robbins, despite the sedation, fainted and had to be attended to by the doctor that accompanied her to the service.

Not one of the nearly two hundred mourners could recall an event that was so heartbreaking. Jeremy asked the attendees to celebrate Paul's life but instead they continued to mourn his passing.

Chapter 40

□ □ □

How High Is Up

by Bill Sundrick, Special Correspondent

What gives with crude at $135 a barrel?

What gives is that this rise in the price of oil has nothing to do with supply and demand, other than the demands of some big oil companies, abetted by a group of greedy hedge fund managers seeking to increase their already bloated bank accounts. The DOE, Department of Energy for those new to my column, released the latest statistics on global oil consumption and production. The way I read the figures—and granted I'm no energy economist—is that there is more than enough black liquid sloshing around than we need. Want more proof? The daily average value of all crude contracts that traded on the various commodity exchanges over the last two weeks approached $20 billion. Sounds like a lot, doesn't it? Darn right it is when you consider that the world only uses $12 billion of the stuff each day. That means $8 billion worth of crude contracts trade each day without any demand attached to it.

One can only conclude that it is the speculative investor that is driving up the price of crude, to the benefit of the billionaire hedgies, our friends in the Middle East and the big oil companies who are getting so fat with profits that they send their retiring CEO's into the sunset with a few-hundred-million-dollar nest egg. Whatever happened to a gold watch?

I caught up with—and I do mean caught up with since he was trying his best to avoid me—the President's energy czar, Bill Lindsay. I asked him why the President isn't doing anything to control the speculative bubble being fed by the commodity traders?

"I don't know if you noticed, Mr. Sundrick, but we are a capitalistic society that believes in free markets as does the commodity exchanges in London and Tokyo and everywhere else in the world. But over time simple economic principles such as supply and demand take care of unnatural pricing."

It was what I expected. He ran off before I could follow up but I would have liked to ask him how much longer we have to wait. Until half the population can't afford to heat their homes, or drive their cars to work, or until every product that uses oil as a raw material gets so expensive that we go into a recession?

The hedge funds took down Lehman Brothers and Bear Stearns. And guess where they get their funding from? You got it: the banks and investment banks. Now they are using their leverage to hurt Main Street again. Who will be the John Paulson of the oil markets, making billions of dollars while the average family struggles to pay their energy bills?

Maybe the hedge fund guys will loan us some money. At usury rates of course!

Chapter 41

□ □ □

Vernon had come back to work after the weekend, while Jeremy took an extra day. Vernon wasn't pleased since the markets only closed to mourn Presidents, not chief operating officers of hedge funds.

Arriving at his customary time of 5:30 a.m., Jeremy resumed his routine and went straight to the gym. He couldn't recall the last time he had worked out without Paul by his side. After a halfhearted ten-minute effort on the treadmill, Jeremy headed for the showers and was at his desk twenty minutes later.

Settling into his chair, he logged onto the computer and went through his emails. Half of the emails were condolence messages, most of the senders having read about the murder in the newspapers. They were brief with little deviation in content, but reading them made a tough morning even tougher. Jeremy decided to let his secretary screen them, weeding out those that she thought he should read personally and required a response. He would never see the message of sympathy from Mr. Datatech.

"Glad to see you back in the saddle," Vernon offered, standing in the doorway of Jeremy's office. "We have a lot to talk about. Stop by my office after you settle in."

"Now is as good a time as there will be." Jeremy rose from his chair, grabbed his coffee and accompanied his partner down the hall.

Albright removed his suit jacket and hung it in the armoire that stood against the far wall. "Paul was an extremely important part of our lives as well as an important part of our firm. I know you're going to miss him as will I."

"Nice words, Vernon, thank you. It won't be easy getting through this."

Vernon agreed. "Definitely not—for you, the firm, or for that matter, for me either. Perhaps I took him too much for granted."

"I appreciate that, Vernon, but I'm surprised to hear you say it," he noted, trying not to send skeptical. "You never seemed like you were such a big fan of what Paul did around here."

"The value that I may have ascribed to his position has nothing to do with how I regarded him on a personal level but let's move on. That seat should not be empty for even one second."

Man, that was a quick transition, Jeremy thought. "I agree and have been thinking about our options. For the sake of immediacy, I have a solution that is tentative at best and, candidly, one that I'm not entirely comfortable with."

"You're not thinking about Marty, are you?"

"I am."

Surprised by the suggestion, Vernon took a minute before responding. The idea made him uncomfortable, as it would Jeremy if he knew the true circumstances that brought Marty to the firm. Vernon wanted an exit strategy for his largest external investor, not a promotion for his cousin. "Interesting thought but, frankly, I had assumed that you would want to get someone more senior in that position as quickly as possible. You've always been the big proponent of the importance of that role."

"And you've never really seen the value in having someone as seasoned as Paul in that position. I'm surprised you're not all over this." Jeremy paused. "I'm sorry; that didn't come out right."

"No apology necessary. You've had...I mean...we've all had a rough few days."

Vernon reconsidered the concept of increasing Marty's responsibilities. Going along with Jeremy's idea would help repair the fraying edges of their relationship, and, despite

Marty's connection with Buck, he was sure of her loyalty to him; a belief borne of arrogance and conceit. Even if he misjudged her allegiance, her ability to affect Parthenon was minimal. To him, the back office represented a necessary evil of overhead expense. *All they do back there is shuffle paper*, he reasoned in his thoughts. *And I can pay her a lot less than Paul. What the hell, it's only temporary.*

Jeremy continued with the sell. "On a strictly stopgap basis—and I underscore stopgap—she's the logical choice in spite of how new she is to the firm. She has the smarts and Paul seemed to think she was doing a pretty good job. It will give us some breathing room while we look for someone with more experience as a permanent replacement. Otherwise, I have to get more involved in that department and I don't have either the time or inclination to do that."

"That's ridiculous. You can't make money for the firm by pushing papers in the back office." Left unsaid by Vernon was that he had no interest in Jeremy getting closer to his portfolio. Jeremy was smarter than Paul and had a broader knowledge of the business, so his ability to pull all the pieces together was a potential danger.

"As I said, I have no interest. Marty isn't perfect but she could be a decent number two."

Vernon continued to warm to the thought. It was a convenient choice. As a lesser of evils he would rather keep Jeremy away from his portfolio whereas Buck already knew the down and dirty. If Marty violated the firm's confidence and shared information gleaned from her new role with him, it would scarcely matter. Vernon tried to see the downside to the idea but couldn't come up with a good enough reason to disagree without raising Jeremy's suspicions.

"It's your call on this one as it was when we hired Paul. All I ask is that you find a permanent replacement as soon as possible." Vernon continued. "Just make sure you keep an eye on her. It means more work for you but with everything that's happened, being too busy won't be a bad thing."

"Agreed on all points. I'm not ready to turn the operation over to her completely; she's still fairly green." He stood. "If there's nothing else pressing, I want to have the conversation with her before the market opens."

"That's a higher priority than anything else I had on the agenda."

Chapter 42

□ □ □

The tightly drawn shades held the room in darkness. Candles emitted faint flowery scents as a CD offered the soothing sounds of a running stream. Buck lay prone, face down on the massage table, naked under a warm fluffy towel, his mind taking him to a quiet place after a grueling workout with his trainer. The beautiful masseuse ran her deceptively strong hands up and down his legs, occasionally getting wonderfully close to his private parts. Buck's ego never let him wonder if it was accidental or intentional—of course it was intentional—and he loved the sensation. He looked forward to his daily, hour-long respite and gave Carla very specific orders never to interrupt. However, there was one exception, one person who Buck always wanted to be able to reach him at any time, day or night. His calls always translated into money, big money.

Carla knocked on the door. "Sorry to interrupt but you have a call waiting."

Buck evolved out of his state of relaxation, rolled over and sat up.

"Should I wait?" the masseuse inquired.

"Nope. The moment has passed but you were great, as usual. Same time tomorrow."

Buck threw his legs over the edge of the massage table, wrapped the sheet around his body and dropped his feet to the floor. After as the masseuse left the room he lifted the portable phone from its cradle.

"Hope this is more important than the meeting you pulled me out of."

"You can be the judge of that. There was a mishap at one of the major oil fields in Riyadh and production has been completely shut down."

"How come I haven't heard anything? I have some of the best sources in the world."

"And I'm one of them which is why you're hearing it now. You know how the Royals are in this country. It's a closed society and information can take a while to leak out. They want to craft the public message perfectly, so my guess is that the wire services won't get the story until tomorrow or the next day. The cause is a mechanical failure at two of the country's most productive wells so there was nothing to draw anyone's attention to the problem—no explosions, no fire, nothing at all."

"How long will they be out of commission?"

"Don't know for sure but the best guess from my sources is one to two weeks. Could be more depending on if replacement parts are available or if they have to be specially molded. But even if it's a week, given how tight the market is, prices are going higher. Much higher."

"And I'm pretty damn sure the Saudis don't feel a burning sense of urgency to rush the repairs."

"Not at all. They could play this out for a while, which I'm sure won't break your heart."

"You just earned yourself a raise, amigo."

"You are too kind and too generous, my friend."

Hendricks pushed a button on the phone's console to open a new line. "Back up the truck, Chuck. I just spoke to my contacts in the Middle East and if I got the story right my best guess is that we're looking at one forty-five."

Nettles was a bull on crude but one forty-five a barrel was aggressive. "I don't know; it's already had a pretty good run and likely due for a pullback. How good do you feel about this info?"

"Let's put it this way. I'm wiring another two-fifty to your fund and I want it all put to work right away. Lever it up by two and don't be price sensitive."

Nettles let out a low whistle. "I'm going out on a limb here but my guess is that you feel damn good about this information."

"I got oil in my veins so I know good info when I hear it. I've never been wrong and I'm not about to start screwing up now."

Buck had a similar conversation with Brendan McNamara. He smiled, knowing that they would be slugging it out in the trading pits as their floor brokers went head to head putting the billion to work.

"Hey, Vern. You ready to make some real dough?"

"I'm already doing fine but thanks, Buck," Vernon responded coolly.

"I'm sure but I have something extra special for you today."

"I said we're good, Buck. The portfolio is long enough oil."

"I don't think you're paying attention, Vern. I said this was extra special, meaning it comes along about as often as a pregnant rooster."

"Okay, let me hear it. Is it time to reverse our oil trade and sell some of those shit companies?" he asked with a touch of sarcasm.

Buck laughed. "Sell? No sir. They ain't ever going to pull enough crude out of the ground to keep everyone happy. The price is going a lot higher and here's today's reason why: my sources tell me that the Arabs are experiencing serious production issues and spigot is off for a week or two. When you add that to the two mega fields in the Gulf coming up dryer than a ninety year old whore, well—we have a major imbalance on our hands."

"Spare me the vision. What Gulf projects? The Barnett Shale? Are we going to get hurt?" Concern was evident in Albright's voice.

"Nope. The big boys own those wells and they're damn good operators—except BP that is—so a dry well here and there doesn't matter all that much. It actually helps us. But

BP is my favorite company. Their fuck up helped the cause. Less drilling means higher prices where I come from."

"I love the oil business," Albright remarked. "Companies screw up their drilling programs and what they already took out of the ground goes up in value because the commodity just got scarcer. The small companies we own should trade up nicely. It would be great if big oil found all the dry holes first. Then we could sit back and watch the panic."

"Amen!"

Vernon called Jack Knowles with instructions to increase their holdings in a number of small cap oil producers. Comanche Oil was a particular focus because of their significant amount of proven reserves. Jack was already uncomfortable with their exposure but knew it wasn't his place to voice any concern. He had to assume that Jeremy, being the other senior partner and a voice of reason, was up to speed and in agreement with the strategy. If it was okay with Jeremy and Vernon, both of whom Jack greatly respected, who was he to question their strategy?

After Nettles and McNamara finished battling it out on the London exchange, they transferred their bidding war to New York when the overseas market closed. Some of Buck's other minions joined in. The last price they paid hovered just above one thirty-seven a barrel. Fahnstock and Smythe, the two brokers on the London exchange they employed to handle most of their orders, piggybacked on their trading. Although not entirely acceptable, it was legal; brokers were allowed to trade on any information they received as long as it wasn't done in front of a customer's order. And it would be foolish not to capitalize on the trades of someone who had yet to be wrong. Then the momentum traders followed. The herd mentality was alive and well. For the moment, no one seemed to care that momentum traveled in both directions. By the time the parasites were finished, crude would end the session at just a hair below one forty, an all-time record.

Chapter 43 □ □ □

Marty took a seat opposite Jeremy.

"I am so sorry about Paul—"

Jeremy motioned for her to stop. "I appreciate your compassion but I don't want to discuss Paul." Jeremy had heard enough expressions of sympathy. Especially from people who barely knew Paul. "Let's get right down to it, Marty."

Marty was surprised at Jeremy's harsh tone and wondered if her time at Parthenon was coming to an end.

"You know what we have in your department—a bunch of well-meaning and hardworking people, but, unfortunately, none of them are capable of stepping up to fill the void created by Paul's passing."

Marty immediately experienced relief upon the realization that her tenure at Parthenon was not the subject of the discussion. "Don't take this the wrong way—I'm not trying to be patronizing or denigrating to anyone, but I agree," she said with perhaps a bit too much enthusiasm. "Isn't that the nature of the operations beast? One Chief and lots of Indians?"

Chief and Indians? The phrase resonated with Jeremy but he couldn't recall why. He pushed the thought to the back of his mind and continued on. "Yes it is, which is why you're sitting here now. You're the most educated employee in that room by a mile, which makes you the most qualified so I'm putting you in charge until I can find a more senior, permanent replacement. Paul was your biggest fan and I'm relying on his judgment. I'm counting on you to rise to the occasion."

"I don't know what to say," Marty responded, outwardly astonished. "I really appreciate the opportunity, even if it is only temporary. I hope I don't let you down."

"Just work hard and I'm sure you won't," Jeremy offered, in a more friendly voice. "If you have any questions or problems with the job or with the people—I don't expect everyone to accept you as their boss so readily given that you are one of the youngest and newest employees in the firm—I want to hear about it. But spare me the little stuff."

"I know what my role is and I have no delusions about my experience. There's no way I can take Paul's place."

"Here's the first piece of career advice for your new role: don't patronize me. I don't respond well to it. I want everything straight without editorial content," he admonished her as he stood. "Let's go back to your office and I'll make the announcement." As they strode down the hall, Jeremy decided to lighten the mood. "I'll offer you one more pointer before you start. Being in charge of payroll comes with the turf. If you want to make sure that no one spikes your coffee when you're not looking, be sure to get everyone their check on time."

Marty laughed politely, although her mind was now elsewhere. A nice bonus would accompany this promotion, but it wouldn't only be coming from Parthenon.

Chapter 44

□ □ □

Jeremy's mood turned somber as he reflected on the most recent conversation with Vernon. With his conscience gnawing at him, he returned to Vernon's office. "There's something that we need to discuss."

Vernon kept his eyes glued to the monitors on his desk as he responded quizzically. "Okay. And what's that?"

Jeremy took a seat across the desk from Vernon.

"It must be pretty damn important if you're settling in as the market's getting ready to open." Vernon settled back in his chair, placed his elbows on the armrests and formed a steeple with his fingers under his chin, his interest clearly piqued.

"I received a couple of threatening letters from some crank. Normally I wouldn't be concerned but they mention Jenn and the kids by name."

"Tell me more." His expression turned from one of curiosity to concern.

"It's about Datatech. Apparently, this guy read the interview...."

"The interview I didn't want you to do."

"Look Vernon, we can make this about you or we can make it about protecting my family." Jeremy paused to collect himself. "I know the interview was a mistake but that's water under the bridge. Lesson learned. Right now I've got some psycho threatening me and my family."

"Have you spoken with the police?"

"No. I thought it would be better to speak to Tom. I gave him copies of one of the letters."

"Suzie's fiancé?" Vernon asked, not outwardly nervous but feeling a knot in his stomach. He didn't need the FBI involved with his people or his business. Good assistants were hard to find but if her husband was always going to be in the background, maybe it was time to start looking.

"Yes. He's looking into it. I also asked Joseph to stay in the reception area as a precaution."

"If I were you I wouldn't be too concerned. In fact, you should tell Tom to forget it. He's one of the Bureau's top agents and only agreed to get involved because Suzie works for us. That's not exactly fair to her or him." Vernon paused to assess Jeremy's reaction. "I've been on the receiving end of a number of angry letters and phone calls over the years but I'm still here, alive and kicking. Regard the experience as a lesson and a nuisance and move on."

Jeremy held his tongue; he had never become accustomed to Vernon's self-centered view of the world. A third trophy wife didn't make him a family man and he never had children, not wanting to sacrifice a minute of his time for someone else.

"You don't appear to be in your usual rush to leave so there must be something else on your mind."

Jeremy shifted uncomfortably in his seat. "There is one more thing."

"Go on."

"When you asked me if anything out of the ordinary occurred the night I went to Robin Hood with Buck, I told you no."

Vernon tensed. "Go on," he repeated.

"Well, I wasn't being a hundred percent candid."

"Just get to the point, Jeremy."

"Hendricks offered to back me in my own fund."

Vernon's facial features hardened. "That son of a bitch did what! What did you tell him?"

"What do you think I told him? I told him I wasn't interested."

"And how did he respond to that?" Vernon inquired, regaining his composure. "He's not used to the word no."

"That's an understatement. He went from being extremely friendly all evening to being an asshole. But even before he turned into an asshole there was something unsettling about him. What's the story?"

"You just told me the story. He's successful, rich and is used to getting his own way. He's spoiled. Should that be a news flash?"

That's the pot..., Jeremy thought. Seeing that the conversation had reached a dead end, Jeremy glanced at his watch then rose from his seat. "I have to get back to my post."

Jeremy settled back into his office and turned his concentration to his screens but nothing seemed right. Since when did Albright become protective of someone else's time or relationships? Shouldn't the threat to his family be more of a concern? And who was this Hendricks guy? He got the sense that Vernon was afraid of him. Otherwise he would have launched into a tirade and likely even picked up the phone to call him and throw him out of the fund.

Emotions that had been relegated to a feeling of annoyance about the shroud of secrecy surrounding Hendricks morphed into grave concern. What did Hendricks have on Vernon to essentially render him impotent in response to an attempt to steal his best asset?

Chapter 45 □ □ □

The market followed the early indications, down a half percent by mid-morning. Jeremy's portfolio was in the green, thanks to his short positions in consumer companies, which were trading as if they were about to file for bankruptcy. With energy prices continuing to rise, it would still take some time for investors to act with more intelligence and less emotion.

Jeremy's neck and shoulder muscles were taut from the stress of watching the carnage on his monitors; his knuckles almost white from gripping the computer mouse so tight. Between the markets and Vernon, he needed a break and made his way to the pantry at the end of the hallway. Jack Knowles had the same idea and was already sipping a cup of coffee when Jeremy pushed open the swinging door. Jeremy took a cup and saucer from the counter while the butler stood ready to pour him a dose of hi-test.

"Another down day, Jack."

"I'm sure it is for most but not for us. You and Vernon did a great job getting in front of this mess."

"A little luck never hurt anyone."

"I would hardly call it luck. Vernon's timing has been incredible. Seems like as soon as he gets done giving me a buy order, crude makes a new high and some company that we own announces a huge find."

Jeremy came to take a break from the market, not to hear Jack ramble on about Vernon. "Timing is everything."

Undaunted by Jeremy's short responses, Knowles continued. "When Vernon threw a bunch of buy orders at me this morning, I got a little nervous but with oil still moving up, it's all working out just fine. More than fine, actually."

"I haven't had a chance to speak with Vernon yet. Was he buying across the board?"

"Nah, picking his spots. It does get nerve wracking since we're already pretty damn long energy but I'm sure you guys know what you're doing. I mean, oil keeps going up but if it ever collapsed, we'd have a tough time getting out of some of the smaller companies. But, as I said, you two are pros so I have zero concern. Between your shorts and his longs, we're cleaning up this year." He paused to take a bite of a fresh baked muffin. "I'd never have the balls to make such big bets, especially the way Vernon does." Jack caught himself. He didn't want to offend Jeremy by only extolling the virtues of Vernon. "Maybe that came out wrong, but it's just that Vernon traffics in companies that are a lot smaller and less liquid than those in your portfolio. Take Comanche Oil. We must own thirty percent, and from what I see, that's not the only company where we own such a significant piece of the float."

Traders were not usually known for lengthy conversation or long attention spans. They spent six and a half hours a day talking in short sentences, pressured by the moving markets and always anxious to catch constantly changing prices. Before Jeremy could respond, Knowles' brought the conversation to an end. He didn't want him to think he had nothing better to do than hang out in the pantry all day gossiping or that he wasn't on board with the firm's investment strategy.

***

Back in his office, Jeremy examined his P&L, which changed tick by tick with the stocks he held. For most, this would be unbelievably distracting and at times, very unnerving—imagine seeing your net worth changing every second—but for a person who did it every day, it was just white noise. After the conversation in the pantry, Jeremy's sense of urgency climbed a few notches. Clearly, the issue with Vernon's exposure hadn't gone away; it was getting worse. He decided he had to find Paul's analysis.

The knock on his open door drew him from his thoughts. It was Marty.

"Can you spare a second?"

"Sure. What's up?"

"I thought it would be a good idea to have access to Paul's computer. I'm sure his hard drive has files that I will need and probably some emails from investors that need a response."

"Sounds right."

"Thanks but I can't gain access unless I know his password."

"You can have it after I go through his emails and files and delete the personal items."

Marty wanted to say *why does it matter, he's dead*, but wisely thought better of it. "Ah, I didn't think about that. When do you think you'll get to it?"

"Maybe later or tomorrow. But don't worry. I'm sure the real time sensitive matters would have found us already. Unfortunately, our investors aren't known for their patience."

Chapter 46

□ □ □

The large four-poster bed was framed by two fixtures that provided the perfect amount of light for reading before falling off to sleep. There they sat, propped up on pillows, she with a Kindle, he with an iPad. He was more staring at the words than reading them, his mind elsewhere, deliberating the wisdom of discussing Parthenon's issues with Jennifer. Having spent four years at a top management consulting firm, she was a trained problem solver and he valued her input. His trepidation, however, was rooted more in a desire not to further burden his wife; she was still struggling with Paul's murder. He labored under the same emotional drag.

"That must be the most complicated book ever written."

Jeremy looked up. "Why do you say that?"

"Because you've been reading the same page for twenty minutes." Jenn took the device out of her husband's hands and placed it on the night table. "Thinking about Paul again?"

"Paul and other things."

She snuggled up to Jeremy and lifted his arm, placing it around her shoulder. He locked her in tight. "Want to talk about it? You know it will make you feel better."

"I guess so. There is so much going on at work that I don't know where to start."

"I can only imagine," she said in a tone full of compassion. "It must be so empty without Paul. I know how bad I feel, so I can only imagine what you're going through. And forgetting the emotion of it all, he was such an important part of your business. My poor baby." She caressed his cheek.

Jeremy listened to Jennifer's words, deciding if he should hide behind her rationale for being out of sorts instead of discussing the other issues he was facing. But he couldn't; they were in a partnership, thankfully different than the one at Parthenon, and he owed her more honesty.

"I do miss him a lot, but there's more to it than that. It's the business in general. It's what's going on at the firm."

"I don't understand."

"I'm really concerned that Vernon may be putting the entire company in jeopardy with all the risk he's taking in the portfolio."

"More than usual? Doesn't he usually swing for the fences?"

"We all do to some extent, but in small doses, not to the extent he apparently is."

Jennifer sat up straight, Jeremy's arm slipping off her shoulder and falling behind her. "Did I hear you say *apparently*! Why don't you know? We have a lot of money tied up in that fund not to mention your career."

"I already spend too much time at work. Can you imagine what my day would be like if I had to focus on his portfolio too? Besides, don't you think I should be able to trust my partner?"

"Absolutely. But obviously you have some concerns about what he's doing, so you have to look into it."

"I have been, and Paul was helping me. I didn't want to speak with Vernon about what I was thinking if I was way off base, so I had Paul do an analysis on his portfolio. He was working on it before...." Jeremy paused, choking up. It was late and he was tired, a perfect time for emotions to surface. "... before he died but I never got to see the finished product. And with all that was happening, I pretty much forgot about it."

"And you just remembered it tonight?"

"No, of course not, Miss Sarcastic."

"So when?"

"I ran into Jack Knowles in the pantry. He mentioned something that made me think that my instincts were dead on."

"What's he thinking?"

"Vernon's greedy. Can't think of any other reason. The more money he makes, the more he wants. And the more he makes the smarter he believes he is. His arrogance has convinced him that he will know exactly when to get out and that it will be before anyone else. He's like everyone else who flamed out—they never thought it could happen to them."

"Maybe you're wrong. You always told me that Vernon is able to distill information almost instantaneously with its release, take a position and then get out quickly with a nice profit."

Jeremy looked at his wife quizzically. "I'm pretty sure I never said that. Maybe you read it somewhere like the National Enquirer."

She smiled. "Hmm, maybe I did embellish a bit." She slid down on the headboard and Jeremy put his arm back around her shoulder.

"Here's something else that bothers me. Vernon had Jack Knowles increase an already large position in a company right before they released new."

"Let me guess—the news was good and the stock shot up."

"Yup."

"So what's your plan?"

"I started a discussion about risk with Vernon but it became acrimonious very quickly. And you know how he can be when his feathers are ruffled. That's when I asked Paul to get involved. I needed more complete information."

"You're in a tough position. He's been good to us. And he's your partner, not some stock position that you can write off if you're wrong because you moved too soon on too few facts."

"Wow! A dagger through the heart. You're ruthless." Jeremy playfully gripped his chest feigning pain. "So that's what you think I do?"

"That's exactly what you do. You may have that teenager that Vernon hired fooled but I know better," Jennifer laughed.

Chapter 47 □ □ □

At five o'clock in the morning, the office was all but deserted except for the skeleton crew that staffed the overnight trading desk. Not even the early bird politicians, who thought the recipe for success was beating the boss into the gym, had arrived. Jeremy went straight to Paul's desk, not bothering to stop by his office to drop his jacket. This was the first time he had been there since the funeral, but he was unwilling to fall prey to another wave of emotion. Short on time, he persevered. He reached under the desk and powered up the computer. The machine easily navigated through the startup applications prior to the appearance of the Parthenon logo, which was accompanied by a request for a login and password. Jeremy entered his administrative override. Only he, Paul and Vernon had these codes, although he doubted Vernon knew his. It was an interesting paradox; Vernon was an incredibly astute investor in technology stocks yet probably couldn't distinguish his iPod from a Walkman. Suzie logged him on and off his system every day.

Jeremy impatiently tapped his fingers on the keyboard as the screen populated with multiple icons. His first inclination was to go to the Recent Documents file, hoping that the report on Vernon's holdings would be one of the last projects that Paul had worked on. This folder held fifteen files. By title, nothing grabbed his attention so he opened them one by one, ultimately coming up empty. It dawned on Jeremy that perhaps Paul wanted to ensure confidentiality and may have used a non-descript label for his work. He sat back in the chair and thought about how he could short cut the search. As if a switch had been flicked on, Jeremy had an "ah ha" moment. Excited, he opened an Excel folder and ran through each of the files. He got the same result.

Yawning repeatedly—it was early, he hadn't slept much and the task was boring—he knew he didn't have much time. The back-office employees would be arriving soon and so would Marty. He didn't need her looking over his shoulder. After a few seconds of thought, he navigated to the documents folder and rolled the cursor over each file, revealing the date and time of their most recent update, and narrowing his search to Paul's last day in the office.

Jeremy looked at the clock on the bottom toolbar; thirty minutes had elapsed and he was growing short on time and patience. He had assumed this would be a quick, simple undertaking. He leaned forward on his elbows and rested his head on his hands. *Where the hell did he hide it?* Key words such as energy, Vernon, Jeremy, immediately came to mind but were too obvious. He ran them through the search function any way hoping to get lucky. Nothing popped up. Then another thought. While in the pantry, Jack Knowles had mentioned a company that Vernon had been buying, Comanche Oil. He searched "Comanche." Surely it would show up somewhere.

"Good morning," spoke a cheery voice.

"Morning, Marty. You're in early," he responded without turning around.

"Not really. I always arrive this early. I get so much work done before everyone shows up." She pointed to Paul's computer. "Anything turn up that I have to respond to?"

"Don't know yet. It just finished booting up."

"No problem. I'll be over at my desk if you need me."

Jeremy resumed his search. The scan of the C drive came up empty. There was one more place to look. He went to the "Recycle Bin" hoping the document was accidentally deleted but could be recovered. Again, nothing. Completely stumped, he had no choice but to surrender. He told Marty that he had more files to review before allowing her access.

***

Jeremy knew he had no choice but to consult Parthenon's CTO, Chief Technology Officer. Five minutes later, Lauren Wilkes arrived at his office. In her mid-twenties, with close cropped hair and light brown skin, she had already been at Parthenon for two years following a similar tenure at Microsoft. Lauren had completed her graduate studies at MIT's Sloan School of Management at the age of twenty-one, when most students are just finishing college. Despite being a brilliant technologist, her refined but attractive looks and tailored clothes allowed her to avoid the appellation of chief geek. But a geek she was. She was recruited by Paul, but now reported to Jeremy. Lauren was too senior to be under Marty and had little aptitude for administrative functions.

She was also oblivious to office protocol, walking right into Jeremy's office without pausing at the door. "What's up, Jeremy?"

"Good morning to you too, Lauren."

"Oh! Good morning." Long on looks and smarts; short on personality.

"Have a seat," he said as he walked over to shut the door. "I have a job for you to do. Simple data retrieval and system check." As he spoke the words, he felt a bit foolish attempting to mislead someone with an I.Q. exceeding one hundred forty, but now was not the time to go into details regarding the true purpose of the exercise. He barely knew her and was unsure how she would react. "I was looking for a file on Paul's computer but couldn't find even a remnant of it—not even in the Recycle Bin. It has to be there. Maybe it was encoded, or he put it on a different drive than the one I was searching, but either way it has to be found ASAP."

"I'll get on it right away. I know just who to give this to. The guy's a whiz...."

Jeremy interrupted. "I want you to handle this personally—without any help. Also, this stays between us, which means that under no circumstance do you discuss this with anyone else."

"Did Paul do something wrong? He wasn't embezzling money or something like that?"

"Oh God, no! Paul's the last person who would do anything dishonest."

Lauren breathed a sigh of relief. "I'm really sorry; I hope you don't think I was saying that Paul could... could," she stammered nervously.

"No, no, of course I don't think that," Jeremy interceded. "I shouldn't have been so cryptic."

"Tell me what you're looking for and I'll do my best to find it. If it's not on one of his hard drives, it could be sitting on the backup server."

"I knew you would understand. He was working on an analysis of one of our portfolios. It's likely on a spreadsheet. If you need key words, use energy, oil, gas and so on. I'll also give you the name of a couple of companies that may help the search."

Lauren started to get up. "I'll let you know right away if I find anything."

"Hold on. I'd also like you to back up all of Paul's emails and personal files on a separate disc and then erase that information from his hard drive. I want to give Marty access to his computer after you finish with your search, but she doesn't need to see anything that's not related to business."

"I completely understand. I'll only go into those files and emails to the extent I need to tag them." Lauren again got up to leave.

"You're an impatient one, aren't you?" Jeremy asked rhetorically, smiling. "One more request and then you can get going. Wait until everyone clears out this evening before you get started. So much traffic goes by Paul's desk that I don't want to take a chance on anyone asking you what you're doing or looking over your shoulder."

"No problem. I don't have plans for tonight anyway." She paused. "But I still don't understand."

"Don't understand what, exactly?"

"I get the fact that Paul's personal data is confidential and I also understand why you prefer that I clean it off his system. But why do I have to do it after everyone leaves?"

"There's good reason but I don't have the time to go into it now. We can talk about it tomorrow, but for now you're going to have to trust me."

"That's fine," Lauren demurred, feeling somewhat foolish that she had questioned one of the two senior partners. "I don't even know why I asked." She turned to leave then stopped. "Actually, Jeremy, I don't need to sit at Paul's desk. I can access his computer from the network using my workstation, which connects through the main hub."

"Perfect." Jeremy responded with a simple smile, pleased that he was in good hands. "Lauren?"

"Yes, Jeremy?"

"I'm sure you're thinking 'what did I just get dragged into,' but there really is nothing for you to worry about."

Despite Jeremy's assurance, Lauren would worry until she knew more.

Chapter 48

□ □ □

Confident in Lauren's discretion and expertise, Jeremy turned to his normal routine but his heart wasn't into the more mundane tasks, such as scrolling through the research notes emailed to him each morning, although it was usually nothing more than an exercise in deleting worthless messages. He looked forward to the shot of adrenaline he always felt when the market opened for trading. As he scanned the first report email, a report on the earnings prospects for General Motors, the phone rang.

"Hello Mr. Cranford. How are you today?"

There was a lack of quality in the voice, an insincerity to the question. "Who is this?"

"You can call me Mr. Datatech."

"You! What the hell do you want?"

"I wanted to give you a clean bill of health. You lived up to your end of the bargain and now I'll live up to mine."

"This conversation is over."

"Wait!," Varko shouted. "Don't hang up. You want to hear what I have to say."

Jeremy froze; he had already pulled the receiver away from his head, preparing to slam it down into the cradle. With some trepidation he slowly brought it back to his ear. "I'll listen but only if you tell me who you are first."

"I'm not ready to do that yet, but when we do finally meet you'll realize how good I am at this game and you will beg me to come work with you at Parthenon." Varko chuckled ever so slightly. "We would work well together since I'm a lot like you. We don't let the game control us; we control the game. But that's not why I called."

"Why did you call? To threaten me again?"

"No sir. This call is only good news. Since Datatech stock had such a great week, consider yourself out of the penalty box."

"I'm happy for you," Jeremy said with as much cynicism as he could muster, "but I don't give a shit about Datatech. The only thing I care about right now is finding out who you are so I—"

"Easy there, Cranford. I just told you things are going to be okay."

"Great. That's just great. Are we done now?"

"Almost, but first I need a little advice. I'm thinking of buying more stock. What would you do if you were me?"

"Are you kidding? Go to hell!"

"That's not nice, Mr. Cranford. Or can I call you Jeremy?"

Jeremy considered the opportunity. "You're right. I apologize. I'm sure a smart trader like you bought it well and has a good gain in the shares. The right thing to do is to sell it. You never go wrong taking a profit."

"You're damn good at what you do so I guess I should take your advice."

"It's the only thing to do. Now if it's okay with you, I have another call waiting."

"Thanks for the tip. People like us have to help one another out."

It only took a minute or so for Jeremy to get Tom Wichefski on the phone and recount the conversation.

"Don't take any solace from that phone call, Jeremy. In fact, by calling you he's exhibiting more aggressive behavior. And if the stock trades down, what will he do then?"

"Believe me; I'm not taking any comfort from that madman's call. I have to see that whacko behind bars before I feel any relief."

Distractions were the Achilles heel for most investors. Not Jeremy. He turned to his screens with no other thought on his mind except how he was going to make money.

***

Varko felt good about the call and the personal connection he had formed with Cranford. Traders had to stick together. He admired how smooth Cranford was. Maybe a bit too smooth, actually. It had to be a trick. Traders make money competing against one another not helping each other. That's what all the investment books said. Cranford was probably still short and was trying to get him to sell it to pressure the price. *That scumbag! Does he think I'm stupid?* Varko banged the receiver against the phone booth's metal wall, frustrated, angry—not knowing if he should buy or sell. He decided that Cranford's fate was out of his hands. Whether Cranford lived or died would depend on the direction of Datatech's stock price.

Chapter 49

□ □ □

Lauren returned to her office and sat down at her workstation, the most powerful at the firm. Her office connected to
a much larger room that housed the firm's technology systems, including the mainframe, network backbone and tele-
com switches, all of which could be accessed from her desk.
This broad entitlement was necessary for trouble shooting
and remedial action should a fault occur, as unlikely as
that was with so many redundancies built in. The downside
of this convenience was that it required an extra level of
security to prevent unauthorized personnel from hacking
into the system. Parthenon's system was impregnable.

Lauren logged onto the network using Paul's password.
This was the simplest route and a replica of his desktop
appeared on her screen. She performed essentially the
same search as Jeremy had by skimming all the folders
on Paul's C, D and U drives hoping for the obvious, but
experiencing the same empty result. She fared no better
with the keyword search. All that remained of the simple
analyses was a review of the deleted documents and files in
the Recycle Bin. Lauren was sure this would also be a waste
of time. It was.

She sat back and gathered her thoughts. Despite the
advancements in troubleshooting, diagnosis and search,
simple trial and error was still the best method for resolution. Analytical almost to a fault, Lauren opened a new
Word document and put down the fact pattern: 1) Jeremy
had given Paul something to work on shortly before he was
murdered; 2) Paul had told Jeremy that the project was
substantially complete; 3) Paul was most likely working on

the project in his office since all the inputs that required access to the firm's database were so sensitive that they would only be available on site; and 4) the document was most likely an Excel spreadsheet since that would be the best way to illustrate the information.

Lauren wondered if she had reason to worry. Sure Jeremy was a partner but there was no doubt that it was Vernon's firm. Should she tell Vernon about this or was he aware of it? How did she know she could trust Jeremy? Lauren defaulted to her instincts. She had loved working for Paul, her direct boss, and trusted him implicitly. His integrity was irreproachable and she believed, through Paul and her own observations, Jeremy was cut from the same cloth. Vernon, on the other hand—well, she never got to know Vernon; he was extremely aloof. It was unlikely he even knew her name or what she did.

The mental gymnastics on incalculable inputs were so exhausting for her analytical mind that she decided to leave the politics aside. She used her administrative pass code to access the firm database and commenced a search of the firm's entire archive of documents, commencing with the reports that were authored a month before Paul's death. Lauren knew that using a single keyword such as energy would be too broad. Using trial and error, she kept narrowing the search: "energy Albright" brought up over two hundred documents; "Robbins Albright Energy" narrowed the results further. Then she limited it to only Excel programs and the number of possibilities declined measurably to a manageable number. She double-clicked on each file and...BINGO—there it was.

The desk printer only accommodated letter sized documents so she forwarded the file to the large Xerox machine located in the photocopy room. Excited, she hurried to retrieve a copy of the spreadsheet on the way to Jeremy's office but was disappointed to see that the particular Xerox she had sent the job to was busy printing out other documents; her request was apparently still in the queue. A copy from her desktop printer would be good enough for now.

As usual, Jeremy's attention was completely focused on his four flat panel screens. Lauren decided this was important enough to interrupt.

"Done," she said.

Jeremy looked up from his computer. "You found the file?"

"It really wasn't that difficult." Lauren said then quickly caught herself. "Sorry, I didn't mean—"

Jeremy laughed. "Don't worry; no offense taken. You're the tech genius, which is why I needed you to get involved."

Lauren stepped around the side of Jeremy's desk and placed the pages listing Vernon's portfolio in front of him. "I'll make sure you have a better copy, but this should provide the gist of what you wanted."

Jeremy scanned the list. Only three columns were legible but they told most of the story. From eyeballing the information, a reasonable guess would put the weighting of energy stocks in Vernon's portfolio at ninety percent. As if this weren't alarming enough, Parthenon's ownership stake in some of the companies exceeded twenty percent. Worst of all, those entities had to be fairly small since Jeremy was unfamiliar with most of them.

Despite Jeremy's strong suspicion that Vernon was ignoring conventional risk management by taking concentrated bets, he had hoped to be proven wrong. Paul's analysis quashed that thought. For the first time since his misgivings about Vernon surfaced, Jeremy felt very nervous—a completely foreign emotion. Still, he was able to keep his poker face.

"Thanks, Lauren. Great job. I'd like to see a copy of the complete file as soon as you can produce it."

***

Lauren returned to the photocopy room and looked through the paper tray that contained the output from the Xerox machine. The only documents it held were from the job that was being printed before she went to Jeremy's office.

The spreadsheet should have been on top, being the last job produced. A glitch must have occurred. She made a mental note to look into it later, but Jeremy was waiting for the final copy of the analysis. Lauren returned to her office and printed another copy.

Chapter 50
□ □ □

The bottom started to fall out for Varko around noon with a knock on the door of his basement apartment. No one ever stopped by to visit unless it was the landlord, and his arrival was announced with more of a bang than a polite tap, tap, tap. Whoever it was, he had no intention of letting them in. It was the middle of the trading day and he was busy watching the market.

"Who is it?" he growled.

"Detective Sean Fischetti with the New York City Police."

"What do you want? I'm busy."

Fischetti moved tight to the closed door so he could speak without shouting. "Please open the door, Mr. Varko. I need to speak with you for a few minutes."

Varko contemplated telling Fischetti to come back after the market closed but thought better of it. No cop could possibly understand the implications of interrupting a trader's concentration during market hours. He opened the door and stepped outside the apartment.

A short military haircut, non-descript black shoes with rubber soles, light gray suit that had a sheen from too much wear, white shirt and bland striped tie almost made the identification card Fischetti was holding an unnecessary confirmation of what he did for a living.

"Are you Ernest Varko?"

"Nobody else lives here so I must be him. What has my wife told you guys now? That witch never stops harassing me."

"It's not about your wife this time, Mr. Varko." The detective knew about the restraining order from a review of Varko's rap sheet. "This concerns something even more serious. Mind if I come in?"

"We can talk out here."

"Do you have a problem letting me inside?"

Fischetti took a small step, placing his foot on the door saddle allowing for a near unobstructed view of Varko's studio. It was routine for Fischetti to request entry into a potential suspect's home since even a cursory look at their surroundings could provide insight into their personality, or even better, clues. But Varko's living quarters were small enough that he could see all he needed to by quickly scanning the room from the doorway.

"Nope but it's no more comfortable in there than out here. I don't have anywhere for you to sit down."

Fischetti observed a tight space containing only a cooking area and a place to sleep. The television, volume turned up too loud, was tuned to CNBC. He couldn't imagine that this guy had enough at stake in the market to suffer through the boredom of watching those talking heads babble on. Varko's brokerage account at Tinker Blistrom revealed ownership of only a few shares of a penny stock.

"Look officer—"

"Detective."

"Okay, detective," Varko responded, clearly unimpressed. "I don't have all day to stand around getting acquainted. What do you want?"

Fischetti wondered what else Varko had to do. It was daytime and he was a night watchman. That was in his domestic incident file, too. He pulled a small spiral pad from the pocket inside his jacket. An equally downsized pencil, similar to the stubs used to keep score at a golf course was stuck in the spine. "You're obviously very busy, so why don't we get right to the reason for my visit. You were the last person to meet with Al Manero before he went to lunch."

"Yeah, so?"

"Apparently, the meeting didn't go all that well. It seems that you got a little upset and had to be escorted from the premises."

Varko betrayed no indication of nervousness. His expression didn't change, no sweat formed on his brow. "Don't take this the wrong way but obviously you never played the markets. I have a lot of money at stake and Manero was being a prick. You can't blame me for being a little hot with him."

Fischetti took the statement down verbatim before asking his next question.

"Besides, what's that got to do with anything? Is it illegal to yell at your broker?"

"After you left Tinker Blistrom, where did you go?"

"I came straight home. Why?"

"Did anyone see you come home?"

"You see where I live. I live in this fucking basement. I have no neighbors down here. Nobody ever sees me come home just like no one ever sees me leave and I like it that way. What's the difference?"

"Roughly ten minutes after you were escorted out of Tinker Blistrom, Mr. Manero went to lunch."

"Yeah, so? What happened? Did he get food poisoning?"

"Not quite, Mr. Varko. I told you this was a serious matter. On his way to lunch, Mr. Manero was hit by a bus and died from his injuries." Fischetti paid close attention to Varko's reaction.

"He's dead? I'm not happy he's dead but I'm also not going to shed any tears for the prick. But what does this have to do with me? Sounds like an accident; that is, unless you think I was the driver." Varko let out an unintentional chuckle.

"I'm glad you can find humor in this, Mr. Varko. I'm not sure his wife and kids look at it the same way. And frankly, I don't either."

"I wasn't laughing but I also wasn't driving the bus. What else do you need to know from me?"

"You admit to arguing with Manero in his office. From what witnesses told me you were pretty aggressive. Did you continue to fight with Manero outside the office?"

"Wait. Isn't this an accident? Sounds like you're making it out to be more than that."

"Not really. This is a pretty routine investigation but we're not ready to label the death accidental until the investigation is complete."

"The streets are very crowded around lunchtime. You should be able to find a witness. He was pretty fat and unsteady on his feet. Or maybe he was in a hurry to eat lunch and didn't pay attention to the traffic."

"You're a funny guy aren't you?"

Varko raised his voice. "Listen, buddy, I said I'm sorry the dude's dead but I had nothing to do with it. If you're telling me I'm a suspect then I'll get a lawyer, but if not, I have to get back to my business. I've already taken too much time away from the market."

"Oh, who's your new broker? Or does a guy like you have a zillion of them to manage all your money?"

"Who's being funny now? And that's none of your business."

"I'll let you get back to work but I may have more questions for you as the investigation unfolds. In the meantime, if you recall seeing anybody after you left Manero's office that could provide an alibi or if you suddenly recall anything that can be helpful, please give me a call." The detective handed over a card before turning to leave.

As Fischetti walked out, Varko shouted after him. "That's why my taxes are so high, because you waste time on nonsense. Go find some real criminals and harass them."

Fischetti hadn't come expecting a confession. In fact, before he met Varko, he had been positive that the visit would be routine, a waste of time. The most likely explanation for Manero's death had been an accident but something about this guy told him that he couldn't discount the homicide theory so easily. As the door slammed behind him, Fischetti had a sense that he hadn't encountered Ernest Varko for the last time.

Chapter 51

□　□　□

Jeremy stared at the finished copy of Paul's analysis. He perused the data, troubled by what he saw. Periodically, he would input a company's ticker into his Bloomberg and go through the holder's list to see who the other shareholders were. Some he recognized; they were large mutual funds. Others he had never heard of, but this wasn't particularly alarming. There were thousands of money managers in the world and no reason for Jeremy to know them all. But one name did cause some concern: Hendricks Capital.

Next, Jeremy looked at the total value of the holdings and almost became physically ill. The value of the portfolio investments approximated three times the actual cash balance; Albright was on margin for more than twice the amount of cash invested. If his bets were wrong, they would be wiped out! Even if he was correct about the direction of crude but some exogenous shock took the market down, such as another terrorist attack on U.S. soil, they would suffer the same fate. The banks wouldn't wait for the market to recover, they would exercise their margin calls as soon as the stocks dipped below a certain price and automatically liquidate the portfolio. Parthenon would be left with no equity and only mega losses. Jeremy's personal balance sheet would be decimated.

Everything was at stake. His livelihood was Parthenon. As good as he was at what he did, if Parthenon ever got caught up in some impropriety the taint would wash over his reputation, rendering him unemployable. But not only was his job at stake—so were his life savings, since he always reinvested most of his bonus back into the firm. And, not insignificant, as a partner in Parthenon he was equally responsible for any illegal activity that went on at the firm. He knew he had to do something.

"Wichefski."

"Tom. It's Jeremy Cranford. Got a minute?"

"Sure, Jeremy, but I don't have anything new for you. I'm still trying to track down something on this Mr. Datatech. We're waiting on the SEC to provide a report on trading activity in the stock."

"That may turn out to be a dead end if his broker is holding it in the firm's name. That's pretty standard for retail investors."

"True, we thought of that but we have to investigate every potential lead. It's also likely that he doesn't trade enough stock for it to show up anywhere."

"I appreciate your help on that but that's not why I called," he said while taking a step toward the window to deal with the fading cell phone signal.

"Then what's up?"

"I'm afraid I have another favor to ask of you, but I understand if you're too busy. I don't want you to think that I'm trying to make the FBI my personal detective agency."

"No worries. It's not as if you're a disgruntled husband asking us to follow your wife around town because you suspect she's sleeping with the tennis pro. This Datatech situation is right in our wheelhouse, so you shouldn't think that it's a favor."

"Well then you're a great guy to be taking a personal interest. I'm sure you could push it off to someone a lot more junior. I can see what Suzie sees in you."

"You're going to get me in trouble; flattery can be considered a form of bribery." They both chuckled.

Jeremy turned serious. "Please don't share this with Suzie. I don't want to possibly put her in a difficult position with Vernon."

"No problem but if it does concern Suzie I may have to step away."

"Of course that's your call, but I don't think it will be an issue." Jeremy delved into his suspicions concerning Vernon's portfolio and his reason for not approaching him directly. "The bottom line is, I don't know if he is doing anything illegal, or, if he is, whether he's even aware of it."

"It's important not to jump to any conclusions but level with me. What are the chances that if Vernon is doing something beyond the pale that he doesn't know it?"

"Slim."

"Exactly. He's been around this business too long and is too bright not. . . ."

"Agreed. I'm just trying to give him the benefit of the doubt."

Tom was intrigued. "So from what you're telling me, you believe I should be looking into this Buck Hendricks character?"

"Spot on, Tom. I've only had limited contact with him and he didn't exactly leave me with a favorable impression."

"Suzie's never mentioned his name, which I would guess pleases you. I'm sure the last thing you would want is one of your employees revealing company secrets to an outsider."

"Very true," Jeremy agreed.

"Why don't I run a cursory check on him and see what turns up. You must have his Social Security number and legal name in your files for tax purposes. Buck has to be a nickname, don't you think?"

"Has to be. What parent would name their kid Buck? We should have every investor's tax information on file but nothing would surprise me at this point. In the meantime, I may have a conversation with Vernon, but I'll leave your involvement out of it."

"You may want to have more information before you do that. Just owning the same stocks as one of his investors or being plugged into the oil business doesn't make Vernon, or Buck for that matter, a criminal. And selfishly, I don't want you alerting them to any issues which would cause them to destroy any potential evidence."

"You sound like my wife. I'll take that under advisement. Thanks, Tom. I really appreciate your help."

"As I said before, I'm just doing my job."

Chapter 52

□ □ □

Buck's black Ford F-180 pickup was waiting in its usual parking space when he deplaned at Midland International Airport. Even though Buck loved the good life and being the center of attention when he was socializing, when he was trying to do business in Texas, he knew a lower profile worked best. A limousine would be too flashy and folks might treat him with suspicion—some city slicker instead of one of their own. He wanted to be perceived for what he thought he was: a down-home good ol' country boy who knew the oil business.

Buck steered the pickup through the gates of the property where Comanche Oil was headquartered, slowing for the security guard to recognize him and wave him on. The asphalt road weaved through the oil fields where large drilling rigs operated around the clock, extracting oil from deep below the surface and feeding it into pipelines that sat on low stilts above ground. "These fields haven't changed much since I worked here," he said aloud as he did every time he visited, nostalgia bringing back fond memories of his teen years. Almost everyone who grew up in the energy business in Texas spent some time in Midland, which served as the unofficial capital for the Permian Basin, an area extremely rich in oil, natural gas and coal.

He pulled up to the main office building. Despite new windows and a fresh coat of paint, it held the same appearance as it had when it was erected forty years ago. Buck steered into one of the visitor's spots directly opposite the front door. He made his way to reception, where the secretary manning the front desk instantly recognized him.

She placed a call to Wayne Goody, Jr. before Buck made it through the second set of doors. Goody had been Chief Executive Officer of Comanche since his father, Wayne Sr., passed away nearly three years earlier. In his day, Wayne, Sr. was regarded as one of the best wildcatters in Texas, able to find oil where others had failed. However, he was also known to use that talent more often to suss out a good time, almost drinking the company into oblivion. When Junior finally assumed control he realized that he needed to find a lifeline to rescue the business that was now in default on much of its debt. He approached Buck with a deal he couldn't refuse. In return for a controlling interest in Comanche, Buck would pay off the bank. Once the oil markets turned around, Buck cashed in, taking the company public in an Initial Public Offering (IPO) and making himself a small fortune. He was still the largest shareholder.

Bordering Comanche's field was Hawk Petroleum, another oil and gas exploration company. Since their fields intersected at certain points they granted each other an easement allowing their pipelines to run next to one another through both properties. Often they would share the costs—and risks—of drilling an exploratory well. Deposits ran underground and were not delineated as well as ground acreage, so significant cooperation was required. Comanche and Hawk had more than neighboring fields as their matchmaker. The CEO's became very close for another reason; they each had Buck and his friends as their largest shareholders.

Wayne Goody Jr. and Harvey Simmons were seated at a small conference table, the sheen from the old wood long gone. They had formed a kinship borne out of similar near-death financial experiences. Having been so close to bankruptcy, and the shame and humiliation that would accompany financial ruin, Goody and Simmons were eternally grateful to Buck for his financial assistance and business counsel. Buck entered and warmly greeted the men he had come to regard as friends.

"Hey guys. Y'all look well."

Goody, paradoxically referred to as Junior by all who knew him, pushed his chair back from the table. Employing great effort, he lifted his massive body from the chair, his five foot ten inch frame struggling to support three hundred pounds of unconditioned body mass. His large stomach jiggled as he pumped Buck's hand in a welcoming handshake. Junior was an extremely unattractive man with a pock-marked complexion and comb over that would tempt anyone with a pair of scissors make him own up to inevitability. Never married and never intimate with a woman unless she was generously remunerated it, he worked 24/7 just to be able to support his hooker habit. Harvey Simmons, on the other hand, was a handsome man, but he labored under an affliction of a different sort; he was dumber than a two by four but talented enough to be a graduate of the lucky sperm club. His wife and three kids were no impediment to an insatiable appetite for other women.

Junior began. "Hundred thirty-seven crude looks good on me, don't it?"

"With your model good looks, anything looks good on you," Buck responded to guffaws.

Simmons dried the tears of laughter from the corners of his eyes. "Not that we don't like havin' y'all visit, but what brings you here on such short notice?"

Buck went over to the credenza and poured himself a cup of coffee. Ignoring the pastries that always seemed to be in plentiful supply in Junior's office, he opted instead for a piece of dry rye toast that was put out for his benefit.

"Y'all have to stop eating this garbage. I don't want to have to look for a new CEO." Buck took a few sips of the tepid coffee. After refilling his cup and taking a bite of the cold toast, he joined the others at the table. "So you boys like the price of oil where it is, huh?"

Junior jumped on the question. "Better than a sharp

stick in the eye but I'm pretty sure it can go a helluva lot higher. Actually, I'm disappointed that it's still below one fifty."

"And if it weren't for the damn government riding everyone's back to keep pumping more, it would be," Simmons concurred. "We can't keep pushing the men and the equipment so hard without an implosion. The infrastructure wasn't built to run without any downtime."

"And y'all will love this. My buddies in Washington told me the President has been jawboning the rag heads to get them to start pumping more, too." He loved tweaking these guys.

"Why would the rag heads agree to that?" Goody asked, clearly confused. "They don't like low prices any more than we do."

"Simple, my large friend," Buck smiled, amused by his own words. "They want more jets. Anytime we want a favor from them, they ask for fighter jets in return. Damned if I know why they need them; the only ones they would use them on are the Israelis, but they know sure as shit that those Jews would kick their asses in a straight up fight."

"Not to mention that they'd catch a lot of shit from us if they ever used those jets for anything else than killing a bunch of those hellkeeta scum," Simmons added in agreement.

Buck smiled at the editorial license with al Qaeda. "I don't want to beat around the bush, so here's the deal. You guys hit the nail on the head. We've never run the equipment—or the men for that matter—this hard for this long. I'm afraid something is going to give and knock us out of commission. And if the Saudi's and their buddies do jack up production, prices are going lower. A lot lower. Don't know about you boys but I'm not happy about the prospect of either."

"Nothing we can do about them rag heads," Simmons said with resignation.

"Course not, but there is something we can do about the supply," Junior suggested.

"I don't know about that. We're the little guys, a drop in the bucket compared to the Saudi's."

"All true but look at it this way. Between your two companies—our two companies," Buck corrected himself, "we account for almost a half percent of total U.S. production. That may not seem like much until you consider that the market is pretty damn tight. But the other point is contagion. When your production shuts down it will spook the market into trading higher since every trader will start thinking that every company's operations are vulnerable."

"But what's our reason for shutting down? Don't you think everyone will be bitching if we say that it's to offset the cuts or drive up prices?"

Junior playfully slapped Harvey on the back of the head. "You can be really dense sometimes, you know that?"

"What if something happened to one of the pipelines?" Buck asked. "It connects the production from both properties. In this business accidents happen all the time."

"The bottom line is that if we were in a different line of business we could raise prices as much as we wanted without every damn politically correct asshole in Washington getting on our backs. This is fucking America for chrissakes, and ain't nobody telling me how much money I can make. The damn government wasn't there with a check for me when oil was priced in the teens so I damn well don't give a shit what they're saying now."

Harvey nodded his agreement. "But how long do we have to be out of commission for?"

Neither Junior nor Harvey ever disagreed with Buck and he liked it that way. Between the stock that Buck owned directly and the shares that he owned indirectly through Vernon and others, he held their wellbeing in a tightly clenched fist. They kept their jobs and high incomes at Buck's discretion and they knew it.

Harvey had another thought. "Say something does happen to the pipeline. Won't some folks around here become suspicious?"

"Number one, who gives a flying fuck? It's our company and none of their damn business," Buck said, clearly losing patience with the debate. "And number two, no one has to know. BP got away with it and they're a helluva lot more important and well known than Comanche or Hawk. Hell, they contaminated the entire Gulf and the only concern anyone had was for sunbathers and birds. No one even mentioned higher oil prices."

"You got my vote. Gotta make hay while the sun shines," Junior added.

Harvey nodded in agreement. "What's the next step?"

"Hey, there is no next step. I just wanted to see what y'all were thinking; wanted to rile y'all up a little, but I did notice while I was coming down the driveway there was a tractor a little too close to the pipelines in zone four."

Chapter 53 □ □ □

Jeremy put aside the analysis and returned to the market. He would pick it up later when there was a lull and when the emotion about seeing his concerns confirmed in actual data subsided. As he looked at the scrolling headlines cross his monitors, one story was of more than passing interest. *"Hack Proof Systems to be acquired by private equity concern."* Parthenon held an interest in the stock and Jeremy smiled, knowing they would make a nice profit on the position. He double clicked on the headline and read through the text that appeared. Then a thought hit him; an uncomfortable thought. He picked up the phone.

"Lauren Wilkes."

"It's Jeremy."

"Was everything okay?" She asked enthusiastically.

"The copies came out fine. Do you have time to come to my office?"

"On my way."

Turning the corner in the hallway, she collided with Marty who was coming the other way. "Sorry, I'm in a bit of a hurry."

"Where's the fire?"

"No fire. Jeremy wants to see me."

"During trading hours? What's going on?"

Lauren continued walking. "I'm sure it's a systems problem," she responded, instantly regretting that she mentioned where she was headed.

"Must be a serious glitch if he called you instead of the help desk," she surmised as Lauren quickened her pace down the hallway, ignoring the comment.

"Come in and shut the door, please." Jeremy gave Lauren a minute to get comfortable. "Something has been bothering me about this data." He held the spreadsheet in his hands.

"I can lay it out another way or size the columns differently," she offered, tensing at the hint of a mistake on her part.

"No, there's nothing wrong with how it's presented."

Lauren relaxed.

Jeremy continued. "I still don't know why Paul would have deleted this file from his computer, even from the Recycle Bin. It's not as if he erased his entire drive when he left the office every night. Why just this file?"

"It struck me as strange too," Lauren offered in agreement, "particularly since there were other files in the Recycle Bin that were time stamped earlier than when he began work on this project."

Jeremy took a breath. "Before I go on, let's clear the air. I know you're in a tough spot. Vernon runs the firm, so ultimately he's your boss, and here I am essentially asking you to check up on him."

"I can't say I'm not at least a little confused, not to mention stressed, but I'm relying on Paul's seal of approval and my instincts. He always used to joke that if you and he ever started your own firm that he would take me along."

"And how did you feel about that? Would it be tough to walk out of Parthenon?"

"As long as we're sharing confidences, Vernon hasn't said two words to me since I started here. I don't think it's any secret that he doesn't see a lot of value in any function except managing money." A light seemed to go on behind Lauren's eyes. "Is that it? Are you starting your own firm? Count me in." Her face flushed with embarrassment. "That was pretty forward. I don't even know if you want to hire me."

"I'm flattered but I don't have any plans to go anywhere. Let me try and clear this up. I haven't done the best job of staying on top of Vernon's portfolio and recently some issues have come to my attention that I probably should look into. I don't want to quiz Vernon—besides this being his firm, his ego wouldn't tolerate being questioned. But as part of my fiduciary responsibility to our investors, I have to be more involved and better informed. The data that you recovered is the first step."

Lauren had a look of bewilderment. "I appreciate the candor but it sounds like you want something else from me. I'm not clear what it is."

Jeremy continued. "A lot of this doesn't add up. For example, I don't know why Paul would have deleted the file when he hadn't even given it to me yet. Maybe someone else hacked into the system and erased it. I need you to look into it. Knowing when it was deleted would also be helpful."

"Shouldn't be a problem. Getting into our system leaves a trail like a fingerprint on a mirror. Access is time stamped and identified by password."

"Perfect. Let me know as soon as you have something."

Lauren started toward the door as Jeremy remembered something else. "And Lauren, I also need some information on one of our investors, Buck Hendricks. Get hold of his Social Security number. We're required to have it for tax purposes so it should be in his electronic file."

"I'm on it."

Chapter 54 □ □ □

Buck pulled the thin Blackberry from his back pocket as the ring tone broadcast a few bars of Willie Nelson's "On the Road Again."

"Hi Buck. How's the homeland?"

"Damn good to be back here in the real world. What's going on in the big city?"

"I came across something pretty interesting."

"Always working for me; that's what I like. What is it?"

Marty groaned, not entirely unhappy that she was about to cause a shift in Buck's mood. "I was in the Xerox room and came across a copy of Vernon's portfolio."

"So what? Vernon could have told Suzie to print out a copy. He reviews his holdings all the time. That's what any good portfolio manager does."

"Do you think I would call unless there was something more to it than that? This is more than a copy of his portfolio. It's a very thorough analysis of everything he owns."

"Damn it! What the hell happened? I thought you were taking care of that. Who the fuck printed it out?"

"You knew there was a risk that the data was backed up. I told you that. Now calm down so we can think this thing through."

"Don't fucking tell me to calm down. It's my neck on the line here."

"And you don't think I'm caught up in this? I'm pretty damn sure I have less to gain than you. The price just went up or I'm outta here."

"All right, all right. I get it. It's not your fault. Tell me what you're thinking."

"We know Jeremy is behind this. He was the one who asked Paul to do the work. But as smart as Jeremy is, after watching him search Paul's computer, he's clearly no techie. And earlier today, I saw Lauren Wilkes running to his office."

"Who the hell is Lauren Wilkes?"

"She's the CTO, so she has access to everything at the firm."

"Maybe you're jumping to conclusions. Maybe he was just having some computer problems."

"Let me spell it out for you."

"Watch it, girl," Buck cautioned, clearly annoyed. "I can add two plus two; I just don't want to jump to conclusions."

"Okay, okay, I'm sorry but I don't have a lot of time to go through this now and it would be a lot more helpful for you to listen for a second instead of jumping down my throat."

"Go ahead."

"I was able to wipe the file off Paul's drive but there was no way for me to get into the system and erase it from the backup files."

"Why didn't you mention this to me before?"

"Are you kidding? You need me to tell you that Parthenon has done everything possible to keep out hackers and that it has backup copies of its files?"

"No, course not. Go ahead. Finish your thought."

"So if I was in Jeremy's position and wanted to retrieve data from the system involving a potentially sensitive issue, I would go straight to the person in charge of tech." Marty paused to allow Buck to digest her thoughts. "See where I'm going with this?"

"Yup. I sure do and I'm not feeling great about the direction."

"So the only reason Jeremy would see Wilkes during the middle of the trading day was if he had something major to discuss. That's all. There you have it."

Buck whistled into the phone. "Sounds like we have a problem but nothing that can't be fixed."

"Hold on for a second. Right now, the only thing Jeremy knows is that Albright owns too many energy stocks. That seems to be the extent of our problem. Jeremy is very direct and not afraid to speak his mind. My guess is that the next step he takes is to bring his concerns to Albright."

"What concerns? They're making a ton of dough. Even if oil prices come down a bit, they're still way ahead of the game. They should be happier than pigs in shit."

"You really don't get it, do you? You may have good reason to believe that oil prices are on a one-way trip higher, but for those not as enlightened, they perceive substantial risk. Jeremy has to be concerned about how much of the firm's assets depend on one investment theme."

"Okay, I agree with you. Let's see how Albright handles this and keep tabs on Jeremy's reaction. He really has no recourse other than to leave the firm and that would damn sure be the best result for both Albright and me."

"I'm not so sure Albright will agree."

Buck laughed. "I know Vernon a lot better than you. Plain and simple; he's just a greedy bastard. And on top of that, with an ego the size of Texas, there is no way he's letting Jeremy Cranford or anyone else tell him how to run his fund. Trust me, I've tried."

***

Buck considered placing a call to Albright; he didn't want him taken by surprise when Jeremy raised the topic for discussion. Deliberating the pros and cons of the phone call, he ultimately decided not to do anything out of fear of jeopardizing her cover. He was sure Albright would not take kindly to the concept of having a spy in his employ. Instead, he would wait for a further update and hope that Albright would inform him if a bigger problem were brewing. But if Albright kept him in the dark, Buck was more than willing to deal with Cranford on his own. He called in Rock to discuss the options.

Chapter 55 □ □ □

It took Varko most of the afternoon to recover from the interruption. He was fairly certain that George Soros never had to suffer such indignities. The government always picked on the little guy, but he took comfort in knowing that he would not be little forever.

Varko had been doing research on a couple of other stocks. Once Datatech hit his price target, he would sell it and use the gains to invest in other companies. They would, of course, also be great investments. He expected to make enough money to get his wife back, even though it wasn't her that he really cared about; without her, he would never get the kids.

The water for his spaghetti started to boil and he put in half a box, breaking the long strands in half to fit in the undersized pot. Dinner was timed perfectly every night to be eaten during his second favorite television show. Varko couldn't wait to be a guest on *Marketline* and exchange thoughts with his favorite commentator, Lou Lindshel. He often rehearsed for his inevitable appearance on television, sitting on his bed while watching the show, muting the volume when Lindhsel's guests were responding to a question and substituting his own dialogue instead. Varko was often impressed by how quick witted his answers were to Lindhsel's probing questions. After watching some of the nitwits that the producers forced upon him, Lindshel was sure to ask Varko to become a regular. He just didn't know if he wanted to take that much time away from his children since they would have so much catching up to do.

The metal handle was hot to the touch, but Varko didn't

seem to notice as he lifted the pot from the single, portable electric burner and brought it over to the sink to drain. Butter was all the garnish he used, Parmesan cheese an unnecessary luxury. He emptied the spaghetti onto a plastic plate and placed it on the chair that doubled as a dining room table. He then sat on the edge of the bed to eat while he watched Lindshel espouse his market views.

Lindhsel's guests were that prick Sundrick, who interviewed Cranford for the Wall Street Journal, and Taylor Karassik, a small cap hedge fund manager described by Lindshel as a market guru. Sundrick was first on the agenda and Lindshel started off with a lob question. "Bill, I've read your series of articles on the rising price of crude. What's the latest, and will we ever see prices retreat?"

"The latest is that crude is touching an all-time high around $140 a barrel and the consumer is getting absolutely killed at the pump."

"Tell me about it. My wife drives around in a Suburban that gets about seven miles to the gallon—and that's going downhill. Painful."

"And you've got a high-paying television job. Think of what it's doing to families that are just eking by."

"What's the most recent catalyst underlying the move?"

"Production issues mostly. The Kuwaitis took down a pipe for maintenance, BP had that major blowup in the Gulf of Mexico and a couple of companies in Texas had a mishap curtailing their ability to deliver product. Funny how this all happened at pretty much the same time."

"I notice a bit of skepticism in your voice. Doesn't it make sense that if every company is running full out that something may go wrong?"

"You're darn right I'm skeptical. Maintenance updates are carefully scheduled so unplanned outages almost never happen, yet now we are seeing a rash of them. Let me put it to you this way: if you walked into your local drug store to buy a bottle of aspirin, and they told you they were out but come back in a couple of days, the price would not go up just because they temporarily had less supply. The store's owner would actually risk making less money because he didn't have product to sell you. But with crude, if they just knock out supply for a bit or even utter that there may be a supply interruption, the commodity becomes more valuable."

"There must be more to it than that."

Sundrick continued. "The hedge funds keep piling into oil contracts at higher and higher prices, essentially marking up their investment, making it a self-fulfilling prophecy. But here's a word of caution to those playing this game, particularly the ones getting in now, chasing the momentum and hoping a greater fool comes along to buy their position. When this ends—and just like the dotcom and real estate bubbles it will end—a lot of people will go broke. They won't be able to close out their positions fast enough. It'll end very ugly. They may even have to go back to flying commercial like us other working stiffs."

"Fuck them," Varko shouted at the television. "Can't wait for it to happen."

"That's small consolation for today's high prices." Lindshel stood to shake Sundrick's hand signaling it was time for his next guest. "Thanks for stopping by Bill."

Taylor Karassik of Kara Capital hailed from North Carolina, talked in an excruciatingly slow drawl and looked to Varko like the nerdy type that all the kids used to pick on when he was young. With a full head of unruly hair, a loud bow tie and oversized tortoise shell eyeglasses, he played the role of an intellectual well, using big words in sentences that went nowhere.

"Excuse me, Taylor. I have to interrupt. I've been listening to you very intently but I'll be darned if I don't feel like I've walked into the middle of a conversation. I don't mean to be rude but if you can take the syllable content of your words down from eight to four—at the most—our viewers should better be able to understand the message you're trying to deliver."

"Sure, Lou. My apologies. All I was saying is that the inverse correlation of the delta and gamma effects of the derivative hedges makes for a very exciting time in the market. Even though I love stocks, the options market is the tail that wags the dog. No doubt about it."

Varko sensed that Lou was losing patience with this joker.

"Okay, whatever you say. Why don't we talk stocks? You're having a great year. Where do you see the opportunities going forward?"

"We are having a really great year but it is far from over. The way the market has run it may be tougher in the second half for some of our less skilled competitors but I still see plenty of opportunities in small cap stocks."

"What a conceited asshole," Varko said out loud.

"Why don't you share some specifics with our viewers?" Lindshel didn't particularly like Karassik but his colorful attitude and conceited personality kept viewers enthralled.

"Be glad to, but let me warn your retail constituents not to try this at home." Karassik laughed. He was the funniest guy he knew. "Just kidding, Lou. The best way to have positive performance in this environment is on the short side. Valuations have become stretched and as is common in a rally, a lot of really bad companies have benefited from a sympathy move."

"A rising tide lifts all ships," Lindshel added.

"Exactly, Lou. Take a nifty little number like Datatech." Karassik said, clearly tongue in cheek. "This baby was on life support and now it seems like it's on a one-way trip to the moon. It goes up every day."

Varko spit out his food. "That fucking asshole! What the hell is he talking about?"

"The price action must be telling you something. Stocks generally go up for a reason." Lindshel responded in his best devil's advocate voice.

Varko was glad to see Lindshel come to the rescue. He'd shoot this moron down.

"All it's telling me is that there are a lot of idiots out there who don't know what they're buying. I love seeing this because it creates more opportunity for me when I short it."

The plate of food flew across the room, crashing against the opposite wall. Spaghetti flew everywhere. Varko stood and shouted at the screen. White foam bubbled in the corners of his mouth and spittle shot out as he ranted.

Karassik continued. "You can read more about Datatech in next week's newsletter."

"Not if I can help it, scumbag," Varko barked.

"Thank you for your thoughts, Taylor." Lindshel turned back to the camera. "There is much more to come tonight, including our panel at the end of the show. Taylor Karassik and the *Marketline* staff will be available, live, to answer any of your questions. Please call the number that appears at the bottom of your screen if you have a question or comment."

Varko was going to set this joker straight. He dialed the number and received a busy tone. He continued to dial non-stop for fifteen minutes before reaching a recording. "Please stand by while an operator answers your call."

Another two minutes passed before a screener came on the line. "What's the question for our panel?"

Varko was not a novice when it came to getting on the air. It was a lesson that took repeated attempts to learn. "I am a retiree with most of my 401k in stocks. I would like to ask Mr. Karassik what he thinks about a potential rebound in the technology sector."

It was the same question Varko heard someone ask on another show. "Excellent question. You will be caller number three."

The sound portion of the program was broadcast over the telephone lines for callers to listen to while they waited. Varko again became more irate than a wolf caught in a bear trap as he listened to Karassik berate the first caller for his "sophomoric approach to investing." The second caller, an older lady with a question about her husband's pension, was treated slightly better.

"Caller number three, this is Lou Lindshel. I understand that you have a question about technology stocks. Which one of our panel members would you prefer to address it?"

"Taylor Karassik."

"Go ahead."

Varko had trouble controlling his emotions. "What makes you such an expert on technology stocks, Mr. Karassik?"

Lindshel had no love for the arrogant Karassik so he allowed the question. He wanted to see how the pompous ass, who was all of thirty years old, would reply.

Karassik responded snootily. "My track record in this sector speaks for itself."

"Your track record is about to come to an end."

Chapter 56

□ □ □

Varko looked at the clock on the bottom of his television. It was three hours earlier on the West Coast allowing for sufficient time for Varko to call his source at Datatech and find out if the company knew why their stock was down on the day. That's what professionals did. They did research. Even though the constant dialing of the company's phone number had been forever etched into his memory, out of habit Varko extracted a tattered piece of paper from the back pocket of his well-worn, dark gray chinos. He looked at the ten digit, toll-free number and dialed.

"Investor Relations, this is Rebecca Sinclair."

"I'm calling to make sure everything is okay."

Rebecca immediately recognized the voice and wondered why she always seemed to answer the phone when he called. "Everything is the same as it was yesterday, Mr. Varko. The company is doing fine."

Rebecca was the most junior employee in the Investor Relations department at Datatech, placed in her current position because she had a friendly personality and the patience to deal with the large retail investor base that owned most of Datatech stock. Part of her job required convincing the callers that she was well informed about the company's activities. In reality she only knew what her bosses wanted her to know which wasn't much more than what was offered on Datatech's web site. The professional money managers and analysts dealt directly with the chief financial officer or other members of senior management.

"There's another jerk shorting your stock out there. Some guy named Karassik."

"We've had experience with Mr. Karassik before and it has never been pleasant—I personally don't like the man— but I have no clue as to why he is shorting our stock. As I said, our current outlook is consistent with what we have said in our latest reports. The business is performing well."

"Maybe you should give him a call and tell him that. He's not doing us any good by going on television and lying about you folks."

"That's not really my job, Mr. Varko, but I'll mention it to senior management."

Varko looked at the scrolling tape and saw that DTCH had declined by fifty cents in the aftermarket.

"When will they call him? They need to do it right away."

"They may not reach out to Mr. Karassik. Management believes that the stock price will follow the company's performance. The company continues to perform within our plan."

"That's good to hear but in the meantime I'm losing my shirt."

Rebecca read from the script provided by her manager. "I'm sorry but we can't be responsible for the stock price on a day to day basis. The management of Datatech is committed to increasing shareholder value over the long term."

"Well, the short term matters to me and a lot of other people, too. I've been at this trading business for a long time and have some good ideas for you to tell your bosses about. I have a way for them to handle the shorts. Maybe they'll even give you a raise."

When Rebecca took this job, she never thought she'd have to deal with creeps like Varko. Her patience was wearing thin. "I don't think they would be interested. They stopped taking calls from Karassik and Cranford a long time ago."

"Jeremy Cranford from Parthenon?"

"Yes. Everyone knows Cranford and Karassik are the biggest shorts in the stock."

Varko was having trouble controlling his anger. "But Cranford told me he wasn't short anymore."

"I've already said more than I should. Have a good day, sir." *Maybe he'll leave me alone and start bothering them.*

As he hung up the phone, the Datatech logo, accompanied by a chart of the stock price, crossed the screen. He reached over and turned up the volume in time to hear the voiceover.

"On a day when the overall market is up three percent, Datatech shares have reversed its earlier gains and are now trading down ten percent. Company sources say business is going well but a guest speaker on our *MarketWrap* segment disagrees. Be sure to watch at eight o'clock tonight when we visit again with Taylor Karassik of Kara Capital, who will share his thoughts on this and other short ideas."

Varko paced back and forth across the floor, wringing his hands, shaking his head and mumbling aloud. Deciding that sufficient time had passed for Karassik to have returned to his office, Varko retrieved the phone number for Kara Capital from Directory Assistance. It was still only six o'clock, too early for a hedge fund manager to call it a day.

Disguising his voice, he spoke with the receptionist. "I have Mr. Ernest Varko calling for Taylor Karassik."

Varko was transferred to Karassik's personal secretary and repeated the announcement.

"Will Mr. Karassik know what this call is about?"

"He will want to speak with Mr. Varko. Mr. Varko is a very famous trader."

The response was polite but cool. "I am sorry sir but Mr. Karassik is very busy and does not wish to speak with strangers. Good-bye."

Click.

Varko was furious. He resumed pacing back and forth across the worn out remnant. Then he had a thought. Varko grabbed the one suit that he owned, the one he wore on those long ago Sundays when he used to go to church with his family. He put on a wrinkled polyester dress shirt with fraying cuffs and collar, age having turned it more gray than white. He attached the clip-on tie to his collar, patted down his hair and headed out the door. It would be a great *MarketWrap* segment: point and counter point. Karassik was sure to agree. Varko had practiced his role many times.

Chapter 57 □ □ □

After the market closed, Jeremy reviewed the day's action, studying various screens on his Bloomberg in search of any patterns among certain sectors or the general market that he could turn into profits the following day. He reflected on the opportunities he had missed and mistakes he had made. Second guessing went with the job. The market was an unrelenting critic.

Jeremy's concern over Vernon's portfolio and his relationship with Buck Hendricks hadn't dissipated with the market's absorption of his concentration. He pulled the spreadsheet from the drawer where he had placed it as protection from prying eyes. He reviewed all the columns again and the cryptic notes he had written in the margins. A nagging thought still held his mind at bay. The incoming call offered no respite. It was Lauren.

"Sorry Jeremy, no luck on Buck Hendricks."

"What's that mean?" he responded, clearly baffled. "We don't have information on our largest outside investor? That doesn't sound right unless he's investing through a holding company or similar entity."

"I had the same thought, so I reviewed our database of individual investors. We have complete information for everyone."

Jeremy continued to be impressed by Lauren's initiative and wondered why he hadn't noticed it before. "That's disappointing."

"Well...there's more. I came across a large corporate investor who has an address at Banque de Union of Switzerland in Geneva."

Jeremy slapped the side of the desk, "Of course. I should have thought of that. Why wouldn't he try to shelter as much money as he could from paying taxes and at the same time hide his identity through a corporation? And Swiss banks add another level of secrecy."

"I'm not a tax attorney but how can a U.S. citizen do that? Why wouldn't everyone do the same thing to avoid paying taxes?"

"Aside from the fact that it's illegal, these are very sophisticated financial shenanigans."

Lauren's expression darkened. This entire episode was more than a little unsettling for someone who until just a day ago was more concerned about a systems crash than the ongoing viability of Parthenon. "I don't mind telling you, Jeremy, that as much as I'm trying to be levelheaded about this, it is getting tougher."

"Believe me, I don't feel particularly good about pulling you into this but I have no one else to rely on, and there's too much at stake to not look into these issues. We owe it to our investors and employees, including you. Hendricks's tax issues are his problems and not ours."

"That's not making me feel better. I never pictured myself as a superhero or martyr. I can't afford to be out of work."

"You won't be. Either things work out here or I'll start my own firm and bring you with me. Look at it this way: if there are issues with Parthenon, they would come to the surface anyway, so all we're doing is getting in front of them. Isn't it better knowing what's going on than walking in one day and being surprised?"

"Thanks, but I'm not sure that makes me feel any more comfortable, but I do appreciate your candor." Lauren paused, reflecting on the situation. "For some reason, I'm not sure why, I trust you."

"You trust me because Paul trusted me and knew me forever. I'm also a no BS person. Now take a deep breath and tell me what else you found."

Lauren inhaled, then slowly let the air release from her lungs. "The company that stuck out for obvious reasons is Bronco Partners, Inc. It actually struck me as a strange name for an account domiciled in Europe—so out of place. Gaucho, maybe," she said in a rare show of humor, "but Bronco is such an American word. And the size of Bronco's investment in Parthenon really caught my eye."

"Good work. Thanks. We'll talk more later."

***

Jeremy reached out to Tom Wichefski. "Hendricks' social is not on file with us."

"How do you report his investment income to the IRS if you don't have his social security number?"

"Because we think that he's using a corporation as his investment vehicle, although we only have the company name and transfer agent so far."

Wichefski was trained in white-collar crime and knew all the dodges—both legal and illegal. "Interesting. I'm going to take a guess and say that the nominee for his interests in the fund is a Swiss Bank."

"You nailed it. But at least we have the company name. It's Bronco Partners, Inc."

"Must have taken him awhile to come up with such a brilliant alias," Tom chortled.

"Guess he doesn't have the most creative imagination."

"Yeah, well his lack of creativity and the fact he's still in a Swiss bank could be a good thing." Wichefski sounded optimistic. "He's probably had that account for a while since the Swiss have recently begun to share information with us when we can convince their courts that one of their depositors is a tax cheat. I'll ask the foreign desk to investigate the relationship between Buck and Bronco."

"Great. Thanks."

"Have you spoken with Albright yet?"

"No, I haven't," Jeremy responded, slightly defensive about not providing a more definitive answer. "Still debating the pros and cons. But I'm coming down on the side of confronting him, particularly as we bring more people into the discussion. Information always seems to slip out despite the best intentions. He would really—and understandably—be pretty pissed off if he heard about this from a third party rather than directly from me."

"If and when you do have a conversation, I'd appreciate a heads up beforehand."

"Sure but why do you need to know before we speak?"

"Who knows how Vernon will react, or Buck if he finds out? They could destroy any evidence or become violent. I've seen it before—even with people you'd never imagine were capable of flying off into a violent rage. I'm more concerned with Buck, since we hardly know anything about him except for what you told me about his reaction when you told him to stuff his offer to set you up in a fund."

"I appreciate the concern."

Jeremy again weighed his alternatives. Sit on the sidelines and wait for Tom to uncover additional information that may provide some clarity, or confront Albright now and risk alienating his partner with suspicions that may be unfounded. No matter what he decided, his career and, possibly, his considerable savings, were at risk. With most of his liquid net worth invested in the fund, a disaster at Parthenon would mean financial ruin. He couldn't just quit and take all his money because if the fund subsequently blew up he could be accused by Parthenon's investors of "knowing something" and putting his interests above those he had a fiduciary duty to protect. Tom's yellow flag about Buck's potential reaction also gave him pause; they hardly knew what Hendricks was capable of.

As it would turn out, Tom's words were more than cautionary—they were prophetic.

Chapter 58

□ □ □

Kara Capital, LLC was based in a townhouse on Sixty-Seventh Street off Park Avenue. The bottom two floors were converted into office space while Taylor Karassik used the upper two levels for his living quarters. As impossible as it was for an outsider to distinguish where Karassik lived versus where he worked, it was harder for Karassik to separate his professional life from his personal. Running a hedge fund was all he cared about. Despite his ego, or maybe because of it, he was a fast rising star among money managers and had already accumulated a net worth in excess of two hundred million dollars.

Varko had thought about storming into the offices of Kara Capital and debating the merits of investing in Datatech but knew there was no chance of getting past the front door if he couldn't even get through on the phone. Karassik would be leaving for the studio soon. Varko crossed to the other side of the street, sat down on a stoop and waited.

At seven fifteen the shiny mahogany door opened and Taylor Karassik appeared in the vestibule of his building, atop the small staircase that led to the sidewalk. Varko rose from his makeshift seat and crossed the street. As Karassik came toward the curb, a stretch limousine pulled up and its driver hopped out. Varko cursed his luck. Now he would never get to reason with him. But good fortune finally found its way to Varko's side as Karassik waved off his driver.

"It's been a long day, Dwayne, and I need some air. I'll walk."

Dwayne got back in the car and drove off.

"Excuse me, Taylor, but could I have a few seconds of your time."

Karassik kept walking, ignoring Varko's entreaty. He tried again. "Excuse me, but there is something we need to discuss."

Karassik was in his own world, at first paying no attention to the person trying to get his attention. On Varko's second attempt, Karassik responded after slowing to regard the stranger's nearly threadbare attire. "Get a job," he sneered.

Did this arrogant prick really think he was asking for spare change? Karassik had no idea how much he could learn from this conversation. "I'm not looking for anything from you. I'm trying to make you some money, or at least stop you from losing it."

"Oh, I get it. You're a fan. Look, if *you* want to make some money, watch me on *MarketWrap* tonight. Maybe you'll learn something."

"I don't think you understand. You're about to make a fool of yourself bashing Datatech again. It's a great company—I just spoke with them and things couldn't be better."

Karassik had run into at least one of these losers after almost every television appearance, but it was usually a more lighthearted conversation and took place in some upscale restaurant during a meal.

"The company's full of shit. That baby's a zero. I hope you don't own it because if you do you're fucked."

Varko poked Karassik in the chest. "You think you're a better trader than me just because you talk on T.V.? You're not. If scumbags like you stopped bashing the stock, Datatech would be trading at fifty by now."

Karassik didn't take to being talked to in that manner by anyone. He sized up Varko's slight frame and figured that if it came to it, he'd have no trouble with him. Still, he was due at the studio and didn't have the time to get into it with this bozo.

"No, I'm not better than you. I just have a different view. Why don't you call my secretary and she can schedule us for lunch. You seem like an engaging fellow; I would love to hear your views on the market."

"Don't patronize me. It's important that I know what you're going to say on Datatech. That's all I want."

"What do you want me to say?"

"Say the truth. That it's a great company and that you were wrong about what you said earlier."

"I've really got to go." He turned and quickened his stride. "Let me do you a favor. You've got twenty minutes to find some third market buyer to take it off your hands before I crush it in front of a national audience."

"I can't let you do that."

Varko thrust the thick hunting knife into the middle of Karassik's back, pulling it out and plunging it back into the tensing mass four more times. The cuts were so deep and came upon him so swiftly that Karassik didn't even have the time or strength to scream out in pain. His victim fell to the sidewalk and lay there in pain, blood seeping out of the multiple wounds, but Varko was not finished. He reared his leg back and kicked Karassik with all his might. That was the final act, stilling the body.

As Varko stood over his victim, smiling, he realized with certainty that he held the power. Not that he ever doubted it, but this proved his power once and for all. And he knew he wasn't done. One more loose end to tie up and Datatech shares would rise to their true value. Growing impatient waiting for the natural forces of the marketplace to take effect, he decided to help them along. He had seen it time and time again; sentiment could change on a dime, but before it could reverse course the selling pressure would have to abate. His opponents didn't fight fair so neither would he. After all, the smartest traders didn't wait for events to occur, they made them happen. It was within his power to remove that one remaining impediment to his ascension to the pinnacle of Wall Street and getting his family back.

Chapter 59 □ □ □

Jeremy walked into Vernon's office and sat in a chair facing the desk. He marveled at how, despite the late afternoon hour, Vernon could look as fresh as when he began the day. Not one hair was out of place, no five o'clock shadow and not one wrinkle on his starched white shirt—no visible scars from his daily battle with the market.

Vernon turned his attention from a document he was reading to Jeremy. "Are we starting tomorrow's morning meeting early, or do you have something on your mind?"

Jeremy smiled but said nothing.

"Judging by your furrowed brow, there's something on your mind."

Jeremy delivered his opening discourse with absolute sincerity. "I took your criticism to heart about being too absorbed in my own portfolio to care about the rest of the firm."

Albright drummed his fingers on the desk. "Can the details about your catharsis wait until tomorrow? I'm trying to get—"

"No, it can't wait," Jeremy firmly interjected, "Let's have this discussion now." He continued without pausing for a reaction. "As I was saying, I have decided to shoulder my share of the management responsibilities. In fact, I am well into my first high level initiative."

Vernon twirled a twenty-four carat Mount Blanc pen between his fingers. "I've got a dinner engagement. Would you mind skipping the preamble and getting to the punch line?"

"Of course. The punch line is that I'm very uncomfortable with your massive exposure in energy. If the market has more than a slight correction, we're toast."

As if struck by a lightning bolt, Vernon shot upright in his chair. Jeremy sat firm and waited for the eruption. He saw the tension build in Vernon's neck, watched his shoulders stiffen and thought he could feel the impact of the gold pen being slammed to the desk, breaking it in half. But Jeremy didn't flinch, didn't react at all. He had witnessed similar outbursts before, although being both the cause and the target was new to him. And this was early in the conversation; it was certain to get more confrontational.

Even their respective demeanors were in conflict; Jeremy's stoicism versus Vernon's struggle to reclaim his composure. Vernon fought hard to contain his anger at being called on the carpet by Jeremy, by anyone for that matter. But there was more at stake here than showing his young charge who was the boss. He had to find out if Jeremy's concern was limited to poor risk management or was the beachhead for larger issues.

Vernon consciously relaxed his angry expression, subconsciously turning it into an unattractive smirk. "Is that so? And exactly how do you define massive?"

"I would classify a thirty percent allocation to a particular sector as aggressive; fifty percent would be reckless and anything above that would be irresponsible." Jeremy steeled his look. "I hope that gives you an indication of the parameters for my discomfort, since you appear to be in the ultra-uncomfortable zone."

"I don't recall providing you with a copy of my portfolio, not that I've tried to keep it a secret. How did you get it?"

"Now that you mention it, I was surprised that I couldn't find a copy of it on the system, but I didn't want to bother you while you were in Monaco. Instead, I had Paul construct a very general outline of your holdings from some bits of data we had."

"So you're in MY office, challenging MY control over

MY portfolio based upon a few crumbs of cobbled-together data? But assuming your detective work has some legitimacy, it's not unusual for us to make a concentrated bet particularly when our research is so strongly supportive. Energy is as close to a sure bet as I have ever seen."

"Let's cut the bullshit. No amount of research could justify the size of our position. And you know as well as anyone that there are no sure things in this business. That is unless someone, say a Buck Hendricks for example, was helping you with your research."

Vernon sprung to his feet as his chair flew back, crashing against the wall. He jammed his finger in the air, directly at Jeremy. "Who the hell are you to question my integrity or that of our largest investor? Buck Hendricks was part of Parthenon long before you." His voice rose in volume. "And who the hell are you to check up on me? You work for me; I don't work for you. I did pretty well before you joined Parthenon and I'll do just as well after you're long gone. This is my fucking firm and I'll do what I damn well please with my portfolio! And with yours too for that matter. If I want to put one hundred percent of the assets into technology or metals or energy, then that's what I'll damn well do."

Jeremy stood, face to face with his partner, mentor and boss. "It may be your *fucking firm* as you put it, but I have a responsibility to the investors, of which I am one. I'm not going to sit idly by while you take unconscionable amounts of risk. And I'm damn sure not going to pretend I don't know what's going on while you put the fate of this firm and my career in the hands of Buck Hendricks."

"Incredible! You've been doing this for all of a few years and now you're the expert. I give you a taste of success and suddenly you know what's best for *MY* firm. You don't wear greed well, my boy, not well at all."

"Ha! That's rich coming from you."

Vernon took in a breath and sat down. "Before we do any more damage to our relationship, let's take a step back and cool off. We can pick this up in the morning after we have each had a chance to collect our thoughts. I know I could use the respite."

"At least we can agree on that. We both have enough to reflect on at this point."

Chapter 60

□ □ □

Jeremy returned to his office, grabbed his jacket and left. He had no desire to revisit the discussion with Albright, which was sure to happen if he stayed in the office. As he moved along with the rush hour traffic, he reflected upon the confrontation and quickly concluded that he had handled it poorly. He regretted being so confrontational, so out of control. He violently slapped the steering wheel in frustration. With his fingers tingling, he decided he had spent enough time wallowing in the self-pity of second guesses and that it was time to pursue a more constructive path. He mentally jotted down the pluses and minuses of his tenure at Parthenon. Sure, Vernon had hired and mentored him but, as Paul had repeatedly said, he had already repaid that debt many times over. Sure, Vernon generously compensated Jeremy, but that was in direct correlation to the profits he had generated. Loyalty did not extend to taking the verbal abuse that Vernon was prone to dishing out, even if Jeremy received, until recently, much less than others at the firm. And finally, who was owed greater loyalty: Jeremy's family and Parthenon's investors, or Albright? That issue, Jeremy reasoned, couldn't be separated from his fiduciary responsibility, which was a legal principle that held much more significant penalties than anything Vernon could do to him.

There really was no debate. Jeremy had wanted to voice his concerns for a long time. He was tired of being a partner in name only, tired of being an appendage to a massive ego that was abusive to loyal employees such as Larry Janowicz, the night trader, and Don Jackson, the junior PM,

and the scores of people that Vernon had churned through
Parthenon's doors. He had no interest in an association with
anyone who skirted the law, if that in fact were the case. It
was all coming to a head.

***

Although he had hoped that this day would never arrive,
Vernon had also known that a confrontation was inevitable.
While he cared for Jeremy, he cared more for being the
unchallenged master of his domain. He had risen to the pinnacle of fund management without Jeremy's help and didn't
need him to maintain his stature. Smart and industrious
employees—and make no mistake about it, Jeremy was an
employee—came with a price. They were prone to outliving
their usefulness, becoming a distraction, a management
headache, wanting more than they were worth. And this
was worse. Albright understood his vulnerability and what
was at stake; how some overreaching SEC minion bent on
teaching the rich and powerful masters of the universe
a lesson, from the perch of their forty-thousand-dollar-a-
year public servant job could misinterpret the customary
standard of "maintaining an edge."

No one was going to bring Vernon Albright down, least
of all someone whom he had made a very rich man. But
firing Jeremy or letting him resign wouldn't necessarily
make this problem go away. Were Jeremy to start his own
firm, as he was sure to do, there was a good chance he could
take a significant number of the limited partners with him.
The implications could be disastrous. Losing the fees and
earnings on more than half the assets would surely hurt, but
that was the least of his concerns. Jeremy's departure would
fuel speculation that something was amiss at Parthenon.
For hedge fund managers, the downside of operating under
a cloak of secrecy was that investors would turn tail and
run at the first hint of trouble. Investors were loyal only
to the extent that they believed their money was safe and
they were earning a good return. Once their confidence
waned, they headed for the exits; no one wanted to be the

last one out since there was no guarantee any funds would be left to redeem their interests. Parthenon would likely buckle under a wave of redemption requests. And, as often happened, someone in government would seek to prop up a waning political career by calling upon the SEC to launch a full scale investigation since the failure of a multi-billion-dollar hedge fund benefiting only rich people could have a devastating effect on the working family and their nest egg. Shark-like hedge funds, aware that Parthenon would have to liquidate at least a portion of its portfolio, would look at the public filings depicting the firm's holdings and beat those stocks down by selling them short, compounding their loss in value. The losses would spiral up at an intense rate.

The worst-case scenarios danced through Albright's imagination like a series of nightmares: financial ruin, social ostracizing and court ordered pin stripes. It would all happen at breakneck speed. And perhaps most damaging, Jeremy would talk.

Albright had worked himself into a rage. He picked up the phone and called his other partner, his true partner, Buck Hendricks.

***

Buck slammed the receiver into the cradle, furious at Albright for not being able to control his people. The worry in Albright's tone exacerbated his own concerns. The plan had been going so well; crude was reaching new highs on an almost daily basis. He was getting wealthier, literally by the minute, as world commodity markets traded around the clock. He went over to the bar in the living room and withdrew a bottle of Chivas. He filled a shot glass to the top and threw it back in one gulp. Then he had another.

Buck sat on the sofa and tilted his head back against the cushion, clasping his hands behind his neck. He closed his eyes tight and put his mind to work. Deciding he had no choice but to act quickly and decisively, he dialed Rock's

number. Rock would handle it. That's what he was there
for.

Chapter 61

□   □   □

Under the cover of darkness, he knelt behind the hedges and lay in wait for his target. The house was dark, providing a sense of relief that the target had not yet arrived home. He was careful not to draw notice in the quiet neighborhood. The treetops, thick with leafage, caught the illumination of the streetlights interrupting their descent. With the houses so far apart, he could easily retrace his path back through the yard undetected.

Growing weary from the boredom of surveillance, he put the gun down and closed his eyes for a few seconds. Fresh eyes were of vital importance. Each shot had to count; there was no margin for error. The gunman's brief respite ended with the sound of footsteps echoing from the pavement across the street. The shooter steeled an elbow on his bent leg and aimed. Two bullets whispered through the attached silencer. That was all he needed to bring down his target. There was no doubt. He was dead.

Chapter 62

□ □ □

The wail of sirens unceremoniously broke through the silence, emitting a sound rarely heard in the affluent neighborhood. Every available police car, six in all, converged on the Cranford home, joined within minutes by an ambulance from each of the two local hospitals. The medical technicians from Saint Barnabas Hospital gave way to the crew from Overlook, respecting their territorial advantage. A gurney was pulled from the rear of their vehicle and the aluminum legs snapped straight. A portable defibrillator was placed on top of the thin foam mattress and rolled toward the sidewalk, where a cop was weaving yellow tape around tree trunks to cordon off the area.

"Save your energy. All you need is a body bag. Guy was dead before he hit the ground. And watch where you walk. This is still a crime scene."

The paramedic looked at the large pool of blood that surrounded the upper part of the victim's prone torso, a reflection of the hovering trees visible in the shiny dark liquid illuminated by the portable strobes.

"Yup, he's long gone. Let us know when the techies are finished and we'll take him away." The driver went back into the ambulance and pulled out a bag from McDonald's. Grease stains spotted the white paper sack.

The cop looked on in disbelief. "How the hell can you eat, watching this? I'm ready to puke."

"Hey, I'm starving and I'm not about to waste a good meal." He paused to take a bite and then continued with a mouth full of a Big Mac. The cop backed up to avoid the flying bits of food coming his way. "Besides, I've seen worse on CSI."

It was another twenty minutes or so until the detectives finished combing the area for unspent bullets or casings and photographing the crime scene. As the last flash went off, Jennifer drove up in her hunter green Suburban, stopping at a Town of Summit saw horse that formed a makeshift roadblock three doors down from her house. Confined to their car seats, Melissa and Alexandra strained to look out the window at the flashing red and blue lights.

Melissa was particularly captivated. "Ooh, Mommy, those lights are so pretty!"

Alexandra, being older, had a more acute sense of the scene. "What are all those policemen doing at our house?"

"I'm sure it's nothing girls; probably just a little traffic accident," Jennifer responded, her voice trembling slightly. She struggled to hold herself together. "You two wait in your car seats while Mommy speaks to the policeman." Jennifer alit from the car and ushered the cop away. Imagining the worst, she didn't want the children to overhear the conversation.

"Are you Mrs. Cranford?" the officer inquired.

"Yes! How did you know? Did something happen to my husband? Is he okay?" Tears formed in her eyes.

The cop took her by the arm, turning her away from the scene as the body was being hoisted onto the stretcher. Thankfully the children focused on their mother and not the activity in front of their home.

"Look at Mommy. She's holding hands with the policeman."

"Why is she crying?" Melissa asked, concern in her young voice.

"I know who you are because one of your neighbors pointed you out as you drove up. We checked your house and no one is home. Our best guess is that the victim was shot during a dispute of some sort."

The tears flowed in relief and she grabbed the cop's arms

with both hands, a grip so tight that he flinched. "You're saying that's not my husband? That's not Jeremy?"

The cop looked puzzled. "You thought...oh. I'm so sorry. I didn't realize. No, thankfully that's not your husband."

"Thank you. Oh my God! Thank you!" She could have hugged him.

"Victim's driver's license says his name is Ernest Varko and he's not from around here. Do you know him?"

"Never heard of him. Poor guy. How did he die?" Jennifer sighed.

"I'm not sure I would hold a pity party for him yet. Judging from the size of the knife he had concealed in his waistband, he was up to no good."

"Oh my God!"

Alexandra banged on the window, catching Jennifer's attention. She wiped her cheeks, smiled and waved at her daughter. "One second, honey," she said before turning back to the officer. "I don't get it. It sounds like you're describing a scene from a movie, except this is Summit, New Jersey. Nothing ever happens in this town."

"I'm with you. There hasn't been a homicide here for more years than anyone can remember, but you read the local papers. The town's had a number of burglaries and I'm betting that Varko was involved. He and his accomplice likely had a disagreement and I'll give you one guess who won."

"But he's not dressed like a burglar."

"The stationhouse gets a ton of calls from homeowners every time they see someone in their neighborhood who they don't know, particularly if the stranger doesn't look like he belongs. Varko probably thought he was being clever by dressing in a suit."

Jennifer nodded toward the body bag being wheeled away on the gurney. "He doesn't seem so clever now."

The cop leaned one hand on his nightstick and the other on his holster, both affixed to a utility belt that hung low on his waist. He threw his head back and laughed. "I guess he doesn't, does he?"

Alexandra expressed her growing impatience by banging on the car's window and shouting, "Mommy!"

Jennifer turned to her and smiled again. She held up one finger before turning toward the officer, "When will I be able to get into my house?"

"The forensic team is going to be here for a while, doing their thing." He paused. "Could I offer some advice?"

"Absolutely. I'm new at this crime scene thing."

"I'm happy to hear that," he chuckled. "For what it's worth, I don't think you're going to get much rest if you stay here tonight. It's probably a good idea to take the family to a relative's or a hotel for the night."

"Yeah, I guess the girls have seen enough of this activity for one day. I should get going before they have a meltdown. Thanks."

"Glad to help."

She opened the car door and posed one last question. "Is there a chance the shooter could come back here?"

"Only if you think you're living in a Hitchcock movie. This isn't the type of crime you hang around for. Whoever did the shooting is getting as far away from this place as possible."

***

Charlie Morris hadn't investigated a homicide since his days as a New York City detective. After twenty years on the force, tired of the gangs, drug dealers, politics and low pay, he retired with a full lieutenant's pension. Moving to New Jersey to be closer to his parents and siblings, he quickly became bored with his new idyllic existence and joined the Summit Police Department, filling a need they had for a veteran detective.

Charlie appeared to be bothered by something. "Why would a guy from New York be walking around one of the best neighborhoods in town with a hunting knife strapped to his waist?"

"Seems like he was looking to jack someone up," offered his rookie partner, Ben Sullivan.

"Could be but what bothers me is that he has a couple of bullets in his heart. I saw these types of shootings in the Bronx but never thought I'd see one here."

"Maybe he picked the wrong dude to screw with or had a fight with an accomplice about splitting up the booty."

Morris rubbed his chin in thought. "I doubt that. According to forensics, there's no gunpowder residue so he clearly wasn't shot at close range. Assuming that's correct, the shooter was damn good. He put slugs right into the victim's heart." Morris spanned the immediate area, trying to picture what vantage point the shooter may have used. "My guess is the victim didn't even know he was a target. If he did why would the knife still be in his pants?"

"Maybe a neighbor shot him; thought he was too suspicious."

"How the hell did you make detective? Is your Daddy the mayor? Does this look like the type of place where people fire guns out of their windows at strangers? Besides, we took statements from everyone on the block and they're either too old to notice or too young and rich to give a shit. And just how many of these folks are expert marksman?"

"Sorry, that was pretty stupid. Guess I have a lot to learn."

"You can start learning when you get back to the station. Run this guy's name through NCIC."

"I learned about that database in training."

"Yeah, the FBI does a great job with it. It's not always totally current but at least we should be able to find out if there are any outstanding warrants on this character or if he has a record."

"I'm on it."

"I'm sure this isn't the first time Ernest Varko has been in trouble, although it's definitely going to be the last."

Chapter 63 □ □ □

When Vernon heard the news from Buck, his first thoughts were of regret. He had regret for how close he had become with Jeremy; regret for not controlling him better; regret for starting the chain of events that led to his death. He sat in his study and stared at the pictures that framed the room. His eyes rested upon a photo taken at Parthenon's annual partners' dinner. Vernon sat between Jeremy and Paul, each with a glass of champagne in their hands and a large Cuban cigar in their mouths, smiles on their faces. A tear came to his eye, although he was unsure if it was because he lost a friend or because he feared losing his freedom.

But Vernon soon rallied to his own defense, rationalizing his complicity. After all, one of them had to go and he was Vernon Albright. Neither losing his fortune nor his freedom were options he was willing to face. Cranford was an ingrate; he spoiled a good thing; he was disloyal. He forced Albright's hand with Buck. Besides, Jennifer and the children were very well provided for. They would get by wonderfully—all because of Albright.

Chapter 64

□ □ □

Jennifer drove a few blocks from the scene and pulled over to the curb. Although experiencing relief from her most dire thoughts, her nerves had not yet leveled off. She looked at the dashboard clock and dialed Jeremy's cell.

"Where are you now?" Her words touched together, concern quickening her speech.

"About ten minutes from home. You sound a little edgy. Everything okay?"

"We're all fine; just a little shaken. There was an incident outside our house."

"What sort of incident?"

"Someone was murdered."

"What! Anyone we know? Were you and the girls home when it happened?"

"No. We arrived after but I don't think we missed it by much." Jennifer spoke quietly as the girls intently watched a video on the screen that dropped down from the car's ceiling. "I spoke with one of the cops on the scene. He didn't have a lot of information but seemed to think that the man was going to break into a house—could have been ours for all he knows—but before he could do anything, he got shot."

"The cops shot him?"

"No. They believe he had an accomplice and that they probably got into an argument."

"How do they know that?" Jeremy asked.

"Since it just happened, I don't think they really know anything yet. My biggest concern is the killer coming back to the area, but the police were very adamant that he wouldn't. They also suggested that I take the girls some-where else for the night since they're working right in front of our house and it's going to be pretty busy. We're on our way to the Hilton but I don't have any fresh clothes for anyone; I just wanted to get away from there as quickly as possible."

Jeremy's stomach fluttered and he felt unsettled. There was way too much going on and none of it was good. His instincts gnawed at him; these were more than a series of isolated instances.

"I'll stop home to pick up a few things and meet you at the hotel. We'll make it an adventure for the kids, a mini-vacation with room service."

As frazzled as she seemed, there was no point in re-counting his conversation with Albright. There would be plenty of opportunity for discussion after the children were asleep. Together, they would decide what to do next. Jeremy realized that his career at Parthenon was most likely coming to an end, although he had seen Vernon act irrationally before only to do an about face and come to his senses later on. This time, however, was different. He was fairly certain that he would be moving on. He parked his car abreast of the bright orange cones that were set out to keep traffic away from the crime scene. He walked the remaining half block, pausing to speak with the investigators outside his house. They repeated what Jennifer had said, which didn't ease his sense of foreboding. He continued into the house and packed an overnight bag. Pajamas for the kids, a few stuffed animals, fresh clothes for him and Jennifer, and toiletries.

Back in the car, he called Wichefski. "I have a new name for you to check out. Ernest Varko. He was gunned down right on my block, actually in front of my house."

"Was he a neighbor?"

"Nope."

"For such a good guy you seem to have an awful lot of gray clouds following you; way too many for it all to be a coincidence." Wichefski sounded incredulous. "I'm starting to get a little worried myself."

"No kidding. How would you like to be me right now? The police seem to think that it was part of a botched robbery attempt, but I don't have much faith in what they're saying. I don't think they do either."

"Tell you what. I'll run his name through NCIC and see what comes up. How was your conversation with Vernon?"

"To say it didn't go well would be an understatement, but I don't have time to give you the details. Bottom line is that Vernon denied any improprieties and was incredibly pissed off that I had the gall to challenge him."

"I'm not surprised, and I'm sure you're not either."

"Of course not. Suffice it to say that my days at Parthenon may well be over. I'll find out when I show up for work tomorrow. Right now I'm on my way to meet Jennifer at the local Hilton. There was too much commotion outside our house."

"Smart idea."

"Thanks but I can't take credit for it. Let me go and I'll fill you in on the conversation tomorrow. I'll be on my cell if anything new comes up on your end."

Chapter 65

□ □ □

It was a slow news day, so all the local stations led with the same story about a homicide in the exclusive enclave of Summit, New Jersey. Comedian Jon Stewart added his commentary on The Daily Show, blaming the murder on the resident investment bankers desirous of maintaining their suburb's exclusivity. The town's police force and those in neighboring communities, such as Short Hills and Chatham, were flooded with calls from homeowners reporting suspicious people loitering in their neighborhoods. Most of the time it was a neighbor who they had never met or a meter reader from the electric company. Buck's phone rang with a different type of concerned caller.

"Have you read the paper this morning? I thought you said it was taken care of."

"I don't need this shit now. I was told it was."

"Nice job. Now we have to worry about him connecting the dots. No good is going to come out of this. That's for damn sure."

"You're not usually one to overreact, Vern."

"Stop calling me Vern, damn it! My name is Vernon— not Vern, ol' Vern or any other quaint appellation."

"Whoa there, cowboy," Buck responded, refusing to be chastised. "Let's take a step back and figure out where this is going. From what the news reports say, the cops believe that the shooting was part of a botched hold-up. That sounds about right to me. And the Summit police won't ever be confused with the Texas Rangers. They have to be more like Inspector Clouseau. Besides, there's nothing to tie this to you."

"Tie it to me? I had nothing to do with it."

"Yeah, right. Like it or not, partner, we're joined at the hip."

Vernon needed a solution, not a reminder of his stupidity. He stayed silent while he considered Buck's words.

"Don't go silent on me, Vernon. We still need a resolution to this mess."

"Don't you think I know that?" he shot back. "As far as Jeremy goes, I can buy some time. His biggest gripe is that I own too many energy stocks, but that's because he lacks our level of confidence. He has no basis for it. I can mollify him by paring back the exposure—not by much, a showing that's all—until we come up with a permanent solution."

"Don't do anything to kill the commodity. We worked too long and hard getting it to where it's at."

"Relax! I'm not going to sell enough to turn the momentum. I'm talking about a purely token gesture in a couple of stocks. Once Jeremy sees the exposure is moving in the right direction, I'm sure he'll settle down. Our positions are way too illiquid to sell much anyway. There are really very few I could even trim without killing them."

Buck sighed. "Do what you have to but don't fuck me over. Rock went wrong somewhere and I'm going to figure out where, then maybe take another run at it. That's still the best solution."

"Well, you do what you have to."

***

Albright clenched his fists and brought them down on the desk, a loud bang reverberating through his office. He had learned nothing from his prior mistake when he took a hugely concentrated position in corporate bonds. Hendricks' information turned out to be way too good, greed grabbing hold of him and not letting go, like an addict having a relapse. The initial sensation of multiplying the gains on his investment and of being so right was infectious, feeding on itself and driving careless decisions. Albright kept pressing the trade, making it bigger, unwieldy, but he never gave the same degree of thought to an exit strategy. His original plan had been to sell into strength as the stocks moved higher, but instead the pull of besting the market fostered more irrational behavior as he increased the size of each holding. Albright reflected on all the missed opportunities when he could have severed ties with Buck instead of becoming more entrenched.

"Damn it!" he said aloud, repeatedly banging his fists on the desk.

Chapter 66

□ □ □

"Homicide. Fischetti."

"This is Detective Feuerman from the nineteenth. I read in the papers about an accidental death case and checked the database to see who was working it. Still you?"

"Yeah. Got something for me?"

"Don't know if I do or don't but I was hoping we could compare notes. I got a high profile murder on my hands and not a lot of leads. Happened earlier this evening and the brass is already all over me to get it solved, like I frickin' need them breathing down my neck. I'm sort of grabbing at straws but figured since both victims were Wall Street types it was worth checking in with you."

"You must be handling that Karass-something case?"

"Yup, that would be me. Karassik was the dude's name. Taylor Karassik. The New York Post said that even though your guy got delivered to the underside of a FedEx truck on a busy street corner, you weren't ready to call it an accident." Feuerman knew it was ridiculous that he got more information from the newspaper than the police database.

"That's just me," Fischetti responded. "My captain thinks I'm crazy but I'm not ready to close the file. How about if I tell you the facts and you tell me what you think."

"Sure."

"Here goes. The incident took place on a crowded corner. You know, one of those corners in mid-town where they put up a fence to cut down on jaywalking and improve the traffic flow."

"Yup. It funnels everyone to one crosswalk."

"You got it. Well, everyone was packed in, waiting for the light to change so they could cross. My guy's probably at the front of the crowd. All of a sudden he supposedly slips, but I think he gets pushed off the curb. Bang! A bus takes him out—he's probably dead already—and then gets run over by a truck. It wasn't very pretty."

"I remember a case like that. Middle of the business district and everyone's rushing around at lunch so they can get back to work on time. One thing leads to another, and all of a sudden an old lady gets thrown into the street and run down."

"This is different. This guy, Manero's the victim's name, wasn't some little old lady. He tipped the scales at about two-fifty. No way is a dude that size going to be jostled into the street. He had to be pushed pretty deliberately. And he may not be twinkle toes but it is kind of tough to slip when you're standing still."

"Pretty tough to accidentally move two hundred fifty pounds of dead weight."

"That's exactly my point. We're not talking about a major commotion or people panicking. If we were, I'm pretty sure that a couple of people would have wound up in the street. We're talking about only one person; someone well above average weight. I don't buy it."

"You mind holding on while I grab my file?"

Nah, go ahead. I'll grab a cup of joe. I'm working a double and starting to fade a little."

"I stopped drinking that stuff two years ago. It wasn't doing my ulcer any good."

Fischetti returned to his desk, chipped ceramic coffee cup in hand, NYPD logo emblazoned in blue letters on the side. He hated how the Styrofoam cups made the coffee taste but thought about switching back. Washing out his mug was getting to be a real pain in the ass.

Fischetti kicked off with the details. "First the easy stuff. Both victims made their living from the stock market, but that appears to be where the similarities end. Karassik was a hot-shot money manager and Manero was apparently your garden variety stockbroker."

"Karassik was also a pretty arrogant fuck. Master of the Universe syndrome but, other than rubbing a lot of folks the wrong way, he didn't seem to have any real enemies. At least that's what his secretary said."

"Neither did Manero. He was your typical salesman. Back slapping, hard drinking, life of the party type. Everyone's best friend. Good family man, too. But right before he went to lunch and took that unscheduled bus trip, he had a dust up with one of his customers who dropped into the office to see him."

"I guess that's not unusual. Most brokers have lost an awful lot of people an awful lot of money. How ugly was it?"

"Enough to draw a crowd. Security got involved and tossed the guy to the curb."

"I'm sure you questioned the customer."

"Of course. Paid him a visit. You should see where this joker lives. It would be a stretch to call it an apartment. His wife threw him out and obtained a restraining order. He's a night watchman and a real beaut. Definitely seems capable of going off the deep end, but I don't have enough to even bring him in for questioning. I'm trying to complete a background check but our links to the database have been down since Monday. NYPD technology at its finest."

"What was the argument about?"

"Seems Manero's customer had been losing money hand over fist in one particular stock. To make matters worse, he apparently used the shares he already owned as collateral for a margin loan to buy more shares. When the stock headed south, the broker sold the collateral to get his firm's money back. All that's left is a few shares of crappy stock."

"I'm guessing that's not the way the customer saw it," Feuerman added.

"Far from it. He can't understand why his broker

wouldn't give him more margin so he could buy more stock."

"What's the broker doing loaning money to a dope like that? Sounds like they should be investigated for taking advantage of a customer."

"That's the game. The brokerage firms make money on the margin interest and hold the stock as collateral in case the loan isn't repaid. The law doesn't require them to administer an IQ test to someone before they buy stock, any more than a mortgage broker requires one before a customer overpays for a house."

"How's this story end?"

"So the poor shmuck wants more money from the broker so he can double down, but they said "no way, Jose." Apparently, he wouldn't take no for an answer and got pretty vocal. By this time, the account wasn't generating any commissions, so between that and the customer being difficult to deal with, Manero stopped taking his calls."

"Typical damn broker. They run your account to zero and then you can't get them on the phone. For them, it's onto the next patsy."

"Manero wasn't quite like that. His boss wanted him to boot the guy a number of times but Manero felt sorry for him. But it got to such a point that even a good guy like Manero had enough. However, the guy decides to pay Manero a visit."

"And let me guess. Manero won't see him so the nutjob barges in and confronts him. They have words and he gets thrown out. Later, Manero leaves the office never to return."

"You got it."

"Not all of it. You never mentioned the suspect's name."

"Varko. Ernest Varko."

A grin formed on Feuerman's face. "You're shitting me! Someone named Ernest Varko kept calling Karassik's office the day he was killed, but the secretary wouldn't put the call through. She said the guy sounded a bit wacky."

"Sounds like the secretary knew her shit."

Chapter 67 □ □ □

Jeremy had another restless night. The hotel bed was comfortable enough but it just wasn't home. Under the best of circumstances—in his own bed—he found it difficult to get a full night's sleep. Added to the mix of random thoughts that held restful slumber in abeyance was the blowup with Vernon and the shooting in front of his house. Long before dawn, Jeremy knew he was sentenced to another night of intermittent sleep and staring into the darkness. Ultimately, he accepted his fate of facing the day on very little rest. Long before the alarm sounded, he rose from bed and began his day.

Jeremy was at his desk sorting through emails when Vernon appeared. He braced himself for a continuation of the prior day's discussion. As Vernon pulled up a chair, something he had never done in Jeremy's office, Jeremy realized that this was going to be a different type of meeting. He braced for the showdown.

Vernon seemed calm and pensive, his fingertips braced against one another, propping up his chin, his elbows resting on the fabric armrests. "I've given a lot of thought to yesterday's conversation."

"So have I," Jeremy responded tersely, clearly in no mood to be on the receiving end of an Albright lecture.

"Please let me finish," Vernon responded in a surprisingly mild tone. "Your feeling that the fund may be too heavily weighted in energy has some merit."

Shock was Jeremy's first response but he kept his mouth shut and his features expressionless. A poker face.

Vernon continued. "I've decided to start paring down the exposure. I still have unwavering confidence in my thesis, but taking some risk off the table is prudent."

"I've never known you to be this conciliatory, Vernon, not that I don't appreciate it. But you seemed so resolute in your position and, I should add, pretty damned upset at me for delving into it."

Albright bit his tongue; this was getting tough. "Let me put it this way. I'm not happy about how you got us to this point, but in fairness, you did try to talk to me directly and I pushed you off. So the way I see it is that we can each shoulder some blame for our little skirmish yesterday. But none of that matters now. All that matters is that we get this behind us so that we can go back to focusing on making money. If reducing the exposure gives you some piece of mind, then it's worth it."

"Piece of mind for me? You miss the point entirely. Limiting the exposure is for the good of the investors; it's the right thing to do. End of story. It's got nothing to do with my personal feelings; I have no emotion about the portfolio. You should know that by now. If anything, you are the one who should be concerned because, as you have reminded me many, many times, this is your firm. A couple of minus ticks in crude and this company could be wiped out. Particularly since you haven't hedged the risk at all. For chrissakes, Vernon, we're a hedge fund and our investors justifiably believe that we've taken out protection on the portfolio, but we haven't."

"I misspoke," Vernon stated, trying to add some realism. "While I care about you personally, I could care less about your personal feelings in regard to *my* investments in *my* fund. However, in this case you've made good sense and I'm smart enough not to have an ego about the idea to pare back the exposure. As to hedging...well, hedging in this case would be moronic. Asinine. All it would do is make the opposite bet and kill the alpha. Cutting back on a few positions is a better solution."

"I disagree but appreciate the olive branch. If I were to anticipate your next comment, it would be something to the effect of telling me to get back to work making money. That's a strategy I do agree with so if you'll excuse me, I have to prepare for the day."

***

Buck was waiting on the phone when Vernon returned to his office.

"How did it go? Is he going to be a problem for us?"

"To be honest, I don't know but I think he's okay. Time will tell."

"Time, you old fool, is one thing we don't have. You may be content to leave things to chance but I'm not!"

The line went dead.

Chapter 68

□ □ □

It was an unusual treat for Jennifer to pick up from only one play date location. It always seemed that Alexandra's and Melissa's friends were on the opposite sides of town. She often joked that she spent more time in her SUV than she did at home, which wasn't far from the truth, particularly on Tuesdays and Wednesdays when each child had different afternoon activities. The girls piled into the car and jumped into their car seats. Jennifer went to strap in Alexandra but the little girl resisted.

"Mommy, I'm a big girl now. I can do it myself."

"Okay, baby. Let me see what you can do." Jennifer stepped back. Accomplishments help build confidence.

While Alexandra fumbled with the straps and locking mechanism, Jennifer fastened Melissa into her seat. Unlike her big sister, she was content to let someone else do the work.

"Mommy?" Jenn recognized the 'I need help' voice.

"Well, let's see. You did great! You got most of it worked out. Just let me untangle this and then you can finish the job." Alexandra slid the buckle into place.

Jennifer had not noticed the two different colored vans that had followed her on an alternating basis since she had left her house almost fifteen minutes earlier. Both drivers knew that if they were patient, sooner or later she would stop to pick up the children, consistent with her routine over the last couple of days. Then it was just a question of finding a quiet street. They got their break soon after she left the play date.

Similar to the block on which the Cranfords lived, the homes in this neighborhood enjoyed large setbacks and protective landscaping. Raoul thought the setting was ideal. He called ahead to Dwyer, telling him to pass the SUV. Noticing the New York plates of the van that just whizzed by, Jennifer slowed her vehicle and checked the rearview mirror hoping that there was not another crazed driver coming up behind her. *Damn New York drivers; don't they know there are kids on this block*, she remarked in silence.

As Raoul continued west on Bellevue Avenue, he provided further instructions. "We'll make our move on the next block."

Maybe the idiot came to his senses, Jennifer thought, as the van in front of her slowed down.

Dwyer came to an abrupt halt at the stop sign and scanned the area for other vehicles.

"This is a good lesson on how not to drive, girls. First this man races past me, then he slows down, then he stops short and won't move. Mommy is going to take another way to the hotel. Remember this when you get older—drive defensively," she said laughing, realizing that her kids had no idea what she was talking about. At least they were a captive audience.

Jennifer turned left at the next corner. The parallel road would work just fine. Raoul cursed at the inconvenience before realizing that it wasn't a problem. He instructed Dwyer to speed up, go two more blocks and then make two left turns.

The black van had come around the corner too quickly for Jennifer to negotiate her way around it. Instead, she braked fiercely, applying as much direct pressure to the pedal as the muscles in her leg would allow. The four wheel ABS system kept the vehicle from swerving but wasn't able to prevent a collision with the van that came directly at her. Thankfully the impact was minor. She immediately turned around to check on her girls. They were both laughing hysterically.

"Fun, Mommy, fun," was Melissa's reaction.

"Weee, weee. Do it again," Alexandra added.

Relieved that everyone seemed to be okay, she got out of the car to speak with the driver of the van. "What's wrong with you, driving like that? I've got children in my car."

Those were the last words she would speak for hours. Raoul had come up behind her and placed a towel soaked with chloroform over her nose and mouth. She went limp and he caught her as she fell. They quickly transferred her into the silver van while keeping an eye out for other cars and nosy neighbors. Next, they moved the children, still in their car seats. Dwyer ran a rope through the back of each car seat, fastening them to a metal bar that helped frame the inside of the van. After testing the rigging, he sat on the metal floorboards and positioned himself between the two children. Raoul applied a small strip of surgical tape over Jennifer's mouth and used a plastic handcuff tie to secure her arms. The girls sat in their seats, mouths agape, surprised but not terrified—yet. Satisfied with his work, he climbed into the driver's seat and quickly drove away, abandoning the other stolen vehicle.

"Mommy's asleep," Melissa observed. "I want her to wake up." Her little eyes welled with tears but she somehow knew it was not the time for full-blown hysteria.

"Did you hurt my mommy?" Alexandra asked, her voice quivering with concern.

Dwyer spoke the lines they had rehearsed. "Your mommy is just resting. She and your daddy planned this surprise for you. We're going to take you to a big, big building where we have lots of candy and toys."

The chloroform kept Jennifer asleep as they reached their Jersey City destination. The empty warehouse occupied a one block stretch in a nearly abandoned industrial area located a few blocks from the Hudson River. Dwyer exited the van and opened the large, metal freight door allowing Raoul to drive into the building where he would park. In the center of the vacant building was a gray metal staircase, its handrails showing traces of red paint. The steps led to an office held in suspension from the ceiling by four thick metal posts. A makeshift playpen constructed from pieces of cardboard boxes sat nearby. In the center were a few stuffed animals and a couple of toys. Rusted machinery, long idle, broken office furniture and debris covered most of the cement floor throughout the cavernous space.

Alexandra and Melissa were lifted out of the van and placed into their temporary home. They were each given a bag of miniature Famous Amos chocolate chip cookies and went about making them disappear. Jennifer was then placed in one of the chairs that sat nearby. A rope was looped around her chest, securing her to the back of the seat. Her head rested on her chest while she remained under the influence of a drug induced sleep.

Raoul gently patted his captive's right cheek until she began to surface, at first finding it difficult to focus. She quickly realized her predicament and her eyes widened with rage as she struggled to free herself. While the tape across her lips muffled her words, her emotions could not be held in check as easily.

Raoul spoke in a calming tone, his guttural accent consistent with his appearance. A hulking figure, his pock-marked face evinced a threatening image. "Now, now," he said tauntingly. "Calm down. We don't want the children to get excited or you to hurt yourself. If you promise to be a good girl, I'll have your restraints removed. Nod if you will cooperate."

Jennifer stared at her captor, willing him to die. She bobbed her head up and down in assent. Raoul moved his hand toward her face, and she braced for pain as the tape was pulled from her mouth. Surprisingly, the white surgical fabric barely caused any sensation. Her face was slightly red but that would fade soon enough. He cut the plastic ties with a knife he pulled from a sheath on his belt and did the same to the ropes that bound her to the chair. She immediately rushed over to her children, jumping over the flaps of the brown cartons that formed a scant protective perimeter.

"Are you two okay? Did they touch you in any way?" The panic in her voice caused Melissa to cry. She softened her tone. "Are those cookies? Can I have one?" She put it in her mouth and rubbed her stomach. "Yum, yum. These are good."

"Mommy funny," Melissa giggled.

Raoul pulled Jennifer by her arm, leading her back to the chair so he could deliver the message he was given. As she sat down, she noticed a gun protruding from the waistband of his pants; fear took the place of anger. It was now about survival.

Chapter 69

□ □ □

Lauren was anxious; she had to speak with Jeremy but he and Vernon were deep in conversation. Nervous energy took her on a few laps around the office. She nonchalantly peered into Jeremy's office each time she passed. Tired of pacing, she waited down the hall and leaned against the wall, the nervous tapping of her foot muted by the Persian rug. The wait wasn't long from there as Vernon appeared in the hallway and walked in the opposite direction toward his office.

"You'll never guess who's behind all this." Lauren waited, purposely building suspense.

"You figured out who erased the file from Paul's computer?" Jeremy asked as he leaned back in his chair, clearly pleased.

Arms folded across her chest, Lauren nodded, the widest Cheshire cat smile decorating her face.

"Nice going. Who was it?"

"Marty Jagdale. It's all here," she said while waving the disc in the air, "the exact times she logged in and out, and what operations she instructed the system to perform." Lauren waited for a reaction from Jeremy. "You don't seem shocked."

"I'm not. Maybe that's the surprise. I've never been completely comfortable with her."

"But you just promoted her."

"Who else could do it? Lucy Rodriquez? I don't think so. Now what else do you have for me?"

Lauren spoke to the evidence. "Seeing her name pop up definitely provided clarity on a few things."

"Such as?"

"Such as why Marty tried to put me through the third degree when she interrupted my coming to your office, and why you didn't want her to see the data." Lauren collected her thoughts. "But knowing it was Marty and knowing that she was hired by Vernon doesn't make me feel very comfortable."

Jeremy looked directly into Lauren's eyes. "I told you before that you have to trust me and that you won't be disadvantaged by anything that happens here. That train left the station long before I got you involved and has nothing to do with the work you've done."

"Meaning what?"

"Meaning that the issues with Parthenon were already in motion and would have eventually surfaced without your involvement."

"I guess you're right," Lauren said.

"Staying here won't be an option for either of us once all dirty laundry comes out. No firm could withstand the fallout from this mess so I'm either going to start my own firm or join with someone else, and you will be part of what I do."

"So then why are you doing this? You have options. At this point I'm sure Vernon would redeem your interests and let you go. I overheard part of your discussion with him this morning. There's suspicion on both sides. Why wouldn't you just pack up and leave before this all blows up?"

"Every once in a while you have to do what's right," Jeremy stated without hesitation. "I have an obligation to the people who invested in this fund and put their trust in me to do what's right. We've got college endowments, pensions, trust accounts that I'm obligated to. People think hedge funds are just for rich people and it's a buyer beware mentality—screw them if they lose money, they can afford it—but that's not how it is."

"Wow, I'm almost tearing up," Lauren appeared starry eyed.

"Before you nominate me for Man of the Year, my motivations are not completely altruistic. I don't want to see all the money I have tied up in this place evaporate nor do I want to go to jail for something that I had no part of."

"Still, I feel inspired to—" Still young and not far enough removed from academia to lose her idealism, she was on the cusp of pledging her undying support to the cause but the phone intervened.

"Hold that thought for a second," Jeremy interjected as he picked up the phone. It was Tom Wichefski.

"I'm pretty sure that the shooting victim outside your house is none other than Mr. Datatech. His real name is Ernest Varko."

Mindful of Lauren's presence, Jeremy appeared stoic although he found the news he just received to be more shocking than Lauren's revealing Marty as Parthenon's own Judas. He held his hand over the receiver and spoke to Lauren. "You're not going to believe this but the news I'm getting now is almost as important as your discovery. This may take a while. I'll give you a call when I'm done."

"You mean there's more? Incredible! I'll be in my office"

"Thanks, Lauren. I really appreciate it."

Jeremy continued the conversation behind closed doors. "Varko is Datatech? How do you know?"

"I spoke with the officer in charge of the case in Summit, a Lieutenant Morris. He's a former NYPD detective and seemed pretty knowledgeable. Anyway, Morris filled me in on what they found at the crime scene and the angle he's taking on the investigation. After he gave me the low down, I went through NCIC. I started by looking at recent criminal activity in this area to see if there were any unsolved murders. It turns out that another hedge fund manager, someone named Taylor Karassik, was murdered earlier today. I'm sure the story will be on the evening news."

"Karassik murdered! I know him, not well, but we've spoken on occasion. Actually we recently compared notes about Datatech. We've both been short the stock forever. How was he killed?"

"Stabbed. Morris said they found a knife on Varko and there was dried blood on the blade. We won't have the lab report until tomorrow but we can both guess what the findings will be."

"There but for the grace...." Jeremy's voice trailed off.

"There's more. Varko may have put another notch in his belt. His broker met an untimely demise right after Varko stopped by his office. The incident is labeled an accidental death pending further investigation, but I would be very surprised if they don't reclassify it as a homicide. The broker's name was Al Manero."

"Never heard of him. How did he die?"

"There's no reason why you should know him. He was a small time retail broker at Tinker Blistrom. Anyway, Manero was on his way to lunch and while waiting for the light to change, he slipped off a curb and was hit by a bus and then run over by a truck. It happened around the corner from your office."

Jeremy felt a chill run down his spine. "So if I didn't get into it with Vernon last night, there was a chance I could be the one laying on a gurney at the morgue. I don't know whether to feel relieved or scared shitless," he said, matter of fact. "If you're right about Varko it means he was a serial murderer. I guess I should feel pretty fortunate to have ducked him twice—last night and when he tried to shove me in front of a truck."

"I'm not so sure about that. Manero was a lot heavier than you and apparently Varko had no trouble pushing him off the curb. If he wanted you dead that day, you would be dead."

"I guess none of that is relevant now. I feel terrible for those men and their families. I can only imagine what Jennifer and the girls would be going through if it were me instead of Taylor or Manero. This business isn't supposed to be life threatening."

"After speaking with the detectives working the Manero and Karassik cases, it seems clear that Varko was likely the common thread connecting those two and you. He had to be the one behind those letters."

"It's a relief not to have to worry about my family's security anymore," Jeremy reflected. "Kind of scary, actually, that I could have been next." He went quiet, sorting through his thoughts before continuing. "Something doesn't add up."

"You don't have the full story yet." Wichefski hesitated, deciding how to deliver an uncomfortable message. He had rehearsed it before the call but now wasn't sure how much to say. At this point his conclusion was largely based on conjecture.

"It certainly doesn't seem like I know everything. For example, I get why Varko was outside my house—but random murders don't happen in towns like Summit, New Jersey."

"Varko wasn't the target, you were."

"That's ridiculous. It doesn't make any sense. I'm not important enough for anyone to want to murder—aside from Varko, and he was a psycho. How many mass murdering nuts are on the loose? I would love to hear your thesis."

"Man, you are one cool customer. If anyone else had heard that they came so close to catching a bullet in the chest or a knife in the back, they would be a lot more flustered, not asking for the analytical justification."

"It's my training and desensitization about being murdered. After all, I've been killed by the market many times." Jeremy joked, alleviating some of the tension.

"Good point," Tom said, chuckling then turning serious, "but do yourself a favor and don't underestimate the seriousness of what happened."

"Right now I'm still in the relief phase. I'll get to the worried phase soon enough." Jeremy ran a nervous hand through his hair.

"Maybe now is a good time since this isn't over yet. Want me to take you through my thought process?"

"Absolutely," Jeremy responded without hesitation.

"Okay. Let me start with a question. Have there been any significant changes at the office?"

"Such as?"

"Come on Jeremy. Has anything changed to the point that someone is really pissed off at you?"

"I think you know the answer to that question. In terms of drama, Parthenon could win an Oscar for best film. There is so much unusual shit going on I don't even know where to start."

"Let me hear it all."

Jeremy began taking Tom through the chronology of events from the letters, Marty's hiring, meeting Hendricks to Paul's murder, Marty's promotion and the about-face Albright did on his energy exposure earlier in the day.

"...After last night I would have laid down odds that he was going to cut me loose today," he finished.

"From what you've told me in the past it's always been his way or the highway."

"That's the truth."

"Do they have any leads on Paul's killer? The database didn't seem to be current."

"If they do," Jeremy answered, "they haven't told me. Maybe you can get an update directly from the homicide investigators. I want that bastard brought to justice."

"Will do. Now tell me more about meeting with Hendricks. The first time he meets you he offers to stake you in your own fund? Wouldn't that require a substantial amount of capital?"

"Yes, billions actually, but I'm a pretty impressive guy when you first meet me."

"And don't forget modest," Tom joked. "You guys make way too much money."

"Hey, I'm not even close to being in Vernon's galaxy when it comes to making money."

"I don't think we'll need to hold a benefit for you anytime soon."

"Point taken."

"Back to Hendricks and the job offer," Wichefski said, turning serious again. "Do you think he planned to pull money out of Parthenon to fund a venture with you?"

"I don't see how he could. Not only is Vernon's portfolio much too illiquid, but apparently Hendricks also owns a lot of those stocks personally." Jeremy twirled the phone cord around his fingers as he replied. "The price of those shares would get crushed under the selling pressure if Parthenon had to liquidate for any reason. Hendricks wasn't going to be the catalyst—at least not by choice."

"So then it's safe to conclude that Hendricks has incredible access to capital. Hopefully the background check I ordered will shed some light on where his funding comes from."

"When will you have it?"

"They just dropped it on my desk. How's that for timing?"

"What does it say?"

"Finish your train of thought and then I'll take a look."

"Where was I? Oh, yeah. Putting me in business. We're talking billions; that's with a '*b*'. It doesn't make sense that I had never heard his name before."

"Lots of things don't make sense about this case, including the four deaths."

"Tell me something, Tom, and be straight. How worried should I be? I mean... we're a hedge fund, not a drug cartel, but people are dying left and right."

"I'll answer it this way. If I were you I'd definitely be a lot more aware of my surroundings. I would prefer to tell you that this is a typical white-collar crime but it's not. White collar crime doesn't include murder."

There was silence on the line as Jeremy came to grips with how close he came to being the victim instead of Varko. But it wasn't concern for his own wellbeing that dominated his thoughts; it was his family and their safety that he grappled with. He silently cursed himself that concern for his family's safety had taken so long to surface to a point where he was ready to do something about it. Adding to his self-loathing was the guilt.

"This is all my fault. Paul's murder is on me. I'm probably to blame for that stockbroker and Taylor, too." Jeremy's voice began to trail off. "I have a nexus to all three."

"Don't jump to conclusions," Tom offered in a reassuring tone. "Manero and Karassik clearly had nothing to do with you. In fact we don't even know that Manero was murdered."

"Come on, Tom. It's too much of a coincidence that the same thing almost happened to me."

"Manero's and Karassik's deaths don't have anything to do with you. Varko was a complete nutjob."

"I buy that," Jeremy said, his voice regaining some strength. "But what about Paul? You can't tell me that there is no connection between the issues I'm dealing with at Parthenon and his death."

"Put that aside for a second and get back to Paul's analysis of Vernon's portfolio, and what happened to it."

"Paul was putting the finishing touches on it the night he was murdered."

"So he never showed you a copy?"

"No. I did see it after he died but had to jump through hoops to finally get a look at it. I had no luck retrieving it from his computer so I enlisted our CTO to help. Apparently, the file was erased from Paul's local drive, but whoever deleted it was either unaware that everything is backed up on the network or couldn't hack into that system."

"And you confronted Vernon with the analysis you finally retrieved?"

"Yes. He went ballistic but seemed to have calmed down today although I'm skeptical."

Tom asked his final question. "Were you or your tech person able to determine who erased the file?"

"Lauren Wilkes, the CTO, told me just before you called." Jeremy paused to deliver the punch line. "Marty Jagdale. The funny thing is that I'm not the least bit surprised."

"This case has so many twists and turns that nothing shocks me either. Bear with me a second." Tom wrote down some more notes. "In fact, the way Marty mysteriously showed up, her involvement in this mess is logical but also brings up another issue."

"Such as?" Jeremy stood behind his desk, pacing three steps to the left and then reversing, three steps to the right.

"First finish up."

"Sure. I believe the next data point is Varko being murdered, which you think was an attempt on my life." Jeremy fell silent as the realization hit him. "Holy shit! Vernon's behind it all! That motherfucker tried to kill me to keep me quiet! He has to be behind Paul's murder too."

"Hold on a second." Tom said, more measured. "That's an easy conclusion to jump to, but it still leaves us a long way from being able to secure an arrest warrant for Vernon. Keep in mind he's still pretty well connected, and his lawyers will shred the case unless we have more substantial proof than the fact that he owns too many energy stocks. Honestly, I'm not completely convinced that he's complicit in anyone's murder. What about you? Do you think Vernon is capable of murder?"

"I wouldn't have thought so before, but now I'm not so sure. If he's done something illegal regarding the fund, then he's facing the loss of his fortune. He's about as greedy as they come, and greed does some very strange things to people. Would he commit murder for a few billion? That's a real good question that I am very hard pressed to answer. But a number of people would do it for a lot less."

"Losing money could be the least of his worries," Tom noted. "I doubt he would survive in jail for too long, particularly since they stopped sending white-collar criminals to country club prisons. They get thrown in with the worst scum of the earth in the toughest Federal prisons."

"I doubt he could survive a week without his personal tailor and hair stylist."

"Let me ask you another question, Jeremy. Is Vernon a good actor? I mean, if something is really bothering him, something really gets in his craw, is he capable of pretending nothing happened?"

"What are you getting at?"

"You mentioned that when you confronted Vernon with the spreadsheet that he teed off on you, got very angry. Marty knew about the spreadsheet because she had deleted it from the system. So it follows that if Marty is working for Vernon, she would have already shown him a copy. He would have been prepared for your conversation and therefore a lot more restrained in his approach to you."

"I get it; good point. He would have been prepared for the conversation and at that point offered to pare back the exposure instead of doing it today."

"Exactly."

"I really doubt that even DeNiro could bring out that amount of rage on cue. Marty's clearly working for someone else. The question is who. My bet is that Hendricks is behind the entire mess. He has a ton of money invested in the fund and is someone who would stop at nothing to protect his interests."

"Hendricks wanted to have his own person on the inside. And from Vernon's standpoint, he knew he couldn't push you or Paul around, so he needed someone else in the mix more aligned with his interests. Or maybe he couldn't say no to Buck."

"One thing is for sure; I'm no longer feeling calm and collected. I may seem calm on the outside but inside I'm officially scared shitless. Paul was murdered. And I was supposed to be next and still may be!" Jeremy's façade was crumbling. "And what about my family?" He asked as he sat back down behind his desk.

"Your family should be fine. We're dealing with some bad guys but not indiscriminate killers. You don't believe Vernon would do something that stupid or rash, do you?"

Jeremy thought it over. "Vernon? No. He wouldn't, but I really have no clue about Hendricks. I only met him once and he struck me as capable of anything. I'm sure it's not lost on him that the best way to get at me is through my family."

"Good point. As a precaution, and I really do believe it is only a precaution, I'm going to attach a security detail to your family. They are very good at being unobtrusive."

Jeremy expressed his appreciation but was still clearly bothered by a nagging thought. "Vernon may occasionally take on a lot of risk but he's not a completely irresponsible investor. There is no way he would bet his entire fortune on one theme—and make no mistake, that's what he's consciously doing—unless he had a real edge."

"Hendricks is a Texas oil man. That's got to be helpful."

"Helpful, yes, but insufficient. He may have insight into crude production but that alone would never provide Vernon with enough confidence that he has a leg up on other hedge funds."

"I guess it isn't that easy, is it?"

Jeremy continued. "Not at all. Hell, I can think of a dozen big oil companies that spent a fortune on buying other companies at the last top in the market and regret it now. And when you're a $100-billion energy conglomerate like Exxon it's a good bet you have better intelligence than Buck Hendricks."

"Your point," Tom interjected, "is that if Exxon can't predict the price of oil then how can Hendricks?"

"Exactly. Texas is filled with oilmen. But Texas is responsible for less than two percent of the world's oil production. Even if Buck were wired to sources throughout the U.S., which I doubt, that would only account for eight percent.

That's like the tail wagging the dog when you consider that OPEC controls over forty percent of production and eighty percent of the world's oil reserves. Nope, Vernon would need more. He'd need better information. Only a guarantee written in blood would suffice, or something damn close."

"I'm far from a commodity expert but I did learn a few things from a prior case I worked on, but correct me if I'm wrong."

"Shoot."

"When a commodity is so tightly in balance, can't eight percent, maybe even two percent, sway it either way?"

"Good point," Jeremy offered, impressed, "but the oil market is so fickle that it can be tight one day and the next day the Saudis open the spigot and bang—no more tight market. Like most markets, commodities, stocks—all of them—they trade on expectations, not what the set of facts at that particular point in time. Nope. That would not good be enough for Vernon. Not for him to put the entire firm at risk."

"I'm not one to believe in conspiracies—I'm not even sure there was a grassy knoll in Dallas—but with crude hitting a new high every day and Vernon and Buck being up to their necks in energy investments, at least one of them feels like he's guaranteed."

"That's for damn sure. How about opening that report now?"

Tom inserted a scissor in the flap of the large manila envelope and pulled it across the top, careful not to damage any of the documents inside. The dossier was about fifteen pages long. It contained Buck's picture and a history that went back to his college days, those years illustrated mostly through articles that appeared in the local newspapers about his family. Tom took a cursory look through the file before returning to the beginning of the report.

"First off, you're going to love this. Tough old Buck's real name is actually Wendell."

"Wendell! I guess I would use a nickname too if my name were Wendell."

"We all would. Give me some time to go through the rest of this report and I'll call you back..."

"That's all right, I'll hold," Jeremy said hurriedly before Tom could hang up the phone.

"That's okay with me if that's what you want to do but there's a lot here," Tom replied, his voice trailing off as he began to focus on the document.

"I really don't mind holding."

"Suit yourself. I'll try to read through this as fast as I can. There's also an executive summary that should hit most of the high points."

Jeremy nervously drummed his fingers on the desk, anxiously waiting for Tom to come back on the line. His gaze rarely strayed from the digital clock located on the bottom of his monitor, the numbers clicking away at an interminably slow pace.

"Almost finished," Tom offered as he turned to the summary.

"I'm not going anywhere," Jeremy responded. Nervous energy ratcheting higher, he wound the phone cord around one finger, then another, then repeated the movement over and over.

Finally, Tom's voice broke through the tense silence. "He does come from money; that much is very clear. It seems his father was a very accomplished wildcatter. Very charitable, endowed the library at SMU. If I were a cynical person, I would say that Daddy wanted to make sure that his son graduated. After Dad died, Buck took over the family oil business which, up to that time was very successful."

"Why do you put it that way?"

"Keep in mind I just did a cursory review of what's in front of me but it seems pretty straightforward. The early tax returns for the business don't show any interest payments for outstanding loans, meaning that it was in pretty good financial shape. But a couple of years after Earl,

Buck's father, died, the interest payment line kept getting bigger and bigger for a few years. Hell, it gets huge! Then it slowly starts going back down."

"So Buck turns out to be a smart businessman?"

"Well, maybe a better investor than businessman and here's why I say that...." Tom turned back to the summary pages and read the pertinent part to Jeremy. "What do you make of all this?"

A trained financial analyst, it didn't take long for Jeremy to distill the information that Tom had relayed to him. "Buck couldn't make a go of it in the oil business but figured out a way to make it in the commodity trading markets. From the dates you gave me it seems he caught the last spike in the price of crude just right and kept piling in. But he needed money to make money. So instead of reinvesting the revenues from the family business back into the company, he invested them in the commodity and stock markets where he could get a much higher return— providing he was right. And he was."

A thought occurred to Tom. "But his personal tax return doesn't show any huge gains and I'm pretty damn sure these corporate tax returns don't show all the money he has made. It's as if that money disappeared." Tom leafed through some more papers. "Wait, this may explain it. He apparently transferred funds to the Banque de Union."

"How much?"

"Actually, it looks like about a hundred million. Not a lot in the total scheme of things, but at least it gives us a paper trail. But there is another transfer. This one is to... You're going to love this. SHAM."

Jeremy laughed. "What the hell is sham?"

"It's appears to be an acronym for Scott Hallwood Asset Management."

"That name rings a bell. Hold on a second." Jeremy opened a browser window and typed the name into the Google toolbar. Almost instantaneously, he found what he was looking for. "I remember the story about this guy

Hallwood and his firm. He was a high flyer at one point, a regular talking head on CNBC, Bloomberg, the whole nine yards. Always bullish on every stock and commodity. Then the market began going through a very tough phase and he was nowhere to be seen. I had heard he went belly up."

"Maybe he did until Hendricks came to the rescue. And if Hendricks siphoned off revenue and transferred it to Hallwood and apparently, also Parthenon, I'm guessing there's more."

"Absolutely," Jeremy concurred. "Anything else in the report about Hallwood or others he may have put money with?"

"Nothing. The trail runs cold. I guess his interests became so big that he decided to take it all off shore and hide it in the Swiss banks to take advantage of their secrecy laws."

"Certainly appears that's what he did, but hasn't the U.S. put a lot of pressure on the Swiss to share information with us on tax cheats?"

"Yes but corporations are still well protected. For example, he could have a subsidiary or separate entity domiciled in Luxembourg. The real money for these banks is with the big entities, and corporations usually have more business to do than individuals, which is probably why Hendricks formed Bronco Partners. Forget about his stupidity in selecting a name that is synonymous with cowboys and Texas. Might as well have just drawn a line to Bronco from his personal accounts."

The puzzle only got bigger and the pieces more irregular, making it increasingly difficult to put together. Everything was conjecture, the facts at this point playing a minor role. They needed more direct information.

Jeremy offered a thought. "Is there any way for you to pull Vernon in for questioning? You're the expert, but aren't there enough data points to justify a warrant or, at the very least, the opening of an investigation? Vernon would be scared shitless and fold like a cheap umbrella. He could give us all our answers."

"There are a few issues with that," Tom responded as he considered the suggestion. "The first is that the FBI is usually brought in by the SEC because they are the ones that have jurisdiction and regulatory authority over the markets and market participants. The SEC isn't involved here yet and it may take a while to get them up to speed. Secondly, Albright is a very high profile person so this decision will be made at the highest levels of the Bureau. And finally, since we are fairly certain that money has been shifted overseas, we don't want to give Buck or Vernon a heads up that we're onto them and risk having them transfer money to another bank and then another until the money trail goes cold. Right now we know, or believe we know, where some of the assets are."

Jeremy felt worse as the conversation continued. The fact pattern more complicated, the interpretation more difficult.

"What about Marty," Jeremy mentioned, almost as an afterthought. "We hardly know anything about her."

"Good point. I'll run a check on her. Hopefully, since she's an employee, the firm has her social security number."

"I wouldn't bet on it being correct. If we have it, I'll send it over."

Chapter 70

Tom Wichefski walked into the New York office of the Deputy Director of the Federal Bureau of Investigation, Giovanni "Joe" Pflucek. Pflucek was not your typical agent, if one even existed anymore. A first generation American, he was the product of an Italian mother and a Polish father. He started his career in law enforcement as a New York City police officer and attended law school at night, joining the FBI after graduating. Owing to a twenty-five year career filled with numerous high profile cases, he was promoted to run the Bureau's largest office outside of Washington. Befitting his importance, he occupied a large corner office. However, he was still a government employee and the sparse furnishings that struggled to fill the office were clearly institutional; non-descript wood furniture and black vinyl chairs that could have been purchased at Staples or some other office superstore. The focal point of the office was Pflucek's trophy wall covered with pictures of him posing with each of the last three Presidents and numerous cabinet members, senators and other politicos. Two flags stood in the corner, crossing in the middle of their shafts and extending to just below the ceiling tiles. One was the American flag; the other displayed the FBI emblem inscribed with the words *"FIDELITY BRAVERY INTEGRITY."* Pflucek wore a replica of the flags on the lapel of his jacket that he never took off while at work, even on hot summer days when the air conditioning was barely functional.

"I think I'm onto something pretty big, Director."

"Let me hear." Pflucek was efficient with his words.

"I've mentioned Suzie's job working at a large hedge fund."

"You have. You said she works for a heavy hitter in the business who makes more money than God."

"That's correct. Well, it seems as though he's had some help making all that money. And it's the kind of help that we don't like to see."

"I'm listening."

"At this point most of the evidence is circumstantial but I feel pretty good about it."

Pflucek had no problem trusting Wichefski's instincts. He was one of the best agents under his command.

Wichefski continued. "The thirty-thousand-foot view is that Vernon Albright—that's Suzie's boss—seems to be violating multiple securities laws including abetting someone who is rigging the energy markets." He provided Pflucek with an abbreviated download of the facts.

"Timing sure is everything. I was just on a conference call with my counterparts at the SEC and Justice. The SEC is being pushed by the White House to look into oil prices. The President's energy czar, Bill Lindsay, is convinced that supply and demand are in check and that there is no fundamental reason for the run up so they want all three agencies to investigate. The SEC suspects collusion in the commodity pits which jives with your thinking."

"There's more to the story, including a few homicides." Wichefski went into detail.

Pflucek was more concerned about the edict from Washington. "Work with the locals on the homicides. Until we get more information they have jurisdiction. Put your focus on the insider trading and market rigging. Get hold of the key players—Albright especially—and put them through the interrogation process. Let's see if he's tough enough to withstand the good old third degree. I'm willing to bet that he opens up to us."

"Be prepared for some pushback from Washington. Albright's been a major donor to both parties and is very well connected."

Pflucek took a second to digest Wichefski's comments. He hadn't risen up the ranks without being politically astute. "Okay. Proceed carefully with Albright. If he gets wind of our involvement before we're ready to arrest him, he could make a few calls and completely shut down the investigation. For now, just make sure that you keep tabs on him."

"I have a source away from Suzie—Albright's partner— who can be our eyes and ears. He may already have enough information to take to Justice for an indictment."

"The guy's clean?"

Wichefski nodded. "Without a doubt. In fact, he's the one who brought everything to my attention."

"And strong enough to handle the pressure?"

"Like you would not believe. One of the coolest customers I have ever seen."

"This is your investigation to manage as you see fit but keep me up on any developments. Meantime, I'll look into Albright's standing in D.C. We may decide to bring both him and the Texan in for questioning. I can't imagine Albright's connections will matter much once Washington realizes what's at stake."

Chapter 71

□ □ □

Jeremy was purposely quick on the phone earlier in the morning, when he told Jennifer it was best to stay at the Hilton for another night since their front yard remained a crime scene. A longer conversation might have led to a discussion that would have been more concerning to her; a conversation he saw no point in having. But he realized during his conversation with Wichefski that Jennifer needed to be told that she had to be more vigilant in protecting herself and the children. She would feel more secure with the FBI providing protection after she got over the initial shock of actually needing a security detail. Not connecting with his wife at the hotel, he tried her cell, also to no avail. He left two voicemails; she was never out of touch for long. Jeremy repeatedly glanced at his watch, his concern increasing with geometric progression as the minutes ticked away without a return call. He tried to steady himself by recalling the false alarm of the other night when he arrived home to an empty house.

His desire to uncover the truth about Albright's involvement continued to build and he fought off the temptation to march into his office and bring it all to a head. The last confrontation almost got him killed, although he still grappled with the concept that his mentor and friend would have gone to such lengths to shut him up. Not that it would be a saving grace, but Jeremy hoped that Vernon was only involved in the financial aspects of this debacle and ignorant of everything else. Jeremy felt like he was losing his mind. His thoughts raced back and forth between worry about the safety of his family to Vernon's aptitude for murder.

The ringing of the phone broke Jeremy from his thoughts. His relief at seeing Jennifer's cell number on the caller ID was palpable.

"I've been trying to get in touch with you. Is everything okay?"

Jennifer fought the urge to cry when she heard her husband's voice. "No one's hurt but everything's not exactly okay. We're being held hostage. They want to speak with you."

"What? Are you okay? Are the girls with you? Where are you?" Remaining calm was not an option.

"I don't know. Some warehouse—"

Raoul pulled the phone from Jennifer as Dwyer placed a hand on her shoulder, keeping her seated.

"Hello, Mr. Cranford."

"Who the hell is this and what do you want with my family?" Jeremy seethed.

"Call me Max. I got a message for you and you'd be smart to pay attention."

"If you harm any of them," Jeremy said through gritted teeth. "I will hunt you down and kill you myself."

"Calm down, buddy. Just listen to the message and go along. That's all you need to do to keep your family healthy." Raoul remained even-keeled, reflecting a detachment to the human elements of his work.

"Okay, okay. What do you want from me? I'll do anything…just you don't harm my family."

Jeremy bordered on frantic but knew he had to regain his composure. Nervously tapping his foot, he strained to listen for a telltale sound, anything that would give him a clue as to their location.

"First of all, this stays between us which means no police. Remember I have three bargaining chips here, not just one. Two of them are freebies."

The cold matter of fact tone put Jeremy on notice that

the captors would have no problem doing anything that was necessary to attain his compliance.

"If you harm any of them, you won't be able to run fast or far enough."

"Shut up and listen."

Through clenched teeth Jeremy acquiesced, realizing it was not the time to be aggressive. "Go ahead. I'm listening."

Raoul motioned Dwyer to loosen his grip on Jennifer. "First, keep your mouth shut. Stop spreading lies about the people I work for and their interests."

"Who do you work for?"

"That's not important. All you need to know is that we know everything you do." Raoul looked at the notes he was given to make sure he conveyed the scripted message, that he didn't leave anything out. "Taking your family is a warning to keep your mouth shut. It is the only warning you will receive. Go about your business and only your business."

"So that's it. You work for Albright!"

Raoul roared with laughter. "Ha. No, we work for one ruthless son of a bitch. It's a waste of time for you to keep guessing."

"And if I agree, you will release my family?"

"In a couple of days. After we see how you behave."

"A couple of days!" Jeremy shouted. "I'm not agreeing to anything unless you release my family now. If you don't, I'm going to the police."

Jennifer didn't need to hear both sides of the conversation to understand the message. She was afraid, more so for her children than herself. She struggled to get free but Dwyer's coarse grip tightened around her arm, causing her to scream. As she did, the children started to cry.

"What are you doing to them? Stop it. I'll do whatever you ask," he said, reconsidering his approach as his concern reached new heights.

"Your wife is a frisky woman but she would be smarter to stay calm." Raoul paused and contemplated his captive.

"Have I told you that she is very lovely? I haven't been so close to a woman this beautiful in a long time."

"Please don't touch her," he begged. "Your issues are with me, not them. Take me and let them go!"

"Why would I trade you for her? You cannot be as sweet or soft. Besides, I have my orders and they don't include negotiating with you. I'm done talking. Your family will be fine if you do what I say. Mind your own business and stay away from the cops."

Tears in his eyes and a tremor in his voice, Jeremy pleaded. "Wait—" But it was too late. His tormentor was already gone.

Jeremy collapsed into his chair, afraid for his wife, his daughters, fear taking its toll, breaking him down. His family was in danger and he was responsible. He felt guilty, helpless. One phrase from the conversation, four words, resonated most loudly: "three chips to play," the voice had said. The message was much too clear; that bastard could kill one of his girls to show he meant business, then another and still be in control. Jeremy took some deep breaths hoping to slow his heartbeat, to calm his emotions, allowing him to think rationally.

Who was behind this? Who was ruthless enough to involve his family, to terrorize his wife and children? Max, if that was his real name, said it wasn't Vernon but why should he believe him? Vernon would never harm Jennifer and Melissa and Alexandra; Jeremy was sure of it. Then he wasn't. He wasn't sure of anything. It had to be Hendricks. He had to be involved. Then it hit him. Jeremy froze at the thought. He had no reason to believe that anyone knew of Tom Wichefski's involvement but maybe he was being naïve. What if they had sources in the FBI? Jeremy was told to keep his mouth shut but he had already involved the FBI. Maybe it wasn't too late to stop Tom from involving others in the Bureau. He prayed that was the case. If Max found out would he really take one of their lives? Jeremy was overcome by a wave of nausea at the thought of being responsible for.... His hands shook, his body nearly convulsed. Would they kill Melissa? She was the youngest and probably the most difficult to control. Or would it be Alexandra? Or maybe Jennifer? She would be the strongest witness once this was over. Different scenarios ran through his mind, each picture more mentally debilitating than the last.

Jeremy considered his options—some barely plausible, others completely unrealistic. He could try to find his family by himself but without any leads it would be impossible. He could confront Hendricks, but what if the scumbag panicked and told his henchmen to get rid of the evidence? Every option he considered was flawed. There was nothing to do but contact Wichefski. He had no choice; it was a risk he had to take. Besides, Wichefski was already involved. The privacy function on his office console was usually reliable, but, at this point, Jeremy was suspicious of everyone and everything. He grabbed his cell phone and dialed.

Jeremy took a breath, endeavoring to regain his composure but it was an impossible task. It took him awhile to recount the conversation, fighting back a complete collapse as he relayed the threat to kill his family. He ended by saying, "I thought you said they would be safe."

"That *is* what I thought. I am so sorry, Jeremy." There was clear remorse in Tom's voice.

"I'm not blaming you, Tom. You've been more than helpful, but right now the only concern I have is for my family. I could care less about Vernon or Hendricks. What should I do now?"

Tom carefully considered his reply. "I don't want to sugar coat it."

"I'm not looking for comfort. I'm looking for help in getting my family back."

"If Vernon is responsible then this is probably a scare tactic, albeit a desperate one, but I can't imagine him thinking he can get away with this. So, let's take him out of the equation. That leaves us with Hendricks."

"I can't believe I put my wife and children in this position. I'll do anything to get them back. Anything!"

"They'll be okay, Jeremy. As soon as we get off the phone I'll update the Director and we'll do all we can to bring them home."

"You can't do that. They may have people in your office. Hendricks is worth billions. He can get to anyone." Jeremy spoke so quickly his words ran together, barely intelligible.

"There are only two people in the Bureau who know about this and that's me and Pflucek. I can guarantee that neither one of us is corrupt."

"Okay, okay, but what will you tell him?"

"That time is not on our side. That Buck and Vernon should be brought in immediately. Vernon will buckle when we question him. And so will Hendricks. They're both looking at serious felonies. Whichever one of them is less culpable will turn on the other in a heartbeat at the prospect of spending life in a federal prison."

"Okay but assuming Hendricks is behind this, what if he gets spooked and hurts them? Or worse!"

"That won't happen because he'll be wrapped up so tight he won't be able to contact anyone. But let's start with Vernon and see what we learn. We can decide what to do with the cowboy after. We don't want to spread the net too wide and give whoever is behind this an opportunity to find out that you're not obeying orders."

"And what about Marty? What should we do with her?"

"Same thing as Hendricks for now. I'll put a top surveillance team on both. Meanwhile we'll see what we can wring out of Albright. Trust me, he'll roll over as soon as we get him in here."

Jeremy offered a final thought. "If there is a conspiracy to rig the oil markets, there has to be more to it than just Vernon buying stock in a bunch of small companies. Someone has to be pushing up the price by trading the underlying commodity. All trades taking place in either London or here are recorded. Between the FSA in London and the SEC, you should be able to get those records and track them to the settling broker."

"Already being done. The data is being culled to see if there was any irrational buying of crude contracts, any abnormal buying patterns. They're doing the same with the stocks in Vernon's portfolio, even checking to see if the timing of the purchases of both instruments overlapped. If there's any suspicious activity, rest assured they will find it."

"I'm really worried, Tom, I'm so afraid for them. I just hope Jennifer can hold on and that she doesn't try anything foolish."

Chapter 72

□ □ □

Jeremy had reason to be concerned. At that very moment, Jennifer determined that she would not sit idly by and wait for this nightmarish episode to play out. Slowly and carefully, she surveyed her surroundings, not wanting to make her thoughts of escape obvious. In the brief conversations that she had had with her captors she had acted demure and afraid for the safety of her children, hoping her submissive behavior would cause them to relax their guard.

Observing entrances on all four sides, Jennifer surmised that the large warehouse occupied an entire city block. Each opening was wide and high enough to accommodate a decent size truck. She noticed that rust had started to eat away at the hardware on the doors and the remaining fixtures that hung from the ceiling, the broken windows accelerating the work of the elements. The multi-paned windows that surrounded the long vacant building had served as target practice for a group of kids testing their accuracy with a handful of stones. She had little difficulty recognizing the odor that hung in the air, the stench clearly emanating from a nearby body of water. This made sense since warehouses were often built close to major transportation routes such as waterways and railroads. Looking at her watch, she worked backward from when she picked up the kids from their play date, estimating the length of time that she had been in the warehouse and then how long she had been unconscious. Jennifer also deduced that her captors were unlikely to travel over a toll road and risk being stopped. The Hudson River, she was sure of it. The Hudson was likely mere blocks away which placed them in close proximity to Manhattan. It had to be. Great information but to what end?

Alexandra snapped Jennifer out of performing any further analysis for the time being. "I'm thirsty, Mommy."

"Me too." Even in the middle of this nightmare, Jennifer couldn't help but smile at the adorable predictability of Melissa copying her older sister.

Seizing the moment, Jennifer turned to one of the two guards. "I need some water for my babies. They're also going to get hungry for dinner pretty soon."

"We'll get food later. There are water bottles in the truck."

In her most timid voice she asked, "Could you please get them for us?"

"Yeah, right. Get them yourself."

Jennifer stepped over the cardboard walls of the playpen and entered the van through the side doors. She moved toward the rear where the water bottles lay loosely scattered on the floor. Bending over, she noticed a jack handle under the spare tire. Her heart raced as she tried to dislodge it by wiggling it back and forth under the heavy tire. It barely moved. To gain leverage, Jennifer squatted, sitting back on her haunches, spreading her feet slightly past the width of her shoulders. She tightened her grip on the jack handle and pulled hard. It came free but her momentum carried it over her shoulder and into the side of the van, metal hitting metal.

"What are you doing in there?" Dwyer shouted at her as he moved around the van to peer inside.

Jennifer had placed the jack handle on the floor and was already moving toward the door of the van. "I dropped one but don't worry, it didn't break." She held four bottles precariously in her arms and offered one to Dwyer, which he accepted.

Suddenly and without warning, the girls screamed. Jenn feared the worst and turned to look.

"Mommy, mommy, look! I'm scared of that thing."

Alexandra pointed at a large rat running across the floor. The sisters began crying hysterically.

"Shut them up." Raoul said firmly, covering his ears with both hands.

"They're tired. They missed their nap."

"Then put them to sleep."

"I don't want to lie down here," Melissa responded, crossing her arms in defiance. "That thing will eat me."

"With those rats running around, the only way they'll nap is if I put them on the floor of the van. Otherwise they'll just keep crying."

"Do it. Just stop the noise. If they were my kids they would feel the back of my hand."

"You probably don't have kids."

"They're a nuisance," Raoul snarled.

Jennifer picked up Melissa and held her close. As she carried her to the van, she whispered in her ear. "Be a good girl for Mommy. I really need you to pretend to go to sleep. Let's make a game of it. See how long you can keep your eyes closed."

"Okay Mommy." Melissa wrapped her arms around her mother's neck and then kissed her on the cheek three times. Everything in threes. Jennifer nearly melted, holding back the tears.

Next, she lifted Alexandra and whispered the same thing.

Chapter 73 □ □ □

Each time the phone rang, Jeremy was hoping to hear Jennifer's voice telling him they were safe and unharmed. Sadly, that call never came. But the phone did ring. It was Wichefski.

"Is Vernon in the office?"

"He should be. Why?"

"I'm going to run him over the coals and see what he knows about your family. It's pretty obvious he's in this shit neck deep, so anyone he knows in DC will be the first to bury him when this story breaks. I'm in the car and on my way to your office."

"No way, Tom," Jeremy protested. "They were pretty clear about what they will do if they find out I brought you into this."

"They won't find out. The only people who know about this are you, me, my boss and Vernon and he won't have a chance to tell anyone."

"What if he asks for a lawyer?"

"With his activities in wire fraud, money laundering and driving up the price of oil which feeds the treasuries of countries that fund terrorism, we can make a case that he's violated the Patriot Act. That means he has forfeited his right to counsel. If we wanted to, we could lock him up at Guantanamo and no one would even know he was there."

Silence. No reaction.

"What's wrong, Jeremy? You're okay with this, aren't you?"

"No. It's too big a risk to take and is too big a stretch. Albright's not a terrorist so I don't know how you can take away his rights. I'm not defending him; I just want to make sure you can do what you say you're going to do and that one of his high-priced lawyers doesn't get in the way."

"There's more to this than you think," Tom responded firmly. "Deputy Director Pflucek wants me to bring in both Albright and Hendricks."

Jeremy seethed. "Fuck him! It's my family that's at risk!"

"Hold on a second. No one is interested in taking any chances with your family's safety and we're not going to do anything that puts them in further jeopardy. Trust me on this; questioning Vernon now is the right thing to do. It's the best chance we have of finding your family without alerting their captors. We can leave Buck for later."

Jeremy considered Tom's approach. He was on the verge of going to see Vernon before Tom's suggestion that they do it together. Maybe having a seasoned FBI agent by his side would provide the appropriate amount of pressure to extract the information they needed.

"I see your point," he offered in a much calmer voice. "Having you there in an official capacity should put Vernon in the right frame of mind to come clean with what he knows."

"One more thing," Wichefski added. "When Deputy Director Pflucek called D.C., he was told that the SEC had already begun their investigation based upon their systems being triggered by some unusual trading patterns in both crude and certain stocks."

"What did they find?"

"A few minor leads. There are a handful of floor brokers that seem to be price insensitive when buying large amounts of contracts on behalf of their customers. The SEC's systems also determined that these same brokers were usually active on the same days. You're the pro. What do you think?"

"Guaranteed those brokers and the accounts they are trading for are conduits in the scheme. Even the greediest traders don't keep buying size positions in an up market.

In fact, they're more apt to sell into the momentum, particularly with commodities that are the absolute riskiest instruments since they use the most leverage. There has to be some pretty deep pockets behind those traders as well as some sure-fire information."

"Is Albright a likely candidate to fund this scheme?" Wichefski asked.

"Unlikely. He hates the commodities market. Convinced it is absolutely rigged."

"I have news for you—he may be right. But what if he is one of the people rigging it?"

"Extremely unlikely but it wouldn't matter," Jeremy responded definitively. "Besides, if he knows the direction of the energy commodities, he can make a fortune buying stock in the companies most affected, which appears to be exactly what he is doing."

"Seems that way. Let's change direction for a second. What about Marty? Is she in the office?"

"You're not thinking about bringing her in for questioning, too, are you, Tom?"

"Not yet. I don't want to raise her antenna but I do want to make sure we know where she is in case we do have to get to her. She is clearly not an innocent observer in all this."

"Innocent? She's guilty as sin."

Jeremy owed a good deal of his success managing money to risk management, paying attention to detail, even small details. He should have paid more attention to who was standing outside the open door to his office.

Marty realized she should have acted sooner but perhaps it wasn't too late.

Chapter 74 □ □ □

Tom parked his government issued Chevrolet on Park Avenue and left the FBI placard in the windshield. Rushing into the building, he didn't notice Marty as she hurriedly exited from a different door. He took the waiting elevator and pressed the button for the sixtieth floor. Standing at the ready, he stepped into Parthenon's lobby as soon as the doors parted. His pace quickened as he moved past the receptionists, ignoring their entreaty to stop. Non-employees were not allowed beyond the entrance hall without being announced, although they had little concern about Tom's intentions. If Suzie's fiancé, an FBI agent, couldn't be trusted, who could?

"Got here as quick as I could," he said to Jeremy as he closed the office door. "You still good with questioning Vernon?"

"I don't see any other way." Jeremy responded, resigned to moving forward.

"Are Vernon and Marty in their offices?"

"Vernon is but Marty apparently just left. She told the receptionist she was going downstairs to grab a bite."

"I'm not going to count on her coming back. As a precaution I'll station a team outside her apartment in case she shows there. I want to know where she is at all times until we have your family safe."

"I appreciate that, Tom."

"Now let's go pay your boss a visit."

Their stride was purposeful and deliberate but in no way rushed. The last thing they wanted to do was create a commotion. Suzie was finishing a call as they entered her area outside Vernon's office.

"Tom!" Suzie exclaimed, a wide smile forming on her lips. "What a nice surprise. I like this new habit of yours, dropping in for a quick visit."

Neither Jeremy nor Tom had shared any information with Suzie, leaving her totally in the dark. Early in their relationship, Tom had been very direct, telling Suzie that if they ever got serious, the nature of his work made any discussion about it off limits. However, neither one envisioned that one of his most important cases would involve her boss.

"We're here to see Vernon."

No kiss hello, no smile from Tom meeting her smile. Suzie was confused. She suspected trouble but knew not to delve into her concerns. "He's finishing a call but he shouldn't be long."

Tom agreed, not out of deference to office protocol but out of a desire not to raise an alarm in case Vernon was on the phone with Hendricks or someone else involved in the case.

"Vernon will want to know the subject matter before he sees you," Suzie said, her eyes pleading for her fiancé's cooperation.

Tom softened, knowing that Suzie's professional world was about to implode. "I'm sorry, but I can't say. All I can tell you is that this is official government business. I really hate putting you in this situation but there's nothing I can do."

"I understand."

"Once we are in his office, please hold all his calls. Tell everyone he's in a meeting and cannot be disturbed under any circumstance."

Suzie didn't press the issue, beginning to understand that the circumstances were far from business as usual. She turned to Jeremy. "You know there will be fireworks."

Jeremy just nodded. It was an uncharacteristically muted response from someone whom she had come to expect more of. They all stood in uncomfortable silence, their eyes focused on the phone console, waiting for the red light to die, indicating Vernon's call was finished. Less than a minute later, Suzie begrudgingly gave them the okay to enter. Albright was startled to see them invade his sanctum.

"Is Suzie not at her desk?"

Staying with their plan, Jeremy stood silent and let Tom take the lead. "She is and she tried to stop us but this is not a social visit."

Vernon didn't have to be told that he should be concerned; he realized he was there for one reason and one reason only. He had no intention of allowing Wichefski to intimidate him. "I don't take unannounced meetings; my time is much too valuable. Now march the hell out of here and make an appointment with my secretary."

Tom ignored Albright's admonition and helped himself to a seat. Jeremy occupied another chair, catching Vernon's steely stare, an expression of contempt for the act of betrayal that would surely be at the root of this conversation.

"And what brings you into my office, you damn ingrate." Albright's words were laced with venom. "Are you here to ask for a raise because the millions I pay you each year aren't enough?"

Jeremy slowly rose from his seat, transforming his normally stoic persona into a menacing presence. Leaning over Vernon's desk, palms pressed firmly on the surface, muscles taut, he responded with disdain. "It's not always about money. Right now it's about my family. And you are going to tell us what we need to know or...." He held his words, realizing that he was deviating from the plan, that threats shouldn't be the first course of action.

Albright didn't allow his shock at Jeremy's uncharacteristic insolence to put him on the defensive. Instead he tilted back in his overstuffed leather chair, a smirk across his face. "Well, well. Finally showing some balls. It took a while but maybe your training is now complete." He leaned forward,

402 □ STEPHEN L. WEISS

resigned to a discussion. "As long as you gentlemen have decided to grace me with your presence I may be able to spare a few seconds. But before we start I have one piece of business to attend to." Vernon again fixed his stare at Jeremy. "Jeremy, you're fired."

Emotions boiled over and Jeremy flew around the desk. "Why you cavalier piece..."

Feeling vulnerable in his chair as Jeremy looked down upon him, Vernon quickly stood. Tom responded, coming around the massive desk and positioning himself in between them.

"That's enough, Jeremy. Let's do what we came here to do and not make a bad situation much worse."

"You're absolutely right." Jeremy said, perhaps more shocked at his loss of control than were the others.

Vernon smoothed the front of his shirt, tugged on the French cuffs of each sleeve, patted the sides of his hair and sat back down. They each took their seats.

Tom started the conversation again. "Since you've already dispensed with the niceties, Vernon, I'll get right to the point of our visit. We have good reason to believe that you are involved in the disappearance of Jeremy's family."

Albright's poker face faded into an expression of surprise and then concern. His anxiety had much less to do with the Cranford's safety than with being accused of a serious criminal offense.

"What do you mean, disappearance? I would never do anything to harm them. That's crazy."

"One of your friends," Jeremy responded, clearly disgusted, "is holding my wife and daughters and threatening to hurt them if I don't keep my mouth shut. I need you to tell me where they are and who else is involved."

"You think I would do something like that? I may be a lot of things, but I'm not a common, violent criminal. I'm not a criminal at all."

Vernon's focus continued to be solely on his predicament. He thought about asking for a lawyer and then discounted the thought as quickly as it popped into his head, not wanting to create the impression that he had something to hide. Clearly, the seriousness of the circumstance still avoided his grasp. He was Vernon Albright and invulnerable. He could take on all comers.

Tom became impatient with the opening dance sequence. "Here's the deal," he said, laying out the facts. "We know you've been involved in some bad shit between manipulating the small stocks you own, trading on inside information, manipulating the oil markets and various other violations of securities laws as well as the Patriot Act. And those are just the appetizers before we get to the main course, kidnapping."

"That's a joke," Albright responded, his voice trembling. "Kidnapping? What the hell are you talking about? I would never harm anyone. And as far as the other items on your fishing list, my reputation is unassailable. I have never needed to do anything illegal to make money for my investors. And I have never, ever invested in commodities. This discussion is over until you either produce an arrest warrant or my lawyer gets here. I've got too many friends in Washington to be treated like this by some low level field agent."

Out of the corner of his eye, Jeremy could see Tom bristle at Vernon's rebuke and waited for his response.

"Since you asked, here it is." Tom withdrew an arrest warrant from his coat pocket. "I don't think you completely grasp what's going on so let me simplify it for you. You are being accused of multiple violations under the Patriot Act. Maybe you aren't particularly familiar with the particulars of that law since it is relatively new. Being a low level civil servant I have been charged with the mandate of enforcing its provisions and would be more than willing to provide you with a brief tutorial on how it affects your rights."

Vernon fell silent, physically deflated at the sight of the warrant that now sat on his desk.

"Under the Patriot Act," Wichefski continued, "you

404 STEPHEN L. WEISS

have no right to an attorney, no right to a phone call, no right to do anything except accompany me to prison. I can even go through every file in your office without a search warrant. Now do you understand the Patriot Act and what deep shit you are in?"

Vernon's expression no longer concealed his concern. The first image that popped into his mind was walking out of his office in handcuffs and shackles, being led into prison and confined in a small cell with murderers and rapists. But any letting down of his guard was momentary. He rallied back quickly, restoring his ability to logically sort through his options, still unwilling to admit to anything. He wasn't going to be baited into a confession or an acknowledgement of complicity; at least not yet and definitely not without a deal. He reasoned that if Wichefski had significant proof, he'd already be in custody. *Damn it! I'm Vernon Albright. I've got friends in high places. Do you really want to fuck with me?*

"I appreciate the tutorial, but I happen to be familiar with the Patriot Act although I am still puzzled why you mention it since I have not run afoul of its provisions. However, I am concerned about the Cranford children and Jennifer although I don't know what I can do to help." The words rung hollow; Albright's ability to care about anything outside of himself was a significantly underdeveloped character trait.

Absent tangible and crushing proof, or a pair of stainless steel bracelets around his wrists, Vernon wasn't going to break easy. And hauling him from the office just wasn't an option. By the time they entered Federal Plaza to book him, every paparazzi and reporter in the city would get wind of his arrest. No doubt the kidnappers would also find out, putting Jennifer and the children at significant risk.

"Maybe I shouldn't have lost my temper but you can certainly understand my frame of mind," Jeremy offered in a conciliatory tone. Pandering always worked best on large egos. "You wouldn't feel any different if it were your wife and children that were kidnapped."

"We're not clicking, Jeremy," Albright sneered, "so let me try a different approach. If Jennifer and your children are in some sort of danger, then I want to do anything in my considerable power to help, but I am appalled that you believe that I am in any way involved."

"This isn't about you, you pretentious ass," Jeremy shot back. "This is about my family."

"I don't have to sit here and take this garbage from either one of you," Albright countered. "Get the hell out of my office." He stood and pointed to the door. "NOW!"

They were working against the clock, trying to get information from Albright before the kidnappers found out that Jeremy had violated the conditions for keeping his family alive. Wichefski could see that a more proactive stance was required and took the only course of action that remained viable, hoping that Vernon would finally realize the gravity of his predicament. Wichefski stood and reached behind his back, extracting a pair of handcuffs from the small leather case attached to his belt.

"Vernon Albright, I am hereby serving you with this warrant for your arrest for violations under the Patriot Act. Please place both your hands behind your head and stand up."

The color drained from Albright's complexion. "Wh-what?" he stammered. "Are you ... are you kidding? You have no reason to arrest me."

"You have the right to remain silent. Anything that you say or do...." Even though it was not required under the Patriot Act, Wichefski thought a reading of the Miranda warning would add drama, feed into Albright's fear of arrest. He wasn't done. "It is also my duty to inform you that you are a person of interest in the murder of Paul Robbins."

The word murder had a whole different ring to it. Albright instantly conjured up a life in prison and possibly execution. "That's preposterous. I wouldn't harm anyone. I want a lawyer."

As Jeremy stood by, Wichefski gave no quarter. "If you don't do as I say, Mr. Albright, you will leave me no choice but to use physical force."

"Wait. This has gone far enough. I'll tell you what I know. Hendricks," he blurted out. "Buck Hendricks is who you want."

Jeremy cut in. "Where's my family? Is Hendricks behind this? Does he have my family?"

"I really don't know. I've never harmed anyone and despite what you think of me, I'm not about to start now with your family."

"Would Buck?"

Albright collapsed. For the first time in his life, he felt helpless. His ability to intimidate was gone. In an uncharacteristically empathetic rush of emotions, he feared that this situation was going to have a very ugly ending for the Cranfords. More so, in his pitifully demented mind, he feared for himself.

Chapter 75 □ □ □

By the time the FBI had mobilized a team, Marty had already been to her apartment and left with what she needed. Her next stop was The Carlyle Hotel where she found Buck alone in his study ransacking his desk. A briefcase lay on the floor, bulging at the seams.

"Going somewhere?"

"Hey, Marty," he answered without looking up. "Taking a quick trip back to God's country. Got some issues to deal with that just sort of popped up."

"And those issues require bringing all your files?"

"Not all, just a few, but Carla must have been straightening up in here because I can't find some that I need. You didn't happen to see any floating around this place somewhere?"

"I don't really pay much attention to your business in here. What sort of files are you looking for?"

"Forget it. Not important." Buck went back to his search.

Marty listened for other noises in the apartment but heard nothing. "Where are Rick and Carla?"

Buck straightened up and rubbed his lower back. It was tense from bending over the low hanging drawer. "You taking attendance?" he said without the smallest trace of a smile.

"Nope. Just curious. It's not like you to leave yourself without a servant."

"Servant? That's kind of harsh," Buck responded with a quizzical look. "I treat my people well. Carla's running an errand and Rick is on his way out to Jersey to take care of a few things."

"What's in Jersey?"

Buck decided to fill Marty in on the latest developments. Since she would undoubtedly find out as soon as she returned to the office, he decided it would be better to put his own spin on it.

"Seems Cranford is alive and kicking. He's gumming up the works a little so I had to take out an insurance policy."

"What type of insurance policy?"

"I'm holding onto the Cranford kids and his wife until that boy realizes how good he's had it. He's throwing all sorts of threats at Vern and I can't let that happen. If he starts talking to the police, then you and I have some real problems. And Vernon isn't the strongest guy in the world either, so I'm just looking to help him out. Sort of give him the gumption to do what he has to. If he sees that I'm serious with Cranford, he'll think twice about turning over on me."

"Is that what Rock is doing?"

"He is going to check on them. I don't like him getting his hands dirty too directly. He found some boys to do the heavy lifting."

Marty stared at Buck with utter contempt. "Your stupidity knows no bounds. There were other ways to handle this."

"Why you no good piece of trash," Buck shouted as he moved toward Marty, his hand raised and ready to strike. "Who the fuck are you to—"

Marty met Buck's threat with a silver handled revolver she pulled from her purse, halting his advance.

"That's my gun," he said in disbelief. "Put it down before it goes off."

"How inconsiderate of me to not have asked your permission to borrow it, but don't worry... you're about to get it back."

"Please don't...don't...," he stammered, pleading in a voice devoid of his usual bravado. "Be careful with that thing." He opened his arms, welcoming Marty into an embrace. "I'm sorry for yelling at you. You know I don't mean to hurt your feelings."

"Sit down and shut up."

With a steady hand, Marty kept the gun aimed directly at Buck's center. He was unsteady as he lowered himself onto the closest chair.

The steely resolve in Marty's eyes signaled to Buck that she had no qualms about pulling the trigger. His concern heightened as her appearance took on an entirely different aura than he had ever noticed. This was not the same young woman who he had reigned over so effortlessly.

Marty continued. "You really carried things one step too far, Buck. I was so in the money. The price of crude was flying and I was about to make enough money to be done with this crap and done with you."

He squirmed in his seat. "I'll give you multiples of anything you were making trading crude. Just don't..."

"No you moron, I was onto something much bigger. It was the perfect plan until your stupidity brought the cops into it. You're weak, Buck, real weak, and I'll be damned if I'm going to risk you opening your mouth."

"What cops?" Buck bordered on dazed, his confusion evident. "What are you talking about?"

"The FBI is onto you, you idiot. They're sitting outside my apartment waiting for me and at Parthenon questioning the old man."

Buck began to stand.

"Sit your ass down."

"Listen, Marty, if they want anyone, it's me and Vernon. We're the big dogs. They have no interest in you. I'll keep my mouth shut and triple what I was going to pay you."

A smug look replaced Marty's angry expression. "Please don't be angry with me," she offered in a mocking tone, "but I've already settled our business. You're not too careful about keeping your passwords and account information secure. Actually, I've been remiss in not showing my appreciation for the nice bonus you paid me. It should make it a lot easier to retire to some faraway place where no one will ever find me. I may even buy a small island and get a new identity. Hmmm, I almost forgot that I have one already. For the brief time we are going to know each other please call me Bridgette." Marty paused; Buck's body appeared to deflate, shrinking his large frame into a mass without structure. "Put your hands behind the chair and clasp them together," she said, motioning with the pistol as she spoke.

"Wh-wh-what are you going to do?" His voice shook with fear.

"Just shut up and do it if you want to live. I'm running out of patience."

He did as he was told.

"Now clasp your hands together."

Again, he complied. Marty moved behind the chair and took out a long plastic tie, similar to what the police used in place of metal handcuffs. With one hand she threaded the plastic through the lattice of the chair back and tied Buck's wrists together.

"I'll give you more? How much, how much do you want?"

"Shut up, Buck. You're really getting on my nerves."

Buck struggled to free himself but it was useless. Marty remained behind the chair, out of his vision. She quickly extracted a handkerchief from her pocket and in one swift move, placed the cloth on top of the gun and the barrel against Buck's temple and pulled the trigger. The handkerchief kept her clothes free from splattered blood. All signs of life trembled from his body as Buck gave one last gasp. Working efficiently, she removed the plastic ties that bound his wrists then pulled another gun from her bag, similar in all respects to Buck's weapon but for the decorative handle and a cylinder filled with sand attached to the barrel. This device would catch the second bullet. She positioned the weapon in Buck's hand and forced his finger to pull the trigger, an act that would have been impossible were he still alive. This would satisfy forensic testing for gunpowder residue on his hand and confirm suicide as the cause of death. As the final step, Marty exchanged her pistol for Buck's, again positioning his hand and finger as if he pulled the trigger. Ballistic tests would confirm that the gun he held fired the bullet that caused his death. With the duplicate gun back in her bag, she hurried around the desk and quickly fanned through the files in the briefcase and what remained in the desk, making sure that she had not previously left anything behind. Satisfied that everything was as it should be, Marty pulled a longhaired brown wig from her bag, placed it back on her head and flew down six flights of stairs, picking up the elevator where it had dropped her off. When police questioned the lift operator, he would respond that no one had ridden his elevator to the Penthouse the entire day.

Marty had a few other loose ends to secure, to ensure that no one would be able to connect her to Buck. Once out of The Carlyle, she headed downtown walking at a leisurely pace so as not to draw any attention. She stood on the corner of seventy-second street and flagged down a cab to take her back to the office. With the meter still running, the taxi came to a stop abreast of a row of black radio cars for hire that idled curbside, waiting to take their customers to the airport or other destinations. She paid her fare, leaving a normal sized tip, hurried into the building and took a seat in Starbucks where she could observe the elevator bank. And then she waited.

Chapter 76

□ □ □

Wichefski had seen it multiple times; the suspects that had begun their interrogation with the strongest resistance would often capitulate most easily. They were the ones so used to getting their own way; pampered rich folk like Vernon or poor kids from tough neighborhoods who still had momma taking care of them, making dinner, doing their wash. The bravado was always false, their fortitude quickly spent. With time continuing to be a consideration, Wichefski pressed his subject.

"We've got one primary concern at this point, and that's Jeremy's family. Tell us what you know about their situation."

"Before I say anything I need some assurances." Albright responded, reflexively calling upon his first instinct of self-preservation.

Jeremy was poised to lunge at Albright again but Tom saw it coming and held him at bay, softly straight arming him in the chest.

"Hold on Jeremy, I'll handle this." He put his arm down. "How about this for assurance? If anything happens to the family, I guarantee you that the government will seek the death penalty."

"That threat doesn't intimidate me at all," Albright said, catching a second wind. "I told you I had nothing to do with the kidnapping and I meant it."

Jeremy noticed the glint in Albright's eyes. Incredibly, he was now looking at this encounter as a battle of wills, as a game. "Tom, can I speak with you a second," he said as he dragged Wichefski off to the far side of the office. "We're not going to win by brow beating him. He's too arrogant and too smart. He realizes that if he tells us anything that his leverage is diminished. As much as it pains me, we have to negotiate."

Wichefski nodded his agreement. There was a bigger picture to consider and right now Albright represented their best shot at pulling it all together. "I don't have the authority to make any deals with you but I give you my word that if your information proves helpful I will speak with the prosecutors on your behalf."

"You really do take me for a moron, don't you?" Albright threw his head back and laughed, his conceit returning in full force. "I suggest that you speak with one of your superiors who possesses the appropriate authority. Otherwise I believe that we have a stalemate." He turned to Jeremy, contempt in his voice. "You may want to chime in here at some point, Cranford."

Jeremy used every ounce of self-control to hold himself back. Through gritted teeth and clenched jaw, he said, "Do what he wants, Tom. We have no choice."

"That's the good servile employee I remember," Albright chortled.

Wichefski pulled his gun from the holster on his belt and handed it to Jeremy. "I'm stepping out to call my office. If he tries to leave, aim for the leg so he can still talk."

Albright didn't blink as he and Jeremy stared at one another. "It didn't have to turn out this way, Jeremy. All you had to do was mind your own business. Instead you betrayed me and in the process killed the golden goose. I knew you would fail at some point. Sure you're smart and have good market instincts but at the end of the day, you're too weak for this game."

"Weak? Is that how you define not using inside information to boost returns? I did just fine, thank you, without resorting to the shit you did. But you? You're a complete fraud. Probably was never able to make any money without having someone whispering in your ear, telling you what to do. That is your legacy; what will follow you to prison and to your grave." He continued to deride his former mentor. "The great Vernon Albright, the legendary investor, reduced to prison stripes instead of pinstripes. I can't wait to see your picture in Forbes. Maybe you will make their new list of the four hundred biggest has-beens. And the folks on Page Six should have a party with you, too. Wonder how long that trophy wife of yours will hang around?"

Tom came back into the office, reached across Vernon's desk and dialed the phone. Pflucek came on instantly. "Go ahead, Director."

"This is Giovanni Pflucek, Deputy Director of the FBI and Agent in charge of the New York Office. I am authorized to offer you a plea arrangement."

Chapter 77 □ □ □

Perhaps it's the innocence of young children that allow them to fall asleep virtually anywhere, under any conditions. The Cranford sisters were no exception. In virtual synchronization, they fell asleep on the floor of the van. Jennifer wasn't expecting them to stay out for long since their internal alarm clocks would soon let them know that it was time for dinner.

"It's been a long time since their last meal so they'll need to eat as soon as they wake up. If they don't have food they'll start crying again. Is there a store nearby?" Jennifer asked innocently.

"I don't know but a McDonald's is never far. Dwyer will take the truck and bring us food."

"He can't take the van because if I have to wake the children from the deep sleep they're in, they'll be miserable and I won't be able to stop their whining. You won't like that very much. There has to be a store within walking distance. We don't need a McDonald's; we can probably make do with a few snacks like chips or crackers."

Raoul laughed. "You assume you'll be leaving here soon but I'm not so sure. You may want more than a snack. I know I do."

"All I know is that waking my children from a sound sleep isn't a good idea. It will be better for everyone if they can finish their naps and get up on their own. But when they do get up, they will need food. It could be anything. It's up to you but if I could suggest something.... " Jennifer waited for permission to continue.

"Continue." Raoul folded his arms across his chest signaling his impatience with the conversation.

"How about going to the local store now and once my daughters wake up Dwyer can drive to a McDonald's?"

"I like that idea," Dwyer concurred. "I could use the fresh air."

"Fine, but hurry," Raoul concurred. "If they start that damn whining again, I'll shut them up myself."

"You're a big man around little girls and women," Jennifer said, disgusted. "Aren't you?"

"Don't push me, bitch. I'm not your husband."

Raoul raised his hand to strike, but Dwyer grabbed his arm. "Don't do it, Raoul. Not yet."

"I'm sorry," Jennifer said meekly, more fearful yet imbued with greater resolve to control the fate of her family. "I didn't mean to insult you."

Raoul shook his arm loose from his cohort's grip. "I don't like babysitting. If my orders weren't to keep you unharmed for now, you wouldn't be talking to me this way. As long as your husband obeys orders, and you keep your mouth shut, you'll be okay. But remember, two hostages work as well as three. Now be a good girl," he ordered in a condescending voice, "and don't cause any more trouble."

A reservoir of tears filled Jennifer's eyes. "I'm sorry, I'm just so afraid for my babies. I'll do whatever you say but please don't hurt them."

"That's better. You learn quick." He turned to Dwyer. "Get going. I'm hungry."

Raoul was feeling like this was going to be an easy job after all. Dwyer would soon be bringing him food and that skinny bitch finally understood her place. He returned to his chair on the other side of the makeshift playpen while Jennifer, clearly dejected, sat on the edge of the van keeping watch over the children.

It was quiet and hot in the large warehouse; along with boredom, it provided a near perfect setting for nodding off. Raoul fought the urge to close his eyes but quickly lost the struggle. Each time his chin fell to his chest, he would briefly stir into a state of wakefulness. Jennifer noticed that each interval of sleep stretched out for longer periods. She repeatedly looked at her watch, growing more anxious with each revolution around the dial. There was no way of telling how much time she had before Dwyer returned. She inched her way further into the van. Alexandra began to stir and Jennifer whispered instructions in her ear. Next, she gently rubbed Melissa's back. As the younger child started to wake Jennifer repeated the instructions.

The children began to cry. Raoul shouted from his chair. "Be quiet."

The crying became louder and he became more annoyed. "Shut those kids up. I warned you."

"I can't. Melissa's hurt. She got her arm stuck under the spare tire when I wasn't looking. I need some help."

Raoul stormed across the floor. "I'll help you. I'll help you shut those kids up," he growled in disgust. He grabbed the side of the van to lift himself inside.

Jennifer swung the jack handle with all her strength, catching Raoul flush in the face. His cheekbones shattered and his nose gave way to the force of the blow, receding into his skull. He grabbed at his face as blood spurted everywhere. Overcome with pain he fell backward to the floor.

Jennifer leapt from the van and administered blow after blow to Raoul's head until he was still. Blood splattered on her clothing and a stream of crimson liquid seeped from Raoul's prone body into the cracks of the concrete, following their jagged path along the warehouse floor. As they had been instructed in her whispers, the children never so much as stole a glance at the body as it lay on the floor, instead using all their concentration to climb into the front seat. Alexandra was in charge of pulling the seat belt across their small bodies and snapping it into the locking mechanism.

Jennifer wasn't at all apprehensive about searching

Raoul's lifeless form for the key to the van's ignition. But as she did, Raoul reached up and grabbed her ponytail. Despite her shock, she held her scream. His grip was firm and he reeled Jennifer in toward his prone body. She was close enough to feel his spittle as he cursed her but Jennifer did not flinch. She braced one arm against his chest, locking her elbow, keeping space between them. With her other hand she clawed at the hand that held her hair but his clenched fist wouldn't yield. As her left arm began to fold, she wrapped her right hand around the metal bar that lay on the floor beside them. In one lightning quick move, she raised it up and thrust the chiseled end down into Raoul's neck. His eyes popped and he flailed around, trying to extract the jack handle from his throat but the life drained from him before he was able to succeed.

Jennifer stood over her conquest. "I guess you get the point now, fat boy."

Jennifer looked herself over and was disgusted by what she saw. She removed her blood soaked outer shirt; the tank top she wore underneath would have to do for now. Keys tightly in her grasp, she slid into the driver's seat as Alexandra finally completed fastening the seat belt that she shared with her sister.

"See Mommy, I told you I could do it."

Jennifer smiled as she reached over and further tightened the nylon belt around her daughters' midsections, securing them into the lone passenger seat.

"Weee!" Melissa excitedly exclaimed. "We get to ride in the front seat."

"Hold on tight to each other," Jennifer said smiling, relieved that they were oblivious to what had transpired with Raoul.

She turned the key in the ignition and the engine immediately kicked in. Her hand reached for the gearshift and pulled it down past reverse and neutral into drive. The next few minutes were critical as she hurried to leave before Dwyer returned.

Not sure which of the four exits was still in working order, she decided on the garage door that surrounded the opening Dwyer had used to exit. It was also closest to where the van was parked. Jennifer applied slight pressure to the accelerator as she turned the steering wheel to the full extent of its range lining up with the exit. She drove fifty feet, stopping just short of the large aluminum door. Hopping out of the vehicle, she ran the last couple of steps and crouched to grab the handles on the bottom. As she prepared to lift, she heard footsteps on the other side of the door and watched in fear as the knob began to turn. Jennifer turned and sprinted the short distance back to the van and jumped in. She threw the vehicle into reverse and allowed it to quietly idle backward a few feet before she applied the brake and shifted into drive once again. Jennifer placed both hands on the steering wheel and ducked below the dashboard.

Dwyer stepped into the warehouse where his attention was immediately drawn to the van, surprised that its engine was running. *We're leaving*, he thought. Dwyer surveyed the cavernous edifice looking for his partner and the hostages. His eyes finally settled on of Raoul's lifeless body, tire jack handle still protruding from his neck. He immediately turned to the van.

"You fucking whore. I will kill you and then your children."

Dwyer reached into the waistband of his pants, pulled a gun and pointed it at the truck's windshield, aiming directly at Jennifer as she lifted her head over the dashboard.

Jennifer spoke quickly and calmly to her children, not a hint of panic in her voice. "Put your heads down and close your eyes. Don't open them until I say or you won't get your surprise." It was a rhyme they had heard many times before and had always been well rewarded for playing along.

Jennifer tightened her grip around the steering wheel, her knuckles white from tension, and turned it slightly to line up her target. She lifted her right foot off the brake and jammed the gas pedal to the floor. The tires screeched on the cement and the smell of burning rubber filled the warehouse. As the van lurched forward she lifted off the accelerator before crashing into the wall. Dwyer wasn't as lucky. He felt every ounce of the two ton mass of machinery as it hit him full force, throwing him against the cinder block structure. Jennifer shifted her foot from brake to gas pedal and eased the vehicle forward, more slowly this time, crushing Dwyer against the building. Only the upper half of his body was visible, appearing suspended on the windshield. Blood poured from his mouth as his eyes rolled back into his head. She lifted the shift into reverse and backed away. Leaving nothing to chance, Jennifer took careful aim at the crumpled body on the warehouse floor and rolled over her once threatening captor, crushing his head under the large wheels

"Mommy, what's that bump? Can we look?"

"No," she screamed, wiping away tears. "Sorry, Mommy didn't mean to yell. There will be an extra special surprise if you can keep them closed just a teensy while longer."

"Okay, Mommy. I want three surprises."

The truck rolled forward stopping no more than two feet away from the garage door. Jennifer once again got out of the truck, grabbed the handle and lifted. The door barely budged. She tried a second time but it didn't move.

Jennifer looked around for something to use as leverage. Having no choice, she ran to Raoul's body. With single minded purpose, she averted her eyes, braced her foot against Raoul's chest and yanked the piece of metal from his neck. Then she grabbed the jack from the rear of the van and positioned it under the worn rubber strip at the bottom of the door. She inserted the bloody end of the handle into the base of the mechanism. After a few downward strokes the door lifted, rolling along the path of its rusted tracks.

Jennifer searched for a landmark as she exited the building and spotted the Empire State Building rising into the skyline across the Hudson River. She exhaled with relief but resisted the urge to feel completely safe until they had driven a further distance away. She had no idea where to find the nearest police station but wanted to be out of the neighborhood before asking for directions. After driving for only another minute or two she pulled over to the curb, her trembling hands unable to firmly grip the steering wheel. She closed her eyes, finally overcome with the realization that she had just taken two lives. Alexandra interrupted any further reflection.

"Mommy, can we open our eyes now?"

For the first time all afternoon, Jennifer laughed. "Of course you can."

It was the release she needed to continue on. Minutes later they were on Erie Street in Jersey City at Police Head-quarters. Jennifer scooted around to the passenger side of the van and opened the door, unbuckled the girls' seatbelt and lifted them out. Holding hands they ran inside, stopping at the front desk where a duty sergeant suspiciously spied her appearance, vestiges of blood still on her pants and two young kids in tow. His immediate thought was that they were the victims of domestic violence.

"We were kidnapped. I need to call my husband."

Chapter 78

□ □ □

The terms were verbally agreed upon but that wasn't good enough for Albright. "I want our agreement in writing and I want my lawyer to review it."

"Listen, Mr. Albright, you really are pushing this a bit too far." Pflucek had tried to be the voice of reason during the relatively quick process but his patience was fading. "I've made every concession I'm prepared to make. You have my word that we will live up to our end of the agreement providing that you live up to yours. There is no time for an attorney review."

Albright sat back and crossed his legs, relaxed and confident. "I guess that's the difference between the public and private sector. You people," condescension underscored, "are content to deal with matters of importance on an informal basis. These inefficiencies never work in the real world. Every deal of significance that I have ever entered into has been committed to paper so that there is no mistake in its interpretation at a future date." Albright continued on his soapbox. "Judging by the relative success of each of our careers, you would do well to take what I suggest under advisement. However, to show you how magnanimous and nurturing I can be, I will leave my attorney out of this and work directly with you to draft an acceptable document." Albright grinned at his own flippancy.

Suzie knocked on the door to Albright's office and listened carefully for a reply. With none forthcoming she knocked again and then tentatively poked her head into the office. "I am so sorry to interrupt but Jennifer is on the phone. Jeremy, do you want to take it in here?"

Jeremy's hopes skyrocketed then dove just as quick. Where was the leak? How did they know Albright was being questioned? He had no intention of allowing Albright to witness him groveling for his wife and children's wellbeing. "I'll take it at your desk."

Suzie handed Jeremy the receiver. "Jenn? Are you okay? What about the girls? We are trying our best to—"

Jennifer cried at the sound of his voice. "We're okay, honey, we are all fine! We got away!" Her cries turned into sobs. "I did some terrible things but we're safe."

"That's all that matters, Jenn. You did what you had to. Where are you? I'll come get you." His relief was manifested in slight tears of joy.

"We're at a police station in Jersey City on Erie Street. I'm still pretty shaken up. I don't want to leave here without you."

"I'll get there as soon as I can."

Jeremy gathered himself together, straightening the sloping shoulders that had been carrying the weight of his family's fate. He spun on his heels and strode into Vernon's office, so clearly a different person. The pen was in Vernon's hand, the sardonic smile across his lips, in stark contrast to Wichefski whose appearance offered testimony to his deal with the devil. Wichefski had just finished affixing his signature to the bottom of the hand written document when he offered it to Albright.

"The government sure knows how to fuck up a good thing," Albright stated unequivocally. "Buck and I are the best thing that ever happened to the economy. People have to spend more money on their energy needs; shocks them into learning how to do with less; teaches great fiscal discipline. And don't forget ecological conservation," he added with an insidious laugh.

"I do have to hand it to you Vernon," Jeremy interjected. "You certainly did have a good thing going, making far more money than any other hedge fund manager. I would be lying if I didn't admit to being awed by you and the relationships that helped you achieve such incredible success."

"I've always tried to impart to you that relationships are where we derive a true competitive edge."

"It's just that Buck didn't strike me as a particularly good partner for you."

"As long as we have our deal," he said, reaching for the agreement to add his signature, "I'll let you in on it. Sure Buck could be a bit overbearing at times but he was great to me. He bailed me out years ago and had me go long a ridiculous number of oil stocks. I resisted at first but everything he said worked out, so what the hell! You know I've always believed that commodities markets are rigged and it's nice to be on the right side of it."

"I'm sure that thought hasn't changed."

Albright laughed again. "You are right about that. Buck knows everything that goes on in that market. Hell, he is the oil market. He has tentacles into so many hedge funds that when he makes a call it's like mobilizing the marines. They all get on the phone and do what he tells them. And guess what? It's worked every time."

"What do you think about that, Tom?"

Wichefski crossed his arms and placed his fist under his chin. "I'm not surprised. We suspected massive collusion. It's too bad we couldn't put you away for life but at least we'll get Hendricks and the rest of his gang."

Vernon focused on the document and rotated the solid gold barrel of his Mount Blanc pen to reveal the point. "We don't share the same perspective on my fate, but with this get out of jail free card I'm about to sign, it doesn't matter what you think any more, does it?" Albright brought the pen over the agreement.

Jeremy ripped the papers from Albright's grasp. "Not today, asshole, not ever. Say goodbye to freedom."

Now that the safety of Jeremy's family was assured and the government's interest in the case out in the open, the FBI moved quickly. Jeremy was anxious to go to his family

428 □ STEPHEN L. WEISS

but waited to see what the next steps would be. He enjoyed watching Vernon's arrogant façade crumble after he tore up the document that would have conferred immunity on him. The shredded bits of Vernon's flirt with freedom now lay beyond his grasp.

With most everything going in the right direction, Jeremy was on his way out the door. "So long Vernon. I guess the next time I see you will be when your patrician profile is plastered across every newspaper in the country."

"Not so fast, junior," he said, exhibiting the difficulty in keeping an inflated ego deflated. "I don't think that your friends here realize what that image can do to their careers."

"I don't see how it can do anything but earn them promotions."

"I wouldn't be so sure. The boys in D.C, won't be too happy when the markets start getting destroyed. Do the words 'Lehman Brothers' ring a bell? The government fucked up when they let them go out of business and the economy still hasn't fully recovered. Once this story hits the financial press it will destroy any confidence that is left in the markets and they'll drop faster than Jeremy's net worth, which is likely going to zero."

Jeremy laughed. "Full of yourself to the end. And delusional, too. I don't think Parthenon is a Lehman Brothers. We're just a pimple on an elephant's ass but you do raise another good point. I can't wait to see what your arrest does to energy stocks and crude, particularly when word really gets out. Your net worth will go up in smoke. You won't be able to afford an attorney. At least I'm young enough to make it all back. And I'm not nearly as pessimistic as you are. Between what you and Buck have in the fund, there's a lot of cushion for the rest of us investors."

"I've weathered bad markets before and I can withstand a temporary dislocation this time, too. But you forget how powerful the oil companies are. They won't let the price of crude go too low and neither will our friends in the Middle East."

"The difference between you and Exxon is that you're on margin; debt up to your eyeballs. You'll be wiped out by the time the markets close tomorrow. My only concern is handling all the calls that will come flooding in from the banks and investors when they hear the news. With both you and Marty indisposed," Jeremy smiled broadly, "the office will be a little understaffed."

Jeremy extended his hand to Tom before heading out the door.

***

Marty, fingers dancing on the tabletop, foot tapping on the floor, kept her eyes focused on the bank of elevators. It had taken longer than she would have liked but her patience was rewarded as Jeremy stepped into the lobby. She donned a pair of oversized but stylish sunglasses, which combined with the brown wig to make her unrecognizable. His steps were quick so she hurried from the restaurant and fell in behind him, lagging by twenty paces. As he approached the entrance to the garage, she closed the gap and reached into her bag. The long, winding driveway to the belly of the building would provide the perfect place to tie up one more loose end. Then only Vernon would be left.

Chapter 79 □ □ □

Alone in the room with Albright, Wichefski took the first jab as Pflucek listened on the phone. "I'm not one to give advice to one so highly revered and accomplished, but I believe less pontificating and more action would have served you a lot better today. You were just one swipe of the pen away from being off the hook."

Vernon was shaken. "We...we...we have a deal. You agreed to it."

"There is no deal. But I am indebted to you."

"Why is that?"

"I decided to take your suggestion to heart. I agree with you that informal verbal agreements are meaningless." Wichefski preened for Albright, straightening his tie and pulling his cuffs from his sleeve. "I feel so much more successful already."

"Wise-ass," Vernon muttered under his breath.

"And while we're on the subject, given what you had said earlier, I have to believe that your agreement with Buck is also written down somewhere. We'll be subpoenaing all your documents and searching every residence and office. You're finished, Albright. The only question is how far down we take you. And that will be a function of your cooperation so the sooner you start talking the better."

Pflucek broke into the conversation. "Handcuff him and bring him in. Since the Cranfords are out of danger, we should also round up Buck," he said with a chuckle. "Sorry for the play on words."

"He's at The Carlyle," Wichefski noted. "He's been

known to have protection so I'd suggest sending two teams."

Albright couldn't bear the specter of public humiliation, an issue that seemed to resonate more immediate concern for him than financial ruin. "At least let me walk in under my own power without the handcuffs. It can't hurt and won't be as negative an image for the markets. No one may even notice."

"That's not the way we do things now," Pflucek stated firmly. "Orders from the top. No dispensation because you're a rich, uh, formerly rich, felon. You're still a felon and it's important to let the public know that no one is accorded special treatment. In fact, we want to make sure every news service in the country gets word of this. And I'm really looking forward to the press conference. Bring the prick in, Tom."

"You're both looking at this the wrong way."

"I think my analysis is actually spot on," Wichefski countered. "If oil gets crushed, the President's popularity polls will show vast improvement—probably in direct correlation to the decline in crude prices. And since shit rolls downhill in Washington, my boss gets happy and then I get happy. We owe it all to you. You will be responsible for having a very positive impact on my career. I may even get some offers from the private sector," he said wistfully.

Pflucek and Wichefski laughed in unison.

Wichefski continued. "I'll wait here until back up arrives but there's still the issue of Jagdale and Hendricks. We need to bring them in."

Pflucek agreed. "Do we know where they are?"

"I put a team outside Jagdale's apartment. They haven't reported in yet so I'm assuming she hasn't shown up. We didn't do anything about Hendricks, figuring he always had security around him and would be sensitive to any surveillance."

"My guess is that she's long gone and may have given

Hendricks a heads up, which means he's likely on his way too," Pflucek responded.

"Could be but I hope not. Once she's out of the country it will be much more difficult to track her down,"

***

Marty's hand curled around the grip of the gun as her index finger found the trigger. She felt no onset of nerves, only a steely resolve to take out the man who had never shown the least bit of interest in her and now represented a threat. Her escape and disappearance was well planned, of that she was sure, but Jeremy was still a liability. There were only two people left at Parthenon who would know that the tens of millions she had wired to her off-shore banks was missing from the firm's accounts. The Fed's had taken care of Albright for now; he wouldn't get anywhere near close enough to Parthenon to notice the missing money. But Jeremy—he was a real issue.

Just a few more steps and he would be turning down the ramp. Her hand tightened and began to pull the pistol from the deep recess of her satchel. But then Jeremy stopped short of the garage. She heard the car coming up the ramp and surmised that he was being cautious. Halfway into the street, the car came to a stop and the attendant got out. Jeremy, having called ahead, handed him a five dollar bill, got in and drove off, unaware how close he was to death.

Marty cursed her luck but swore to finish what she had set out to do. His time would come soon enough but now was the time for preserving her options. She walked a few blocks to the subway station and boarded the next train. She switched trains twice more, not out of necessity but as a function of careful planning, before arriving at her station. Walking briskly but not fast enough to draw attention, she arrived at the apartment she had maintained for just such an emergency. It was in a large, nondescript building with many units, comfortable enough but lacking relative to the luxury she had become accustomed to. She hoped she wouldn't be there long. She couldn't be. She had all that money waiting for her; the nearly hundred million she had taken from Buck and the tens of millions she had embezzled from Parthenon. However, despite all precautions, high tech thievery left a trail. But unless someone knew the money was missing, they wouldn't search for it. They would never discover Buck's loss since he had already done such a good job protecting it in numbered accounts— that's why his files had been so helpful. And with $20 billion sitting on Parthenon's books, and the market carnage sure to ensue, it would take Jeremy awhile to realize their loss but eventually he would. Marty was not about to let that happen, not with all the planning she had put into this and the humiliating acts she had endured with Buck.

Chapter 80

□   □   □

Jeremy had slept peacefully for the first time in quite a while, intertwined in his wife's arms, who had vowed to never let go. But once the digital clock clicked 5:00 a.m., she had no choice; it was time for him to go. Jeremy rolled over on his side and threw his legs over the edge of the bed. His feet sunk into the deep pile carpet as he made his way across the room where he grabbed a pair of gym shorts and running shoes. He had decided that his routine would be different this morning, and every morning going forward.

Before leaving the second floor master bedroom, Jeremy deactivated the motion detectors that fed into the alarm system. He then stopped in each of his children's bedrooms, kissed them gently on the forehead and bounced down the stairs to his basement gym. Once there, he strapped on a heart monitor, aiming to quadruple his resting pulse to one hundred sixty beats per minute. He looked forward to the intensity of his workouts. A large flat screen television occupied the entire wall opposite the cardio equipment. He pointed the remote control and changed the channel to CNBC. Then he began to run on the treadmill, hiking the elevation to fifteen degrees, the maximum. Cleaning up the mess at Parthenon was going to be a monumental task but despite this, Jeremy felt more at ease than he had in a long time. Deep into the night, he and Jennifer had talked about the future. He felt rejuvenated.

As he hit the midpoint of a sixty minute run, a familiar face came across the screen. Hair unkempt, clothes disheveled, suit jacket draped over his clasped hands in a poor attempt to conceal his new stainless steel bracelets,

Vernon Albright was being led into Federal court accompanied by four FBI agents.

The CNBC commentator spoke over the image. "This video was taken last night as Vernon Albright, one of the true pioneers of the hedge fund industry, was being led into his arraignment. The details are still breaking but perhaps our own Lou Lindshel can shed some light on this important event."

"Thank you. Apparently, Albright did not act alone. According to government sources, one of his alleged co-conspirators, Wendell Hendricks, who used the nickname 'Buck', was found dead in his apartment at the very exclusive Carlyle Hotel. Hendricks is thought to be a billionaire investor from Texas who had a large investment in Albright's firm. The authorities are categorizing the death as suspicious pending an investigation. My source, who has access to the crime scene report, told me that the first impressions of the forensic team indicated suicide but that this seemed inconsistent with the fact that a number of files appeared to be missing from the desk drawers as well as the general condition of the apartment including a packed travel bag. An FBI spokesman said they are looking for a person of interest in connection with this incident who most recently went by the name Marty Jagdale, apparently an alias. Fingerprints collected from her office indicate that her real name is Sonia Jha. Miss Jha has also been named a person of interest by Interpol and UK authorities for her alleged role in the bankruptcy of a large hedge fund in London approximately eighteen months ago. However, the Europeans had never issued an arrest warrant. The FBI further stated that the crime scene at The Carlyle is similar to what Scotland Yard investigators found at the home of the founder of the hedge fund in London, Sir Martin Simmonson. The death of that individual had been classified as a suicide but I would be surprised if the investigation into Simmonson's cause of death were not reopened. The New York City Police department and the FBI caution that

Miss Jha could be armed and that her appearance, which you now see on the left side of your television screen, has likely changed. I will keep you up on this story as details emerge. Back to you in the studio."

Jeremy widened his stance to straddle the sides of the treadmill while the black conveyer belt kept rolling. Despite halting his pace, his heart beat faster and the color drained from his face. He reached for the phone and called Wichefski.

"Tom! I just saw the news and heard what you guys apparently uncovered on Marty or Sonia or whatever her name is. She may have killed Buck? Why didn't you tell me any of this?"

"One second Jeremy," Wichefski responded as he sat up in bed. He placed his cell phone on the night table and rubbed the sleep from his eyes. He shook his head from side to side dissipating the fog that inhibited clear thinking. "Sorry, but I only got to bed a few hours ago which is about the time we found out about Marty. Europe is five hours ahead of us so the inspector in charge of the investigation had already left for the day. We had to wait until three a.m. our time to get any real information. At that point I didn't want to wake you."

Jeremy felt foolish that he had not been more thoughtful before awakening Tom at six a.m. "Sorry I woke you but the news hit me like a brick. What should I make of this? Apparently she's already killed twice. Why not a third or fourth time?"

"Meaning do you and Vernon have anything to worry about with her on the loose?"

"No, I mean me and my family. I could give a crap about Vernon."

It was Wichefski's turn to feel foolish. "Right, right. Sorry, still waking up. Look, I think she's on the run and long gone but until we find her, we don't know for sure. It seems unlikely she would do anything because we now know enough that her eliminating any more witnesses wouldn't serve any purpose. And it's not like you witnessed her doing anything. Vernon, on the other hand, may have reason to be nervous but I doubt anything happens to him either. He's got his own security team plus we'll be watching him when he gets out on bail."

"Well we don't have our own security team and I don't have the FBI watching out for us." He paused. "I don't like playing the odds with the safety of my family. What would you do if you were me?"

"Probably worry as much as you are now but that doesn't mean that such a response is rational. I'm very comfortable that you and your family are safe but I don't want you to worry. You've been through a lot so I'll assign people to watch you and your family until we put more distance from what's gone down."

"That's great. Thanks so much and I'm sorry to have called so early. I'm sure you'll let me know if you hear anything new."

***

Miles away, in a different part of the city, Sonia Jha had been watching the same news report as Jeremy. She had known it was only a matter of time before they linked her to the incident in Europe but that figured into her plan. They could reinvestigate Simmonson's death all they wanted but the conclusion would be the same: suicide. She was that good. Contrary to the news reports she had seen, she didn't regard herself as a killer. She was doing the world a favor. Simmonson, Hendricks, Albright and Cranford were only different from her in how they got what they wanted, but to her and to them, the end justified the means. Sonia remained confident that, like Simmonson's death, Buck's demise would ultimately be ruled a suicide. Thus all that mattered was protecting her fortune and removing any trace of the embezzlement. Sonia understood that she couldn't rely on that alone. Unfortunately, the Parthenon situation required more remedial action than the much smaller operation in London. She remained fixated on Cranford; he represented a risk she was unwilling to take. He was too damn righteous and would have the accountants review every transaction until he accounted for every dollar Parthenon's investors had entrusted to the firm. Getting rid of him was just good risk management. Wouldn't Paul be proud?

***

Jeremy's desire to resume his exercise routine momentarily waned as he digested the latest information. He focused on Tom's steadfast belief that Marty—damn it, Sonia—didn't represent any kind of threat. Throughout the entire ordeal, Tom's primary concern had been the safety of Jeremy's family. He had actually been incredibly conservative about how the FBI proceeded, even putting his career at risk to a certain extent. If there were the slightest chance that he or Jennifer and the kids were in danger, Wichefski would have said so.

Chapter 81

□   □   □

Trading began in London at a furious pace, sending the price of Brent Sea Crude down five percent on the opening bell. Shortly into the session, the price stabilized briefly as traders stepped in to support their positions hoping to fend off a rout. As the price ticked up a few nickels, others reloaded their sell orders seeking to preserve some profits. A number of speculators who had unhesitatingly and enthusiastically bought the upward momentum in oil prices never took the time to quantify their risk. Unlike the forces of gravity that pull all objects back down to earth at the same rate of speed regardless of weight, markets have variable rates of descent. This was one of the fastest price declines on record and the most effective strategy was to sell at any price. Every time the price of crude declined ten dollars, exchange rules required the suspension of trading for five minutes.

Exacerbating the downward move were the speculators who bought crude on margin, putting up on average only fifteen percent of the contract price. With the price decline erasing the only equity they had in the commodity, the brokerage firms that held these margin accounts sent out liquidation notices to the borrowers. As the market continued to trade down, the margin accounts were automatically liquidated, wiping out a number of traders within the first twenty minutes of the opening bell. They had no hope of recouping their investment. Brokerage firms are very similar to banks foreclosing on homes; their only interest is in recouping their capital, not maximizing the sale price. Financial institutions are in the money lending and commission business; they have no desire to own investment risk by taking possession of any stocks or commodities.

The price of any energy related commodity would decline for five successive days. Eventually OPEC would announce production cuts putting a floor under the price but not before Brent touched sixty dollars a barrel.

***

Global stock markets were decimated in early trading, a tsunami washing around the world as the opening bell rang in each market. First the Asian markets and then Europe. By the time the U.S. markets opened, the foreign indices were down ten percent. Investors were rightly concerned that commodities and stocks could be so easily manipulated and rushed to liquidate their investments before they collapsed as oil did. Jeremy, ever rational, took advantage of the emotional reaction to the headlines. When fear or greed, rather than fundamentals, dictates market direction it usually results in an overreaction. He acted quickly, opportunistically covering the short positions in companies that suffered from higher energy prices and buying stocks that were compellingly cheap. Over time the market would become more rational in its valuation; reversion to the norm is what the experts called it. Besides, if anyone took the time to think about it, collapsing energy prices were a good thing for just about everyone except oil companies and OPEC. Consumers would feel flush with cash and pour that into the economy.

At 4:00 Jeremy nearly collapsed from exhaustion. He barely had the strength to smile as Jack Knowles came across the speaker. "Unbelievable job, Jeremy. If this is how my career ends at Parthenon, I'll be a happy man. I've never seen someone make so much money in one day. Check that. You made more money today than you made in the prior six months."

"Thanks, Jack. You and your team were tremendous. Every order was executed flawlessly. Unfortunately, we didn't make enough money to offset the losses in Vernon's portfolio."

"Screw him. That's his problem."

Jeremy laughed loudly. "You're right, Jack. You're absolutely right. As long as the investors are made whole, screw him."

Epilogue □ □ □

Jeremy walked into his children's bedrooms and gently prodded them awake. "It's time to get up for school, girls. You don't want to miss the Daddy bus. First stop is at the bakery."

Melissa and Alexandra popped out of bed and rushed into their bathrooms to brush their teeth and wash the sleep from their eyes.

"I want a big chocolate chip cookie for breakfast, Daddy," Melissa announced with her mouth full of toothpaste.

"And I want to bring Munchkins for everyone. It's my teacher's birthday." Alexandra loved her kindergarten class.

Jennifer stood in the doorway. "I had these kids on much better diets when you worked in the city," she joked.

"Yeah, but the tradeoff is worth it. You have me to drive car pool in the morning."

After driving the two miles from his children's school to downtown Millburn, Jeremy walked into the offices of Cranford Capital a touch before nine o'clock and threw his gym bag in the corner. He would not need it until four-thirty when he left the office. He stopped in the kitchen for a cup of coffee and ran into Lauren Wilkes, his chief operating officer and Larry Janowicz, one of his traders.

"Good morning, Jeremy."

"Morning, Larry. How goes it?"

"Working the same shift with Jack is a pure pleasure. I was never much of a night owl and now I actually get to see my wife and kids every once in a while."

"Those hours you kept at Parthenon were appropriate only for vampires and rock stars."

Lauren chimed in. "I don't know how you did it all those years. If I don't get my seven hours a night, I'm toast the next day."

"I'll leave you two to discuss healthy living. I have a few things to do before the market opens. Important stuff, like read the sports section."

Lauren chuckled. "My how things have changed."

Jeremy walked into his office just in time to answer his phone on the last ring. It was Suzie, his assistant. "Hi Suzie. Any day, huh?"

"And it can't come soon enough. These babies are kicking like crazy. The expectant father is on line one for you."

"Morning, Tom. What's new?"

"I wanted to get in touch with you before two news stories hit the wires. First, the ballistics test showed that the same gun was involved in the murders of Paul and Buck. So for now it appears that Buck shot Paul and ultimately killed himself but no one here is wedded to that fact pattern. The forensic team is still investigating."

"Any leads on Sonia's whereabouts?"

"None, but we're still looking. Women can change their appearances a lot easier than men and it's only been two months since everything unfolded. We'll get her."

"Well, it seems you were right," Jeremy conceded.

"Meaning?"

"Meaning that my fears about her coming after us were way overblown. She's probably far, far away at this point. I guess I'll be closing out my account with SOS Security. I'm spending a fortune on guards."

"And Jennifer has never found out?"

Jeremy chuckled. "Nope. If she knew I had someone watching her and the girls 24/7, no amount of security would be able to protect my sorry ass. What else you got?"

"The second piece of news isn't going to knock you off your chair either. The government has dropped the case against Albright. You knew it was coming but I wanted to make sure that you had the official word."

"The only surprise is that it didn't happen sooner."

"Everything went his way. The prosecution team went through three different lead attorneys in a month; each left public service for the greener pasture of a hedge fund. With the SEC's talk of increased focus on regulation, hedge funds all seem to think that having a former prosecutor on their payroll as general counsel is tantamount to slapping the Good Housekeeping Seal of Approval on their door. But the real difficulty with the case was that we had no one to testify against Albright or any paper trails to connect him to Hendricks. He certainly knew when to be discrete."

Jeremy picked up where Tom left off. "And it didn't help matters that he never met with any of Buck's other stooges, who thankfully were less cautious in protecting themselves. Those guys will be away for a long time. I still can't believe the law hasn't changed regarding insider trading. It's ridiculous that there isn't any tangible proof of a link to Vernon's buying of those oil companies and Buck's information."

"Vernon owned so many of those little companies that the percentage of his portfolio that overlapped with Buck's direct ownership was actually negligible. They may have been his biggest positions but there weren't enough of them for us to take a credible case to a jury. Predictably Albright hired some pretty good lawyers and they would shred the case in front of twelve people that were unsophisticated in finance."

"I still have a hard time believing that they would not allow testimony from either one of us about his confession," Jeremy said.

"What can I say? He has a great legal team. They convinced the judge that this does not fall under the Patriot Act and therefore his statements are inadmissible because he was refused counsel. And the prosecutor doesn't want to rely on your testimony alone since you are such an interested party."

"Let's face it, Tom, Washington is gutless. The bottom line is that the case is a political hot potato. The government can grab enough headlines with the prosecution of Hallwood, Nettles, McNamara, and the others. Those are much easier cases to prove. They don't want to risk a long drawn out legal battle with Albright that they could wind up losing. Meantime, the administration is continuing to trumpet their role in bringing down crude so all is well in the world."

"It's a bit of a sad commentary but that's the way it is," Tom concurred. "I wish I had better news to deliver."

"At least we hit him in the wallet and that's where he hurts the most. His energy portfolio was decimated. The leverage killed him. He'll be paying back the brokers for years and years to come," Jeremy offered in search of a silver lining. "Thanks, Tom. I appreciate the call."

Jeremy reached across his desk for the New York Post. It had the most thorough sports section of any newspaper in the city. As he finished Peter Vescey's column, a sportswriter who he regarded as the best in the business, Lauren walked in and placed a copy of the Wall Street Journal on the desk open to the front page of Section C, *Money and Investing*. Jeremy couldn't believe what he saw. The headline on the column read "Vernon Albright Is Back!"

Vernon Albright is back in business with the launch of a new hedge fund. He claims to already have commitments totaling four billion dollars. Reached for comment, Albright had the following to say. "I'm glad the government finally came to their senses and realized I did nothing wrong. Small minded bureaucrats targeted me because I was the poster boy for success but I refused to be used as their stepping stone to higher office. I will not apologize for being an aggressive hedge fund manager who has done very well for investors and in turn, made some money for myself. My new fund is already oversubscribed. Who wouldn't want to invest with me? I'm the best there ever was. My track record speaks for itself. I'll start with four billion and grow it to thirty."

"This morning is full of surprises that aren't surprises," Jeremy remarked to Lauren after he read the article. "Want coffee?" he inquired as he pushed away from his desk.

"Nope," she responded, smiling, "still not a coffee drinker."

It had become a running joke between them. Every day, mid-morning, Jeremy went out for a cup of coffee. Every day he asked and each time Lauren politely declined.

Jeremy walked the half block to Bagel Chateau. In case Jennifer happened to be in town, his bodyguard trailed a step behind, wearing khakis and a polo shirt. Jeremy pulled open the door and moved past the usual crew of locals who occupied the same tables each weekday morning with their laptops and newspapers.

A red headed woman, conservatively dressed in a skirt that fell below her knees, baggy long sleeved shirt and large reading glasses observed the two men walking past her table as they did every day.

"One day soon, Jeremy, one day soon."

About the Author

□ □ □

Stephen L. Weiss's circuitous route to Wall Street took him from financial planning to tax law to the entertainment industry, where he represented some very well-known personalities, providing both career and investment advice. But the investment business was his first love, and he finally answered its call—first in institutional equity sales, where he dealt with some of the most accomplished professional investors at both mutual funds and hedge funds, then in senior management positions at Salomon Brothers, SAC Capital and Lehman Brothers (he played no role in its demise). He is currently Managing Partner at Short Hills Capital Partners, LLC. Mr. Weiss lives with his wife, two daughters and three dogs. He is also the author of the well-received investment book *The Billion Dollar Mistake: Learning The Art of Investing Through The Missteps of Legendary Investors* (John Wiley and Sons, January 2010) which has been translated into Chinese, Korean and Japanese; and *The Big Win: Learning from the Legends to Become a More Successful Investor.* (John Wiley and Sons, May 2012).

Made in the USA
San Bernardino, CA
16 December 2014